Refle(

BY STUART BONE

Humorous Fiction

Driven to Distraction

Nothing Ventured

Long Shadows

Reflections

Stuart Bone

Best wishes

Copyrights

ISBN: 978-1-8382770-0-0

For the Chalkleys and the Faulkners
My Canadian family who have given me a second home.

Still Missing

by Karen Taylor

Chapter 3 (First draft)

As we have seen from the earlier chapters, people go missing all of the time. Even with today's technology it's still possible to disappear. But what of a child's disappearance? That's a completely different story. In the case of a missing child there's a sense of urgency to find them, a fear of what's happening to them the longer they are gone. There's a euphoria of elation when the child is found unharmed and a sense of utter desolation as worst fears are confirmed when a body is discovered.

But what happens when the child or their remains aren't found? How long should a search continue? To the family it should never end but to those on the outside, perhaps with a feeling of guilt, they must wonder if manpower and money should be thrown at something that now seems like a fruitless search. And what happens after many years have passed? Are those that were involved still affected by the past or are they able to move on with their lives?

Emma Burrows was five years old when she went missing on 24 September 1980. There appears to have only ever been one suspect for the crime, a twenty-five year old man with learning difficulties. The fact that he too disappeared on the same day looks suspicious but surely a mentally disabled man with a five year old child wouldn't have been able to evade the police for this long.

Emma Burrows lived in Little Tenwick, Essex with her parents and elder brother. Sylvia Burrows, 39 was a housewife and part-time cleaner. Daniel Burrows, 41 was an unemployed factory worker. They were a normal family, liked in the village and their fifteen year old son, Ray apparently doted on his sister. Why then, did Emma disappear?

She was taken to school that morning by her brother but disappeared soon after when teacher, Caroline Willis, 23 stepped out of the classroom. She was never seen again.

Jimmy McGill, the twenty-five year old man with learning difficulties, was known to wander around the village on his own. His mother and younger brother, Joey both worked and his father, Tom was well known as a drunk and bully who rarely took an interest in his family or village life. There was no one, therefore, to prevent Jimmy taking his daily walks.

He apparently liked watching children playing. When Emma disappeared the village turned accusatory eyes onto him and his family. But why would a man who had always been harmless suddenly decide to abduct a child? If he'd killed her, would he have been able, on his own, to hide the body from the police and the entire community who took part in the search that followed? That seems unlikely, so what really happened that day? Did someone else take the child? Were others involved in making both Emma and Jimmy disappear or was the whole thing just a tragic accident?

Chapter 1

Mother

Sylvia couldn't help smiling to herself as the bus pulled away from the stop on its journey out of Maldon. She'd never made love during the day before and she felt a little naughty. It had been years since she'd had someone special in her life and at seventy-eight, she'd thought those years were behind her.

Ken had been a complete surprise. She'd seen him several times at the retirement home while visiting her friend, Marjorie and they'd often smiled at one another. It was two months ago now that they'd found themselves together on the patio area at the back of the Home. Marjorie, like Ken's ninety-two year old mother, had Alzheimer's disease and while she'd sat in her wheelchair, staring out at the garden, occasionally mumbling something unintelligible under her breath; Ken's mum had fallen asleep, leaving their visitors to chat to one another. They'd talked so long Sylvia missed her bus. Instead of waiting an hour for the next service Ken had driven her home even though it was completely out of his way, their easy conversation continuing on the journey, like they'd known one another for years.

The only reason he hadn't driven Sylvia home today was because he had to go to work. Sylvia thought it a little odd that a man of seventy still worked as a security guard but Ken had told her,

"I sit behind a desk on the ground floor of an office block in Chelmsford. I don't exactly chase criminals down the street.

I'm a glorified receptionist really, handing out passes and telling people which floor they need to go to."

While the Home his mother was in wasn't exactly a palace it still cost a lot of money to be a resident. Perhaps that was why Ken still continued to work. Sylvia didn't like to ask. She knew what it was like to have money troubles although fortunately, those years were far behind her.

The practically empty bus left the outskirts of Maldon and its estates of recently built housing and travelled on through the flat, open countryside of Essex with views across to Northey Island in the distance where the River Blackwater met the North Sea. Even on the single decker the view was still impressive. Some thought the landscape stark but Sylvia had always loved it, the wide open spaces, the richness of the colours from the grassy marshes to the crops in farmers' fields; ever changing in the light and through the seasons.

The area was rich in history, Northey Island itself being involved in the Battle of Maldon over a thousand years before when the Vikings had invaded. A poem had been written about the event although the beginning and end of it were lost in the mists of time.

Sylvia didn't really like history though. That meant looking backwards, into the past, something she didn't like to do if she could help it. The landscape she was currently looking out onto once had a large, medieval building on it that had begun to sink into the soft marshes as soon as it was built. It quickly became a ruin and, passing here as a young girl, Sylvia had thought what remained of the building looked sad and desolate. There was nothing left of it now as far as she could see and that was better. For Sylvia the past was just another ruin that shouldn't be looked at if at all possible.

A moment later and the bus passed a bank of trees by the

roadside and Sylvia caught herself looking at her ghostly reflection in the window instead of at the landscape. As she turned to face forwards she couldn't help another smile escaping onto her face. Ken had often told her she was beautiful and didn't look anywhere near her seventy-eight years. She liked him saying that and several times she'd caught herself looking at her image in the mirror more intently before tutting and telling herself she was a silly old woman and that she should remember the sin of pride. Ken was just being kind. She always saw the grey hair peeping out at the roots between salon appointments and the lines around her light blue eyes and across her pinched cheeks.

Her thoughts returned to the stolen afternoon of passion. It hadn't just been to fit in with Ken's work schedule. Sylvia was worried about what other people would think of her dating again, especially a man eight years younger than herself. While Ken was grey haired with a matching moustache that aged him, he was still noticeably younger than her, Sylvia felt, and that was a worry.

She could imagine the things the villagers of Little Tenwick would say, whether they were just joking or being judgemental. The village might have grown substantially since she'd first moved here but it was still an out-of-the-way place where little went on. Gossip was always something to listen to and Sylvia didn't want to be its subject, not again.

Then there was Ray to consider. It wouldn't be so bad if he was still in his own place but living back at home again in his old room that still had the same single bed in it and the display cases on the wall with his toy soldiers in them, Sylvia felt she couldn't have Ken staying over while her son was in the house, especially as he was there after another relationship breakup. She'd felt sure he'd cracked it this time with Jackie but apparently, according to Ray, she'd stopped noticing him.

It was only a temporary stay, although it had been over a year now. While Sylvia liked having her son there she was worried about him. All he seemed to do was work and then come home, choosing to spend his evenings in front of the TV with his mother after she'd cooked dinner rather than going out with friends. Of course Ray was fifty-four now and not exactly of an age to go out pubbing and clubbing. Sylvia sometimes forgot he was older. While she'd miss him she felt it would be better for Ray to get a place of his own again. She certainly wouldn't miss sharing her house with his cat, having to empty its foul litter tray each day.

The bus continued its journey down the country lanes of rural Essex, barely stopping at the remote stops as it passed open fields and the occasional property, from Tudor cottage to Victorian terrace, sixties bungalow to new-build executive home. Eventually it reached the village of Little Tenwick.

Another new housing development was nearing completion on the far side of the village on the road leading out towards Great Tenwick but at least the centre remained unchanged. Sylvia alighted from the bus by the pleasant, triangular-shaped village green at the stop opposite the pathway that led up to the primary school where she'd been a dinner lady and where both of her children had gone to school.

As Sylvia faced the green the small Norman church stood serenely to her left behind the yew trees. Between the wall of the graveyard and the green was the terrace of white clapboard houses, the first two housing the village shop, and beyond that was the local, redbrick public house, The Fox and Huntsman, with it's two large bay-fronted, diamond leaded windows looking back at her.

She stepped across the grass and then crossed the other road that helped give the green its shape. Unlike the houses beside the shop in the terrace most of the properties in the heart of the village didn't face onto the road but instead, had their front doors facing onto small alleyways that led away from the centre.

Sylvia walked carefully between the parked cars (the only sign in the centre of the village that showed it was larger and busier than it had once been) and made her way up one of the narrow footpaths to her own house, another white clapboard semi.

The house next door had once belonged to her friend, Marjorie in the retirement home and her late husband. Now it was rented out but tenants never seemed to stay long due to the difficulty with finding a free parking space in the village centre. It was currently empty again.

Inside Sylvia hung up her jacket and went straight through into the compact, square kitchen at the back of the house. The afternoon with Ken had put her behind schedule. On the round dining table in the middle of the room was the list of business phone numbers she'd promised the vicar she would call up regarding getting the trestle tables, bunting and lighting delivered on time for the upcoming harvest festival at the church. She'd also promised Ray a chicken pie tonight and that took a while from scratch. She began with making the pastry first. Once the pie was in the oven she made a start on the phone numbers, hoping none of the people she wanted to speak to had left work early on a Friday afternoon.

It was a lot to do but then everyday had become like that for Sylvia. For years she'd thrived on it. Working hard meant there was less opportunity to think about the past. But today, for the first time, she wished she did have a bit more free time, some leisure time for herself and Ken. She really enjoyed being with him. Ken made her happy. With him there was no past, just the present and whatever future was left in this life. Perhaps that was why she'd delayed introducing him to Ray or some of her friends in the village. They mostly all knew about Emma. Ken didn't and Sylvia liked it that way. That couldn't go on forever, she knew that, but perhaps it could carry on for just a bit longer. There was no reason for him to know everything about her yet. Ken could remain her secret and she could take her time telling him everything about her. There was no rush.

Chapter 2

Father

Daniel enjoyed going to the restaurant for lunch. Friday was always fish and chip day, usually cod or a nice piece of haddock. It saved him having to cook for himself in the evening. There was always someone there he knew and could chat with. There were about sixty residents in the retirement village and he knew the majority of them. Daniel was aware of who he should sit with in the restaurant or the communal lounge and who to avoid. As soon as one of the annoying residents descended, Daniel would leave and return to his own apartment.

As he passed the communal lounge today after his lunch, leaning on his stick, he peered inside through his square, black-rimmed, thick spectacles and wondered whether to stop and grab a coffee but then he heard one of the staff members announce those immortal words, 'It's time for bingo' and Daniel shuffled off quickly. Afternoon bingo signified being old and Daniel refused to be thought of as a stereotypical old man.

Outside there was a definite nip in the air and he pulled his cardigan tighter around him before heading off towards his apartment, wishing he'd brought his trilby to keep his head warm and to stop his wispy bit of grey hair from blowing in the breeze. Daniel had been here two years now, one of the first residents of the newly built retirement village. He'd been in two minds whether to move to somewhere like this but Tania had persuaded him.

"It's future-proof dad," she'd told him, "You can still be as independent as you want now, bussing into Stow for shopping and a pint, but you can also get care if and when you require it."

That was Tania, ever the practical person. It was still a wrench to move out of the house he and his late wife, Alice had shared for years but he had to admit, it had proved to be a good move. The apartment buildings were only two-storeys high and had been built to blend in with the traditional properties in Stow on the Wold, using the distinctive Cotswold honey-coloured stone. While it gave them character, to Daniel they still looked like what they were, modern apartments trying to blend in.

He made his way along the wide footpath to his own ground floor apartment, holding onto the black iron railing along the edge to help him move that little bit quicker. He was puffing when he arrived at his own front door and, not for the first time, he cursed the pneumonia of several years before for turning him into this weaker version of himself.

As he opened the front door he heard a voice call out,

"Don't be startled Mr Burrows, I'm in here cleaning."

Daniel smiled. It was Jessica. He always liked it when Jessica came to clean.

He walked into the airy main room of his apartment. The sunlight streamed in through the French windows behind the small, square, oak dining table and bounced off of the white walls. The room always seemed welcoming whenever he returned to it, his familiar, slightly battered, three-seater, grey sofa facing the electric fireplace with white, faux-marble surround; the long, low, oak coffee table that stood between them matching the dining suite he and Alice had picked out together for their old house. He rarely watched the small TV that stood to one side of the fireplace and spent most of his time sitting in his comfy armchair that was sat on the other side.

At the far end of the room, beside the dining area was the ushaped, white kitchen where Jessica was stood waving at him across the countertop, a damp cloth in her hand.

"I'm just wiping over the surfaces in here and then I'm all finished," she told him.

"In that case I'll put the coffee on."

"Oh Mr Burrows you're naughty," she said, "You know you always make me late for my next appointment."

"It's just a coffee, it won't take long."

Jessica smiled.

"Well I do enjoy the proper coffee you make. My Gary only likes instant."

Daniel pulled a face as he hobbled past her without his stick.

"Terrible stuff that instant," he told her, taking a packet of filter coffee out of the top cupboard, "It rots your gut."

Jessica laughed. She was always in a good mood. That was one of the reasons Daniel liked her. Plus she was a decent cleaner, like Sylvia, his ex-wife had been. Sylvia had always told people she enjoyed cleaning and so took pride in the results. Daniel knew Jessica felt the same way. She'd told him how much she enjoyed her work, making places look nice for people. She enjoyed being around the 'old folks' here at the retirement village too, she'd told him on more than one occasion.

"Surely not Dorothy Berkley," he'd said to her, trying not to wince at being included in the 'old folks' reference, "No one likes being around her, not even her husband. That's the only reason he died."

"Mr Burrows, you're wicked," she'd replied, still laughing.

She'd only been working at the retirement village a couple of months but to Daniel, it felt like he'd known her for years. She was around forty and had told him she had three children. The eldest son was at university and her daughter had only just started school.

"A bit of a late surprise," she'd explained.

Jessica finished washing down the countertops while the coffee brewed. When it was ready they both sat down at the dining table.

"How's the little one settling in at school," he asked.

"Okay," she replied, "There have been a couple of tearful mornings but she's made a few new friends now so that's improved things."

"Good. I remember my little girl being just the same when she first started school. She was a shy, little thing."

"Your Tania?"

"What? Oh, no, Tania never had a problem. She's always been confident. I think she made sure she was friends with everyone by the end of her first day. No I'm referring to my elder daughter."

"Is that her in the photograph over there?"

Jessica indicated the photos on the glass-topped, side table beside the armchair. There were two silver frames stood side by side. It was obvious neither photo had been taken recently. In one was a picture of a lady in her prime. The other was of a little girl.

"Yes," Daniel said, "That's my Emma."

"She's beautiful."

"She's dead."

Jessica's eyes widened.

"Sorry," Daniel said, "I didn't mean to blurt it out like that. She disappeared when she was five years old and was never found. She has to be dead."

"I'm so sorry."

"That's my wife, Alice beside her, who passed away five years ago."

"There's a definite resemblance between them," Jessica said.

"Oh Alice wasn't Emma's mother."

"No? Oh, I'm completely confused. Sorry, you don't have to explain. It's me nosing into your personal life again."

An image from a couple of months back passed through Daniel's mind. It was Jessica's first time cleaning the apartment. She'd been chatting away to him while cleaning in the bedroom, her lengthy, fair hair pulled back into a ponytail, the long fringe that almost hid her eyes bouncing about as she moved around the room dusting. Daniel had been standing in the doorway, laughing at something she'd said that he couldn't recall now. When she'd pulled the suitcase out from under the bed he'd shouted out,

"Don't touch that!"

"I'm sorry," she'd replied, startled by the sudden change in his demeanour, "I wasn't going to look or anything."

Daniel had instantly apologised.

"That's some of my personal belongings," he'd told her, "From my past. They're sad things really. I shouldn't keep hold of them."

"No need to explain," she'd said, gently pushing the case back under the bed, "I was just going to vacuum under there but I can always leave that until you're able to move anything you don't want me to touch."

Daniel had realised how silly he was being. The case was locked after all.

"No, it's fine," he'd told her, and apologised again.

"My two eldest children I had with my first wife, Sylvia," Daniel told her now, "That's when I lived in Essex. Sylvia and I divorced after we lost Emma. I'd already started working here in Gloucestershire and that's where I met Alice. Tania is our child together."

"Oh right," Jessica replied, "I hadn't realised you had other children besides Tania. I've only ever seen her visiting you. She's very nice isn't she. I've only spoken to her the once although I've seen her here at other times. She's quite striking with that long, dark red hair. What product does she use on it, do you know, it's so shiny."

"Oh, talk of the devil," Daniel said, as his mobile phone rang.

He pressed the cancel button.

"Oh, shouldn't you have taken that?"

"No it's fine, let her leave a message. We're having a nice chat."

"Won't she be worried if you don't answer?"

"Tania? No she won't be worried about me. Besides, I often leave my phone here when I'm over at the lounge or restaurant and she's always busy at work so we're used to speaking to each others answerphones. So tell me, what is it your eldest is studying at university again?"

After Jessica had gone, Daniel had a nap. It was only later, as he was thinking about what to have in a sandwich, that he remembered Tania had left him a message. It was short and to the point, as always. She was popping in to see him that night. She had something she needed to discuss.

Daniel felt a bit miffed.

Why tonight and not some time over the weekend? I might have been going out, he thought to himself.

Not that he was. It was unusual for her to actually visit him during the week. Well, it wasn't like she visited every weekend either. Her job often took her away on business trips. Then there was her boyfriend, Raj. They liked to spend time together at the weekend. Daniel still didn't know why they didn't just move in together.

He sighed. There were times when he didn't understand his younger daughter. He wondered what she wanted. He hoped she wouldn't stay too long, there was football on later.

Tania arrived to see her father at six thirty.

"I won't stay long," she told him, after kissing him on the cheek, "I've stopped in on my way home from work."

Daniel would have known that without her telling him. His daughter was dressed in a black skirt suit with a grey blouse. Her long hair, which was much more red than ginger these days, was neatly pinned up and still perfectly in place after a long day in the office.

"Oh, okay," Daniel replied, sadly, even though he was relieved, "You could have said that earlier though. I might have been going out and have changed my plans for your visit."

"Then you could have rung me back and told me that, couldn't you," Tania replied calmly, removing her smart jacket and sitting down on the sofa.

Even though she hadn't raised her voice there was something in Tania's demeanour that made Daniel feel like he'd just been scolded by a parent. He folded his arms and sat back in his chair, waiting for her to speak.

"If you want to get your dinner dad, don't let me stop you," Tania told him, "I know you have your routine."

"I don't have a routine," he told her, crossly, "I eat when I like. I'm not in some old folks Nursing Home."

Tania sighed.

"I never said you were dad, but whenever I phone at this time you always tell me you're eating and can't talk for long."

She continued speaking before her father could respond.

"Anyway, I'll come straight to the point."

You always do, Daniel thought to himself, moodily.

"I've been offered a new job," she told him, "It's still with the same firm and I guess it's a promotion really. It will be more money and it will definitely challenge me."

"But," Daniel said, sensing there was a but, otherwise she wouldn't be here.

Tania looked across at her father. He thought he saw fear in her eyes but he must be mistaken, Tania didn't fear anything.

"It's in Los Angeles," she told him.

"Right."

Daniel wasn't sure how he should respond. He wasn't really sure how he felt.

"I've worked a lot with the people there already," Tania continued, "But conference calls and business trips are different to being there full-time, although I do at least know a lot about that side of the company and a little about the area where it's based but even so, it's a big step."

She looked expectantly at her father.

"What?" he asked.

"What do you think about it?"

"Well it's up to you, Tania," Daniel replied, "It's your decision."

"But it will affect you too."

"Will it?"

"Of course it will, dad," Tania said, standing up and walking over to the French doors behind the dining table, "I'll be over five thousand miles away, not a few miles down the road. I won't be able to just pop in and see you."

"Well it's not like…" Daniel began.

Tania turned round from where she was looking out at the communal garden.

"It's not like what," she said.

"Well," Daniel began again, "I mean, well I just meant…"

"You think I don't visit you enough, is that it?"

"Well, it's not like you come here each week is it, not that I expect you to."

Tania tutted.

"I might visit more often if I was made welcome."

"What does that mean?"

"I've not even been offered a tea or coffee."

"Well I thought you said you weren't staying long."

"Christ dad, a cup of tea doesn't take long to drink."

"Fine," he said, standing up, "I'll make you a cup of tea."

"Well don't bother now."

"My God Tania, make up your mind."

Tania closed her eyes and took a deep breath.

"Look dad," she said, opening her eyes again and looking at him, "I just want your opinion on what I've told you. While it's a great opportunity, I'm scared. I'm thirty-five years old. I've never lived anywhere except here in Gloucestershire. I thought I was settled here but now suddenly I'm being offered the chance to try something new. I don't know what to do. I'd like your opinion."

"Why?"

"Because you're my dad," she shouted at him, "You're the only relative I have. Don't you have an opinion on it?"

"Well I just think only you can make this decision, Tania. You're a sensible girl, you always have been. Whatever decision you make will be the right one, I'm sure of it."

Tania stared at him for what felt like ages to Daniel. He couldn't understand why she looked disappointed.

"And that's really all you have to say on the matter," she asked, "You don't have your own opinion on your daughter leaving the country?"

Daniel felt confused. What else was she asking him? He

shrugged his shoulders. Tania sighed again.

"Fine dad," she told him, walking past and grabbing her jacket from the sofa, "I'll leave you to your plans."

She headed out the front door, closing it loudly behind her. Daniel still felt confused.

Chapter 3

Brother

Ray enjoyed walking up and down the three aisles that made up the supermarket in Great Tenwick. As manager of the only grocery shop around he thought it good for the locals to see him. Customer service was everything in a small branch. It was his duty to be seen and to interact where needed, no matter whether the customer was one of the many boring, old farts in the town or one of the grubby-looking ones, he had to show no discrimination, unless of course it was to someone like Mrs Barker-Smyth who very occasionally popped in on a Friday for some emergency olive oil for one of her many dinner parties. She deserved extra attention.

She lived in the large, detached home, Treetops at the end of the long driveway just outside of town on the road leading back to Little Tenwick. Ray passed it every day on his journey between work and home and often imagined what it looked like inside. Sheer opulence, he felt.

While he had a little bit of money put aside he was in no rush to leave the house in Little Tenwick. He felt he was doing his duty being close to his mother in her twilight years. Without him, who else did she have apart from a few old dears at the church who cleaned, flower-arranged and generally did lots of unpaid work for that new lady vicar.

Ray didn't agree with all of this volunteering. The church was a wealthy establishment. You only had to look at the amount of solid silver on display on Sundays to know that. Not that Ray attended that often, only when he was bored at home. It seemed to make his mother happy though when he went, that and cooking for him each day and generally taking care of him. Ray couldn't understand why Jackie hadn't been as happy as his mother to have him around. Still, she was in the past now, along with all the others.

Ray didn't think much of Little Tenwick itself. It was still just a backwater. Half the residents didn't seem to realise they were living in the twenty-first century as far as he was concerned. No, once Sylvia passed away, he wouldn't stay there. It wasn't the sort of place for someone of his standing to live permanently. He'd always planned to move further away. So far the furthest he'd gone was South Woodham Ferrers when he was married, which was barely a half hour drive, but Ray felt living in that town had still been a big change after growing up in such a twee village.

Great Tenwick was much the better place, he thought, with its senior school, two pubs and parade of shops that included various fast food establishments, a hairdressers and a newsagents. Ray had been at school with the owner of the newsagents. Naveena Kumar, as she had been before her marriage, had taken over the running of it from her parents. Ray always had the impression that she'd had no choice in the matter. Her older brother, Amrit was the one their parents had wanted to better himself, to go to university and study medicine, but really it had been Naveena that had the brains.

Next door to the newsagents was Ray's supermarket. Well, it wasn't exactly his, it was part of a nationwide chain but Ray always thought of it as his own. Aside from a quarterly visit from the ghastly area manager, Elizabeth Chan who only seemed to come here to moan about his sales, he was pretty much left to run it as he saw fit. He knew what he was doing, having worked here since he was a sixteen year old Saturday boy. He felt the place was vital to the local community. It wasn't all about the amount of sales but more about the quality of them. Of course larger stores would have more but here, it was the repeat ones from the same customers Ray was proud of. He knew he was right about that and was sure he was seen locally as a very successful businessman. It could only be a matter of time until he was invited to a Mrs Barker-Smyth dinner, sitting at a vast mahogany dining table, discussing local politics alongside chairman of the parish council, Geoffrey Delaney.

He was another customer Ray always looked out for. He came in each week to use the self-service coffee machine so it was always the briefest of visits and Ray had only managed to engage him in conversation on a handful of occasions, often shouting his words to the back of the man as he rushed off to get on with whatever important task he had to deal with in his life that day.

Ray hadn't been sure about the coffee machine at first but now he was glad it was there and took the credit for its installation whenever he could. While he always called Great Tenwick a town it wasn't the largest of places and most of the residents still referred to it as a village. It was a bus or car journey away from the railway station at Southminster that ran into London but there had been a glut of new housing and more and more people were moving out this way and commuting daily to the city. They needed somewhere to buy a coffee and the supermarket was a handy place to stop. While Geoffrey Delaney was retired he was still seen as a local bigwig and was often spotted driving about on some errand or other and he'd chosen Ray's little establishment as the place to pick up a beverage.

There had been recent talk again of a large supermarket opening up on the edge of the village within a new retail park but that rumour had been around for years and Ray wasn't unduly worried. As he looked about his empire today he smiled. He knew his customer service policy was a big draw and he was sure his supermarket would survive any competition.

His other reason for patrolling the shop floor was to make sure his staff knew he kept watch over them. His older members were no trouble but some of the youngsters that worked there on a late night or weekend weren't always the most conscientious of workers, especially when two of them were there together egging each other on when the store was quiet. Ray wanted them to see him both as a formidable boss and as a role model. He felt he looked indomitable in his sharp, grey suits with his salt and pepper hair and his manager's name badge pinned proudly to his chest. He was sure the youngsters looked up to him. It didn't matter that they called him Rabid Ray behind his back, just so long as he was Mr Burrows in front of his customers.

Getting out onto the shop floor and speaking with the locals also allowed Ray to hear the gossip. While he professed not to like it (or those who spread it) it did sometimes provide a tasty nugget of useful information, as did today's.

Mrs Dunwoody was the quintessential village gossip. She was a small lady, always in a floral-patterned headscarf and beige mac, no matter what the weather. She would scurry about rather than walk and, being round-shouldered, resembled a sprinter about to cross a finish line. She came in most days, more to chat than to buy. Ray never once saw her heading off with more than one carrier bag and even then there was barely anything in it, even though sometimes she was in the shop for half an hour or more.

Ray hadn't spotted her by the bargain bucket at the end of the bread and cake aisle and he jumped when her claw-like hand reached out for him.

"Have you heard about Eleanor Stanley?" she asked.

Ray's ears pricked up at this. Eleanor was another member of the parish council alongside Mrs Barker-Smyth and Geoffrey Delaney. Ray didn't like her because she always ordered her shopping online from one of those upmarket stores. Perhaps she was dead. Ray was hopeful, the woman looked about ninety.

"What about her?" he asked.

Mrs Dunwoody beamed, pleased that news hadn't reached here before she had.

"She's selling up and moving in with her son in Colchester. I heard it's because of her health; heart I think."

Ray tutted.

"I doubt it," he told her, "I've been past her house when her shopping's been delivered. There's always a loud clanking of bottles. If anything I'd say it was her liver."

Mrs Dunwoody nodded.

"Anyway," she continued, "She's moving next week."

"That's quick."

"I heard her daughter's taking over the house."

"I'd have thought Eleanor would have sold it."

"Me too. Perhaps it's the daughter's inheritance. She gets the house and the son gets her savings. Anyway, she's retired from the parish council."

Ray felt the overcast day brighten. This could be the start of better times arriving, finally. He'd waited years for a place to become available on the parish council. Every year the old fossils on it retained their seats, none of them wishing to retire or to die.

"Yes I suppose she'd have to give it up," he replied, hoping he sounded like he didn't care.

"I guess there'll be a by-election."

Ray grinned as he got ready to tell the old gossip something she didn't know.

"There can't be," he said, "It's less than six months until the next election. That means there can't be a by-election."

"Really?"

"Oh yes. I know all the rules. The casual vacancy will have to be decided upon by the other members."

"Ooh."

Mrs Dunwoody headed off with this extra nugget of information to spread the news further. She didn't buy anything in the shop but for once, Ray didn't care. Finally, all of his years of having to listen to the gossip of the lower class members of the community, ingratiating himself with all of the right people and generally working hard at making himself a pillar of the community were about to pay off. This was his chance. He was going to make sure he got that seat on the parish council and this time, there was nothing that was going to stop him.

Chapter 4

Teacher

Caroline listened to the shouting and laughing out in the principal room and smiled. She imagined the children all running and jumping about before being persuaded back to the trestle tables by the sandwiches, crisps and cake. She looked down at the salad in her Tupperware box and sighed before setting it aside and returning her attention to the spreadsheet on the screen in front of her.

It had proved more difficult to find a site for the new sensory centre than she'd expected, and more expensive. She'd assumed East London would be vastly cheaper than the two sites the Small Hands charity already used in Windsor and St Albans but she'd been wrong. Then again it had been many years since she'd lived to the East of London or given that time in her life much thought. A lot would have changed in thirty-nine years.

She'd finally found the right site and the other trustees were in agreement. The place needed a lot of work before it could open but the new centre was desperately needed. Caroline had analysed the data of just where the families that used the set of facilities at the two current sites came from. A new centre to the east of London would cut down travel costs for many families in Essex and Kent. The offer on the place had been accepted and the sooner the paperwork was sorted the better.

Caroline yawned. She felt tired. Perhaps the stresses of running her own charity were getting to her now she was sixty-two. She felt she looked every year of it as well, spending longer each day in front of the dressing table mirror, trying to hide the bags under her dark brown eyes and getting more blonde highlights added each time she went to the hairdressers to cover the grey. Looking her age was one thing but feeling it was quite another. Perhaps the tiredness was due to the small amounts of food she was eating on her latest diet. She stared again at the salad and pushed the Tupperware container further away from her. The long weekend city break was coming up soon and she really wanted to get some weight off before then. She knew Oliver wanted her to lose a few pounds as well before she appeared on his arm in public in some chic continental city.

Caroline sighed inwardly. It was alright for him. His business meetings were often on the golf course. That was one of the reasons for him getting the membership to the Wentworth Golf Club in the first place. Well, that and the fact that Oliver could relish telling people he was a member of the Wentworth Golf Club, that was definitely the main reason. Caroline's meetings were usually in draughty council offices. He was probably at the exclusive club now, enjoying nine holes of golf on a warm Friday afternoon before buying rounds of drinks for everyone in the bar.

Oliver had asked her many times to join the gym at Wentworth which would sort a programme out for her and help with nutrition but that sort of scene wasn't her. She could just imagine it, a wealthy health club where one had to wear designer training gear and swim the breaststroke with hair neatly pinned up; to have a face full of expensive make-up that was meant to convey a 'natural' look, convincing others that you weren't wearing any and that was how you looked when you got out of bed first thing of a morning. Caroline didn't actually know whether that was a true assumption of the place or not but it was a good excuse to use to prevent her from going.

Not that she didn't appreciate high end fashion and the finer things in life, dressing up in an expensive cocktail dress and having her hair and make-up done for an evening out. She and Oliver had both worked bloody hard to get the lifestyle they had today. Caroline enjoyed the social events held in one of the many beautiful private rooms at Wentworth as well as dining out at various salubrious restaurants around the Surrey/ Berkshire area. She liked their large, detached property in Virginia Water and the winter sun trip, summer holiday and long weekend city break each year.

Right now she was a bit in love with her new Mercedes Roadster which she got to drive to the office everyday. Perhaps the car stood out in the staff car park of a registered charity but what the hell, it wasn't as if it came from charity funds and Caroline's lifestyle meant there were a lot of wealthy friends who were all looking to offload money to charity for either tax purposes, to help their image, or just to alleviate their guilt at their own wealth. Caroline didn't care what the reason was, just so long as they kept giving so she could help others.

Perhaps she ought to think about joining the gym though. While she'd helped Oliver make his accountancy firm a huge success before raising their two children and then going on to setting up her own children's charity, Caroline wasn't so fruitful when it came to her diet. Food preparation bored her. She wanted to eat things ready-made that had taste, like cake; particularly cake. She hated bland salads and vegetables but she had to agree with Oliver, appearances were important when running your own business. You had to look successful as well as providing the figures that proved it.

Oliver worked off his business lunches in the gym and on the golf course and was pretty fit for a sixty-five year old man.

His girlfriends certainly saw more than just the size of his wallet. Not that they hung around long. Caroline knew he got bored very quickly with flighty, young women and when it came to his business, he only wanted Caroline on his arm; a woman that made sure she was up-to-date on all of the latest accountancy rulings and regulations and who could talk business with anyone.

The noise had died down outside, meaning the kids were all settled and enjoying their food. Caroline smiled as she thought about the number of parties they'd given here over the years. The sensory centres had helped so many children. Beside the soft play and sensory areas, Caroline now had full-time, paid counsellors at both centres and had provided a number of amenities for the siblings of the ill children to ensure they didn't feel left out. She'd built up a range of other facilities over the years as she recognised more of the requirements that the families with disabled children needed to help improve their lives. The charity still relied heavily on their volunteers though and Caroline's favourite time was when she was able to read to the children in the chill-out zone. It took her back to her days as a teacher when all she'd wanted to do was make a difference to a child's life.

That hadn't quite worked out as planned, nor had motherhood, with Oliver sending their two children to a boarding school aged eleven because it sounded good to say you'd got your children into that particular one. They'd both done well there but it had been heartbreaking to Caroline when they would call to say they weren't coming home for the weekend, choosing to spend time with other school-friends' parents instead. They'd never asked her for help with homework, having seen her as just the mum, the woman who cooked them dinner and cleaned their clothes. They'd never seen the teacher.

Caroline felt that was probably one of the main reasons why she'd started the charity in the first place. While she'd supported Oliver, working in his office for nothing in the early years, meeting and entertaining new clients, it was still her husband's firm and him that was seen as the success. Caroline wanted to prove she was somebody too, not just the wife, the mother, the drudge. She hadn't needed to earn money for herself from her venture so why not help others and create a charity. It was watching a programme on the television about an autistic child who was also severely deaf and how a sensory room with fiberoptic lights and bubble towers was making a difference that began her research and the eventual setting up of the Small Hands charity and the opening of the first of her sensory centres here in Windsor.

Oliver had thought her mad to take on that level of work, telling her she could be a lady of leisure with the kids away from home, Jemima eventually going on to university in Manchester and settling down there while James had married and emigrated to Australia, but that wasn't what Caroline wanted. Her husband had changed his tune when he got free publicity for his own firm when it was mentioned in various articles about Caroline. Plus he could tell his clients and friends how he was involved in charitable work because he was a trustee and did the charity's accounts for free.

The door to the office opened and Hasanna walked in with a large slice of chocolate cake.

"Here," she said, "You can't miss out on this birthday cake, it's gorgeous."

She placed the plate down on the desk in front of Caroline, who eyed it greedily. After licking her lips she said,

"No I shouldn't, really. I have a salad here."

"Salad," Hasanna blew a raspberry, "That's not a salad, it's a box of lettuce."

She pushed the plate nearer to Caroline.

"Eat this," she said, "You don't have to worry about your weight, you look great."

Caroline smiled at her. Hasanna was forty-eight years old. She was tall and lithe with beautiful big, dark eyes. Her natural afro hair was kept short with the ends currently dyed a coppery-gold colour. Caroline picked up the cake and took a bite.

"Wow, that is good," she said.

Hasanna nodded.

"Told you," she replied, "Oops, you've got some cream on your lip."

She leaned over the desk and gently wiped away a small smudge at the corner of Caroline's mouth with her thumb. She looked into Caroline's eyes and smiled before brushing her lips with her own. Caroline felt a thrill pass through her as she always did when Hasanna was close to her.

"I'll see you after work," Hasanna whispered.

Caroline nodded.

Hasanna grinned before turning and leaving the room.

Chapter 5

Accused

The sun shone down through wispy, scattered clouds. The water rippled from the wake of a passing fishing boat, masking any reflection. Mike McGill barely noticed the bobbing of his own vessel having spent many years out here on Lake Huron. His rod hardly moved. Fishing was poor today but Mike didn't care. It was the solitude he delighted in.

He knew he should have already begun heading back to shore, getting the boat onto his trailer at Sauble Beach and then driving to the cottage to be there for when the family arrived but he just wanted a few extra minutes alone on the boat. Not that he felt alone. Aside from his ten year old golden retriever, Ben currently asleep on his piece of carpet at the back of the boat, Mike could feel Barbara was with him.

Six weeks, that's all it had been since she'd passed yet to Mike it felt like he'd lost her months before. In some ways he had. The pain of the cancer had eventually robbed his wife of her uplifting, happy demeanour no matter how hard she tried to be strong. She'd never been one for crying but the tears had flowed at the maliciousness of the illness and the thoughts about its predictable outcome.

"I feel so guilty," she'd told him, towards the end, "I don't want to leave all of you."

It had taken all of Mike's strength to respond and not to crumble into an inconsolable wreck.

"It's not your fault," he'd said, "Don't ever blame yourself."

In the hospital a week later Barbara had still been hanging on, no longer conscious but refusing to die. During a small gap when the rest of the family weren't there, Mike had whispered into his wife's ear,

"I told you not to feel guilty. You don't have to stay. You've given us the love and strength to carry on. Go and be our angel."

Within ten minutes she'd passed away.

While there were times Mike hated being alone there were others, like being here on the boat today, when he was sure Barbara was with him. It was as if she was just out of his line of vision but still there, patting his back consolingly as she'd often done in life after he'd had a busy day at work or the Leafs had just lost an ice hockey match.

He felt his small ponytail brush his neck as the breeze blew and he smiled. He'd not worried about his appearance much while Barbara was ill and, even though his brown hair was now grey, it was still thick and grew well. It had only taken a few missed trips to the hairdressers for it to become noticeably longer. Barbara had said she liked it, that he would look like a 'surfer dude' after tanning in the sun while out on his boat and so he had kept it, trimming his grey beard short before the funeral so that he didn't resemble Santa Claus in mourning.

Having taken time off from the car assembly plant during Barbara's illness, Mike had returned to his job the day after the funeral. He needed something to take his mind off of the situation he now found himself in and work helped with that. Eddie thought him cold and unfeeling but Mike didn't care. His elder son didn't understand emotion, except anger.

Eddie was probably the main reason why Mike was still out on his boat. It was meant to just be Jill and the two girls coming up today but she'd called this morning to say Eddie was coming too, his soccer weekend with friends having been cancelled last minute. It would be his first visit to the cottage since his mum had died and Mike knew he'd be on edge. He didn't like fighting with his son but there was an inevitability that it would happen at some point over the course of the next two days.

Mike wanted this weekend to be filled with happiness. He was hoping the girls would want to come out with grandpa on his boat tomorrow, laughing at his 'funny accent' and the way he still pronounced some words in a very English way, even after almost forty years living in Canada. His other son, Robbie was arriving with his husband, Graham (or Gray as he'd recently begun styling himself) and they were waiting on news to see if their surrogate was pregnant. It was life going on, just what Barbara would have wanted, but Eddie had a way of sucking any positivity or happy emotion out of a room.

Mike sighed as he reeled in his line and started the engine. Ben barely looked up as the boat gathered speed and ruffled his fur. He knew they were going home. There was no need to move yet. The breeze blew into Mike's face and a sudden image appeared in his mind of the wind doing the same thing to him during a darkened evening when he was stood in open countryside, not far from Northey Island where the River Blackwater met the North Sea. He quickly shook the image away.

Why was his mind doing that, replaying the past so vividly? It wasn't the first time recently that had happened, returning him to a time when he was still known as Joey rather than Mike.

Joey McGill. Most of the time Mike could forget about what that name represented, or rather, the time that name represented. He'd begun using his middle name as soon as he emigrated to Canada. His children had long ago forgotten that his letters were all addressed to Mr J.M. McGill and Barbara had only known that he preferred to use Michael instead of Joseph.

Barbara was the reason the past was coming back, Mike knew that really and it wasn't just because she'd died of the same illness that his mother had, spinal cancer; it was because he'd never told her the truth about who he was and why he'd emigrated to a new country. All she'd known was that he was a wiz with cars and that he liked to keep fit. His parents had both died and he had no other family left. She knew nothing of Jimmy.

Thirty-nine years ago there was no internet and social media. The newspaper stories about a missing girl in rural Essex never made it to the Canadian press. No one knew and Mike didn't feel the need to discuss it. He'd always planned on telling Barbara at some point. Well, maybe not the whole truth but certainly the information that had been reported in the newspapers, but it never seemed to be the right time. Now his chance had gone. He could never tell her now and that made him feel guilty. That was why the past had reared its ugly head again. That was why Mike had returned to work so quickly. Barbara was dead but it was the past that was haunting him.

He arrived back at the cottage to a cacophony of noise. The two girls were arguing in the bedroom as he passed, both wanting the top bunk. Seeing grandpa they rushed to hug him and asked him to choose.

"Well who had it last time?"

Neither could remember.

"Well then you'll just have to sort it out yourselves…but quietly."

The cottage, as it was called, was certainly not like the cottages he'd left behind in England. There was no thatch, no beams or low ceilings. It was basically one long, wooden structure built on top of a garage and storage area on the ground floor. The three bedrooms were small but each big enough to fit a double bed, the kids room having a pull-out bed as well as the bunk. They were created by partition walls and were off a small corridor as one entered the property from the raised deck outside. Aside from the bathroom the rest of the space was one large room, kitchen, dining and lounge. The walls were a dark wood and Mike had wanted to paint them white for years but Barbara had refused, preferring the 'rustic' look. They used to joke that if Barbara went first the first thing he'd do would be to paint the walls white. Mike knew he'd never paint them now.

The main room was no less quiet than the girls' bedroom. Robbie and Gray had arrived as well as Eddie and Jill and they were all laughing, well, not Eddie who was sat on the sofa with a full champagne glass on the table beside him. Jill, Robbie and Gray were stood around the large dining table laughing, near empty glasses in front of each of them. When they saw Mike they shouted louder and all ran to hug him.

"We're pregnant," Robbie told him, "We had it confirmed this morning."

"Congratulations," Mike replied.

He tried to refuse the glass that was shoved into his hand.

"You know I don't drink."

"Come on papa Mike," Gray told him, good-naturedly, "One won't hurt. You had a glass at our wedding."

Mike took the glass and, after a cheers, took a sip. He cast a glance at Eddie who was staring down at his lap. He felt the anger start to rise in him.

Sod it, he thought, this is a time for celebration. He turned to his other son and said brightly,

"So, does this mean you're going to sell your cramped, little condo in Toronto then?"

"What do you mean, cramped," Robbie replied, mocking sounding hurt.

"Well you're not going to fit a baby in there," his father told him.

"They're only small though-eh," Gray added.

Jill snorted.

"But they come with a heap of stuff, trust me," she told them, "The diapers alone need a room of their own-eh."

Both Jill and Gray had that habit Canadians were famous for of ending most sentences by adding 'eh' to the last word, giving it an extra syllable.

"We can't really afford anything bigger in town," Robbie said.

"Well why don't you move back out our way," Mike told them, "I'm in Guelph and Jill and Eddie are in Milton. It would be nice for you to have family close by, wouldn't it? I hate the drive into Toronto these days. The 401 is always so busy."

Robbie and Gray looked at each other.

"We haven't really thought that far ahead," Robbie said.

"Well give it some thought," Mike told them.

"I thought you were going to sell up though papa Mike," Gray added, "Move permanently up here."

"That was my and Barbara's plans," he replied.

The cottage had been in Barbara's family for a number of years and she and Mike had always planned to gift it to the children after Mike retired and then sell their house in Guelph and buy themselves another cottage to live in permanently, somewhere a little quieter either further along the coast or across on Georgian Bay.

"I'm glad someone's finally remembered mom," came a voice from behind them.

All four turned to see Eddie staring moodily back at them.

"It's only been weeks since she died and you're all laughing and joking like she was never here."

"Eddie!" Jill scolded.

"Yeah come on Ed," Robbie told him, "No one's forgotten mom. If she was here she'd be the first to raise a glass to our happy news."

"But she's not here is she."

Mike tried to bite his lip but he was having trouble.

"Well I think she is here," Jill said, "She wouldn't miss this-eh."

"Now you're being ridiculous."

Mike turned round.

"Hey," he said, "This family has had enough hurt and upset these last six months. If there's happy news then we should be able to celebrate it."

Eddie's eyes narrowed.

"Well I still don't feel like celebrating," he said, coldly.

"Then why did you bother coming," his father asked, "Was it just to make everyone else feel as miserable as you? Is that your purpose in life?"

Eddie stood up.

"I seem to be the only one missing mom."

"Oh grow up," Mike shouted at him, "We all miss her. That doesn't mean we can't ever laugh again. Your mother wouldn't want that. Think about what she'd want right now."

"Are you saying I didn't know her?"

Mike sighed.

"Oh God, give me strength," he said, before looking back at his son, "You really are a selfish, little shit."

He heard Jill gasp. It was at this moment that Barbara would usually step in but she was no longer here to do that.

"You can't talk to me like that," Eddie said.

"Yes I can. This is my house."

"It's mom's."

"Well now it's mine," Mike spat, "And I don't want you in it, not if you can't be bothered to be happy for your brother."

"Oh so it's all about Robbie as always."

"For God's sake will you listen to yourself," Mike exploded, the girls rushing into the room to see what the noise was, "You're thirty-five not fifteen. Yes, today is about Robbie. He's going to become a father. Do you remember what that feeling is like because I sure as hell do. Now if you can't be happy for him then get the fuck out of my house."

Eddie opened his mouth to respond but saw the girls standing in the doorway, looking confused.

"Pack up your stuff girls," he called over to them, "We're leaving."

Still Missing

by Karen Taylor

Chapter 3 (First draft)

The disappearance of Emma Burrows stood out for me when researching cases for this book. For a child to vanish from a tiny village which, at the time, was a place where everyone pretty much knew everybody else, seems remarkable. It appears unlikely that a stranger from outside would have just happened to pass through that day and snatched a child, but if he (or she) was local then how did no one else not know anything about it?

I visited Little Tenwick, which hasn't changed much in thirty-nine years. While the centre, where the school Emma attended is situated, is unusual in that there aren't many properties that face the village green, surely, with a shop and pub and the time of day that it happened, there must have been someone that saw something.

Visiting the area raised more questions for me than provided answers. I wanted to speak with those involved in the story at the time, all of those people, still living, that were part of both Emma Burrows and Jimmy McGill's lives. I can't believe an entire village was part of a mass cover-up. At the time everyone was in shock. Today, people all seem to know about the disappearance, even though they weren't all living in the village at the time. The story is still part of everyday life here, a huge tragedy where the after affects are still felt.

Someone must know something. How in depth did the police investigation go at the time when the only suspect was Jimmy McGill? Was there a lack of enquiry or just a lack of evidence; or was there a lack of truth being revealed?

Chapter 6

Mother

So many people hated Mondays but Sylvia felt happy sitting in the vestry. She'd always enjoyed cleaning and never saw it as a chore. While she couldn't get on her hands and knees and scrub the stone floor of the church anymore she was quite happy sitting here polishing the silver candlesticks, knowing they'd be gleaming again on the altar next Sunday.

She was also happy about Ken. They'd been able to spend more time together over the weekend, with Ray working both days, and Sylvia could see their relationship growing ever stronger. She realised the time was coming when she'd have to tell Ray about Ken. She didn't want to keep fitting her boyfriend in around her son's work schedule. Ken had mentioned wanting to meet Ray a few times recently and that was the only worry Sylvia had. What would her son think when she told him she was seeing someone? For the last year, since leaving Jackie, she was all Ray had. Would he see her relationship as another rejection? Perhaps it was wrong not to have told him sooner, when things with Ken had been less serious.

Kerry walked into the vestry with a cup of tea that had two digestive biscuits resting in the saucer. She smiled at Sylvia as she placed it down on the table.

"Thought you could do with this," she said.

"Perfect timing," Sylvia replied, throwing down the cloth and pulling off her latex gloves.

"You always get such a shine on those," Kerry told her, admiring the candlesticks.

"It's just elbow grease with a hint of polish. I've always believed if a job is worth doing it's worth doing well."

"I'll try and remember that the next time I've got my hand in the toilet at home, trying to unblock the u-bend."

Kerry winked and they both laughed. Sylvia like Kerry. She'd started coming to the church and volunteering a couple of months ago, having said she disliked the vicar at the village where she lived. Apparently she had two children but she'd never brought them to church. Sylvia didn't ask why, she didn't like to pry.

Some of the other volunteers had given Kerry a wide berth because she wasn't local, which is probably the reason Sylvia had made an effort to get to know her. Kerry was a kind-hearted woman and always willing to help out with any job at the church. Sylvia had the impression Kerry wore a wig but she couldn't understand why she'd chosen one where the hair was such an incredibly dark shade of black. That coupled with the over-sized glasses that didn't suit her made her friend look like she was wearing a disguise. Whenever Sylvia found herself thinking this she would berate herself for being shallow about this lovely, young woman. It wasn't looks that were important.

"I was sorry to hear about your daughter," Kerry said.

Sylvia was so surprised to hear that unexpected sentence she spat her mouthful of tea back into the cup, sending hot liquid over the rim to splash down onto the biscuits below.

"Sorry, what," she said, sounding flustered as she wiped her top lip with her hand.

"I was sorry to hear about your daughter," Kerry repeated, unfazed by Sylvia's obvious distress, "I heard about her abduction today."

Sylvia didn't reply.

"My heart goes out to you," Kerry said.

Sylvia felt a rush of anger.

"Please don't pity me," she replied, forcefully.

Kerry's expression changed to confusion and Sylvia's rage instantly evaporated.

"I'm sorry," she said, "It's just that you got that look on your face that everyone gets once they've heard about the disappearance. People change towards me once they know the truth."

That was another reason Sylvia didn't want Ken to know.

"I won't change," Kerry began, but Sylvia interrupted her, shaking her head.

"You already have," she told her, "You're going to be worried from now on about what you say in front of me, concerned in case any mention of a child will send me off into a spiral of upset and depression. It always happens. I've experienced it for the last thirty-nine years."

Sylvia remembered the utter shock in the village when Emma went missing. While she often blotted out the events of that day, how she arrived home on the bus from her usual weekly shopping trip to Chelmsford to be told her daughter was missing, how she half-fainted at the bus stop and had to be helped home, how the doctor gave her a sedative that sent her to sleep with a feeling of guilt that she wasn't out there searching with everyone else, but she could always remember the days and weeks and months that followed.

The police and press eventually left them alone as no new leads came in but the rest of the village was always there and while their help in the initial search had been wonderful, the pitiful stares that Sylvia received, or the times when she entered the local shop to silence, knowing that the local residents must have been talking about her before she opened the door, was difficult to deal with. It went on long after the village had returned to normal, Sylvia being the sole subject of village gossip, and it always reignited around each anniversary.

"The news won't change me," Kerry replied, "Not if you don't want it to. You only have to say how you feel."

Sylvia snorted.

"You think so?"

"Of course," Kerry said, seriously, "No one will treat you differently unless you tell them how you feel. Have you ever tried to do that?"

Sylvia felt herself squirm.

"I'm not one to talk about my feelings," she admitted, running the backs of her fingers gently down the side of one of the candlesticks, "I've always thought them private. I suppose I've never really talked about myself because, if I do, people will be looking at me. I don't want to be everyone's centre of attention. That happened when Emma was taken and I hated it. I hated the pity, I hated the sympathetic looks, I hated other people's embarrassment."

"So why didn't you tell them how you felt?"

"Because it was all well meant. It wasn't done to hurt me, and saying it did would have made me seem ungrateful. That's what I mean about talking about your feelings, the situation can very easily get misconstrued and cause arguments or resentment. I just want people to treat me as Sylvia, not as some tragic martyr trying to get through each day since her daughter was taken."

"Don't you want to talk about Emma?" Kerry asked.

"Of course I do," Sylvia replied, "But other people don't. They want to hear about the day she was taken. They're not interested in listening to me telling them how much I loved her and the things we liked to do together when we were at home. They can't see how that would make me happy. They don't want to hear me wonder if that caring little girl grew up to take a job in a caring profession. They don't want to listen to me wondering if she married and had children of her own. They think I want to talk because I still can't cope with what happened, and then I get the pity looks again."

Kerry took the seat opposite Sylvia at the vestry table.

"Well tell me about her now," she said, "I'm listening. I want to hear about who Emma was."

"You're just saying that."

"I'm not. Let's face it, I've already heard three different versions today of the events of the day she was taken from various members of the church ladies. It'll be nice to hear about the little girl they're talking about from the one person who actually knew her."

Sylvia smiled. It had been so long since she'd spoken aloud about Emma she wasn't sure where to start.

"She was a miracle child really," she began, "Daniel, my ex-husband and I had tried for another baby for years before she came along. No one really knew why it took so long for me to fall pregnant and then to keep losing the babies I was carrying. I went through a number of tests. It was a difficult time."

"I can imagine."

"Daniel was ready to give up trying. At the time I was angry. I'd just lost a baby later in the pregnancy than normal and had to give birth to her. I suppose my emotions and hormones were all over the place but I told Daniel it was up to me to decide when we stopped, not him. It didn't go down too well."

Sylvia stared at the half-full cup of tea and the soggy biscuits, unable to meet Kerry's gaze as she spoke about intimate moments of her marriage whilst sat inside a church.

"We stopped the program we were on for conceiving. Well we pretty much stopped…anyway it was a few months later when I fell pregnant accidentally. It was still a stressful time. I was convinced I'd lose this one too."

Sylvia looked up but she was thinking about the past and her gaze was fixed somewhere beyond Kerry's shoulder.

"When they placed Emma in my arms I was overjoyed but still terrified I'd lose her."

A dark cloud passed over Sylvia's face as she now focussed her attention on Kerry.

"I sometimes wonder if I knew something would happen to her, even then. Perhaps my worrying thoughts took on a physical form and I created the situation that caused her to be abducted."

Kerry reached over and patted her hand.

"You can't think like that," she said, "It wasn't your fault. You can't think someone away."

Sylvia conceded the point with a nod of her head.

"Tell me about Emma," Kerry urged.

The smile returned.

"She was an angel," Sylvia said, "A delicate, little angel. She just brought us all such joy. She was so loving. Even when she was upset she would rush to Daniel or I and her hug was so warm and affectionate. Her favourite colour was purple. I've still got her rag doll with the purple hair. It took me ages to find her. There wasn't a lot of purple about back then. It was more just pink for girls and blue for boys with yellow or white as a unisex option. It was her purple hair ribbons that Emma loved the most because she could wear them all of the time. When she went to school she couldn't take her doll with her but she could take her precious ribbons."

Sylvia sighed.

"I barely let her out of my sight before she went to school. She was my, Daniel's and Ray's world. In our house it was only ever the four of us, one unit. I thought she'd always be safe with us…and then she was taken."

"I can't begin to imagine what that's like," Kerry said, "And I hope I'm not making the pity face. I can't tell."

Sylvia smiled warmly at her. Kerry was a very nice person. It had been pleasant to think about Emma the little girl rather than Emma the missing child. And yet, Sylvia realised, she'd still brought up the awful day while talking. Perhaps she was being too hard on the other residents of Little Tenwick. Emma was always going to be linked to her disappearance. That would never change. She didn't like the fact though. That meant she was always going to be 'poor Sylvia.' She'd thought she'd proved herself an upright, respected member of the community years before, having cleaned for many of the residents as well as being a dinner lady at the primary school, going above and beyond with her help for the children there, caring for some after school, taking an interest in their lives and generally helping them with any difficult situation.

It was Marjorie that had got Sylvia the job, having already been a dinner lady herself for many years. She could see her friend floundering after the abduction and had fought hard for Sylvia to be offered the position. Sylvia had been worried about working at the school where her daughter had been a pupil but she took the job and soon realised it was the best thing for her.

"How do you cope," Kerry asked, "I mean, how do you get through each day?"

Sylvia sighed again.

"You just do," she said, "Not at first, obviously. In the first few weeks I felt I wouldn't be able to go on without my Emma. Every time the phone rang or there was a knock at the door my heart would pound in my chest, wondering if there was going to be news about her. There never was any."

"What, none?"

"Oh there were rumoured sightings. Some of them were well meant, others were people looking for attention or just being nasty, thinking it a joke to say they'd seen her when they hadn't. The elation of possible sightings and the utter despair when nothing came of them was exhausting. By the time of the later so-called sightings, Daniel had begun working over in Gloucestershire so it was just me and Ray at home."

"That must have been difficult."

Sylvia shrugged.

"Not as much as you'd think. Daniel and I had been drifting apart for a long while. To be honest we both realised we preferred it when we were on opposite sides of the country and we had a very amicable divorce. Daniel met someone else. Whether that was while we were still married I don't know. It doesn't matter now. Anyway, he had his new life, Ray had his studies and I needed something for me. That's really when I started going to church more."

"And that helped?"

"Oh definitely. I spent most of the time shouting at God rather than praying, wanting to know what I'd done to deserve to be treated this way. Eventually I realised anger wasn't helping to bring my little girl back and I found myself praying for the strength to understand what had happened. It took months, well years really, but eventually I found the strength to forgive whoever took her."

"Really? I don't think I could."

Sylvia shrugged again.

"What other choice did I have? I've always believed my Emma is still alive. I think I'm the only one that does but a mother would know if her child was dead wouldn't she? I've never felt that. I'm sure she's alive just as I'm sure that poor, simple lad didn't take her. He couldn't have. No, someone else took her and I pray that she's been brought up well in a loving family. That's all I can do."

Kerry was silent for a moment.

"I don't think I could be like that," she said, "But I admire you Sylvia. You're a strong lady. No one should look at you pityingly."

Sylvia smiled back.

"Thank you," she said, "I appreciate that."

Sylvia's smile was replaced with a look of puzzlement.

"Why today?" she asked.

"Why what?" Kerry replied.

"Why were the ladies talking about Emma to you today? It's a few weeks yet until the anniversary."

"Oh, I see what you mean. Actually the ladies were talking to each other rather than to me, I just overheard. I think it was on account of the woman in the village asking questions."

"What woman?" Sylvia asked, "What questions?"

"Oh I assumed you must have known," Kerry told her, "Apparently there was some woman in the village asking about the Emma Burrows case. It was this morning I believe."

Sylvia rushed home to phone Ray. She could barely catch her breath. She hadn't asked what this woman looked like or how old she was but what if it was…what if she'd come home?

Ray didn't like being disturbed at work and made that clear to his mother before she could interrupt him. She was shocked by his response when she told him about the woman.

"Oh yes I know about her," he said, brightly, "She's a

journalist and came into the supermarket earlier, quite by chance. She didn't realise who I was."

"You didn't tell her anything did you?"

"Well only a little," Ray said.

Sylvia sighed with relief.

"But that's just because I was too busy. I've said I can talk to her again anytime."

"What?"

"We're going to be mentioned in a book about missing people. Can you believe it? Isn't it exciting?"

Sylvia was exasperated.

"No, it's not exciting," she told her son, forcefully, "It's utterly wrong to bring the past up again. It's upsetting to me, don't you see that."

"Oh mother, it's practically forty years ago."

"And what has that got to do with it? I don't want to be reminded of the past."

"So you're not going to speak to her then," Ray said, sounding downcast.

"Of course not!"

"Oh, because I told her you would."

"You what? Well, you can just un-tell her. I'm not going to have the past brought back to life, nor mentioned in some book, and if you've got the sense you were born with you won't speak to her again either."

Sylvia slammed the phone down. She didn't usually speak to Ray like that but she was scared and upset. Realising this woman wasn't her Emma and was just a journalist made her angry. It was wrong. Who on earth would want to look into Emma's story? There'd been nothing new to add to it in years.

The past belongs in the past, Sylvia thought to herself, the facts and the secrets.

She shivered, feeling afraid. Was it possible that someone looking into the case now would find out she wasn't where she said she'd been that Wednesday morning, thirty-nine years before?

Chapter 7

Brother

Ray had been feeling quite cheerful before his mother's phone call. He'd spent more time than normal that morning parading up and down the aisles in the hope that Geoffrey Delaney would come into the supermarket. While he knew there was now a casual vacancy on the parish council, Geoffrey Delaney didn't know that he knew. Ray wanted to use that to his advantage by casually mentioning all of his merits in passing conversation. He'd spent a lot of the previous afternoon in his office (Sundays were always quiet at the store) preparing ways in which he could achieve this.

Being out on the shop floor though did have its disadvantages. Monday morning was always a busy time and with his assistant manager, Carmel and one of the part-timers, Janine on the tills, Ray found himself being the member of staff customers approached to ask the location of various products, when all he wanted to do was concentrate on watching the door to see if Geoffrey Delaney entered. His frustration threatened to envelop him and when Mrs Bradley asked him, not for the first time, where the tinned peas had moved to, he imagined himself smacking her repeatedly with a can while telling her they'd been in the same place for the last three years.

Just as he was about to give up hope, Ray saw the chairman of the parish council striding towards the front door, his Jaguar saloon parked across two parking bays outside. While Ray was fifty-four, in front of the older, debonair Geoffrey Delaney, he felt like a young, inexperienced teen. The man oozed confidence and success and was very charming. He was everything Ray wanted to be, a popular, well-respected pillar of the community.

At the door Geoffrey stood back to let a couple of ladies out, smiling and nodding at them before entering the shop. He made his way to the coffee machine, pulled out a cup, stood it in place and selected his coffee from the screen. Ray tried to make his walk over seem as casual as possible.

"Oh, hello Mr Delaney," he said, "I didn't see you come in."

"Good morning Roy," Geoffrey replied, reaching for a packet of brown sugar and a stirrer.

Ray decided to continue talking rather than correct him.

"Off somewhere on business?"

"That's right, and I'm later than I want to be."

For the first time he looked at Ray.

"I don't suppose you could do me a favour could you?" he asked.

Ray fought hard to stop his grin spreading ever wider.

"Of course," he replied, as nonchalantly as he could, "Just name it."

"Could I pay for this coffee later," Geoffrey said, "I need to use my debit card and there's a queue at the tills. I really can't afford to be late for my next appointment."

"It's no bother at all," Ray told him, trying to sound like he was chatting with an old friend, "In fact, have this one on me."

"Oh, well that's very kind," Geoffrey replied, placing a lid onto his takeaway cup.

"Well I like to look after a loyal customer."

Geoffrey pulled a face.

"It's only a coffee I get here," he said, "My wife does all our grocery shopping in Chelmsford."

"You're still regular," Ray told him, "I've always instilled good customer service into my staff. It's the most important aspect of running a store. We're only as good as our customers."

"I suppose. Well, thank you. I must go."

Ray chased after him, walking along in his wake as he tried to avoid the other customers in the aisle.

"I've always felt a good store manager serves the community," he called out, "And I've certainly had lots of experience of doing that over the years."

"You have been here a long time," Geoffrey agreed.

"Thank you," Ray replied, taking the comment as a compliment, "There are other ways I'd like to help the community too that one can't do on one's own."

They were at the automatic door now. As it opened, Geoffrey Delaney continued to stride on through it.

"Perhaps we can talk about it some other time," Ray shouted, after the retreating figure.

He was glad to see Geoffrey wave over his shoulder and took that as an affirmative answer to his request. It was just then that a striking blonde lady stepped past him into the store. Ray thought nothing of the stranger and returned to his office, pleased that he'd had a good conversation with Geoffrey. It was barely five minutes later that Janine came in and told him a journalist would like to see him.

He was very pleased with Janine. She'd only started here a couple of weeks ago but she'd fitted in well. She was one of the older part-timers, in her forties, apparently with two children who were both now at school full time, which was why she'd wanted a job. She hadn't had much retail experience but she was proving to be a hard worker. Ray had interviewed her himself. He wished she took a bit more pride in her appearance, like coming into work with some make-up on so that, with her short, mousey bob, she didn't look emaciated, but that was a conversation for another day.

Karen Taylor walked into the office wearing a navy blue trouser suit, which instantly put her into Ray's good books. He liked people to look smart and that was sadly lacking in this day and age where people would go out for a meal in a restaurant in jeans or shorts. She was probably about five foot four but her three inch heels put her at eye level with Ray. She had an abundance of long, blonde hair that she regularly flicked off her face with a shake of her head.

"It's good of you to see me," she said, handing him her business card before sitting down in the proffered seat.

She glanced around the cramped office and made a mental note.

"Well I only have a few minutes to spare really," Ray lied to her, "As you probably noticed, it is one of our busier days."

Karen shrugged indifferently.

"Well, I'm from London," she replied, "That's a completely different level of busy. Anyway, I'll come straight to the point."

Karen told him about the book and the chapter she was preparing on Emma.

"It was an amazing coincidence that I found you," she said, "I only visited Little Tenwick for the first time today, to try and get a feel of the area. It's cute isn't it, a proper village. Anyway, I stopped by here to buy some cigarettes on my way home and thought I'd ask if anyone knew about the story. I was astounded to discover Emma's brother worked here."

Ray sat further back in his seat, a wide grin on his face.

"Yes," he said, "I certainly haven't let our family tragedy prevent me from climbing the rungs of the career ladder."

He saw Karen cast another quick glance around the

cupboard-like office.

"Of course there's always room for expansion," he told her, "Actually I'm…I'm working on some plans to improve our facilities here at the moment. I think we're a vital resource for a town like this."

"I suppose everyone finds a convenience store handy."

Ray frowned but before he could reply, Karen spoke again.

"Now," she said, sitting forward with a pen and a pad of paper in her hand, "You don't mind if I make a few notes do you? I've found most people prefer it to my recording the conversation."

"No, no that's fine."

"As I said, I'm writing a book about various unsolved missing person cases and my research led me to your sister. The case really stood out."

"How so?"

"Well there seems to be very little information about it and a sparse investigation," Karen told him.

"Oh, but the police were here for ages," Ray said, "At least it certainly felt like that at the time. There was a distinct lack of privacy, I can tell you."

"You were fifteen, weren't you?"

"That's right. I was at the comprehensive here in Great Tenwick."

"And you took your sister to her school that day."

"Yes. I always did on a Wednesday. My father was out of work at the time and didn't seem in any hurry to get something else. Money was tight, I've never tried to deny that, and mother used to have to get the early bus to a food store in Chelmsford that sold items cheaply every Wednesday."

"Couldn't your father have taken your sister to school?"

"That's what I said at the time but was told not to be cheeky.

Apparently father had to be home in case he was called about a job opportunity."

He sighed and shook his head.

"It sounds like you're not close to your dad."

"I haven't spoken to him in years," Ray told her, "Once he moved away to the Cotswolds and replaced mum with some tart and had a new family I had no interest in keeping up the relationship."

Karen wrote some notes on her pad.

"I believe he did very well for himself," Ray continued, "Mother has kept in touch, God knows why. He lives in some kind of retirement home in Stow on the Wold now that must cost an absolute fortune."

"Are you expecting him to leave you money in his will?"

"No of course not," Ray said, "Why would you ask? I'm doing very well on my own thank you very much. Besides the house in Little Tenwick will come to me through mother; well of course I'll need to sort out some legalities seeing as it's still left to both Emma and me. Anyway, it was father who paid the mortgage and signed it over to her."

"That was nice."

"It was guilt for the way he treated us."

Karen was aware that Ray seemed to have forgotten all about only giving her a few minutes of his precious time.

"So, you took Emma to school," she said.

"That's right. I left her at the early club they ran and then got the school bus here to Tenwick Comp."

"And how did you discover your sister was missing?"

"I was called out of class by the headmaster. He told me Emma had got lost and a secretary brought me back home."

"That must have been scary."

Ray shrugged.

"I don't really remember," he said, "It was a long time ago. I think it was shock at the time. That often leaves one feeling numb to begin with, doesn't it. I returned home to my mother being in bed, having been given a sedative and father out searching for Emma with the rest of the village."

"So she went missing from the early club."

"That's what I was told. Each morning parents were able to deliver their children to the school from eight o'clock. It was so they could go onto work or get on with other things. It was only Wednesdays that Emma used it. Mother took her to school the rest of the week. She always arranged her cleaning jobs for after nine o'clock."

"And Caroline Willis was the teacher in charge."

"That day, yes. She was also Emma's form teacher. I believe the staff took it in turns to run the early club. It was just children sitting in a classroom as far as I know and there weren't that many of them, so nothing strenuous. It was reported that Caroline stepped out of the room for a couple of minutes and that's when Emma ran off."

"Why did she do that?"

Ray sighed.

"Oh she was always crying about something. I'm afraid Emma was rather spoilt with attention from my parents."

"I read it was something to do with her losing a hair ribbon," Karen said.

"Was it? I barely remember. That wouldn't surprise me though, if someone pulled it out as a joke."

"She wouldn't have lost it then though would she," Karen said.

"What?"

Ray was confused by the question. Why was this woman concerning herself with such minuscule details?"

"Well, if a child pulled it out then he (I assume it was something a boy would do) would have it. It wouldn't be lost, would it?"

Ray shrugged.

"I don't know," he told her, dismissively, "I wasn't there. Perhaps it got thrown away or lost, it really doesn't matter, does it."

"Doesn't it?"

Ray was beginning to get bored with the conversation. He didn't reply to Karen's question and instead continued with what he was going to say.

"Emma would have cried and run off to find a grown-up."

"A grown-up," Karen questioned, "Not necessarily a teacher?"

There she went again, getting picky over minor details.

"Well a teacher was implied, wasn't it," he told her, sarcastically, "After all, she was in a school at the time."

Karen didn't rise to his response.

"It's interesting that you said grown-up and not teacher, though," she told him, "Would she have gone searching for another grown-up if a teacher wasn't available?"

Ray shrugged his shoulders again.

"I've never really given it any consideration," he said, "I mentioned she was given a lot of attention by my parents. She was the miracle child, the daughter they never thought they would have. Emma was kept close by my mother at all times until she went to school. All she had at home were my parents and me, and I was already ten when she came along. She wasn't used to other children. She felt safe with adults."

"Interesting," Karen said, more to herself, writing another note in her pad, "And do you believe she was abducted by Jimmy McGill?"

"Oh undoubtedly," Ray replied, "He was always hanging around the school. He wasn't right in the head; dropped on it as a baby or something like that. His family were very lower class. The father was a drunk and hit his wife on a number of occasions. The mother could barely cope with the husband and the mentally ill son. Both of the parents were dead within six months of the abduction. The village didn't mourn their loss. I'm surprised the brother didn't go off the rails like his father."

"Do you know where he is now?"

"Joey? I heard he emigrated. I think it was Canada but that's all I know."

"And what about the teacher, Caroline? Did she stick around?"

"She finished the school year. I believe she had to due to her contract or something like that, but as soon as she could, she left. Well she was blamed for what happened after all. It didn't look good, did it, losing a child placed in your care. I don't think the headmistress wanted her to stay. She thought it reflected badly on the school."

"How do you know all this?" Karen asked.

Ray snorted.

"You haven't lived in a village before have you," he said, "Little Tenwick remains a backwater. It thrives on gossip. One heard enough conversations. Not that I was an eavesdropper you understand, I detest gossip, but my mother's friend at the time was a dinner lady at the school and she knew what was going on there."

"I don't suppose you know where Caroline went?"

Ray grinned.

"Actually I do," he told her, "By chance I saw her in a photograph in one of the national newspapers last year. She runs a charity of some kind now but she also married a very wealthy businessman. She's certainly done alright for herself."

"You don't happen to know the name of the charity do you?"

"No but I do recall her married name. What was it now, Morton, no Metcalf, that's it. I remember that because of the calf bit. I always thought she was a bit of a snobby cow."

Karen scribbled down a few more notes.

"Well that's all very helpful," she said, closing her notepad, "I'm sorry to have taken up your valuable time."

"Oh you haven't…," Ray began, before remembering what he'd told her when she first sat down, "Well I mean, it doesn't matter. I'm more than happy to chat again at a later date. This book sounds very interesting. Will it just be the one chapter or will it spill over? You know there's lots more I can tell you about my background, if that's what you want to know. I'm sure mother will be happy to talk to you too."

Karen stood up.

"I've found I always need to tread extra carefully with the mother of a missing child," she told him, "The book is still very much in its early stages but I'll let you know if I need more information from you. I know where you are now."

Ray beamed.

"Pop in anytime," he said.

He sat in his office grinning for fifteen minutes after Karen left, thinking how good it would be to be mentioned by name in a book. It would be good to tell Geoffrey Delaney and the other members of the parish council. Surely that would be a plus for his membership, a story about such triumph over a terrible tragedy and his own rise in social standing through hard work and determination.

It wasn't until after his phone call with Sylvia that he began to see things differently. The past could be raked up again.

Karen was a journalist after all and Ray could remember the press intrusion at the time of the abduction. The coverage first of all had been great, getting the story out there and having more people looking out for Emma. They were portrayed as a grieving family. Then, when there was no trace of her or of Jimmy McGill, the stories began to change. Questions were asked about the true home life of the Burrows, Sylvia and Daniel's relationship with each other and their children. Even the divorce was later reported on. That had been less pleasant.

Ray didn't particularly want all of the details of the past to be talked about again, especially if the parish council looked on it with a dim view. Perhaps he shouldn't have mentioned the family's need for money or how he came from a broken home after his father left. Ray just wanted to be seen as a man who was going places, who had dealt with tragedy and won through.

He hadn't liked the way his mother had spoken to him on the phone. She's been very short and rude. She hadn't been like that since Emma was still with them and all of the attention had been on her. It was typical that now she was being remembered again Emma was still taking attention away from him, even though she was dead.

Why wouldn't his mother accept that her daughter was dead? Why wouldn't she have her declared so? That way, Ray could inherit the house in Little Tenwick without any niggling complications. Perhaps **he** could have her declared dead. Ray smiled. He liked that thought very much.

God, he said to himself, I still detest that little bitch!

Chapter 8

Father

Daniel stared around the communal lounge. It wasn't set out like those rooms one saw in a retirement home, all winged-back chairs in the same dull colour, placed around the edge of the room. Here there were various seating areas with different coloured, comfy chairs and sofas as well as high-backed chairs set around small, circular tables.

It was a nice, bright room with a small kitchen area for residents to make their own drinks but Daniel still felt depressed. While the room was quite trendy the occupants were not. The place was filled with old people falling asleep. Daniel hated that. If he wanted a nap he'd stay at home. He wouldn't come out to the communal areas and do it. The room should be full of chatter and laughter but today it felt like a morgue.

Deep down he knew he was being over dramatic. There were only a couple of people asleep but because they were, the other residents were talking in whispers. Daniel wanted to shout out, to wake the lazy bastards up and get a bit of life going in this place. Everyone was well over seventy but that didn't mean they had to behave like they were old.

He'd been out of sorts since his chat with Tania on Friday but he still didn't understand why. It wasn't often she asked for his opinion and whenever she had, she'd always made her own decision anyway. Why was this one any different? She'd decide what she wanted to do in the end so why get shirty with him?

Daniel looked about the room again. He'd come here for a bit of company, a decent chat but he wasn't going to get it so he decided he may as well get the bus into the village and have a couple of pints. He never felt alone with a pint of bitter in his hand.

Daniel thought back to the previous month when he'd turned eighty. He hadn't wanted to celebrate. It was an old age number and he didn't want to be it. Tania though had arranged and paid for a small surprise celebration in the communal lounge for all of the residents. It was an afternoon tea with sandwiches and cakes and everyone on their best behaviour. Many of the residents had dressed up too. They all seemed to enjoy themselves but if Daniel had had his way he would have had a table full of booze and sent out for takeaway food, with everyone letting their hair down dancing to some lively music. As Jessica had pointed out to him when he'd admitted his disappointment, not all of the residents may have survived that event.

In early September there were still plenty of tourists visiting the Cotswolds but at least on this Monday afternoon in Stow on the Wold, they were walking about the village looking at the architecture of the beautiful buildings and browsing in the shops. Daniel had no trouble getting a seat in his favourite pub looking out onto the stunningly picturesque market square. Just after he'd sat down with his pint of bitter a friendly face walked in.

"What a surprise to see you here, Bob," Daniel joked, as his friend sat down opposite with a pint.

"This is the first this week," Bob told him.

Daniel raised an eyebrow.

"It's only Monday," he said.

"What's your point?"

Daniel laughed. Bob took a healthy slurp of his pint.

"So how are things up at the Fading Fast Nursing Home?" he asked.

"It's a retirement village, as well you know," Daniel replied, "Although it certainly feels like a morgue today."

"I don't know how you stand it. Mind you, I might change my mind once I'm nearer your age, in another thirty years or so."

"Hey, Alice and I catered for your fortieth at the restaurant. I know for a fact that was twenty-five years ago."

Bob winked.

"That restaurant hasn't been the same since you two sold up," he said, "Alice was a smashing chef."

"I know," Daniel replied, sadly.

"We all miss her."

Daniel smiled before taking a sip of his beer.

"I still sometimes turn to talk to her if I've seen something interesting or thought of something funny," he confessed.

"I understand," Bob replied, "There are the odd occasions when I wish my Teresa was there."

"She's still alive."

"I know, but mostly we'd rather be on our own."

Daniel couldn't help laughing at his friend.

"But you and Alice," Bob continued, "You were definitely made for each other. I've never seen a couple as happy as you two were."

"That was a surprise to both of us when we first met," Daniel told him.

"Was it?"

"Yes. I was still waiting for my divorce to be finalised and Alice had just ended things with her boyfriend. Neither of us were looking for another relationship."

"Where did you meet?"

"At a small pub down in Bourton-on-the-Water. It's a café now. I hadn't long been living in the area full time. Before that I was still travelling between here and Essex until my marriage ended. I'd worked at a paint manufacturing plant there until it closed down. We mostly supplied to the car industry but when the collapse in car sales occurred I wound up out of a job. A nice way to start the new decade of the eighties."

Bob nodded as he sighed.

"I remember those times," he said, "I was out of work myself for a couple of years. Fortunately it was before I was married and had a family to support."

"Well I had two children," Daniel continued, "It wasn't much fun watching my wife take care of all of us and then going out cleaning to try and make ends meet."

He looked a little sheepish.

"I should have done more at home but it was different back then," he added, "Men were still supposed to be the breadwinners. Most women that had children usually only worked part time if at all. Times were changing but I think we were still influenced by the generation before. My dad was a real dinosaur. I was already a disappointment because I hadn't wanted to go into one of the armed services like he and his ancestors all had."

"I know the type of man you mean," Bob said, taking another healthy swig of his beer.

"I'd worked damned hard to become a supervisor at the factory and I wasn't going to settle for anything less in a new job. Of course a lot of the manufacturing industry was on its knees but eventually a supervisor role came up here in Gloucestershire and Sylvia and I decided I ought to take it. It was a relief really to get away from…"

Daniel realised he was about to mention the fallout from his daughter's disappearance and decided he didn't want to talk about that.

"…well, away from my marriage. It wasn't very stable by then."

Bob didn't appear to have noticed Daniel's pause in mid conversation. He'd just finished his pint and indicated to the barman to pour them two more. He turned back to Daniel.

"What job did you do," he asked, "I only met you once you had the restaurant."

"It was a large company that made lots of products for the home. I was in the arm that produced wallpaper."

"That's a bit of a leap to running your own restaurant."

Daniel smiled.

"That's when I met Alice. Wasn't I telling you how we met?"

"You were," Bob told him, matter-of-factly, as the barman placed two beers down onto their table, "But then you moved into giving me your whole life story. Why do you think I ordered two more pints?"

Daniel laughed.

"Sorry," he said, "I do have a tendency to waffle. Anyway, I'd just had a meal with some colleagues at a small pub in Bourton-on-the-Water when I noticed an attractive woman step out through a 'staff only' door and sit up at the bar. When I went up to order drinks I spoke to her. She told me she'd just cooked our meals and I complemented her on how good they were."

"Is that it?" Bob asked.

"No, there was moonlight and soft music and a choir crooning in the lobby; what do you mean 'is that it.'"

Bob grinned.

"I just meant is that all there was to you two getting together, you telling her you liked her food."

"Well, yes. As I said, both of us thought we were going to have a fling but we fell in love and got married the following year."

Both men fell silent as they turned their attention to their beers. Eventually Bob said,

"Whose idea was it to buy the restaurant?"

"It was both of us really," Daniel replied, "After a few years in my job the housing market crashed. I could see history repeating itself, working for a company that relied on a buoyant housing market. Fortunately Alice's parents had decided to retire from running their pub and we took over the tenancy. I worked the bar and Alice created a new menu for the kitchen. Pretty soon we realised food was more lucrative than drink and so we sold up the house Alice owned and bought the restaurant, living over it for a few years. Alice ran the kitchen and I did whatever else needed doing, waiting tables, working the bar, cleaning. After a while we invested in some holiday lets and that became my job managing and maintaining them."

"Well you certainly made a success of that restaurant. I loved going in there every week. It was always busy."

"That was Alice. She was so talented."

"Just like your Tania."

"Sorry?"

Daniel was momentarily surprised at the mention of his daughter.

"Well she's doing well for herself isn't she, working at that aviation firm. Got a good head on her shoulders. She certainly didn't get that from you."

"Charming."

"How is she, anyway?" Bob asked.

"Same as always," Daniel replied, "She came to see me the other night to talk about her new promotion at work."

Bob chuckled.

"Another one? She'll be running the whole place soon."

"This one will mean a move to the United States."

Bob whistled.

"That must be a tough decision for her to make."

"Sorry?"

"To decide to uproot herself and all she knows to move to a foreign country."

"It's the States, Bob," Daniel told him, "It's hardly that different to Britain. We all speak the same language."

"It's still a huge change. What have you advised her to do?"

"Whatever she wants."

"That's it, is it? That's the limit of your pearls of wisdom?"

"Tania knows her own mind," Daniel told him, "She always has. She probably just wants me to give her my blessing to go."

"And have you done that."

"I think so. I'm not actually sure."

"Well you'd better make sure," Bob told him, "Jesus Christ Dan, she's your only child isn't she?"

"No."

"Well she's the only one you're in contact with. Have you thought about how you'll feel without having her just up the road."

"Not really."

"Well you'd better," Bob told him, "And quickly, otherwise she'll be heading off and not looking back."

Daniel thought about what Bob said as he waited for the bus back to the retirement village. It was only two stops but too far now for Daniel to walk it, at least without having a sit down halfway along. After two pints with Bob he didn't want to risk getting caught short on the way.

What had he said to Tania on Friday night? She'd left in a bit of a huff. Had she wanted him to tell her to go, or not to go? No, that wasn't like her. She knew what was right in her own mind. She'd always been an intelligent, confident girl.

As he stepped onto the bus, Daniel felt guilty that Tania hadn't been planned. He'd thought his child rearing days were behind him after his first marriage ended. Ray was practically grown and Emma wasn't coming back. He knew that. He felt he'd probably known that as soon as he'd walked across the village green that morning to be met by Emma's teacher who was searching for her with the headmistress.

Alice had told him she wasn't that maternal although as soon as she discovered she was pregnant she changed and became excited about the impending birth. Daniel was excited too but when the midwife told him they had a beautiful baby girl he'd felt scared. Memories of Emma came rushing into his mind and of course, her disappearance. Suddenly there was another little girl that was going to call him daddy and Daniel silently struggled to deal with that while Alice fell in love with her daughter.

Tania had always favoured her mother. Daniel was okay with that, especially as she got older but he always felt his Emma would have remained closer to him, daddy's little girl. Ray had chosen to remain with Sylvia and had cut off all ties with his father after hearing that he was going to have another sister. That had hurt, although Daniel and he hadn't seen each other too often after he'd moved to the Cotswolds. Ray had probably only visited three or four times and while Alice had been pure kindness to him, he'd treated her indifferently.

Daniel wondered if that was the reason he didn't make more of an effort to try and patch up the relationship with his son. He hadn't ever returned to Essex after he and Sylvia had decided to divorce but he had ensured she and Ray kept a roof over their heads by giving her the house and continuing to pay off the mortgage. He hoped that atoned for his period of unemployment when Sylvia had been the only one bringing in any sort of income. She still kept in touch with the occasional letter, letting him know how Ray was doing. He appreciated that.

As he walked from the bus stop to the retirement village Daniel realised he needed to make more of an effort with the only child he still had left in his life. He wasn't sure he understood Tania's anger the other night but that didn't matter. If she wanted his help then he would give it. He took his mobile out of his pocket and left a message on her's, telling her to come over anytime and they could discuss her decision together. An hour later she responded with a text, telling him she had a late meeting that night and would come over the following evening.

Daniel went to bed that night feeling contented. The next morning he was still in a good mood and found himself enjoying the game of rummy in the communal lounge that he got cajoled into joining. He treated himself to dinner in the restaurant before returning to the apartment, thinking he could use a nap.

As he entered his lounge the landline phone started ringing. Tania always called his mobile and he rarely got calls from anyone else. He answered the phone gingerly.

"Mr Burrows, my name is Karen Taylor," the voice at the other end of the line said, "I'm a journalist currently researching a book about missing people. I was wondering if I could speak with you about your daughter, Emma."

Daniel struggled to take the words in.

"Sorry, what; who are you?"

"I'm a journalist," Karen told him, "I've worked on a number of newspapers but I'm currently researching a book I'm writing about people that have gone missing. I've found the case of your daughter's disappearance fascinating and wondered if we could perhaps speak about it."

"I don't really think…"

"Oh I don't mean right now," Karen interrupted, "Obviously this is a phone call out of the blue and I understand it will be a bit of a shock. You don't know who I am but as I say, I have worked on a number of newspapers and I'm happy to provide you with more details when you're ready to talk to me. Perhaps you'd like your daughter present?"

"My daughter?"

Daniel felt confused. This woman was asking about Emma and now talking about her being present. What did she know?"

"Your daughter Tania. I believe she lives nearby."

"Yes she does but…look I'm sorry this is all a bit of a shock. You want to ask about Emma?"

"That's right," Karen said, brightly, "I'd like to devote a chapter to her in my book; find out what happened and how you feel now with the case still open. I'm already working on a first draft."

Daniel had now managed to get his head around what this woman was saying.

"I suggest you look at the information reported at the time," he told her, "Nothing else has changed since then."

"Yes of course, I am familiar with the story but…"

"This is no story," Daniel told her, "This is a real event, a distressing event that still hurts."

"I understand that but…"

"Good. Then you'll understand why I don't want to talk

about it and why I don't want the case mentioned in a book. Please don't call here again."

Daniel heard the voice saying something else as he placed the receiver down. He realised he was shaking. What right did this stranger have of raking up the past? Why was she looking into what had happened? It was so long ago, almost forty years. Emma was dead, let her rest in peace.

Daniel flopped down into the armchair beside the fireplace and picked up the photograph of his daughter, his Emma, his pride and joy.

"Oh my darling," he said, aloud, "If only I'd saved you when I had the chance."

Chapter 9

Teacher

Caroline was having trouble concentrating. The figures on the screen in front of her kept blurring and she found herself picturing the night before at Hasanna's apartment in Hounslow. It wasn't the first time today she'd done that and she was surprised she'd managed to get through her speech this morning. It was every few months that the centre had an open day for people to visit. While parents of children that needed the charity's help would always have personal viewings of the centre, Caroline liked to open the place up to the public as well as a way of not only allowing them to see what they did and how they helped but also as a way of educating them, to show that illnesses, whether physical or mental, should not be hidden away and should be talked about openly. It was also a chance to get donations.

Caroline had done so many now that she could practically give the speech in her sleep but she preferred it when she was able to concentrate. She gave up on staring at her screen and sat back in her chair. Oliver had had one of his 'late business meetings' in London and had stopped over, which Caroline knew to mean there was another young woman on the scene. That wasn't a problem for her. She let Oliver do what he wanted. He was usually much pleasanter to be around at home when he had a new conquest. She knew it would be over when he started being moody again.

It had given her the chance to spend some time with

Hasanna. She even took the afternoon off from the office, something Fran, the manager of the centre was glad about. Caroline knew she hated sharing the office at the Windsor Sensory Centre, feeling Caroline was always watching her every move, but screw it, it was Caroline's charity and she wanted somewhere away from home to base herself.

Fran was currently sat at her desk opposite Caroline's. She'd put her fan on even though it wasn't hot in there. It made a regular whiny noise that she was hoping would send Caroline elsewhere. She didn't know Caroline wasn't concentrating on anything except the day before.

Hasanna had taken her walking in Brazil Mill Woods on Hounslow Heath, taking them along a path beside the river Crane.

"This is part of the London loop," Hasanna had told her, "It consists of twenty-four walks that circle the outskirts of the city."

"Perhaps we should walk all of them together," Caroline had replied, grinning.

Although they were on the edge of West London, close to Heathrow airport, for Caroline they could have been in the middle of nowhere, just the two of them listening to the birds singing in the trees on a beautiful clear day. It was a Monday afternoon and in places where there were no other people, Hasanna took her hand and Caroline felt a thrill of excitement and contentment pass through her as they walked along.

At one point she'd pulled Hasanna off of the path and the two had giggled like schoolgirls as they ran among the dense wood, the silence among the trees feeling so thick it was almost visible. No other creature stirred and when Caroline's foot broke a twig the crack echoed like a gunshot. They stopped by an old oak and Caroline crushed her lips against Hasanna's.

She felt the urge to cry as Hasanna kissed her back passionately. She'd not felt that sort of affection in years and she realised how much she had missed it and craved it.

The evening and night together had been magical and when she awoke early, Caroline felt a sadness at having to return home to her normal life.

"Stay longer," Hasanna had said.

"I really can't," Caroline had replied, "I've got the neighbours to think about."

Hasanna had laughed.

"You all live in big, detached houses behind electric gates. Who's going to notice you're not there, unless they have telescopes pointed at your house and drones flying overhead?"

"I wouldn't put that past some of them. But I don't want to alienate anyone. It's those wealthy neighbours that donate the most to the charity."

"I've never seen any of them at our open days."

"No, well they give money so that they can tell people they've given it. They don't want to actually meet the people they're helping."

"I think that's wrong," Hasanna had told her.

Caroline had shrugged.

"To be honest I'm just glad they give. Besides it's not all of them. Some do it because they genuinely want to help but that doesn't mean they want to physically help. We're all different. Some people, like you, get stuck in and work hard to do all they can to help others and will stand up and fight for what they believe in. Others just don't know how to interact with those that need help or they know they wouldn't be any good at providing it. We can't all be the same otherwise the world would stop."

Caroline smiled then and bent down and kissed Hasanna one

more time before dressing and returning home, buying herself a croissant and a large cappuccino with a dash of vanilla syrup in it on the way. After showering and changing she'd headed out to the Windsor sensory centre to begin her day by giving her talk before planning some meetings and arranging a visit to the site for the new centre.

Trying to focus again on the screen, Caroline wondered if she could take Hasanna with her on the visit. It had been over a year since she'd begun volunteering at the centre. She'd grown up with a mentally disabled brother who had sadly died when Hasanna was in her twenties, and she'd volunteered at a number of different places over the years. After the end of her marriage she'd moved to Hounslow and her job at a small social care facility had taken her out to Windsor where she found, and began volunteering at, the sensory centre. She was great with the children and the adults, so patient. That was the first thing Caroline had noticed about her. She was also incredibly efficient. When she lost her job, after the social care facility closed down because of cuts in funding, Caroline offered her the vacant assistant manager role at the sensory centre (over Fran's head) and she'd been working here permanently for the past six months. It was only in the last couple that the two women had begun their relationship.

Caroline was in two minds about taking Hasanna to the site. On the one hand she knew she was the best person to run the new centre as she would thrive on the extra responsibility, but on the other it would mean they would have much less time to spend together, having Hasanna working on the other side of London.

Caroline sighed as the phone rang and she watched Fran answer it. If only Fran wanted to leave that would be perfect.

"It's for you," Fran called over, "A journalist; someone

called Karen Taylor."

Caroline wasn't unduly worried. The charity had been mentioned in a number of publications over the years. A bit of free advertising was always useful.

"Hello," said the voice, "Am I speaking to Caroline Willis?"

Caroline almost gasped. Why was this journalist using her maiden name? She took a moment before replying, quite coldly,

"No, you're speaking to Caroline Metcalf."

"Oh of course," the voice at the other end of the phone said, brightly, "I'm sorry, I've got my notes in the wrong order. I'm Karen Taylor. I'm a journalist working on a book about missing people that have never been found. I'm very interested in the Emma Burrows story."

"Are you?"

Caroline wasn't sure what else to say. Why was this woman doing this, churning up the long ago past?

Her voice must have had a touch of worry in it as she noticed Fran's ears prick up. The bitch even turned off her fan to hear all the better.

"Yes," Karen said, "I've read over many cases during my research but I found myself drawn to Emma. She seemed to disappear off the face of the earth that day with no credible sightings of her afterwards."

"It was a long time ago," Caroline told her, "Surely it shouldn't be raked over again. What about the rest of her family? I'm sure they don't want to relive the past."

"Oh, so you're aware the parents are still alive."

"Well no, I just assumed I…"

Caroline was getting angry with this woman for making her flustered. She wasn't usually like this. She noticed Fran's head was tilted towards her and she cleared her throat loudly. Fran turned and jumped as she realised Caroline was looking at her. She began typing vigorously and staring intently at her screen.

"Obviously Sylvia and Daniel are both elderly and I do need to tread carefully with them," Karen continued, "But the brother, Raymond seemed quite happy that the story is going to appear in a book. It was actually him that put me onto you yesterday."

"Really," Caroline questioned, "I don't know how. I've not seen him since that time. I don't think I ever actually spoke to him."

"What, not even when he dropped his sister at school that day?"

"Oh, well maybe I acknowledged him," Caroline added, quickly, "But I didn't know him."

Perhaps it was a general wariness of journalists but Caroline felt like Karen was being accusatory and trying to trip her up into saying something she shouldn't. She was usually better at handling people like that but the shock of the past being raised had thrown her.

"Well he recognised you from an article about the charity you run. I was able to look you up online. I must congratulate you on making such a difference to so many young people's lives."

If she thought flattery was going to help she was mistaken.

"It's a team effort," Caroline told her, feeling she was now on firmer ground, "My fellow trustees, staff and amazing volunteers all help to make the charity a success."

"I think it's remarkable how you've managed to turn your life around."

"I'm sorry?"

"Well, to be blamed by people for allowing Emma to disappear while in your care, to leave teaching behind you and then to run your own successful charity, it would make a great story in itself."

"Thank you but I don't wish to be a story," Caroline told her, firmly.

She wondered which article it was that Ray Burrows had read. There'd been a few over recent years and Caroline had been glad of the publicity at the time. She never dreamed she would be linked to the past by one of them.

"I was wondering if I could come and chat to you about the Emma Burrows story," Karen continued.

"Why?"

"Well you were a big part of it at the time and I'd like to get your take on it and see how it's shaped you in the years since."

"I don't think that's necessary," Caroline told her, "Everything I have to say about that case was said at the time. You've told me you've researched it so you already have all of the information. There's nothing to add."

"Oh but I'd like to…"

"I'm afraid I must go now, I have an important meeting to attend. Goodbye Ms Taylor and good luck with the book."

Just before she replaced the receiver she added,

"Oh, and I'd prefer it if you didn't use my married name in it or make any reference to the charity or my husband's business at all. If you did I'm afraid I would have to take legal action. Goodbye."

After she'd hung up Caroline wondered if that last sentence had been wise. It made her look like she had something to hide but she didn't want the past affecting the charity and Oliver certainly wouldn't want his company to be associated with it.

He knew what had happened. Caroline had told him as soon as they started dating after she took the job as a filing clerk at the accountancy firm he worked at in Guildford; once she'd finally been able to flee Essex and leave Little Tenwick behind her. Well, she'd told him the facts that had been reported in the newspapers, that was all he'd needed to know.

It was bad enough people blamed her for Emma's disappearance because they thought she'd abandoned her post for two minutes. Only two people knew she'd actually been away from the classroom for twenty, and knew what she'd been doing. That other person was long dead. There was no way the journalist would be able to discover what had really gone on back then, was there?

Chapter 10

Accused

In the end, after Jill had spoken with him, it was only Eddie that left the cottage on Saturday but the weekend was already ruined as the happy atmosphere was impossible to get back. Jill was upset, knowing she'd be facing a big row when she got home, Robbie and Gray were miffed that their good news had been spoiled and Mike was just angry at Eddie for causing all of this upset. The two girls didn't really understand what had gone on but the low atmosphere affected them and they became moody and tetchy with everyone. Mike was glad the following day when they all went off to Owen Sounds to go shopping, leaving him to go out on the boat with just Ben for company.

Mike felt angry every time he thought about the argument. It was now Tuesday and, arriving home after a busy day at the car plant, he received a text from Robbie about going for a scan with the surrogate and that just brought back the rage at how his son's blissful news had been marred at the weekend.

Mike found himself slamming cupboard doors as he got his dinner ready. What was Eddie's problem? Was there more to it than just losing his mother? Yes it was still recent and the pain was raw, but that was the same for all of them. Surely they should be coming together to support one another. He was acting like a spoilt child as far as Mike was concerned and that was Barbara's fault.

Mike was struggling with opening a can of sweetcorn and he threw it across the kitchen. It banged against the wall, leaving a dent; the contents spilling down over the countertop. He cursed before turning and walking out into the lounge.

He was angry at Barbara now too. How dare she leave him. How dare that horrible illness of cancer rob a fit woman of her life. What was the point of both of them going jogging and playing golf and using gym equipment in their basement if one illness could wipe out all of that hard work? Ironically Mike had been exercising even more recently to burn off excess emotional energy and that, coupled with his lack of appetite, had seen his six-pack return at sixty years of age.

But the exercise hadn't assuaged his anger. How was he meant to live without Barbara? How was he meant to cope alone with a son that hated him? Why wasn't she here right now, telling him to make the first move and apologise. Mike would have moaned about it but would have done it to please her. But she wasn't here and this time, he wasn't going to do it. It was Eddie's fault. It was always Eddie's fault and perhaps if Barbara had had a go at him once in a while he would have turned into a grown-up rather than remaining a spoilt child.

Fuck it, Mike thought, let him come to me and apologise and then we can talk.

He returned to the kitchen and cleaned up the mess the sweetcorn had made, wondering if he still had some of the paint colour in the garage to repaint the wall with after he'd patched up the dent. Before he could go and check, the phone rang. It was Jill.

"Look," he said, before she could say anything, "I'm not apologising for the weekend. It was Eddie's fault and he has to realise that. Barbara isn't here now to protect him."

Jill sighed.

"Oh my God, you two need your heads knocking together."

"What do you mean by that?"

"Do you really think that Barbara never called here after one of your fights, asking Eddie to apologise to you? She had to keep on at the pair of you until one of you finally made the effort to talk."

"I never knew that," Mike admitted.

"Well now you do. But just so you know, I'm not going to do that. I'll let the two of you sort this one out on your own, I don't care how long it takes. Anyway, that wasn't why I was calling. I was wondering if you knew a man named Amrit Kumar?"

An image of that dark, windy night near Northey Island flew into Mike's mind again. He was back there, reliving the events and the feelings; the fear, the anguish, the digging. Mike closed his eyes and shook his head vigorously to dispel the past.

"Are you still there, Mike," Jill asked, "Can you hear me?"

"Sorry," he replied, trying to keep his voice from sounding shaky, "Could you repeat that?"

"I said, 'Do you know a man named Amrit Kumar.'"

Jill sounded so calm and rational when she said that name. She couldn't know who he was, surely. Not even Barbara knew he existed. What should he say? Should he deny all knowledge? But how had he got hold of Jill? Surely he wasn't here in Canada. He wasn't sitting in Jill's house now was he.

Mike's heart began thumping in his chest. He took a couple of deep breaths to try and calm himself. He needed more information.

"Erm, the name sounds familiar," he told her, "Why do you ask?"

"Well he sent me a message through Facebook just now," Jill said, "He saw a photo of you on my page and recognised you apparently."

"Oh for God's sake Jill," Mike replied, angry now, "How

many times have I told you that I don't want images of me on your social media."

"I'm sorry, it was a group one from Robbie's wedding. I thought my security prevented people from seeing the image and my comments, but I had it set as 'public,' so everyone could see it. Anyway, do you know him? He referred to you as Joey so I wasn't sure. Eddie said I should check with you before replying. He remembered something about Mike not being your first name. Who knew-eh? I never realised that. So is Joey your real name or is it Josep…"

"Jill please, stop rambling."

Mike could feel his head aching.

"I'm sorry, you're probably trying to recall the name. He said it was from years ago, when you were still in England. That's going back-eh. He's left contact details. Well, he's left a phone number. That seems a bit odd doesn't it; not an email address? Anyway, do you want it?"

"Yes," Mike told her, quickly, "Yes, I do remember him now. Why don't you give me that number."

"Sure. It will be nice to catch up with an old friend," Jill told him, brightly, "Perhaps this is just what you need right now-eh."

That wasn't the reason Mike had told her to give him the number. He wanted to speak to him without going through Jill at all. This was all about the past, about Jimmy, about that little girl, about that damn purple ribbon. He'd never told Barbara the truth and there was no way Mike wanted any other member of his family finding out.

It was too late to phone England that night. All of the next day Mike found it difficult to concentrate at work. As soon as he arrived home he phoned the number he'd been given. It was answered after two rings.

Amrit's voice sounded different at first but then it had been thirty-odd years since they'd last spoken. He sounded alert and awake.

"I thought you'd phone sometime this evening," he said, after Mike told him who it was.

That was an odd moment for Mike, saying, 'It's Joey.' It felt like someone else was talking. He'd quickly added, 'But I call myself Mike now' to try and keep the past at bay. He wanted to talk to Amrit as Mike McGill not Joey.

"Why on earth have you contacted me?" he asked.

"Because I have news," Amrit replied, "I'm sorry I had to contact your daughter-in-law but I really needed to get in touch. I searched various social media sites and found your name attached to a Facebook photo. Well, I found Mike McGill but I knew that was your middle name and I could recognise you in the photograph. I'm glad you've got on with your life and have children and grandchildren. And I'm sorry to hear about your wife."

Mike made a mental note to tell Jill to check her so-called security arrangements on her Facebook page again. How much other information was out there for just anyone to read? It was frightening.

"I didn't want to say anything to your family or to write anything down in an email," his old friend continued, "That's why I sent you my number. I'm happy to call you back if it's too expensive for you to call me."

"Just tell me what you want, Amrit," Mike said.

"I have news."

"Yes, you've already told me that bit."

"Alright," Amrit replied, sounding miffed, "I'm trying to make sure I tell you everything. This isn't easy you know."

"My God you always were a worrier," Mike told him,

"You're still getting yourself into a panic."

"Well maybe you'll be worried when I tell you what I know. I see you're still just as controlling as you used to be, trying to hurry me along."

"I'm not controlling. I just want…"

"Look Joey, Mike, whatever you want to call yourself, please let me say what I need to."

Mike sighed.

"Fine," he said.

Amrit cleared his throat.

"My sister, Naveena runs the newsagents my parents used to own. Do you remember?"

"The newsagents yes, your sister, no."

"You must remember her, she used to fancy you."

"Did she?"

"Yes, she used to hide round corners and stare at you when you were in the shop, usually with a Fry's Turkish Delight in her hand."

"Oh my God, yes I do remember her now, a podgy, little thing."

"Well she isn't any more. She blossomed as she got older. She eventually settled down with…"

Mike lost himself in memories while Amrit spoke. He'd only ever wanted to blot out the last eighteen months of his life in England but he'd actually stopped thinking about all of it. He'd forgotten there were happier times, events like spending time in Amrit's parents' shop and being allowed to serve customers and help put stock out. The couple had been so much in love and had such respect for each other; something that was sadly lacking in the McGill house, even when Mike's father had been sober.

Mike knew all about his dad's other woman, Eileen; well,

most people did including his mother. Only Mike knew where she lived. Everyone else was just aware that Tom McGill would disappear for weeks at a time, only returning after some drunken argument with his girlfriend brought him back home again.

It was only when he'd started work for Peter Tomkyns at the local garage that Mike had discovered where his dad went to, having seen him and Eileen arguing outside a pub in a village towards Danbury when he was test driving a car. He was surprised his father hadn't gone further afield. He'd asked around and discovered Eileen lived in a rundown cottage nearby that had belonged to her late parents.

Mike liked it when his father was away. His mother would smile more when she wasn't trying to cope with bruises after another drunken attack. She never once got medical treatment, too afraid of hospitals after her sister had died in one as a child. No wonder her spinal cancer had killed her so quickly after she'd finally been persuaded to have a check-up.

Mike didn't know when the beatings had begun. He'd been aware of them all of his childhood, sometimes he and Jimmy getting in the way too when one of his father's drunken sessions turned nasty. They became more frequent as Tom's drinking spiralled out of control as the years passed by. At one time he'd been thought of as a decent builder and had worked on many of the local houses, but as alcohol took him over so the work dried up, which just made him hate the world even more. The attacks stopped though when Mike turned sixteen and he was big enough and strong enough to finally beat his dad up. His mother had been distraught and chastised him for it but at least Tom never laid a finger on any of them again after that.

Only Jimmy seemed to miss his father when he was away which Mike always found odd seeing as Tom rarely took an interest in his eldest son and would only sometimes listen to him, other times telling him to 'fuck off and annoy someone else.'

Jimmy didn't understand emotions that well. He'd been starved of oxygen during a difficult birth and had been left with learning difficulties. There hadn't been much help back then in the nineteen fifties when Jimmy had been born but Sheila had proudly shown off her son in the village and vowed to look after him rather than have him end up in some institution.

Backward, that was the term everyone used then to describe Jimmy. He was a sweet boy but struggled with what people said and did. If someone cried with laughter he still associated tears with sadness. If people laughed at him he thought that was a good thing and would laugh along. His father and his drunken mates were the worst at doing that whenever Jimmy passed the pub while they were standing outside.

It was at those times that Mike despised his father the most. He swore he would never be like him but there was always that fear that he'd inherited his genes. Mike hated that he got angry so easily, not that he'd ever hit anyone. He feared for his sons too although Robbie had never given him any trouble. Even when they were old enough to start drinking, Robbie always remained happy-go-lucky whereas Eddie would turn surlier. Mike hated to see that and did his best to deter him from drinking. Eddie hadn't appreciated that.

Amrit had finally stopped talking about his sister and her husband and three children.

"Sorry," he said, "I got carried away."

"It's okay," Mike replied, "Why don't you tell me now why you contacted me."

"A lady came into my sister's shop on Monday. She's some journalist called Karen Taylor and she's writing a book about missing people. She was asking about Emma."

Mike's heart began thumping again. If Amrit could find him after so many years it wouldn't take long for a journalist to locate him. Would she follow the same route and speak to his family? For the first time he was glad Barbara wasn't here. What would this have done to their relationship? He wondered how he would have reacted if he'd discovered Barbara had a secret past that she hadn't told him about. He'd have been hurt and felt like she didn't trust him. What if his family found out about his past now? Could he tell them Barbara knew all along? No of course he couldn't, that was more lies. He'd have to tell them that he kept it secret from her too. Would any of them want to see him again? He could lose everything.

"What does she know?" he asked.

"I don't know," his old friend replied, "I assume just what was reported at the time."

"Good," Mike said, "Good. Well there's no reason for her to discover any more is there."

"I'm scared."

"Why Amrit? This doesn't concern you."

"Of course it concerns me! Don't you remember what I did for you?"

"I didn't mean it like that," Mike told him, "I meant that you're officially not involved. You weren't mentioned in the press. You weren't interviewed. You were just a friend of mine who didn't even live in the village. You're safe."

"I wish I felt like it."

Mike closed his eyes. He was worried about Amrit. He'd kept certain information secret for almost forty years but it seemed like age and experience hadn't stopped him from continuing to be a nervous Nelly. What if he blabbed, even accidentally? Would the police reopen the case? That's if it was ever closed. What happened when a person wasn't found?

"Wouldn't Emma have been declared dead by now," he asked, "Isn't there something about being declared dead after seven years missing?"

"She's never been declared dead," Amrit said, "Her mother believes she's alive somewhere and refuses to have her declared dead. Naveena said her brother, Ray has often moaned about the situation to her. The house his mum lives in is still to be split between the two children and Ray is scared he won't be able to sell it. He's still a self-centred, little shit."

Mike's mind was racing through many different thoughts. Each one came back to what he could do to avoid telling his family the truth.

"Perhaps I ought to come over," he said, aloud.

Amrit must have been taken aback because it was a moment before he replied.

"Are you crazy," he said, "Why would you do that?"

"So that I could talk to the journalist face to face, nip her questions in the bud."

Mike sighed.

"Look, to be honest, Amrit my family knows nothing of my life in England and I want to keep it that way. Maybe this is the best course of action."

"Well what will you say?"

"To the journalist?"

"To your family, about why you suddenly have an urge to travel to England."

"I'll say I want to visit the past. It's not really a lie."

Mike felt this was the best solution and he warmed more and more to the idea.

"Maybe it will be good to settle the past," he continued, more to himself than to Amrit, "I can visit my mum's grave.

It's been almost forty years since she died after all. I could mark the anniversary."

"Why, you haven't marked any of the others."

Amrit sounded miffed.

"What's up with you?" Mike asked, feeling angry again.

"Just promise me one thing," Amrit said.

"What's that?"

"When you come to England, don't try and look me up."

Still Missing

by Karen Taylor

Chapter 3 (first draft)

But what of those people who were, and still are, involved in the story of Emma Burrows. How have the last thirty-nine years shaped them? Have they been able to move on or has the past remained with them always?

For the family members, Emma can't be far away in their thoughts. Sylvia and Daniel are no longer together, their pain and suffering over the loss of their daughter too much to bear as a couple. While Daniel married again and had another child, Sylvia has never escaped the past, choosing to remain in the same home that the family of four once shared with just her son, Ray for company. Back at home after a number of failed relationships he spends most of his time working in an insignificant supermarket in a quiet, neighbouring village.

But what of the other two remaining characters from this tragic story? Are their lives still touched by the past? For Caroline Willis, she inevitably left teaching behind her after being the person many locals blamed for Emma's disappearance. She was, after all, the person in charge at the time and she'd abandoned her post. It only took two minutes for the child to go missing but that was enough time.

Life though, appears to have been kind to Caroline, who is married to a wealthy accountant in Surrey. She now runs her own charity helping disadvantaged children. Perhaps the guilt of the past has stayed with her, spending her life trying to help as many children as she can because there was one she couldn't help. She may have money, wealth and a great lifestyle, but has she found the peace she so obviously craves?

For Joey McGill, life surely had to get brighter. Not only did he have to struggle with seeing the world blaming his brother for the abduction, within six months of the incident, both of his parents were dead, Sheila from spinal cancer and Tom from cirrhosis of the liver. His entire family were gone but there was no sympathy for him not while Jimmy was thought of as guilty for one of the worst crimes most people can imagine; the abduction and murder of a child.

I wasn't surprised to discover that Joey had emigrated to Canada. With nothing to keep him here except bitter memories, a fresh start was surely something he deserved, but he's still being touched by tragedy with the recent death of his wife from the same illness that took his mother.

For those involved there must be a reluctance to talk about the situation but surely it should be faced if there is more to tell. With so many unanswered questions about what went on I can't see how any of the five people involved have been able to let the past truly rest.

Chapter 11

Father

When Tania arrived that evening, feeling happy that her father wanted to discuss her dilemma with her, she found him in the lounge. The light was fading outside but there were no lights on in the room. Scared at first she was relieved when he answered her greeting, even if he had jumped.

"Why on earth are you sitting here in the dark?" she asked, switching on the standard lamp beside the sofa before heading into the kitchen to turn on the lights under the wall units.

"Hmm?"

Daniel looked about him and seemed to realise for the first time that it was no longer the afternoon. He was holding the photograph of Emma. The phone call from the journalist had shocked him. While he'd never shied away from speaking about Emma it was always in the past tense. Karen Taylor had somehow made her seem alive again but she still remained the delicate five year old girl. Daniel thought he'd managed to lock away his culpable feelings but the bloody journalist had found the key and the past had flooded out, the tears, the shouting, the contents of the suitcase.

He'd been devastated when Emma disappeared and blamed himself for allowing it to happen. There'd been that one moment, that instant that he could have saved her, but he didn't and she was gone. Some nights he still dreamed of that day and what might have been if only he'd...Daniel sighed sadly as he sat in the chair, the image of the suitcase appearing in his mind again before he shook it away.

Unlike Sylvia he'd always believed Emma was dead. There was no way that backward boy and his daughter could have been alive and not been found. Dead, they could remain hidden. That part of Essex was close to the marshes and some of the areas were particularly remote. It would be easy for them to get lost and stuck in the mud, never to be seen again. No, she had to have died otherwise she would have found her way back home somehow.

Being unemployed when his daughter disappeared, Daniel had nothing else to do all day except join the fruitless searches until everyone else began to lose hope like he had that first day. There was nothing else to occupy his mind. The stress of Emma's disappearance brought him and Sylvia closer for a short while but it didn't last. After the pain of the many miscarriages before she came along, Emma was the only thing that held their marriage together. With her gone there was nothing left.

"What's wrong?" Tania asked, coming back into the lounge area and crouching down beside her dad's chair, rubbing his arm consolingly, "You haven't got yourself into a state because of my job offer have you?"

"What? No, of course I haven't," Daniel told her, testily, "Why would I?"

"Oh well," Tania replied, standing up, clearly miffed, "I'm sorry if I thought you might have had a feeling about it. Isn't that the reason I'm here?"

"I've had other news since I spoke to you. I forgot you were coming round tonight."

Tania tutted as she sat down on the sofa opposite.

"Well I haven't got long to make the decision. You said you were ready to talk it over, so here I am."

"Well that will have to wait," Daniel told her, "I had a phone call today, from a journalist."

"A journalist? What did they want?"

"She wanted to talk about Emma for a book she's writing."

"Oh."

"Is that all you've got to say on the matter," Daniel said, exasperated.

"Well what do you want me to say," Tania retorted, "This was all from before I was born. It has nothing to do with me."

"Emma was your sister."

"And don't I know it."

Daniel's eyes narrowed.

"What does that mean?"

Tania sighed.

"I've spent my whole life being compared to some five year old girl in a photograph," she said, "And I've never measured up against her in your eyes."

"You're being ridiculous."

"Am I dad? My God, you give that photo more attention than you've ever given me. Even now, I'm sat here in front of you with a problem I want help with but you're still concerned with that spoilt, little bitch."

She pointed at the photo he was still holding. Daniel cradled it to him.

"Don't you call her that," he said.

"Oh my God, are you really going to try and protect a photo from me? Are you concerned about the picture's feelings?"

"Emma was a flesh and blood person. She was lovely."

"Well I've never met her so forgive me if I can't get emotional for you. My God dad, all you've told me is some journalist wants to write about Emma in a book. I'm sure we can check to see if she needs permission from us first or, here's an idea, you could just not speak to her. Have you thought about that?"

"There's no need to be facetious."

Daniel wished Alice was still here. She'd understand what he was going through but a heart attack had cruelly taken her away from him, just after his recovery from pneumonia when they'd decided to retire and had sold the restaurant and several of the holiday lets. They'd planned to go travelling and had even bought the tickets for the first leg of the journey. He felt so alone now. All he had was Tania but they seemed to be so distant with one another. After his wife died Daniel sold the remaining holiday let and gave the money to his daughter. It was what he and Alice had discussed doing once they'd returned from travelling. Was that the only reason she still came to see him, he wondered now, because she felt she had to, out of a sense of duty?

Tania sighed.

"Look dad, if you're really worried about the journalist I'll do a bit of asking around at work. I'm sure someone in the legal department or the press office will be able to tell me if this person can print the story. Then we'll take it from there, how's that?"

"That's got nothing to do with it," Daniel said, still sounding miffed.

"Well what the hell is the problem," Tania responded, "You scare me to death sitting here motionless in the dark, then you tell me you've had a phone call from a journalist and when I try to help, you snap at me."

"My God, you're so thoughtless."

Tania stood up.

"I don't believe you," she said, "Are you actually for real?"

Daniel stared up at her, puzzled.

"What do you mean?"

"Do you have any idea what my life has been like?"

"You've had a very good life," Daniel said, before looking down at the photograph, "Some haven't been that lucky."

Tania crossed the room and yanked the photo from her father's hand.

"What are you doing? Be careful with that."

"Yep, those words have rung in my ears for years," Tania told him, returning to the sofa but remaining standing.

"That's my first real memory of you," she continued, "Showing me this photo and telling me to be careful with it. I had to hear how wonderful Emma was, how precious Emma was, what a super sister Emma would have made. Never once did you tell me that I would have been a great sister to her too. I've had to compete with that sister my whole life to try and wrestle some attention from you and do you know what, even though she's never been here, she's always won. She was the beautiful, cute, little blonde girl with the blue eyes while I was the ginger kid with the short curly hair and glasses with a patch over one eye. I felt like little orphan Annie, and not just because of the way I looked. I hardly saw you and mum, you were always working."

"We were providing a future for you," Daniel told her, "You've done very well because of us."

"And you expect me to thank you, do you? You're my parent, isn't that part of the job description."

Daniel tutted.

"You've always been ungrateful," he mumbled

"Ungrateful am I. Yes I'm ungrateful because you and mum were out at work each day before I was up and came home when I was already in bed. I'm ungrateful because when I was older I was seen as just a handy, unpaid member of staff in the restaurant kitchen. I'm ungrateful that we never even went on holiday where we might have enjoyed some bonding time together because mum couldn't leave the restaurant and you couldn't leave the holiday lets. I missed out dad because you preferred to spend your time making sure strangers had a good holiday, rather than taking your daughter on one."

"We provided you with everything," Daniel told her, angrily.

"Oh yes," Tania mocked, "I had toys to play with as a young child, I had a good education but where was the attention, where was the family time? You hug this damn photo more than you hug me. You spend more time laughing and joking with that cleaner that works here than you do me."

"You've always been strong and capable," Daniel said, "You've never needed hugs."

"Well perhaps I just wanted them," Tania shouted, fighting back the tears, "I didn't get the chance to choose who I was. The occasional times mum found me upset because I felt unloved, she tried to explain to me how you felt about Emma but it was difficult for a young child to understand. I had to become strong and hard-hearted to cope with the lack of love and attention from you. If you think that's a successful upbringing then you're very wrong."

Daniel couldn't think of anything to say. Alice had never told him that Tania had been upset. He'd always thought her so capable. Tania looked down at the photograph in her hand.

"I didn't have anyone," she said, "My brother's never wanted to meet me and I have this bloody sister whom I've had to fight my whole life, my whole bloody life."

She threw the photo down onto the floor. Daniel heard the glass smash. He launched himself out of his chair and onto the floor.

"No!"

He carefully turned the frame over. Emma stared up at him.

"Thank God the photo is okay," he said.

Tania was standing over him. She sighed.

"My God," she said, "Even now, when I've poured my heart out to you, you're still concerned with her. Why am I even bothering discussing my job move with you?"

"That again?"

Daniel was angry. She'd almost destroyed the only photo he still had of Emma.

"You obviously want to take it so why don't you just do it," he told her, not looking up, "Just take the fucking job!"

Tania's shoulders sagged. She fought hard not to let the sob escape from her. She turned and walked out of the apartment.

Chapter 12

Teacher

Caroline slammed the front door behind her and stomped across the driveway to her Mercedes. Oliver was so bloody selfish. None of this was about him.

After hearing from Karen Taylor earlier, all she'd wanted was to talk to someone who knew about the past, someone to tell her to ignore the journalist and say that everything would be okay. She hadn't wanted her husband to go into one and blame her for the untold problems this missing persons book could cause him.

Caroline wished now she'd never told him about the abduction in the first place but when they first began dating she'd felt she had to. She'd been left hurt and lacking in confidence after leaving the primary school in Little Tenwick. While Caroline wasn't accused of killing that annoying, whimpering, little girl she was blamed for allowing it to happen. Some of the parents no longer wanted her teaching their children.

Everyone thought Jimmy McGill had taken Emma and so had Caroline. She thought about her charity and the help the sensory centres gave to children and their parents. There was none of that help all those years ago for poor Jimmy McGill or his family. Caroline felt terrible that, at the time, her opinion of him had matched the other residents of the village. She'd found him a nuisance, a pest that hung around the school playground. You wouldn't always hear him approach and would jump when you saw him. He found it very funny and laughed, which used to put Caroline's back up. Now she would want to help someone like him, not shun him. Had she been such a terrible person back then?

The gossip in the village had raised Jimmy McGill from annoying nuisance to child murderer. It got so out of hand that the majority of the village began speaking about this monster returning to snatch another child. Parents wanted their little boys and girls to be kept in safe hands and they were no longer Caroline's. Overnight she'd effectively gone from being a teacher to an assistant, putting away crayons and paper after the children had finished using them, being responsible for wheeling out the large television on the trolley when a teacher required it for their class, giving out the little pink tickets each day to those kids that received a free school dinner.

If she could have left the school straightaway Caroline would have, but she had to stay the full year. It would have looked suspicious if she'd bolted anytime before that and she had nothing to hide, well, apart from the affair she'd been having.

It was a tough year, being whispered about behind her back or worse, confronted by angry locals, and the school barely helped her. The other teachers were sympathetic but they were all older than Caroline and she sensed they thought her too young to have been left in charge of a class and they'd all been proved right. They were also scared of headmistress, Brenda Goodwin who had once been Caroline's champion, her mentor, her lover; but she no longer wanted to be any of those things, too worried for her own reputation and that of the school.

Caroline, as a young and eager new teacher had trusted this woman, had admired her work ethics and her determination to give the children, especially the girls, the confidence to know they could grow up and be anything they wanted to be. Caroline had loved her and thought the feeling was reciprocated, but when she became a disappointment and an embarrassment to the school, Brenda lost interest in her and Caroline realised she'd just been used.

She shook images of the past away and pressed the button to open the electric gates, speeding out onto the road and heading for Hounslow. Hasanna would provide her with comfort.

Damn Oliver, she thought to herself as she switched on Magic on the radio, when did he become such an arsehole.

Caroline had taken the temporary filing job at the accounting firm because her dreams of what she wanted to achieve as a teacher, making a difference in the lives of the children in her classes, was now dead in the water almost before it had begun. She needed time to reassess her life, and she also needed money.

Oliver told her he'd noticed her the first day she joined the firm but she wasn't sure about that. It may have been true. She'd kept her head down, not wanting to draw attention to herself. The story of Emma Burrows had been in all the national newspapers and Caroline's face had made it onto the pages.

Oliver had been kind and sweet to her. In her vulnerable state she saw a man who would take care of her. After being abandoned so abruptly by Brenda Goodwin, Caroline found Oliver comforting with strong arms to hold her and tell her everything was okay. As their relationship grew he told her of his plans to leave the firm and go it alone, setting up his own company and revelling in the opulence and wealth his success would provide. All she wanted to do was help him achieve that venture.

Had it been love? Caroline thought it probably was. They

were good together and looked good together as well. She told him about the missing girl and her part in it, worried in case it came out at a later date. Oliver told her he understood and said not to worry. She never mentioned Brenda Goodwin or how long she was actually away from the classroom for that day.

"It's old news now, my darling," he'd said, of the story, "No need to worry about it anymore."

Caroline swore out loud in the car now as she approached Thorpe Lea. How different that Oliver was to the one he'd become.

"Don't you realise what this means for me and the business?" he'd bellowed at her, after she'd told him about Karen Taylor's book, "This could ruin everything. I've put too much work into this for you to lose it all for us."

"And what do you think I've been doing all these years," Caroline retorted, "Don't you dare forget all the hours and sacrifice I put in to getting, what you're now calling 'your' business, off the ground. I also raised our two kids, who you seem to have forgotten about in all of this, while you were at work or out on the golf course, supposedly 'networking' or whatever the new pretentious word is. I'm sure you know it."

"I never said you didn't help…"

"Besides, this isn't about you," Caroline interrupted, "This is about me and my reputation. What will our kids say if they find out? How do you think all those people that use the centres will react, knowing the head of the charity misplaced a child in the past; the charity that I built up and that you mention every chance you get to potential clients to make you look humble?"

"My firm does your accounting for free."

"And so you bloody well should. I'm worried about the damage this will do to the charity and the people I'm trying to help."

Oliver had waved his hand dismissively, a gesture Caroline had always hated.

"It's a charity. They'll all keep coming back for their freebie care. But of course I need to be worried too. We're a team. What affects you, affects me and you really ought to be worried about the business. That's our bread and butter. I can't afford to lose any clients."

"Oh I'm sorry," she told him, sarcastically, "Will that put a dent in your three times a week golf habit? Will it stop you playing at an exclusive club and buying God knows how many drinks in the bar afterwards to keep up appearances? Will it eat into your overnight stays in London with some little tart because let's face it, it's not your looks she's after is it?"

"You're one to talk. At least I take some pride in my appearance."

Caroline snorted.

"You really think you're some kind of catch do you, a balding sixty-five year old man who wedges himself into slim-fit shirts and who throws a hip out every time he attempts to climb out of his Porsche 911? You're a joke, Oliver, we're both jokes."

That had been the moment Caroline stormed out of the house with only her car keys and her handbag.

When had she stopped loving Oliver, she wondered now, as she drove onto the A30, was it after their second child was born when she took time off from helping him at the office? He'd certainly stopped noticing her then. She became the 'little wife at home' like a number of his new wealthy clients' wives. He began suggesting she meet them for coffee and having lunches together but Caroline didn't want that. She'd had a taste of business life and wanted to work once the kids were both settled in school. By the time that happened she realised she'd become an appendage, an attachment for Oliver's arm. He could now afford to pay staff to do the jobs Caroline had done before for free.

She was still useful at events and she knew Oliver was proud of her for being able to talk to any of his clients about a range of subjects but he didn't treat her as an equal anymore, no matter how many times he said they were a team. That was probably when she fell out of love with him. It was Brenda Goodwin all over again; Caroline had served her purpose and now she was discarded and her confidence was given a battering.

She'd tried throwing herself into motherhood but then the kids had been sent off to boarding school. With Oliver insisting they must have a cleaner and gardener to look after their new house for appearance's sake, life became boring for her but it took a long time to build up the confidence to realise she could strike out on her own. The charity had helped her as much as it helped others. When Brenda had cast her aside she'd fallen into Oliver's arms. Starting the charity she hadn't needed anyone and it had felt great. It still did.

Turning onto the A315, Caroline allowed her mind to drift to the past. Brenda Goodwin had probably been late forties but she looked older with her sensibly-cut grey hair, dark-coloured cardigans and wraparound tweed skirts that were held together with a large safety pin halfway down the length at the front. She didn't exactly sound like a woman a pretty, young, innocent teacher would fall for but Caroline had admired her so much. Brenda was strong, determined and, even though she was married to a lovely, local man, she was independent and had her own mind and opinions. Caroline wanted to be like her, just with a better haircut and cuter clothes.

Brenda had instigated the relationship not long into

Caroline's first year at the school, asking her into her office for regular meetings to see if everything was okay. There was the occasional brushing against her side, the stroking of an arm. When Brenda kissed her for the first time Caroline had been shocked but not appalled by it. She felt special knowing this woman she so admired was attracted to her.

They had to be careful not to be seen. They were in a small village at the beginning of the nineteen eighties but sometimes Brenda would be playful. As she drove now, Caroline could still remember her excitement when a pupil would bring her a note from the headmistress that mentioned what she wanted to do with her in her office. It had been a magical time, only marred when the school year had ended and Caroline had gone to visit her family in Suffolk. As soon as the new autumn term began, Caroline and Brenda picked up where they'd left off.

But then that morning happened when she was called into the headmistress's office by one of the sexy notes and while there, Emma Burrows had gone missing. Caroline hadn't even seen her come in but the other children told her she'd run off crying just after arriving because her hair ribbon had been pulled out. Caroline hadn't meant to be away so long but Brenda had been feeling particularly amorous since their summer break from one another.

She'd gone back to Brenda and told her what had happened. At first neither was too worried, suspecting the little girl that was always crying to have run off home. They began searching the grounds to make sure she wasn't there before worrying Emma's parents. Then Daniel Burrows had come along, saying he hadn't seen his daughter since she'd left for school with her brother that morning. That was when the panic had set in.

It had been awful after that. Brenda had insisted Caroline lie to the police about where she was, terrified of her husband discovering what she'd been doing. Caroline had to say she'd left the classroom for two minutes to use the toilet. She told the police she'd seen Emma arrive and, when later asked about Jimmy McGill, said he was always hanging around the school, not that she'd actually seen him that day, but she assumed he would have been there.

Caroline trembled in the car as these memories came flooding back. She'd lied to the police about where she'd been and what she'd been doing but what other choice had she had. Brenda was so terrified about the affair being found out that she became really hard on Caroline, blaming her for what had happened and for potentially ruining a school's, and a headmistress's, reputation. Caroline had felt dreadful, realising she'd been no more than a convenience.

As she pulled up outside the apartment block where Hasanna lived, Caroline delved into her handbag and pulled out her foldaway make-up mirror to check her appearance. She sighed at her reflection. She saw every wrinkle and line on her face and blamed them all on Brenda, on Oliver and on that bloody five year old girl for running off and causing all this mess in the first place.

When Hasanna opened the door Caroline felt a wave of emotion and fell into her lover's arms. Finally she was with someone who liked her for herself, who would give her the affection and comfort she craved right now. Caroline kissed her girlfriend passionately and then began to cry.

Chapter 13

Accused

As the plane descended through the cloud the patchwork of green fields emerged and grew ever larger. Roads cut through the landscape like grey rivers, the moving traffic a colony of ants trailing one after another until they slowly became clearer and Mike could distinguish cars and lorries by colour. He didn't feel a warm emotion returning to his homeland, just a nagging fear that perhaps this hadn't been such a good idea after all.

It had all happened surprisingly quickly. Mike checked online Wednesday night to see if there were any cheap seats available to fly to London and then found himself booking a return ticket for a flight leaving Toronto Pearson late Thursday. He had to tell work he was taking a week off and then his family. Work was understanding, knowing he was going through a tough time. Robbie, while surprised, empathised with his dad's need for time to reflect. Eddie couldn't comprehend the situation at all.

"What do you mean you're suddenly going to England?"

Mike had hoped Jill would answer the phone but it had been Eddie. At least their last argument was forgotten as soon as Mike revealed his plans.

"I just feel I need some time to myself."

"Don't you get enough of that already? You rarely come here to dinner, even though Jill's always asking you."

"I just need to be somewhere different, where there are less memories of your mother."

"You want to forget her?"

"Oh for God's sake!"

It hadn't ended well, with Eddie's last words to him being not to bother rushing back.

The queue at customs was surprisingly short and soon Mike was stood on the platform at Gatwick, waiting for a train to take him to London Bridge. It was midday local time, seven a.m. in Toronto. Mike was glad of a cool breeze on the platform to help him stay awake.

From London Bridge he was going to get a cab to Liverpool Street Station and then another train out to Chelmsford in Essex where he'd booked himself into a small, cheap bed & breakfast for the week. He'd made contact with the journalist Amrit had mentioned, Karen Taylor. Well, he'd found a blog with a contact email address and messaged her before leaving for the airport, telling her that 'by chance' he was coming to England and where he was staying in Essex.

He also mentioned how he'd heard from a friend about the book and explained that, while he had nothing to add to what had already been said, she could contact him if she wished. He thought that was a good way of putting it. All he had to remember now was what he'd told the police and the press at the time…well perhaps not what he'd told the journalists. Those words had never made it into print.

Now though, after a seven hour overnight flight, thinking about the past and what had actually happened, he wasn't so sure it was a good idea to speak to a member of the press. What if he gave her too much information and she started asking other questions? What if he got nervous and she realised there was more to the original story than met the eye? It was too late now, unless his email had gone astray. All Mike could do was wait until she made contact.

He hadn't slept on the overnight flight although that wasn't unusual. A plane wasn't the most comfortable of places to try and take forty winks, nor the quietest when there were crying children, snoring adults and announcements coming over the speaker system. He couldn't concentrate on the movies as his thoughts kept drifting to the past. The closer he got to England and to Essex, the stronger those memories became, forcing their way into the forefront of his imagination, breaking free from the mind shackles Mike had encircled them with when travelling in the other direction as he escaped to Canada almost forty years before.

Test driving a car that day for his boss at the garage around the country lanes close to home, Mike hadn't had a care in the world. His dad, Tom had been with his mistress, Eileen for several weeks and the atmosphere at home had become joyous. Then Mike saw his brother. It wasn't unusual to see Jimmy by the stile that led onto a public footpath that crossed one of Garret's fields. It was just outside of Little Tenwick, up the small hill beside the church. The field had a dense copse with a dead, hollow tree trunk right in the centre where Jimmy liked to hide all his treasures. It was mostly stones and coloured glass that he found on the floor although sometimes it was a possession belonging to someone else. He thought it was secret but Mike knew exactly where it was. He'd been there often enough, ensuring anything Jimmy had that wasn't his was returned to its rightful owner.

Even when Mike had seen him that day he wasn't unduly worried. Jimmy was heaving his large frame across the stile. He was wearing his favourite royal blue, woollen jumper that was so old it had several holes in it. He'd decided to match it with a pair of dark brown trousers and a scuffed pair of black shoes. In the glimpse Mike got as he drove past he saw his brother's right hand was held in a fist with something purple hanging out of it, floating gently in the breeze.

Mike continued on his journey. It was only on his return, travelling through Little Tenwick to get back to the garage, that he saw the young teacher and the headmistress with Daniel Burrows, looking ashen and nervous. Daniel had waved him down, asking if he'd seen his daughter. It was only then Mike had begun to feel worried.

As the train made its way into London the rows of houses became denser, finally being replaced by tall apartment buildings and office blocks as they entered the central part of the city. Getting the cab and travelling to Liverpool Street through the busy streets and then locating his platform at the station to head out to Chelmsford occupied Mike's mind with the present, but once he was settled onto the next train, heading to the county he grew up in, Mike's mind returned to the past. For the first time he remembered himself as Joey.

Jimmy was upset when his brother found him in the copse, thinking it was a secret and he'd tried to hide what he was holding in his hand.

"What is that you've got there," Joey asked him.

"Nothing."

"Come on Jimmy, show me; I know you've got something."

Joey had to pull Jimmy's hand from behind his back. It took all his strength, his brother was very strong. He tore the purple material from his hand and saw it was a ribbon. He'd seen it before. That girl who was always crying wore them all of the time, the girl that was now missing in the village.

"Where is she?" Joey asked.

Jimmy appeared confused.

"Where is she," Joey repeated, holding up the ribbon,

"Where's the girl you stole this from?"

Jimmy looked hurt.

"I didn't steal," he replied, "It came off."

Joey was getting more and more worried. How had it come off? Did it fall or was it pulled? Did she let him have it or was she upset? Did he take it from her while she was alive or had he peeled it off her dead body?

"Where is she?" Joey repeated.

Jimmy frowned.

"In school," he said.

Joey shook his head.

"No she isn't," he told him, "She's missing. What have you done with her?"

Jimmy was squirming. He always did that when he knew he'd done something wrong but didn't want to admit it. He was always difficult to handle at times like this.

"Not saying anything," he said, and folded his arms.

"Come with me," Joey said, "We've got to get you out of here."

"No!"

Jimmy shook his head. Joey tried pulling but he couldn't do this on his own, he needed help.

Mike shook his own head back in the present. Going over the past wasn't doing any good, especially the parts that he didn't want to tell the journalist about. Mike hadn't seen his brother since leaving for work that morning, that was the official story. That's what he'd told the police at the time and that's what he had to tell the journalist now, aside from saying he didn't think his brother was guilty.

He felt shattered when his train arrived at Chelmsford and he started to nod off in the cab. At the B&B he managed, with some difficulty, to connect his phone to the free wifi, fully expecting to see a message from Karen Taylor to arrange a meeting. There was a message waiting for him, but it wasn't from the journalist.

Chapter 14

Mother

Sylvia felt on edge as she walked down the alleyway from her house and crossed the road to the green on Friday afternoon. Ever since Kerry had told her about the journalist hanging around the village she felt she was being looked at and talked about again.

In the shop yesterday, Mrs Barton behind the counter had suddenly begun talking very loudly to Maria McCarthy, who had her back to the door, about the British wildlife nature programme that had been on TV the night before. Outside the church afterwards, Sylvia was sure two of her neighbours were giving her the pitying look as they whispered to one another.

It was happening again. People had been reminded about the past and were making it seem like it had all happened yesterday rather than thirty-nine years ago. Sylvia didn't like it. She wanted to be Sylvia the retired-dinner lady, Sylvia the retired-cleaner, Sylvia the local villager, not Sylvia the pitied, tragic martyr. Kerry had told her to tell people how she felt but if she started having a go at people, saying she didn't want their pity, they'd just say she was still suffering and that it was the stress talking.

She walked across the green and crossed the other road to the bus stop that stood beside the pathway leading up to the school. She was taking the bus to Maldon to visit Marjorie. For the first time in years Sylvia looked up that path with trepidation, remembering the last time her daughter had been taken up it by Ray, rather than remembering all of the fun times when she felt happy to go to work there as a dinner lady, the children calling out to her and rushing up to give her a hug.

She turned her back on the pathway and waited in silence for the bus to arrive. She was the only one waiting at the stop and was pleased to be alone for once. When the bus arrived she clambered on and felt glad to be leaving Little Tenwick behind her.

She spent most of the journey worrying about telling Ken all about Emma. She'd wanted to keep the secret a little longer and was angry at that damn journalist for forcing her hand. While she was both surprised and relieved that she hadn't yet been contacted, Sylvia had half a mind to phone Karen Taylor up and give her a piece of her mind. She wasn't ready to tell Ken, she told herself, but honestly, would she ever consider herself ready.

When she got off the bus outside the retirement home, Sylvia was in a panic and was seriously considering telling Ken the relationship was over. It seemed the easier of the options she had. They'd had a nice time together but perhaps that was all she needed at seventy-eight. She could carry on on her own. She had the church still and it looked like Ray was going nowhere. Perhaps she could get used to having his cat around.

It was a late afternoon visit she was making to see Marjorie. Ken was meeting her here later and, after their visit, they were going back to his house for the evening. It worked out well as Ray was covering the late night opening at the supermarket. He'd headed out to work at midday. Sylvia had made pasties that morning and she'd placed one in Ray's lunchbox that he took to work with him as a surprise treat for him to enjoy later. He'd been a bit huffy with her since she'd complained about the journalist and she hoped this peace offering would help him feel better.

Inside she discovered Marjorie was in her room, some of the other residents having complained that her mumbling and staring was disconcerting in the main lounge. She'd been left in her wheelchair at the bottom of her bed. When she entered, Sylvia immediately pushed her towards the window where she could at least see the sky.

"Gosh it's getting quite chilly in here," she said, feeling the radiator, "They ought to start putting the heating on."

She fetched a thick cardigan from Marjorie's wardrobe and put it around the old lady's shoulders.

"There," she said, "That's better isn't it."

Marjorie didn't respond.

"Everyone in the village sends their love," Sylvia told her, brightly, sitting down beside her old friend.

She sighed.

"Oh I wish that was true," she said, patting her friend's hand, "You deserve so much better than this. People do ask after you but it's not the same as visiting is it. This place isn't so far away, especially as most of them have cars."

Sylvia turned and looked out of the window. She had to sit up really straight to see any of the garden and even then it was just the tops of the trees at the far end. It was a lovely, outdoor space but unless you were able to stand up, it was completely hidden to the upstairs residents.

"Do you think I'm making a fool of myself," she asked, not expecting to receive an answer, "Do you think it's silly for a seventy-eight year old woman to have a full-blown relationship with a man?"

She waited a few moments, as if waiting for the response she would have received from Marjorie before the Alzheimer's had taken hold.

"Shouldn't I be looking for just companionship at this age,

someone to go dancing or go to bingo with?"

Sylvia looked back at her friend.

"I've found so much more with Ken and that kind of scares me," she admitted, "He's awakened feelings in me I haven't felt in years, feelings that I thought were gone forever. I can't help worrying about what others in the village will think. I don't want to be thought of as some silly, old woman. It's bad enough that they've started treating me the way they did when Emma first went missing."

She reached over and squeezed her friend's hand.

"You never did that," she said, "You never pitied me. You saved me. You listened to my outbursts, you held me when I was upset, you told me off when I was wallowing in self-pity. I wish I still had all of you here now, Marjorie. I don't know what to do. I've fallen in love with Ken but I fear how he'll react when he finds out about Emma. I don't want his pity. I don't want him being sorry all of the time, I couldn't cope with that. Oh that damn journalist. I bet she's never suffered in her life."

Sylvia let out a long sigh.

"No, that's not a fair thing to say," she admitted, "If I've learned anything from my prayers and contemplation in church it's that we're all on our own journeys in this life. We have different experiences to deal with, both positive and negative. Some of us handle things better than others but that's only because we're all different and have had different upbringings."

She smiled at her friend.

"I wonder if you're still in there somewhere Marjorie, learning from this terrible time you're going through. I guess all we can do is the best for ourselves and stop comparing our lives to others. No one should be envied or pitied."

Sylvia sighed again.

"I suppose I'm not going to know how Ken reacts until I tell him," she said, "And if he does pity me then I know the relationship will be over. I ought to give him a chance though, rather than ending it now."

She smiled at Marjorie who was still staring down at her lap.

"Thank you," she said, "You're still helping me make decisions, even if you don't know it. You're the only one who knows the whole truth about what happened thirty-nine years ago. I'm certainly not ready to share all of that with him yet."

Ken was waiting for her in the hallway when she came out of the lift. He beamed at her and Sylvia felt herself go weak at the knees.

"Are you ready to go?" he asked.

She nodded.

Ken was a great cook and Sylvia always enjoyed having a night off from the kitchen. Today though, her stomach felt knotted as nerves took over, thinking about what she was going to tell him tonight.

Ken's house was a modern property in an area of Maldon that was full of similar properties. It was a three-bedroomed house with an integrated garage and mock Tudor panelling on the pitched roof above the window of the master bedroom. Inside a square lounge led through to a large kitchen diner and conservatory.

Sylvia tried to be upbeat and happy while Ken cooked, putting off their talk until after they'd eaten. He made chicken thighs in garlic and lemon and served it with creamy mashed potato and green vegetables. It was delicious and Sylvia ate everything on her plate despite the nerves. The white wine helped. Ken only had the one glass as he was driving her home afterwards so that she could be in before Ray arrived home. He topped hers up twice.

"You've seemed a little quiet tonight," he said, the second time he added more wine to her glass, "Is everything okay?"

"I've got something I need to tell you," Sylvia replied, "Something about my past."

"Ooh, that sounds racy."

Ken grinned at her but Sylvia couldn't return it. She readied herself by taking a deep breath.

"I've told you about Ray," she began, "My son who runs the supermarket in Great Tenwick."

"Yes, I look forward to meeting him. I hope that will be soon. I'm sure we'll get on well together."

"Well I also have a daughter, Emma."

Ken seemed non-plussed.

"Oh right," he said, taking a sip of his wine, "Is she local too?"

"No."

Sylvia took a moment before continuing.

"She was abducted when she was five years old. I haven't seen her since."

Ken's face took on a shocked expression and he slowly lowered his wineglass onto the table. Sylvia remained silent, her heart thumping painfully in her chest as she waited for his response. Eventually Ken said,

"Jesus Christ!"

He opened his mouth to say something else and then closed it again, as if he was struggling to get the words right. Eventually he looked across the table at Sylvia. She desperately hoped he wasn't about to give her the pitying look and apologise, worrying he'd said something before now to offend her.

"How on earth do you cope with that each day?" he asked.

Sylvia, realising she had been holding her breath, let out a long sigh of relief. She almost smiled at Ken's response, grateful to him for not being full of remorse.

"There isn't a choice," she told him, "You get on with life or you go under. You think about all the other things you have in the world. You acknowledge that the hurt and pain and all those other emotions are still there but with time, you learn to leave them to one side, in a place where you don't allow them to control you. Of course they do at the beginning. You have to experience them all, but then you've got to pack them away and get on with life."

She shrugged her shoulders.

"It's a form of grief. Everyone knows what that feels like."

"Yes but this is different," Ken said, "It's not even the death of a child is it. It's the loss of one without knowing what happened, that perhaps they're still alive somewhere."

He put his arm across the table and took hold of her hand.

"You never got to say goodbye."

Tears sprang to Sylvia's eyes. No one had ever understood like that before. In an instant Ken was by her side and she leaned into his chest as she sobbed. It had been years since she'd allowed herself to show this much emotion over Emma. Of course there were still tears. Every year on the anniversary she cried but the rest of the time she stayed strong. Sylvia was surprised at the level of her emotional outburst now and thought that perhaps she should have given in to it more often.

Perhaps it was Ken too, his understanding, his affection for her, the fact that for the first time in years, Sylvia wasn't alone. There was someone there to ease the burden, to take on the mantel of being the strong one for a short while.

Once she stopped crying Sylvia took herself off to the downstairs cloakroom to wash her face. When she returned

Ken was still sat at the table, the plates now cleared.

"I don't know if you fancy any dessert yet," he said.

Sylvia shook her head.

"Shall we go and sit somewhere more comfortable," she asked, "I'd like to tell you what happened, if you don't mind."

Ken smiled.

"Of course I don't mind," he replied, "Let's go into the lounge."

He picked up her drink and they both sat down on the sofa. Sylvia took a sip of her wine before speaking.

"It was nineteen eighty," she said, "The end of September, almost thirty-nine years ago to the day. It was Wednesday, the same as any other. Ray took Emma to school on that day because I went early into Chelmsford to be first in line at the bargain supermarket. My ex-husband, Daniel was out of work and we were struggling."

Ken had his arm around her shoulder. He was gently stroking her neck and fondling her ear. Sylvia liked his touch.

"When I returned to the village I was told Emma had gone missing and was given a sedative to make me sleep. I slept right through to the next morning."

She sighed.

"I wish I'd refused it. I should have been out looking for my little girl. If she was lost and frightened then she needed to hear her mother's voice calling her. I wasn't there for her."

"So you didn't know what had happened then," Ken said, "First hand I mean."

Sylvia shook her head.

"No. My Ray had taken her to school as normal before catching the school bus to the comprehensive in Great Tenwick. Apparently Emma's teacher stepped out of the classroom for a couple of minutes and when she returned, Emma was gone.

The other children said she'd run off after losing one of her purple ribbons in her hair. That was the last reported sighting of her."

"My God. And there were no leads?"

"No. Everyone thought a local boy had taken her. I say boy, Jimmy McGill was about twenty-five at the time. He had mental problems of some kind, I don't know exactly what. Back then not everything was given a name like today. Everyone described him as backward. He was a kind boy and wouldn't harm anyone. He was nosy, well let's face it, most of the people in the village were that, but Jimmy would come up to your window and look inside your house, not realising that was something you shouldn't do."

"Like a modern day Boo Radley," Ken said.

"Sorry?"

"'To Kill a Mocking Bird?' Never mind, I interrupted you."

"Oh well, Jimmy couldn't help it, bless him. He liked people and wanted to know what they were doing. He also liked watching the children playing in the school playground. I don't see why that day he would have suddenly decided to take one of them."

Ken remained silent, allowing Sylvia to continue at her own pace.

"He went missing too, you see, on that day. I know people thought me an idiot at the time to suggest it was just a coincidence but I really believe that it was. If a mentally ill man and a five year old girl had gone off together they would have been found easily enough wouldn't they. They'd have been found within hours, but those hours passed, then days and weeks, then months and years and there were no clues and no leads."

"That seems strange."

"Oh there were so-called sightings once the story hit the newspapers. Nothing ever came of them. They were both gone, but separately as far as I was concerned. It must have been such a terrible time for Sheila McGill. There was Daniel and I doing a televised appeal for info while her son was thought of as the guilty party. Where was her appeal for her missing son? Where was the outpouring of grief for her?"

Sylvia sniffed.

"I didn't think of that at the time, I was too concerned with Emma. It was only later that I thought about Sheila but I felt it was too late then to go and see her. Well, I felt guilty for not going sooner and by then she'd been diagnosed with cancer and passed away not long afterwards, the poor woman. I sometimes wonder though if maybe Emma was never found because the police only looked at Jimmy McGill as the abductor."

After a beat, Sylvia shook her head and added,

"No, that's not fair. The police did all they could. He wasn't found either. Let's face it, everyone else was expecting them to be together. I guess the search for Emma was a search for him too. I still think something really odd must have happened that day. I just don't know what."

"What happens with a case like that," Ken asked, "I mean, is it still open?"

Sylvia shrugged her shoulders.

"I suppose it's dormant," she told him, "It's there for if any new evidence comes to light, which is hardly likely now. So many other people go missing each day. The police did all they could at the time with the resources they had. Eventually they had to move on. I guess we've all had to move on."

She looked up at Ken and he smiled at her, leaning in and kissing her cheek. She settled herself closer to him, feeling his comforting warmth against her.

"So what did you do," he asked her, "I mean aside from the police investigation. How did you get through each day? What did you do?"

"What didn't I do," Sylvia replied, "I felt so guilty being asleep at the most critical time of her disappearance. I wanted to be out searching. Daniel went out. Well, he was the first on the scene, having walked by the school when the teacher was out looking for her. I was told to stay at home by the phone to await news. It was awful. I felt useless and worthless sat there."

She reached for her wine glass.

"And trapped," she added, "The press were all over the village at the time too, speaking to everyone else about the family because the police stopped them speaking to me. We had to keep Ray at home for a while after they turned up at his school. He felt trapped too."

She took a healthy swig from the glass before placing it down again.

"Eventually the press lost interest. There were plenty of other news stories happening at the time, the Yorkshire Ripper attacks, the increase in unemployment, anti-racist marches that clashed with actual racists," Sylvia sighed, "It seemed such an unhappy world. We usually look back on the past nostalgically, thinking it was a better place, but it wasn't. I really don't think we change as much as we believe we do."

She leaned her head against Ken's chest, feeling the rhythmic beating of his heart against her cheek.

"When you think," she began, "Years ago there were public executions. People would actually go to watch other people die. We think that's barbaric now but really we've just replaced the public executions with TV. Look how violent some of the programmes are, even the soap operas now. There's not a week goes by without a death or a vehicle smash or something being blown up and people lap it up. Then there's these reality TV shows. We sit at home watching people on the screen being forced to eat something disgusting or we see them showing a doctor some body part that's become abnormal. Other programmes bring on these naive young people who aren't usually the smartest in the world and put them into situations where the public can laugh at their ignorance or stupidity. All that is just a modern day version of the Victorian freak shows. I don't like it."

Ken moved as if to get up.

"I'll fill up your glass," he said.

"No don't do that. I've had enough," she replied, "I'm rambling."

Ken laughed.

"You're still making a lot of sense," he told her.

Sylvia smiled and handed him the glass, not wanting to move away from where she was snuggled into him. Ken placed it on the table beside him.

"Where was I?" she asked.

"You were about to tell me what you did to find Emma."

"That's right. Once the press had left and the investigation seemed to stall, I decided I needed to keep Emma in people's minds. I suppose it was natural for the rest of the village to return to their own lives. With the press and police presence gone their lives could return to normal whereas mine was never going to be the same again."

She shook her head sadly.

"I had leaflets printed with Emma's face on them that I would deliver all round the local areas. That took a lot of time, having to rely on an infrequent bus service and my own two feet. I also sent the leaflets to various newspapers to print in their issues, and to radio shows to put out announcements. Some did it for free, others required a payment. Like I said, Daniel hadn't been working and only got a job a few months after Emma disappeared. I therefore couldn't afford to do that too often."

Sylvia sighed.

"It didn't bring any results but I kept going. I had to do something. Oh my goodness."

She stopped talking and sat up.

"What is it?" Ken asked, concerned.

"Is that the reason?" she said, talking more to herself.

"Is what the reason?"

"Why I received the pitying looks from people. Did they watch my fruitless search for my daughter and think I was just deluding myself? Did I make people pity me?"

Ken reached out and stroked her arm.

"Sylvia, people would have felt sorry for you, that's all. It's natural. No one can begin to imagine what you went through unless they went through the same thing themselves. It's not pity."

"I don't know," she replied, "It still looks like pity today."

"Today?"

Sylvia shook her head.

"Don't worry about that," she told him, not wanting to think about the journalist, "Where was I again?"

"You were leafleting the area."

"That's right."

Sylvia sat back against Ken again.

"Well, I felt like I was either on the road with my leaflets or in church, being angry at God for allowing my little girl to be taken away from me. It kind of felt like I was the only one doing anything. Ray had school and exams to study for. I could understand that but Daniel seemed to have resigned himself to Emma being dead and I hated that. Our marriage had been rocky for a while but when he got his job over in Gloucestershire it felt like the first ray of hope for the family. Of course really it just meant we saw a lot less of each other and we finally realised that we preferred the time apart than the time together."

"So you were all alone," Ken said, sadly.

"I had my Ray of course and the church was helping. I realised my anger was getting me nowhere and I started talking to God rather than shouting at him. I asked for help and strength to understand what had happened; to accept it."

"That must have been difficult."

"It felt damn near impossible in the beginning," Sylvia told him, "But over time I did start to accept what had happened. Don't get me wrong, I still hated it and I was still doing what I could to keep Emma alive in other people's memories, but I had to accept that she had been taken. I prayed that she was safe and happy and that she was being brought up with love. It was a coping mechanism I suppose. I had to learn to cope with the emptiness, the wretchedness and frustration of the situation."

She fell silent for a moment as she reflected.

"My Emma is with me everyday, just not in person. That thought alongside all of the other feelings just became a part of me, part of my everyday life, like my grey hair, my wrinkles and the arthritis in my knee. I cope with the grey hair by having it dyed, I cope with the wrinkles by avoiding mirrors, I cope with the knee pain through hot water bottles and rubs; I cope with Emma not being here by quelling the negative emotions. Each one of those things can flare up without warning, noticing the grey hairs peeping through at the roots, looking in a mirror with an overhead, unforgiving light, a sharp sudden pain in my knee; or an overwhelming feeling of grief when thoughts of Emma ignite the emotions."

Sylvia looked up at Ken.

"Learning to cope took years," she said, "My friend Marjorie helped me get a job as a dinner lady. I was still cleaning houses on a part-time basis and I started volunteering at the church. I was busy all of the time but it helped me to take my mind off of things for a while. I made new friends at church and I loved patrolling the school playground with little children walking around with me, all wanting to hold my hand. It was lovely."

Sylvia smiled at the memory.

"I still did what I could for Emma. I still had my leaflets but the announcements in the paper became less often, once a month, once a quarter and then once a year. Eventually I had to stop altogether. Emma was growing up with new parents, I felt sure of that. I'd been praying for the strength to understand and God had given me that. I had to let go and just hope that one day we might be united again but even then it wouldn't be the same, I know that. In my head she's still five years old not forty-four. She's still the delicate, little miracle Daniel and I had spent years trying to have. She's still my beautiful daughter with the purple ribbons in her blonde hair. She loved purple. That's how I know she's safe and alive. Every time I've prayed to God to ask him to keep her safe, I've always seen the colour purple somewhere afterwards. He's letting me know He's heard me. That's how I know she's still alive."

She stopped talking. Ken didn't say anything.

"I suppose some will think that's silly but I know in my heart that she's okay."

Ken kissed the top of her head. Sylvia felt a wave of relief and elation. She'd told Ken and he understood. He didn't pity her, he respected her. It felt good.

"I'm glad you feel that way," he said, "You're a brave lady Sylvia."

"Oh I don't know about that," she replied.

"I do," he said, "You've been through so much and yet here you are, getting on. Being able to tell me all this tonight shows how strong you are."

"Thank you."

Ken gently sat Sylvia up.

"That's why I need to be strong too," he said, "I've got a little secret I need to tell you."

Chapter 15

Brother

Ray sat in his office eating the pasty he'd found in his lunchbox. It wasn't as good without some pickle and he wished his mother had thought to put some in the container. It didn't enter his head to buy himself a jar from stock. He'd turned off the monitor of his computer, fed up of looking at stock lists; his black reflection on the screen matching his current mood.

Ray had been out of sorts all day. He'd been woken early by Bertie pawing at his face in bed at five o'clock, wanting to go outside. Ray didn't know why his mother refused to have a cat flap put in. It would make his life easier.

Sylvia had been trying to be nice to him since she'd been terse in that phone call about the journalist but Ray just found that annoying. He couldn't understand why was she so reluctant to accept the book? It's not like she had to buy herself a copy.

He was also miffed that the gossipmongers weren't spreading the word about the journalist and the book around the area fast enough. Although he detested gossip he'd hoped to receive an outpouring of emotion from people over the past coming back to haunt him, graciously accepting their condolences about losing his beloved, little sister, listening to them telling him how brave he was being and how much they admired him for getting on with his life so successfully, but there'd been none of that. He'd had to work hard to bring it up in conversation with Naveena next door at the newsagents that evening when he'd made an excuse to pop in there for a particular magazine. All she'd wanted to discuss was how the long hours were getting to her and that she had plans in place to retire soon.

Self, self self, Ray had thought to himself, while smiling and pretending to sympathise with her.

His mum had even had the audacity to complain to him that people appeared to be pitying **her** again over Emma's disappearance. Talk about rubbing it in. Mind you, he didn't blame Karen Taylor for his mum's mood, he blamed Emma. She'd known how to twist her parents round her little finger from a very young age and she was still doing it now from beyond the grave.

Ray thought she had to be dead. He hoped she was anyway. She'd been a burden on his life for five years and he'd hate to think she'd been a burden on someone else's for the last thirty-nine. He'd seen her go off with **him** anyway, that backward boy. Jimmy McGill was an oversized oaf and could very easily have killed a grown man let alone a prissy, little girl like Emma. If Jimmy was still around Ray would have shaken his hand. Well, perhaps not actually touched him but he would have been grateful for his part in getting rid of the little gobshite.

As Ray finished off the pasty his mind returned to the past. His early childhood had been happy enough except for the times his mum became ill and she would cry. Ray didn't understand about getting pregnant and miscarrying at the time. All he knew was that his mother would seem very happy and contented and then soon after she'd become upset and weepy.

After a while he noticed his parents arguing more. Then came that time when he was eight and, needing to go to the toilet, he'd rushed into the bathroom to be greeted by his mum crying on the floor and there being blood on the front of her dress. She'd actually shouted at him to get out and he'd fled the room, wetting himself out on the landing.

And then the little bitch had come along and suddenly his parents were all smiles again only this time, it wasn't him they were smiling at. He was only noticed when he did something that might upset the precious new baby.

"Stop shouting, you'll wake Emma", "Don't kick that ball about, you might hit Emma", "Give that toy to Emma, Ray, she wants to play with it. Come on now, don't be silly, she's younger than you, let her have it."

Oh I let her have it, Ray thought to himself now, a grin on his face.

The first time he'd hit his sister was when she started walking and she used to annoyingly follow him round. His parents thought it adorable but even then the attention was on Emma rather than him. "Look at Emma walk", "Look at Emma toddle after her brother", "Isn't Emma sweet, loving her brother so." So fed up with his trailing sister, Ray had hit her, knocking her over. He'd never seen his mother that angry before. She came down on him like a ton of bricks. After that he had to learn to hide what he was doing. It wasn't easy when the spoilt, little bitch cried at the smallest thing but Ray soon became adept at causing her all sorts of pain.

Emma became a very accident-prone little girl, alway tripping over her own feet or some obstacle in her way. Several times Sylvia had taken her to have her eyes tested, convinced she couldn't see properly. Ray had found that hilarious. Of course it also meant his mother became ever more protective of his little sister and he received even less attention.

He convinced his parents that he was the doting brother. Sylvia beamed every time she saw her son reading a story to his sister. Once she was out of earshot those tales of bunnies and teddies became a lot more sinister. Many times Emma woke up in the night screaming and crying because of bad dreams. She was still wetting the bed when she was abducted. Ray hoped that if she was alive now she'd still be suffering with that.

He turned his monitor back on but didn't return to updating his stock lists. His mind remained in the past. It wasn't long after the news of the disappearance had died down that Ray had begun working here in this store on a Saturday. He'd loved it. People had moved on from Emma and he was no longer asked about her. His dad had started his job in the Cotswolds and was away a lot. It was only Sylvia who continued to go on about Emma. Ray had found it embarrassing, especially when she came into the supermarket with those leaflets with Emma's photo on them that he'd kept conveniently forgetting to bring in himself, getting the manager to display one in the window.

After only passing two of his O levels, Ray decided to give A levels a miss and began working in the shop full time at sixteen. Thirty-eight years later and here he was, running that same store. Ray smiled to himself as he thought about what he'd achieved. The shop meant everything to him. It had never let him down like friends, family and women had. Jayne, Sandra, Alison and Jackie; each one of them had betrayed him.

Jayne had lied to him before they married, telling him she didn't want children. Only ten years in and she changed her mind. Well, Ray certainly hadn't. After seeing what happened when a baby entered the family he definitely knew he wasn't going to have any. Even just her thinking about babies became obsessive and soon Jayne stopped paying him any attention.

After the divorce Sandra came along, a woman that described herself as a free spirit. The sex had been amazing, the attention and detail she put into satisfying Ray's desires being an eye-opener to him. But then she'd told him she wanted them to take a year off and travel the world while they were still young. Ray told her that was crazy as he'd just got assistant manager at the shop. He'd thought Sandra loved him and had been shocked when she went off alone.

Alison was mental, as far as Ray was concerned. Just when he'd begun to have feelings for her she introduced him to her two children that she hadn't even mentioned before. He'd dumped her there and then and she'd come to the shop a few times afterwards, making a complete fool of herself. Ray feared losing his job for a while. If the current area manager, Elizabeth Chan had been installed at the time then she would have definitely got rid of him. She was looking for the right excuse to do that.

Ray hadn't expected to find anyone else after that but then Jackie came into his life, his mother's favourite. She rented the apartment above the hairdressers in the parade of shops where the supermarket was, working part time in the salon. She was warm, kind and family orientated. She loved her parents and got on well with Sylvia. She'd never had children of her own and was too old to try now, which suited Ray. A couple of months after moving in together over the salon, Jackie took on a full time role.

Ray didn't expect anything to change but suddenly his partner became more demanding, wanting him to cook meals a few times a week and take his turn tidying the apartment. She worked in the same building she lived in and Ray couldn't see why she couldn't continue to take care of their home (and him) like she always had.

When it was his turn to cook he'd bring home microwaveable meals from the supermarket but that wasn't good enough for Jackie. She wanted him to cook properly for them like she did. Ray no longer recognised this nagging woman who had replaced the Jackie he'd moved in with. She started taking evening classes and not long after, told Ray she was moving out to go and live with her new boyfriend she'd met at pottery.

Ray tutted now. Why did women have to change? He'd stayed the same over the years, why wasn't that enough for any of them?

Well that's their problem, he thought, not mine.

He was better off without a woman in his life. All he needed was the shop and all he desired was that seat on the parish council. That would show them all what they were missing. That would give him the respect he deserved. Even his mum was prone to change. She was doing it again now, being short with him, treating him nastily while her attention was focussed on Emma.

Ray sighed. Everything always came back to Emma. Why couldn't she have ended up as just another bloody mess on the bathroom carpet like all his mother's other attempts to have a child? Why did she have to live? She'd ruined his whole life but he wasn't going to allow her to destroy his future. No, he needed a new plan to get himself onto the parish council. If the gossip about his sister wasn't working because it was old news then perhaps he needed to create some new news. He remembered giving Karen Taylor some old flannel about expansion when she'd eyed up the size of his office. He turned round in his chair (with some difficulty in the space) and looked at the back wall. On the other side was Naveena's newsagents. He smiled.

Still Missing

by Karen Taylor

Chapter 3 (first draft)

Trying to get those involved in the Emma Burrows story to open up to me has proved quite challenging in most cases. I realise my questioning will open up old wounds but surely a fresh look at the past would help those wounds heal for good. Time moves on, technology moves on and police procedures move on. To those not involved, thirty-nine years may seem too far after the event to bother with, but to those that were affected by the abduction, surely a chance to perhaps answer some questions, to re-examine the past, should be an opportunity to grab with both hands.

To me, looking in from the outside, those involved seem scared to even look back at what happened. For Emma's parents that is understandable but for the others that were on the periphery of involvement, their hesitation to speak to me makes my journalistic brain become thoughtful. I've been fascinated by this case because of the lack of evidence and suspects at the time but the wall of silence that I'm up against now actually speaks to me.

Most people believe Emma is dead. Perhaps that is true after the number of so-called sightings diminished as the months passed by after the disappearance, but where there is no proof surely there should be hope. While Sylvia is certain her daughter is alive, why are others so certain she is dead? I can't help wondering if there is other information that never came to light that, if it had, might have had some bearing on the case.

If that's true then there is almost forty years of guilt of not speaking up at the time to be carried around. That would weigh a person down and could make them reluctant to talk now. If the past hasn't been settled then no one can properly move on. Thirty-nine years may have gone by but time alone doesn't provide absolution.

Chapter 16

Father

Daniel wished now that he'd just stayed indoors rather than going out for a ten minute stroll. He'd always thought calling a place like this a retirement village had just been some pretentious advertising but it really was like every village Daniel had ever lived in; you couldn't go anywhere without bumping into someone who wanted a nose into your personal life.

Having been acknowledged out on the main path by Gerald Corkhill, who insisted they needed warming up after being outdoors on a fresh day, Daniel found himself in the communal lounge drinking coffee at a table that also included Cynthia Jameson who was knitting something odd in a lurid blue wool.

"I see your daughter visited you the other night," she said to him, "Tuesday wasn't it, about six? I'd just watched Pointless on the telly and got up to pull my curtains over. She didn't stay long did she."

"It takes you a while to pull your curtains over does it," Daniel replied, not feeling very polite.

"Oh I was up for a second time, straightening them," Cynthia replied, brightly, "It was then I saw her car pass out of the exit gate."

"That's a lovely car," Gerald said, putting his mug down onto the coffee table, "She does well for herself, your Tania. Must earn a good salary up at that aviation firm."

"Next time she pops in I'll ask her to bring a wage slip."

“I was only saying old boy,” Gerald replied, obviously hurt, “I just meant you must be proud of her.”

“An apple doesn’t fall far from the tree,” Cynthia said, smiling at Daniel, “You and your wife were successful in business too weren’t you. I used to come into your restaurant with my Alan. You always kept it nice.”

Daniel smiled as a reply. He felt bad for snapping but then it wasn’t like he’d wanted to come in. Gerald had practically dragged him in, using a grip that belied his eighty-five years. Daniel hadn’t spoken to Tania since Tuesday night when he’d told her to go off to the States. They didn’t speak to each other that often but it was now Friday and he thought she’d have rung to apologise. He was still angry with her for accusing him of being a bad parent and smashing Emma’s photo frame. Hadn’t both Gerald and Cynthia just proved he was in the right, telling him how Tania was successful because he and Alice had been. They’d shown her how to be a good human being by example. If that wasn’t being a good parent, Daniel didn’t know what was.

“Do you think your Tania will ever settle down,” Cynthia continued, finishing a row and switching the needles over in her hands, “She lives on her own, doesn’t she?”

Daniel nodded.

“Yes,” he said, “She has a boyfriend, Raj but they have separate homes. I’ve given up on asking why they don’t move in together. It seems an odd relationship to me, more a convenience.”

“Things are certainly different these days,” Gerald replied, “In our day you courted and then got married. There was no other acceptable option.”

“Everyone seemed to want to get married back when I was at school,” Cynthia agreed, “I always used to wonder who my husband would be and what my wedding day was going to be like. There was never much talk about having a career. I don't mean jobs, we all spoke about those, whether that was working in a shop or a factory, or even going into nursing or teaching but they were always spoken of as temporary, only working until we married and started a family. Back then it seemed like a career and marriage were mutually exclusive experiences for a woman. It's better now. There's so much choice for a girl."

Daniel's mind travelled back to when Emma was born. Had he ever thought about her future, what she was going to be when she grew up? Probably not, even though times were changing. If he was honest he had thought about walking her down the aisle on her wedding day. He frowned as he realised he hadn't had the same thoughts about Tania. Had he always known she wouldn't get married? No, of course not. He hadn't imagined it because of Emma and superstition. He'd thought about Emma growing up and she'd died at five years of age. He didn't want to go through that again with Tania. She had to be treated differently.

"I've just had an email from my daughter," Cynthia continued, breaking into Daniel's thoughts.

"The one in New Zealand?" Gerald asked.

"That's right."

"Is she the estate agent?"

"No that's my other daughter, the one in South Africa."

Cynthia sniffed.

"It's a shame they're both so far away, I do miss them."

Daniel squirmed in his chair, not able to feel comfortable in it anymore.

"While technology is so good these days and I can talk to them over the internet anytime I like," Cynthia continued, "It's not the same as being in the same room together. You can't hug a screen can you."

"No," Daniel said, "No, you can't. Will you excuse me, I'm going to go home for a nap."

Before Daniel left the room the door opened and one of the members of office staff came in with a young, blonde woman who was obviously being shown around the facilities for an elderly relative. Daniel stood back to let them through. The young woman thanked him. Behind them came Jessica who beamed.

"Mr Burrows," she said, "I'll be at your place in half an hour."

"Then I'll get the coffee on," he replied.

Jessica laughed.

"You're terrible," she said, before holding the door open for him.

As Daniel thanked her he noticed the young, blonde woman glance in his and Jessica's direction but then she turned away to listen to what the staff member was saying about the lounge.

Another resident for the Fading Fast Nursing Home, Daniel thought to himself, remembering what his friend, Bob had called the place in the pub the other day. He didn't think about it in an amusing light now. Seeing a person being shown round wasn't a good sign. An apartment becoming available meant another one of them had died.

As he made his way back to his own apartment Daniel thought about Cynthia and her children living abroad. There was a real sadness in her voice when she said that modern technology wouldn't allow her to hug her daughters. Tania had accused him of rarely hugging her. Surely that was just said in anger though, wasn't it?

Daniel's mind raced through his memories of his time in Gloucestershire. He hadn't been the most tactile of people, he knew that. There had been that friend of Alice's who had a daughter with Downs syndrome. She was a delightful, happy, little girl but she liked to give whomever she met a hug. Daniel had always cringed when she grabbed him and then felt guilty. He had no idea where that feeling came from. Perhaps it was just a product of the time he was brought up in when any illness that affected the mind wasn't talked about and the people suffering it were hidden from public view in institutions.

He remembered now that he'd had the same thoughts about Jimmy McGill. He'd had some sort of mental issue, something to do with a difficult birth, Daniel believed. He'd found Jimmy a bit creepy even as a small child. The family had done their best for him, well, not the dad, Tom. What a complete waste of space he was. The mum, Sheila had often looked tired, although the dark circles around her eyes weren't always from tiredness. Tom was a thug after a drink, not that anyone interfered. Back then it was part of someone's private life and no business of anyone else's to get involved. Oh you could gossip about them behind their back but you never got involved.

Daniel always believed that Jimmy McGill must have taken Emma. They both disappeared together the same day. He hated to think what might have happened to his daughter in the boy's care and he knew he would have probably killed Jimmy himself if he'd returned to the village.

He had little sympathy for the rest of the family too after the abduction although he barely ever saw them, especially after he started working here in Gloucestershire. Sheila hid herself away and was later diagnosed with cancer, dying soon after. Tom disappeared back to that lady friend of his and Daniel heard he died as well. Joey, the brother stayed in the area while his mum was alive but he left as soon as she was dead. Daniel's new job came up at the ideal time for him to leave his old life and the bad memories behind.

Up until Emma's disappearance, Daniel had always admired Joey McGill and the way he got on with his life despite the father he had and the fact that the mother had to give all of her attention to her other son. He wondered if Joey ever felt he'd lost out in the attention stakes…

Daniel stopped walking. He was only a few steps from his front door but he stopped dead as his last thought sunk in. Had Tania been right? Had she lost out on his attention because of what happened to Emma?

He cast his mind back again to before the abduction. While never tactile to strangers, Daniel remembered being a hugger to his children. His father had thought that odd but that just made him do it all the more. Ray had stopped enjoying hugs when he was about ten but Emma always loved them. She'd go out of her way to get one but, try as he might, Daniel couldn't recall hugging Tania. Was his mind playing tricks on him? In every remembered hug the recipient was Emma.

He stepped forward, still in a bit of a daze, and opened his front door. His thoughts returned to Joey McGill. He'd grown up in difficult circumstances but how much had he suffered emotionally? He lost his parents and his brother and then emigrated abroad on his own. Had he found love again? In a way the same thing had happened to Daniel. He'd lost his daughter and wife and then his son who no longer wanted to stay in touch, but had he really done anything to try and rectify that? No, he hadn't. What if Ray's termination of their relationship had been a cry for help, a need for attention?

If he was honest with himself, Daniel had felt relieved at the time, being able to leave the past and everyone associated with it behind. He'd been lucky to find love again. He'd met Alice and they'd had Tania. While Alice was gone, Tania was still here. But for how long?

Daniel walked into his lounge and collapsed into his armchair. He realised he'd made a mess of everything. While he hated remembering, thirty-nine years ago he'd had a chance to save Emma but instead, he'd shouted at her in anger, telling her to get out and she'd fled from him, terrified, never to be seen again. Now this week he'd shouted at his other daughter, also telling her to leave. Tania had probably gone off and booked her flights. He'd left his first family behind when things got tough and now his younger daughter was about to leave him behind. Three children and he'd lost all of them. What sort of a bloody idiot and terrible father was he? As he sat in his chair, a lump in his throat, Daniel realised he didn't want Tania moving to the United States.

Chapter 17

Accused

The email was a brief message from his daughter-in-law. 'Phone me as soon as you get this. Don't worry about the time. Jill.'

Mike had gone straight downstairs and asked the owner of the B&B if he could pay to use her phone, worried about what was going on back home.

"What's happened?" he asked, as a sleepy-sounding Jill answered the phone.

"Oh Mike, it's you."

It couldn't be anything too bad if Jill had been enjoying a lie-in. Mike started to feel angry. He'd been really worried.

"Of course it's me," he snapped, "You asked me to call. What's happened?"

He realised Jill usually worked on a Friday. Why was she still in bed? What about getting the girls ready for school?"

"Oh my God, it's not one of the girls is it? Do I need to come back?"

"Calm down Mike, we're all fine," she told him, "I just needed to speak to you before Eddie arrives."

"Eddie? What do you mean arrive?"

"Oh God I shouldn't have drunk that wine last night," Jill said, more to herself, "My bloody head. Look Mike, yesterday after you'd left for the airport, Eddie and I went to your house to collect Ben. The phone rang while we were there and Eddie answered it."

"Oh for goodness sake, that's what the answerphone is for."

"It was a natural reaction," Jill replied, "I'd have done the same. Anyway, it was a British journalist, Karen someone, asking to speak to you regarding an email you sent her. Apparently you'd told her you were going to England but you didn't say when you were arriving. Eddie started asking her questions and she told him about some abduction you were involved in years ago."

"Fuck it!"

Mike closed his eyes. This was all he needed. The whole point of coming to England was to stop his family finding all of this out. Now that bloody, stupid journalist had opened her big mouth. Why didn't she just reply to his email? Why call his home phone number when an email would have cost nothing? Why was she phoning Canada in the evening? What the hell had the time been in England? Was the damn woman an insomniac?

Really though, Mike was angry at himself for not giving her all of the details in the first place. He'd been in a rush to write the email before leaving for the airport and Robbie had set his mails up to automatically add his name and number at the end. Mike didn't know how to turn that off. He preferred to be contacted via his home phone anyway. His latest cellphone seemed such a complicated instrument to use.

"What's going on Mike, I'm worried about you," Jill said.

"You don't have to be," he replied, "It's nothing really, just something from my past. I'll tell you all about it when I return. I'm laying some old ghosts to rest. Just wait until I get back."

"It's too late for that," she told him, "Eddie looked up the story about the abduction online and went into one."

Mike sighed.

"When does he not go into one," he said.

"Come on Mike, he's just worried about you, you can see that-eh?"

"No I can't," he retorted, "Just tell him to mind his own business until I return."

"I can't, I told you; it's too late for that. He's following you to England."

"What!"

"He wants to know what's going on. He left for the airport last night to wait until a seat became available. I tried to tell him not to but you know what he's like, he wants to know the truth and straightaway. We argued. That's why I drank the wine. I've no idea if he's still at the airport or already on his way there and frankly, I don't really care right now. I'm just warning you that he might turn up and I'm pleading with you not to start a fight."

"I won't start one, but if he does…"

"Oh for God's sake Mike," Jill interrupted, "I don't care who tries to start one I'm telling you to stop it, okay? You're both in a foreign country. I don't want the two of you ending up in prison over there. Just stay calm and talk rationally to one another. Remember, he's only following you because he's worried. Please try and remember that."

Mike returned to his room after he hung up the phone feeling utterly exhausted and wretched. He tried to sleep but thoughts about Jimmy in the past and Eddie in the present prevented him from enjoying a decent, deep sleep. In the end he gave up and went out for a walk, finding a fish and chip shop where he could sit in and enjoy cod roe and chips, something he hadn't eaten since emigrating.

Returning to the B&B he entered the residents' lounge, not wanting to sit alone in his room with just his thoughts for company. The TV was on and one elderly person was watching it, so engrossed he didn't even notice Mike. At the dining table sat a blonde woman who appeared to be in her early forties. She looked up from the newspaper she was reading as the door opened and smiled. Not wanting to watch the television, Mike walked over to the table.

"There's a filter coffee machine over there," the woman said, "The owner, Mrs Jessop, only switched it on ten minutes ago. It should still be hot."

The woman had a half empty mug in front of her.

"What does it taste like," Mike asked.

"Like bitter water, but at least it's hot."

He laughed.

"I'll give it a shot," he said, and poured a mug out before joining the woman at the dining table.

"Is this where they serve breakfast?" he asked.

"No, there's another room across the hallway where you can eat," the woman said, "I haven't been there yet, I only arrived this evening. Oh, I'm Sarah by the way."

"Mike," Mike replied, shaking the woman's outstretched hand.

Her face lit up when she smiled. She had very distinctive blue eyes that Mike felt had to be due to wearing coloured contact lenses. Surely they weren't naturally that colour?

"Are you here on business or is it a pleasure trip?" Mike asked her.

"Business I suppose," Sarah told him, "I'm at a seminar for work. It was half a day today and then all of tomorrow. I'm only here for the one night."

"Is it interesting?"

Sarah pulled a face.

"Hardly," she said, "It's a refresher course that I've had to do after taking time out from my job to look after my sick father. It's not like I've forgotten any of it in the last few months."

"What is it you do?"

"I'm an instructor," she told him, "For flight attendants, you know, cabin crew. I'm based at Gatwick but the seminar came up at Stansted so here I am."

"I've just come from Gatwick myself," Mike told her, "Well, Toronto before that."

"I thought I detected a bit of an accent."

"Really? My kids think I still sound English."

"Well you'll probably start sounding more English by the time you return."

Mike shook his head.

"I shouldn't think so after a week."

"That's not long for a holiday."

"Well it's not really a holiday. I'm…"

Mike didn't know how to continue with that sentence.

"Oh please, you don't have to tell me anything," Sarah said, "It's none of my business why you're here."

"No it's fine honestly," Mike replied.

He thought it would sounded sinister, or at least a bit odd, if he didn't say something.

"I'm here laying a few ghosts to rest," he said, remembering what he'd told Jill on the phone earlier, "It's my first time back in England in nearly forty years. My wife recently died and I felt the need to look back at some issues from before I emigrated."

"I'm sorry to hear about your wife," Sarah said.

"And I'm sorry about your father."

"Thank you. He's still with us," she said, "Just. He's in the hospital."

She waved her mobile phone at him.

"I'm hoping they don't need to call me. I had to come on this course now because the next one won't be for six months. He's been in there a few times over the the last few months but the latest stroke means he's not going to come out again. It's only a matter of time, so the doctor says, but I'll be back by his side tomorrow night. I feel bad but…"

She shrugged.

"I'm sure you've already done all you can," Mike told her, "And I'm sure he appreciates it."

Sarah smiled.

"Thank you," she said.

The smile left her face.

"While I don't like him being in pain I also selfishly don't want him dying either. I'll be all alone."

Mike couldn't help thinking about Barbara and his two sons. His children both had their families and right now they had him too. Perhaps he should make more of an effort with Eddie. He looked at the woman sat beside him and his heart went out to her. No one should ever feel alone.

"I know that feeling," he admitted, "Of being alone."

"Oh, didn't you say you had children?"

"Oh I don't meant now. I mean back when I emigrated. I was alone then. I'd lost my parents and my brother. There was no sympathy for me, not that I asked for it."

"That sounds terrible," Sarah said, "Was it an accident?"

Mike shook his head.

"No," he said, "My brother disappeared. He had learning difficulties and it was thought he'd taken a little girl. He hadn't. I know he didn't do it but you can't convince a village full of bigoted people who listen to gossip and believe what they want to believe."

He practically spat out that last sentence as he returned to the past and became Joey again. Sarah seemed lost for words. On the television the studio audience laughed.

"Oh," she said, before adding again, "That sounds terrible."

"It was. He was the sweetest boy in the world, my brother. Well, he wasn't a boy, he was five years older than me but, although he inhabited a twenty-five year old body, Jimmy was still a boy inside; a sweet-natured, kind, caring, little boy."

Sarah smiled.

"You still miss him, don't you."

Mike could feel a tear well up in his eye but he didn't try to blink it away or pretend it wasn't there. He didn't know why he was talking to this young woman sat next to him about it. Perhaps it was because she was a stranger, someone he wouldn't see again after breakfast in the morning.

"I miss him everyday," he said, "And my mother. After Jimmy went missing, everyone blamed him for taking the little girl that disappeared at the same time. I know it looked bad but I also know he wasn't responsible, he couldn't have been. While the parents of the little girl received sympathy, me and my mum were given the cold-shoulder. It wasn't fair. Oh I could handle it. I was out at work all day but mum couldn't face her job so she spent more time at home, having to bump into the villagers every time she needed to venture out."

Mike sighed.

"We weren't a well-thought of family in the first place, what with Jimmy and my good-for-nothing dad who was a well-known, local drunk. He was away with his fancy woman at the time. He came back a week later and barely seemed interested to know his eldest son was missing. He told us he was ill, that he was dying but really, at the time I thought it just a cry for attention. He disappeared back to his woman again soon afterwards. Later we found out he **had** died; cirrhosis of the liver."

Mike shrugged his shoulders.

"I didn't shed any tears for him," he said, "My mum had been having back trouble for ages and I'd finally persuaded her to go to the doctor. After tests were done it was discovered she had spinal cancer and she was dead within a couple of months, just before I heard about dad."

"That's so sad," Sarah said.

She touched Mike's hand. He looked up at her and was shocked to see tears in her own eyes.

"I'm sorry," he said, "All this talk of death at a time when you're worried about your dad."

Sarah shook her head.

"You don't have to be sorry," she told him, "I cry at anything. Mrs Jessop showed me her kitten earlier and I felt myself welling up then."

Mike gave her a sympathetic smile. She looked at her watch.

"Well I think I'm going to head up to my room," she said, "What with the drive up from Sussex today and the first part of the course, I'm rather tired."

"Yes you don't want to fall asleep in class tomorrow."

"Don't worry, I'll sit at the back," Sarah said, winking before standing up.

Mike laughed.

"Well I'll probably see you at breakfast," he said.

"Probably," she replied, stepping away from the table.

She stopped halfway across the room and turned back, speaking a little louder than before to be heard over the theme tune to some programme on the TV.

"I'm very sorry to hear about your brother," she told him, "I hope you find the peace you need while you're here."

She stared at him intently for a moment before smiling and then leaving the room. Mike smiled back, even though she'd already gone. The smile left his face as he remembered Eddie was on his way. If only he would listen to him like the young lady just had.

Chapter 18

Mother

Sylvia slept badly Friday night, tossing and turning until she fell into a deep sleep in the early hours of Saturday morning. She awoke at seven with a heavy head and a feeling of despair. The previous night played out again in her head as she lay in bed.

She arrived home with her heart still pounding. It had been scary rushing up unfamiliar roads in the dark in Maldon, desperately trying to find a main road and cab office. She hadn't wanted Ken to come after her. She was too upset.

After twenty minutes she'd found a street with a Chinese takeaway open. They'd phoned a cab for the distressed-looking, old lady and ten minutes later she was heading back to Little Tenwick. Sylvia was anxious she didn't have enough money on her but thought she had forty pounds in the left hand drawer of her welsh dresser that also contained batteries, old keys and instruction manuals for electrical appliances she no longer owned.

"What are you doing," Ray called out, from the lounge as he heard Sylvia rummaging in the kitchen.

She jumped and let out a yell.

"Goodness mother, what's wrong with you?"

"I didn't expect you to be home yet," she called back, trying to control her breathing and heart rate.

"Didn't you see the lounge lights on? Really mother, you're becoming very unobservant. We had a problem with the tills and had to reboot the system. As there were barely any customers I took the executive decision to send the staff home and close up early. Where have you been? What are you doing now?"

"I'm, erm," Sylvia tried to think quickly on her feet, "I'm just looking for the village newsletter for Kerry. We've been out for some dinner and she's just dropped me off."

"It's alright for some."

Sylvia found the two twenties under the pack of small screwdrivers she'd got out of a Christmas cracker ten years ago that she thought might still come in useful one day. After paying the cab driver the fare and a good tip she walked back up the alleyway, closed the door and leaned her head against the glass panel, taking a few deep breaths before putting her head round the lounge door. Ray had the TV on and was laid out on the sofa, the cat dozing on the armchair. It was the cat that looked up, giving Sylvia a low mew in greeting.

"I'm going straight to bed, Ray," she said.

"Already? It's barely nine o'clock."

"I know, I just feel a bit tired. Perhaps I'm coming down with a cold."

"Well make sure you keep it to yourself," he replied, "I don't want it, I've got far too much on at the moment. Oh I forgot to bring cat food home so Bertie's had the last pasty you made. You didn't want it did you?"

"Er, no, that's fine."

"He seemed to enjoy his more than I enjoyed mine."

Sylvia didn't reply to her son but instead left the room and tried not to run up the stairs to her bedroom. Once there she was able to lose the persona of calm, rational person that she'd put on for the cab driver and Ray. She finally allowed the woman that knew Ken's secret to reappear and fresh tears fell down her cheeks.

Sylvia shook the images of last night away as she got out of bed and ran herself a hot bath, hoping it would relax her. It didn't. Lying in the suds she couldn't help thinking about what Ken had told her. When he'd said he had a little secret she hadn't been unduly worried. After what she'd told him about Emma's disappearance anything he said would seem almost insignificant surely, something to acknowledge and then move on from. As she closed her eyes and sank further down into the bubbles, the whole conversation passed through her mind again.

"What is it, Ken," she joked, "Another woman?"

"No nothing like that," he replied, seriously.

He seemed reluctant to speak. Sylvia, having just shifted a burden off of her shoulders felt light and giddy. She touched his leg, quite high up on the thigh.

"Come on," she said, "It can't be that bad."

He looked into her eyes and smiled.

"I'm growing fonder of you every day, Sylvia," he said.

"I feel the same way."

"That's great," he continued, "Because I have to tell you, I'm not seventy years old."

Is that all, she thought to herself.

"My, my Ken," she said, playfully, "I thought it was only women that liked to take a few years off of their age. I didn't realise you were so superficial."

"I'm not older than seventy," Ken told her, "I'm younger."

Sylvia frowned.

"Why would you add years onto your real age," she asked, "Unless you were a teenager trying to get into a nightclub?"

Ken stood up before turning back to look down at Sylvia.

"When we met I found you very attractive," he told her, "You spoke of the number of years you and Marjorie had known each other and volunteered your age. I thought if I didn't add a few onto mine, you might not want to see me, romantically."

"Well how many are we talking here," Sylvia asked, still not particularly worried, "Four, five?"

"Eleven."

"Sorry?"

"I added on eleven years."

Sylvia did a quick sum in her head.

"You're fifty-nine!"

Ken nodded. Sylvia was shocked. She felt her breath quicken.

"I can't believe this," she said.

Ken knelt down in front of her.

"It doesn't have to change anything, does it," he asked, "I'm in love with you Sylvia, surely that is all that matters."

Sylvia stood up.

"It most certainly is not," she told him, walking past.

He grabbed at her arm.

"Please don't leave."

She shrugged her arm from his grip.

"What else can I do," she said, "This can't work. I'm in my seventies and you're in your fifties."

"Only for one more year."

"Oh so that makes it alright then."

"Really Sylvia, I think you're being a little childish about this."

"Me," Sylvia replied, astounded, "You're the child."

"I am not."

"I'm old enough to be your mother. You're practically the same age as my son. No wonder you told me earlier that you thought the two of you would get along."

"Please Sylvia, let's sit down and talk. This isn't an issue."

"Isn't it," she said, "Then why did you keep it a secret if you're so okay with it?"

Ken took a moment.

"Like I said, I was very attracted to you and I worried you wouldn't even look at me in that way if you knew my age. I thought once we got to know each other…"

He left the sentence hanging.

"Deceit," Sylvia told him, "That's what it is, deceit."

Ken stood up, starting to feel miffed.

"Well what about you," he said, "Coming here tonight to confess your own past."

Sylvia was incredulous.

"You can't compare my heartache at losing my daughter to your lies about your age," she shouted at him.

"I'm not trying to," a desperate Ken replied, "I'm just trying to say we all have secrets and pasts. Let's get through this."

Sylvia was shaking her head, not listening.

"I'll be the laughing stock of the village," she said, "'Look, there goes the cradle snatcher' they'll say. My God I was already a little embarrassed thinking you were seventy."

She looked at Ken.

"I'll be mocked, laughed at, pitied. I'm not going to be pitied again by anyone, do you hear me. This is over."

"Please Sylvia, give it some time."

"I'm leaving."

"At least let me give you a lift home."

"No," she said, rushing into the hall and yanking open the front door, "I never want to see you again."

She'd fled with Ken's voice calling her name.

As she pulled the plug out of the bath and stared at the water as it slowly emptied, Sylvia sighed. She felt as wretched now as she had the night before. Ken had lied to her. She was embarrassed and thought herself stupid. How had she trusted this man so readily and easily at her age? What was it she'd asked Marjorie on her afternoon visit, 'Do you think you can ever be too old to make a fool of yourself?' Well, she certainly knew the answer to that question now.

For once Sylvia didn't relish going over to the church but the flowers for the next day's Sunday service weren't going to arrange themselves and besides, she'd promised the rest of the ladies she'd be there.

Walking down the alleyway from her house to the village centre, Sylvia was still in a daze and only realised she was in the road when a car's brakes squealed. She jumped and turned towards the noise, finding herself staring at a face masked by the reflection of the outside world on the windscreen. She could just make out it was a woman. Sylvia stared for a moment as she realised how close she'd come to being hit, before calling out an apology and continuing on across the green to the church.

Inside the church the calmness of the space did nothing to assuage her fraught feelings. She was petrified Ken would turn up, upset that she hadn't responded to any of his numerous calls and texts that he must have begun sending as soon as she'd left his house. Every time the door creaked as it opened she would turn round quickly to see who it was.

"Are you okay Sylvia," Kerry asked her, after the fourth time of spinning round, "You seem distracted."

Kerry had a sudden thought.

"You're not worried about that journalist coming back are you?"

"Who?"

Sylvia had completely forgotten about Karen Taylor in her distress with Ken. With a start, she realised she'd gone to bed last night without saying goodnight to the photo of Emma, the first time in thirty-nine years. That just made her angrier at Ken. How dare he disrupt her life like this.

"I suppose I am still a bit edgy," she told Kerry, too embarrassed to mention Ken to her.

Kerry nodded.

"It must be awful to have the past brought up, especially so near to the anniversary."

Sylvia was glad the two of them were working on a display away from the other ladies. They were far enough away not to be overheard. As the other ladies still treated Kerry as an interloper, the two were barely acknowledged in their corner of the chancel.

"One year's the same as any other," Sylvia told Kerry, "I try not to think about the number of years Emma's been gone, although that isn't always easy when a significant one is approaching, like next year."

"I can only imagine," Kerry replied, "Has that journalist not been in touch yet?"

"No," Sylvia said, "But I did tell my Ray I didn't want to speak to her so perhaps he told her that."

"Good for you. I think it's terrible for someone to bring up the past like that. It's thoughtless."

Sylvia shrugged.

"I suppose I can understand it to a certain degree," she admitted, "Especially if she's been researching a lot of cases. If you're on the outside looking in, it's just another story, one like all of the others. After all, there are thousands of missing people out there right now, and that's not to mention the number that have disappeared over the years, but to each of the people that are affected by the loss of someone, the situation isn't 'just another story;' it's the worst time in your life and something you'll never truly get over."

Kerry and Sylvia walked out of the church together once the arranging was finished. Outside on the pathway Kerry bumped into an older man with a ponytail who was walking in the opposite direction. As their eyes met for an instant Sylvia thought she recognised him but, after muttering a quick apology, he fled inside the church. Kerry watched the back of him as he disappeared inside.

"Very nice," she whispered, "If he's looking for salvation I'm happy to volunteer to help."

She turned her attention back to Sylvia and began explaining to her friend how she'd had to park her car the other side of the green today, near Sylvia's house. The man was forgotten.

"I'd just reversed onto that small concrete area in front of the pub to turn round and go back up past the church to look for a parking space that way, when a dark blue Ford Focus pulled out of a space right in front of me. I don't know why it's so busy around here today for cars."

"It feels like it's getting busier every day," Sylvia sighed.

They passed the shop and walked over the small triangle of green before crossing the road, chatting all the way. As Kerry pulled her car keys out of her purse she indicated behind Sylvia with her head.

"That's a nice house," she said, "I only noticed it for the first time today when I parked up. A shame it's right behind the pub but it's lovely beyond isn't it, all those open fields."

Sylvia automatically turned, even though she knew the property Kerry was referring to.

"Yes Honeysuckle Cottage is lovely," she agreed, "Wrongly named I've always thought. It's quite a grand-looking Victorian house with it's two large bays."

"Have you ever been inside?"

"I used to clean for an old man that lived there," Sylvia said, "A Mr Prendergast, but that was years ago. It was rather cluttered with all of his collectables but the rooms were large and beautiful with original fireplaces and cornicing. I've not been in it for years. The current owners work in London where they have an apartment. We rarely see them."

"It's a shame for such a beautiful house not to be lived in," Kerry said, "I wonder if they want a house-sitter."

She grinned as she opened her car door.

"I'd probably rattle around in it, even with the kids," she said.

She smiled and waved before getting into her car and driving off. Sylvia waved back but remained standing where she was rather than turning up the alleyway to return to her own house. She looked again at the large, Victorian detached property behind the pub and past memories began flooding back to her. Usually she kept the ones about Honeysuckle Cottage locked deep inside but with that damn journalist bringing the past back to the present, Sylvia was finding it a struggle to keep certain thoughts buried. Thirty-nine years ago, when she told everyone she was in Chelmsford, buying food at the cheap supermarket, Sylvia Burrows had actually still been here in the village when her daughter had been taken. She'd been just across the road, inside Honeysuckle Cottage, stealing from the owner.

Chapter 19

Brother

Ray was becoming more and more frustrated. Why was it so hard to transfer his pencil plans to the computer?

He was pleased with his ideas to expand the supermarket into the newsagents next door. Not only would it give him the size of office he felt he deserved, but it would also provide extra storage space and the potential to add some self-service till points. Obviously there would be costs involved but surely the owners of the supermarket chain wouldn't object to that. They'd trust that one of their best and longest serving employees knew what he was talking about.

Ray had drawn up his final plans in pencil at home and was amazed he'd done such a good job under the circumstances. His mother had been in a funny mood when she came home last night and he'd heard her tossing and turning in bed, which in turn had kept him awake. It sounded like she was crying at one point but he didn't go into her. She was always like this around the anniversary of Emma's disappearance and Ray refused to ask after her, not wanting to hear yet again how sad it was that Emma was gone or listen to Sylvia's fantasy story that Emma would return one day. Her mood was even affecting the cat. Bertie had struggled out of Ray's grip when he tried to hold him this morning.

He was eager to get his plans sent in to head office to be approved but knew he would need them to look a little more professional first. If only the stupid computer would do what he wanted it to do. For two hours Ray had been stuck in his office trying to get the plans laid out and still all he had on the screen was a square and a couple of triangles.

He gave up and decided to make one of his tours of the store. It was pretty empty customer-wise, just a couple of people perusing the aisles; unusual for a Saturday. Mrs Dunwoody was in but, as per normal, she was only spreading gossip, currently chatting to Carmel, Ray's assistant manager, by the tills. She was holding a wire shopping basket but all it had in it was one small tin of spaghetti hoops.

Ray was about to return to the office and give the plans another go when he spotted Mrs Barker-Smyth walking up to the entrance. Her visits were so rare that Ray remained rooted to the spot, staring at her as she came in through the doors and made her way straight to the tills. She must have asked about the alcohol because Carmel turned round to the display behind her and picked up one of the better bottles of whisky they sold.

Finding his feet, Ray started to walk towards them, his shoulder knocking a young woman who was reaching up for a packet of biscuits. He barely noticed and didn't utter any kind of apology.

As he neared the tills he saw Mrs Barker-Smyth converse politely with Mrs Dunwoody who hadn't moved from her spot. That wasn't a problem for Ray, he wanted what he had to say to be overheard by the local gossip.

He didn't quite get his timing right and kind of sprung up in front of Mrs Barker-Smyth who gasped.

"Oh, Mr Burrows," she said, placing her hand on her chest, "You always seem to pop up unexpectedly don't you."

Ray laughed in a way he hoped conveyed that he was used to being in the company of people with double-barrelled surnames.

"Last time it was by the traffic lights at the bottom of the road when you almost jumped on my bonnet."

Mrs Dunwoody sniggered. Ray ignored her.

"Yes that was an accident I'm afraid," he said.

"It very nearly was."

"No I mean I lost my balance as I stepped off the kerb. But anyway, how can I help you today?"

"Your member of staff is already being quite helpful thank you. I'm having a few friends to dinner and just realised I'm almost out of single malt."

Mrs Barker-Smyth turned her attention to Carmel.

"I'll take that bottle thank you," she said, "And if I could also purchase a bag."

"Oh please," Ray interjected, "I wouldn't expect you to pay for a bag, have it on me."

"That's very kind."

"I could use a bag," Mrs Dunwoody threw in.

Ray looked at her like he'd just scraped her off the bottom of his shoe.

"I take it you're still shopping," he said, indicating her basket.

Realising Mrs Barker-Smyth was watching him he sighed inwardly.

"But when you're finished you too can have a free bag," he added, resignedly.

Mrs Dunwoody grinned and winked at Carmel. Ray turned his attention back to his important customer.

"It was lucky I caught you," he said.

"Was it?"

"Yes I was busy in my office, working hard on some expansion plans for the supermarket."

Mrs Barker-Smyth glanced quickly around the walls.

"Yes I'm sure it could be improved," she told him.

Ray grinned.

"My sentiments exactly," he replied, "Anything to help improve the daily lives of our local residents. It's my raison d'être, as it is for you, being on the parish council."

"Yes we do try and do our best for the community," Mrs Barker-Smyth told him, tapping her pin into the card reader.

"And very successfully you do it too. I only wish I could do more but I'm limited here on my own, but being part of a team, like the parish council…"

He left the sentence hanging.

"Have you got any beef burgers in?" Mrs Dunwoody asked.

"What?"

Ray's train of thought was lost.

"Beef burgers," Mrs Dunwoody repeated, "They're meat patties, made of beef."

Carmel sniggered and Ray was shocked to see a smirk appear on Mrs Barker-Smyth's face too.

"They're in the freezer over there," he said, crossly.

Mrs Dunwoody walked off. Ray didn't want Mrs Barker-Smyth's last impression of him today to be one of mirth so he spoke quickly again before she left.

"Have you heard about the journalist that's been here asking questions about my sister's disappearance?"

Mrs Barker-Smyth had just taken the carrier bag with the bottle of whisky inside it from Carmel.

"I did hear the abduction story being mentioned again," she said, "I wondered why that was. A journalist you say?"

Ray nodded.

"Yes she's writing a book about missing persons and wants to include a chapter on Emma."

"That must be hard, having the past raked up again," she

told him.

"Yes it is," Ray replied, adding in a sigh, "But one has to get on, doesn't one."

"I suppose."

He was pleased to see genuine concern appear in the woman's eyes.

"Please convey my good wishes to your mother."

Ray smiled brightly.

"I will," he said, "That is kind of you."

Mrs Barker-Smyth nodded at him before leaving the shop. Ray returned to his office, a huge grin on his face. He felt he'd just taken a huge step forward in his quest to become a member of the parish council.

He sat down behind his desk and stared at the geometric shapes on the screen. The extension plans were good but perhaps there were other ways he could make himself appear to be an upright member of the community. His mind returned to the conversation he'd had with Karen Taylor. He'd told her about that teacher, Caroline Willis setting up her own charity. She must have spoken to her by now. That would make the perfect excuse for him to contact her himself. After all, if he was associated with the owner of a charity, and a successful one at that, it would sit very well with the parish council members. He opened up the internet on his computer and began searching for the article he'd seen Caroline mentioned in.

Chapter 20

Teacher

It's strange how things can change so quickly, Caroline thought to herself, as she made a few final adjustments to her make-up in the dressing table mirror in her bedroom. She and Hasanna were currently not speaking after their first row while Oliver had become more thoughtful and bought her an emerald bracelet to say sorry for getting angry over the journalist contacting her about Emma Burrows.

Caroline looked down at her wrist now where the emeralds shone in their platinum setting and smiled. She was well aware part of the reason for his attentiveness was because he wanted her by his side that evening at a corporate event in the private room of their most expensive local restaurant.

When she walked downstairs in her new black cocktail dress that she'd specifically gone to Harrods to buy that morning, even though she always felt an old frump shopping for designer labels amongst the Saturday shoppers, Oliver smiled at her and told her the bracelet looked wonderful. Caroline knew he wouldn't compliment her on how she looked and felt embarrassed that she'd had to buy a size sixteen. She ought to make more of an effort with her diet. It wasn't such a bad idea to lose a few pounds and get in shape at her age. Perhaps it was time to bite the bullet and join the gym at Wentworth like Oliver wanted her to.

Tonight's event was the usual type of thing Oliver organised, a beautiful room with free bar and a hot buffet.

Caroline had been looking forward to it all day. It had been a while since she'd last dressed up, had a few drinks and conversed with business acquaintances and potential new clients for Oliver. There was always a lot of wealth in the room but Caroline had become comfortable with it over the years. These potential clients could also become future donors to the Small Hands charity so she would make sure to be a kind and thoughtful hostess.

At the event Caroline found it difficult not to think about Hasanna and the argument, even though the room was full of people. She sprang into her mind as she surreptitiously scraped the delicious-looking creamy sauce off of her chicken before eating it, realising that Hasanna would berate her for worrying about calories and fat content instead of just enjoying the food.

With hindsight Caroline knew she should never have suggested having lunch together at the Windsor Royal Shopping Centre on a busy Friday lunchtime. It was a popular place and very touristy, being opposite the castle. It was also a little too close to home. Caroline should have realised she would bump into someone she knew but, when she was with Hasanna, it seemed like nobody else existed.

She'd jumped when someone tapped her on the shoulder in the bistro. It was a neighbour three houses away from her own. They usually only made small talk when they saw each other and they did the same now, asking how each other was, how kids and grandkids were. It was a few minutes before the lady looked curiously across the table at Hasanna.

"Oh," Caroline said, realising she hadn't made introductions, "This is Hasanna."

The two women nodded at one another, the neighbour waiting silently for more of an explanation as to who exactly this person was.

"She works for me at the charity," Caroline added.

Her neighbour smiled, looking visibly relaxed.

"Oh right," she said, "An employee."

After she'd left, Caroline continued tucking into her meal, not realising Hasanna had stopped eating and was staring at her.

"What?" she said, when she finally noticed.

"You don't even see it do you," Hasanna told her, her voice sounding upset.

"See what?"

Hasanna shook her head.

"What am I to you?" she asked.

Caroline looked about her quickly, embarrassed about talking feelings in public.

"You know what you are," she whispered.

"Do I? I thought I meant something to you."

"Ssh, not here, please."

"Why not here?"

Hasanna's voice was louder than before. Caroline blushed.

"This isn't fair on me," she said, "You know this is my local area."

"So I embarrass you?"

"No of course not but remember, I'm a married woman."

Hasanna tutted and stood up.

"Where are you going?"

She didn't reply. Caroline hastily waved at the waitress and passed over money for the half-eaten meal that included a large tip. She followed Hasanna who had stomped away through the centre and was heading out onto the main street. Caroline had to run to catch her.

"What's wrong," she puffed, when she caught up, "What have I done?"

"If you can't see that…"

"Oh don't play those sorts of games with me," Caroline interrupted, feeling angry herself now, "Just tell me what I've done or said because I really don't understand."

Hasanna stopped walking.

"You just treated me like dirt."

"How?"

"Introducing me as a piece of hired help. Don't you think I deserve better than that?"

"Well what did you expect me to say," Caroline asked, "Here's a woman I'm having sex with?"

An old lady passing by at that moment visibly jumped before she moved on, dragging her shopping trolley behind her a little quicker than before.

"You could have introduced me as a friend," Hasanna told her.

"And then I would have had to explain where we met and who you were and where your family are from. That neighbour is a nosy cow as well as a snob. It was just easier to say you work for me, which you do."

Caroline wished she hadn't said that last part as soon as the words left her lips. Hasanna tutted and walked off again. Caroline followed.

"I'm sorry," she said, "But that woman really is an annoying snob. If I'd told her you were a friend she'd have sat down and started asking about your family background and where you live."

"I doubt it. Didn't you see how relieved she was discovering the black woman was just the hired help and not someone she had to converse with in her social circle."

"That's taking things too far. Do you really think I'd hang around with racists?"

Hasanna shrugged.

"I wouldn't put it past you."

"How dare you!"

"Oh I dare. How many of your rich contacts and clients do you actually know as friends? You've already told me you don't care what they think so long as they give you money for the charity. I assume Oliver thinks the same way about his clients. It does matter though, what people think. It's more important than money."

"I'm not that interested in money."

Hasanna stopped and blew a raspberry.

"Hey," Caroline told her, "I'm not going to apologise for having a good lifestyle. You have no idea how hard Oliver and I worked to make his business a success. That's what we wanted, success, to prove we could do it. The money is an added bonus. It's ours, why shouldn't we spend it how we want."

Hasanna turned and began walking again. Caroline followed.

"Obviously you've got a problem with money," she continued, "Jealous are you, that I have it and you don't?"

Hasanna didn't reply.

"You've been okay with me paying for everything when we've gone out."

"You've always insisted."

Hasanna sighed and stopped walking.

"Look," she said, "I don't have a problem with your money. You can do whatever you want with it, I really don't care. What I do object to is being looked down on, just because you have it and I don't. Having money doesn't make you a better person. I just want you to treat me as an equal."

"I do."

"Then you could have told that woman I was a friend from

work. That would have been enough for her and have sounded better for me."

"Yes it probably would," Caroline admitted, "But I was surprised to see her there and had to say something. I'm sorry if I hurt you. You know I think highly of you. My God if it didn't mean we'd be apart I'd be making you the manager of the new sensory centre."

"Why, so I'll be more socially presentable to you?"

"That's not what I meant and you know it," Caroline said, feeling hurt. "Look, let's just remember something. I live near here. I have a husband and a family and a certain standing in the community. I'm not about to risk spoiling all of that by introducing you as my lover."

Hasanna gave a sad laugh and shook her head.

"So not even a girlfriend or partner then," she said, "Just a fuck buddy am I, a bit of fun, a bit of rough in your oh so perfect world."

"Okay fine," Caroline shouted out, "You walk off and be offended by every word I say. I didn't have you down as a snowflake."

Hasanna stomped off. Caroline watched her go before turning round and walking back the way they'd come.

They hadn't spoken since. Thinking about it now, as she thought about having another portion of the delicious chicken but with the sauce this time, Caroline still felt she hadn't done anything wrong. At the end of the day Hasanna was a woman on her own with nothing to lose by having a relationship with Caroline, whereas she had everything to lose. They'd speak again, she knew they would. Perhaps it was the right time to officially offer Hasanna the role of manager of the new East London branch, even though that would mean more time apart. The paperwork for getting the site owned by the charity was almost complete. The trustees had signed all the relevant documents. She and Hasanna could work on how they wanted the centre to look together.

Caroline stepped up to the buffet table again. The waiter was currently assisting someone else so Caroline helped herself to the chicken, removing the lid from the chafing dish, the aroma permeating through her nostrils and making her stomach rumble. She filled her plate and as she placed the lid back on she noticed a woman was standing beside her in the reflection of the highly-polished chrome.

As hostess, Caroline turned and smiled warmly at her. The lady smiled back. She looked to be about mid-forties with an abundance of blonde hair. She was very curvy in her tight red dress and behind her shoulder, Caroline noticed several of the men in the room were looking at her and then grinning at each other while they spoke. For a split second she wondered if this was one of Oliver's tarts but no, he wouldn't bring them here and besides, this one was certainly too old for him.

"Is it Ms Metcalf?" the lady asked.

"Caroline, please," Caroline replied, going straight into hostess mode.

"I'm Karen Taylor," the blonde lady said.

Caroline recognised the name but for the moment, couldn't quite place it.

"Pleased to meet you," she said, shaking the woman's hand, "Are you here representing a company this evening? I'm sorry I haven't had a chance to speak with you yet."

"Oh that's no problem," Karen replied, fishing a business card out of an impossibly small handbag that matched her dress, "And I'm here representing myself I suppose."

"You have your own business?"

Caroline looked down at the card she'd just taken.

"No. I spoke to you on the phone last week. I'm sorry if I offended you. I was hoping we could arrange a proper chat."

Now Caroline realised who this woman was, the journalist who'd brought up the past.

"I'm sorry, this is a private function. It's really not the place to…"

She looked about her, seeing if someone could remove this woman without making a scene. Karen smiled again. Caroline felt like she was mocking her.

"It's okay," she said, "Your husband invited me here."

Caroline's gaze returned sharply to the grinning woman in front of her.

"You've spoken with Oliver?"

"Well I was worried I'd upset you on the phone," Karen told her.

Caroline thought her sweetness sounded more saccharin. Karen continued talking.

"I wanted a chance to explain myself fully so thought it might be better if I approached your husband first who could then speak to you. He invited me here this evening. I'm surprised he hasn't mentioned it."

Caroline doubted whether this story was true. Just then she saw Oliver and called out loudly to him. He looked momentarily confused as he walked across to her but then realisation dawned on his face as he saw who his wife was talking to.

"Ah, Ms Taylor," he said, "I hadn't realised you'd arrived."

He turned to Caroline.

"Darling," he said, "I meant to tell you earlier about our surprise guest."

Caroline couldn't believe what she was hearing.

"How much earlier," she asked, "Before the starter arrived,

before we came here tonight, or, I don't know; how about when she called you in the first place? Why the hell didn't you tell me you two had been in contact?"

"Darling please," Oliver said, looking around him, a silly grin on his face, "Let's keep things relaxed."

"Oh, you mean like how relaxed you were when I mentioned the phone call to you initially, when you went apoplectic."

Caroline stopped for a moment, taking in what she'd just said.

"Why are you so calm?" she asked.

Oliver gave a little laugh. He always did that at events with clients but doing it to her made her angry. It was condescending.

"Well," he said, "As Ms Taylor pointed out on the phone, this is an opportunity for both my business and your charity to receive some free advertising, not only in a book but in the publicity for it on its release. All you need to do is answer a few questions darling."

"It's such an interesting case," Karen threw in, "I think it will make a nice chapter."

Caroline wasn't sure who she was more angry at.

"A nice chapter," she mocked, "A nice chapter?"

Her voice began to rise in volume.

"Do you even realise what actually happened back then?"

Karen gave a laugh very similar to the one Oliver had just given.

"Well that's part of the reason I'm here," she said, "To get the full and up-to-date story."

"A child went missing, Ms Taylor," Caroline told her, firmly, "A family lost their daughter and they still don't know what happened to her. That village lost a member of its community and while they tried to deal with that they had to put up with endless questions from the police and the press. Do you have any idea what it's like to have press intrusion in your life when you're grieving? No I don't suppose you do. You're always outside looking in, eager to get the story no matter what the cost to anyone else."

Oliver touched his wife's arm.

"Keep it down old thing," he whispered.

Caroline wrenched her arm away from his touch.

"And as for you," she told him, loud enough for the rest of the room to notice and turn their attention to their hosts, "Will you stop at nothing to gain more clients and more wealth?"

She was starting to see what Hasanna saw.

"How much is enough for you, Oliver? Does money make you happy? I doubt it because you're always striving for more."

Oliver looked embarrassedly about the room but couldn't do or say anything.

"The two of you are just the same," Caroline told them, "You don't care that so many lives were ruined thirty-nine years ago when that little girl went missing. You don't care that it still affects people today."

Karen's expression had remained unchanged.

"And why has this affected you so much," she asked, "You told me on the phone that only the Burrows family would be affected by my questions."

Caroline had to stop herself lashing out and smacking this woman in front of her. With all of the emotions she was feeling at the moment she might kill her with one blow.

"I've already told you," she said, quieter now yet still with menace in her voice, "I have nothing to say on the subject that I didn't already say back then. I'm leaving now.

"Darling you can't…"

"Yes I can Oliver. If you don't trust me and ask journalists along without telling me then you can do this on your own. I don't care if your business grows or fails. You can go fuck yourself."

There were several audible gasps from the crowd.

"And you," she said, turning back to the journalist, whom she was glad to see took a step backwards, "I will reiterate what I told you on the phone. If my name or anything to do with me is printed in some cheap, trashy book or in some rag, I will sue you for every single penny you've got. Do you understand me?"

Caroline didn't wait for an answer. She threw Karen's business card onto the floor before turning away and stomping out of the room.

Still Missing

by Karen Taylor

Chapter 3 (first draft - amendments)

As we have seen from the earlier chapters, people go missing all of the time. Even with today's technology it's still possible to disappear. But what of a child's disappearance? That's a completely different story. In the case of a missing child there's a sense of urgency to find them, a fear of what's happening to them the longer they are gone. There's a euphoria of elation when the child is found unharmed and a sense of utter desolation as worst fears are confirmed when a body is discovered.

But what happens when the child or their remains aren't found? How long should a search continue? ~~To the family it should never end but to those on the outside, perhaps with a feeling of guilt, they must wonder if manpower and money should be thrown at something that now seems like a fruitless search. And what happens after many years have passed? Are those that were involved still affected by the past or are they able to move on with their lives?~~ How long does it take for people to forget? Perhaps they never do but what is the reason they can't forget the past? Is it the tragedy of events or is the reason more sinister? Do some have secrets to hide or know something that may not have seemed important at the time but perhaps now they realise that they ought to have spoken up about it?

Emma Burrows was five years old when she went missing on 24 September 1980 after running out of school, upset that one of her purple hair ribbons was taken from her. There appears to have only ever been one suspect for the crime, a twenty-five year old man with learning difficulties. ~~The fact that he too disappeared on the same day looks suspicious but surely a mentally disabled man with a five year old child wouldn't have been able to evade the police for this long.~~ Why was no one else investigated?

Emma Burrows lived in Little Tenwick, Essex with her parents and elder brother. Sylvia Burrows, 39 was a housewife and part-time cleaner. Daniel Burrows, 41 was an unemployed factory worker. ~~They were a normal family, liked in the village and their fifteen year old son, Ray apparently doted on his sister. Why then, did Emma disappear?~~

She was taken to school that morning by her brother but disappeared soon after ~~when~~ while teacher, Caroline Willis, 23 ~~stepped out of the~~ was away from the classroom. She was never seen again.

Jimmy McGill, the twenty-five year old man with learning difficulties, was known to wander around the village on his own. His mother and younger brother, Joey both worked and his father, Tom was well known as a drunk and bully who rarely took an interest in his family or village life. There was no one, therefore, to prevent Jimmy taking his daily walks.

He apparently liked watching children playing. When Emma disappeared the village turned accusatory eyes onto him and his family. But why would a man who had always been harmless suddenly decide to abduct a child? If he'd killed her, would he have been able, on his own, to hide the body from the police and the entire community who took part in the search that followed? That seems unlikely, so what really happened that day? ~~Did someone else take the child? Were others involved in making both Emma and Jimmy disappear or was the whole thing just a tragic accident?~~ Why haven't we been told everything by those involved in the story?

Chapter 21

Accused

To begin with the rental car felt strange. While it was an automatic, exactly what Mike was used to, sitting on the right-hand side he'd twice whacked his hand against the driver door as he moved to put the car into reverse.

He really had to concentrate on the roads through and out of Chelmsford but once he hit the countryside they started to seem familiar. Working at Tomkyns garage after he left school, Mike had spent a lot of time driving the local country lanes and many of them hadn't changed. He was surprised at how recognisable they were after so long.

He took the longer route to get to Little Tenwick, wanting to enter the village from the opposite side to the usual direction in from Chelmsford. His journey took him through Great Tenwick, which felt more enclosed than it used to. Only the main section of the high street seemed unchanged with the supermarket and Amrit's family's newsagents in the nineteen fifties parade of shops. The road continued on out of the village and led him on towards Little Tenwick.

Mike hadn't heard anything from Eddie yet. He could be on a plane in the air, on the ground in England or have decided to be sensible and remain in Canada. Whichever of those it was, Mike wasn't going to hang around waiting to find out. He'd already arranged to pick up the hire car this morning and he was going to continue on with his plans.

He wasn't in the best of moods, having eaten breakfast

alone. He'd been later down to the dining room than expected, falling into a deep sleep in the early hours of the morning, and had missed the young woman, Sarah who'd already left for her training course. It made Mike feel annoyed. He would have liked to have seen her again, or at least been able to say goodbye. She'd helped him the night before, whether she realised it or not. Talking out loud about the past for the first time in years had proved cathartic.

He almost missed the turn onto the road leading up to Little Tenwick. Years before the road veered round to the left beside an open field that belonged to the strange old lady with the wart and moustache. Most of the kids had been scared of 'the witch' but the two donkeys she kept in the field were enough to allay those fears for Mike and, as a young Joey, he would often walk his brother down to feed them.

While the bend in the road was still there it was now beside a building site with a sign saying, '2, 3 and 4 bedroom homes arriving soon.' Mike swerved quickly when he realised this was the turning, his tyres squealing as he skidded round the corner. If he'd continued straight on the narrow lane would have taken him down onto the marshes with no place to turn the car without risking it getting stuck.

Once past the development West Road became familiar. Halfway up he pulled over on the left-hand side and looked across to the small terrace of, what had once been, grey brick houses on the right. Obviously they were no longer owned by the local authority as each was now individual, some rendered and painted while others pebble-dashed. Each had a front door opening right onto the pavement with a tall, narrow window to the side and a matching one above it. They weren't big.

Number thirty-seven, at the end of the terrace, looked nothing like it had when Mike lived there. The grey brick had been rendered and painted a delicate yellow. The double-glazed windows were housed in dark, wooden frames making the house look warm and inviting to visitors. There hadn't been many of those when the McGills were in residence, aside from Amrit.

At the time Mike had been surprised that Amrit seemed to enjoy coming to his house. The two had met at the comprehensive school in Great Tenwick when they were both eleven. Back then Amrit was a rarity, an Indian boy in a rural Essex village school. It wasn't just the kids who stared at him. It didn't take long for the prejudices of the adults to seep into the minds of the children and Amrit was often bullied. There was less physical contact, more name calling. Mike, or Joey as he'd been then, made sure there was no physical abuse by beating up anyone who tried to inflict it. He was probably Amrit's only friend. Perhaps he was the only one who came anywhere close to understanding how name calling could hurt. While Amrit was daily referred to as a 'Paki,' Joey's brother, Jimmy had often been called a 'Spastic.'

It was only now that Mike could see the appeal of number thirty-seven for his friend. While he'd enjoyed his sporadic helping out at the newsagents, for Amrit it had been a daily occurrence, work rather than just a bit of fun. His parents had wanted him to become a doctor and, although Mike and Amrit himself, knew he was never going to attain that, his parents had been blind to their sons academic abilities and insisted he have extra lessons. They were always pushing him. Going to the McGill residence must have seemed like a relaxing break from all of that.

He'd always been a polite, respectful boy and Mike's mum, Sheila liked him. Jimmy grew used to this other boy being in the house and would ask matter-of-fact questions, like why his skin was so dark. Amrit would laugh good-naturedly, knowing there was no hate or malice behind Jimmy's words, unlike those said to him in school.

Only Mike's dad, Tom was the fly in the ointment, but then he was a pig of a man to most people so it wasn't really a racist issue, although asking loudly 'is that brown-skinned boy still here eating all our food' wasn't exactly a sign of tolerance.

Mike put his rental into drive mode and continued on up the road. He gasped as he came out into the centre of the village. Aside from the amount of parked cars it looked no different to how it had before he emigrated. The triangular-shaped village green was the same with the small convenience store beside it, set at the end of the parade of white clapboard buildings. It still had its two small windows either side of the door, the glass separated into six-by-six panes.

To the right of the terrace, facing him stood the pub where his dad had spent many hours getting drunk and often getting barred as well. Even that hadn't changed, still a redbrick building with the same green sign telling everyone it was The Fox & Huntsman. Behind the clapboard terrace stood the Norman church where Mike's mum was buried. To the left of where he'd pulled up by the bus stop was the open piece of ground with the pathway leading up to the primary school where Emma Burrows had last been seen.

Just like in the past the village seemed deserted. Mike had always found that strange. The place looked the part of a quintessential, pretty village where Miss Marple might show up at any moment to solve a murder, but to him it had always seemed to lack that sparkle of warmth that one would expect from a close-knit community. Perhaps he only felt that way because of the reputation the McGill's had but, looking at it today, he realised the green was too small for kids to have a kick about on, the walkway in front of the shop was too narrow to stand there and have a chat, the pub only had room for two wooden picnic tables out the front. It meant kids went elsewhere to play, gossip took place inside the shop and drinkers remained by the bar. People only used the village centre as a walkthrough to get somewhere else.

With nothing changed the years fell away and when Mike saw his reflection in the rear view mirror he was momentarily startled by the grey-haired man staring back at him. He sighed as he got out of the car and made his way over to the church, wondering all the way whether his ponytail looked ridiculous rather than cool.

The black, wrought-iron gate still had the familiar creak as he opened it. The two large yew trees either side of the gate plunged the path leading up to the church into shadow. Mike stepped off it halfway along, on the right-hand side, passing by the oldest of the graves. The headstones of these, if not already cracked or fallen, were unreadable. The grass and wildflowers had taken them over but it gave a certain beauty to the tranquil space.

He walked to the end of the row which brought him to the burial site at the side of the church. Two rows up from here and the third one along was the grave of Sheila McGill. This too was overgrown with wildflowers but Mike knew his mother had always preferred them to shop bought. He didn't bother trying to tidy the space, knowing it would soon grow up again.

He stood there for ages just staring at the small, oval headstone. He momentarily wondered where his father was buried but didn't waste too much time on the old bastard. The fact that he was dead and no longer a stain on the planet was all that mattered to him. Stood here Mike thought less about missing his mother and more about the tough life she'd had, married to a drunken bully whose mood swings could never be predicted, practically raising a mentally disabled son alone, having to suffer the looks and stares of the other residents of the village after her boy was accused of abduction. She died not knowing the truth about what happened to Jimmy and an overwhelming feeling of guilt filled Mike's heart and he had to turn away from the grave, like he was turning away from his mother's gaze.

He walked back along the graves towards the path. He needed to think over the past, that was the whole point in coming, but he couldn't do it so close to his mother. As he reached the path he saw the church door was open and headed towards it. Two women emerged and he bumped into the younger of the two. As he was about to apologise he caught sight of the older lady and realised it was Sylvia Burrows. She was older (of course she was older) but there was no mistaking her. She'd always been attractive, not that she'd ever seemed to realise it, and she still looked good now; a smartly dressed, well-preserved older lady.

Mike's initial feeling was of fear. He didn't want her to recognise him, didn't want her to talk to him, not until he'd had a chance to process the past again on his own. Right now he was still Mike McGill. He needed to become Joey. He muttered an apology and then fled inside the church.

There were a few other women in there, talking to each other in a whisper as they made their way to the door Mike had just entered through. They must have just finished arranging flowers as there was a heady, floral scent in the air. A couple of them gave him a cursory look as they passed by the pew he'd just stepped into near the back but that was all. He didn't recognise them and they didn't recognise him.

Mike had never spent much time inside the church. His

mother had come every Sunday but he always felt it was more about keeping up appearances rather than being due to a strong faith. She'd never made her children come with her but then Jimmy wouldn't have been able to have sat still long enough to listen to a whole service and he might have played up. Sitting here now, Mike wondered whether her Sunday morning in church had been Sheila's chance to escape from her life for a short while.

It felt calm and peaceful here and Mike was glad the women had left. He closed his eyes and allowed his mind to travel back again to when, as Joey, he needed help getting Jimmy out of the copse. Of course it was Amrit he'd phoned that day, from the payphone in the next village along from Little Tenwick. Jimmy was still sitting in the copse when he returned. He flinched when Joey walked in but relaxed a little when he realised his brother wasn't about to start telling him off again. Joey sat down opposite his brother with his back resting against the base of a tree and smiled.

"I'll sit here a while with you," he said.

He wanted his brother to be as relaxed as possible. They didn't speak, they just sat there until footsteps were heard and Amrit appeared.

It still wasn't easy to get Jimmy out of the copse, even with the two of them. He really didn't want to leave. Eventually he was bundled into the back of the van Amrit had driven there in.

"Why did you bring your dad's van," Joey asked his friend, "It's got his name on the side."

"Well how else was I going to get here," Amrit replied, "You said it was urgent. I still don't know what this is all about."

Amrit was only about five foot five, a good six inches shorter than both Joey and Jimmy, but he was strong enough to keep Jimmy's arms from flailing and hitting one of them.

"I'll explain on the way," Joey told him, "Let me lock up the car I've been test-driving and then I'll be with you."

After locking up the car, Joey rushed back to the copse and retrieved the purple ribbon that his brother had placed inside the dead tree trunk. There was no way he was going to leave it there to be found if the area was searched. Too many people knew Jimmy walked this way most days.

It wasn't comfortable travelling in the back of Amrit's dad's van. Although he was lying down, Jimmy kept struggling and Joey, trying to hold him, received several bruises to his legs from the kicking.

"Did you come through the village?" Joey asked Amrit.

"Yes. Why?"

"Were you stopped?"

"No. What is this all about, Joey?"

"A girl has gone missing," he said.

"God that's terrible. What happened?"

Joey didn't reply. A moment later Amrit cottoned on.

"Hey wait a minute," he said, "What the hell have you got me into? I knew I was coming to help you calm your brother down, you didn't tell me the reason why."

"He's not done anything," Joey replied, firmly, "At least I hope he hasn't."

"What!"

"Keep your eyes on the road Amrit," Joey called out, as the van swerved.

With his friend back in control, he continued talking.

"He hasn't done anything intentionally, I know that. The girl went missing from school. Jimmy doesn't go into the school. He knows he's not allowed."

"Then why am I currently driving you away from the village

in my van?" Amrit queried, his dark eyes narrowed as he frowned in the rearview mirror.

"Come on, you know what that bloody village is like. They'll blame Jimmy regardless. I just need to hide him until I can get him home later without anyone seeing. Then I can say he's been at home all day. Mum will back me up."

"I shouldn't be doing this."

"Come on Amrit, I've helped you enough over the years."

"Stopping me getting beaten up at school is a bit different from breaking the law."

"We're not breaking the law!"

"Really? You truly believe that do you?"

Joey was silent for a moment. Jimmy had stopped struggling, seemingly resigned to his fate.

"I know that Jimmy would never hurt anyone intentionally. I need to find out more of what happened to that little girl today. Believe me Amrit, if I discover Jimmy is responsible then I'll bring him back to face the consequences, but if he isn't then I need to get him an alibi. I'm not having the village acting as judge and jury before anything is known. I just need some time. Will you help me?"

Amrit sighed.

"I'm already helping, aren't I? I'm driving."

Joey smiled.

"Where are we headed to?" Amrit asked.

"That old barn we found years back on the far edge of Garret's farm, the one that's sunk into the marshes at one end."

"That old place? It's not habitable."

"It's okay for today. It was still dry the last time we used it as our den."

"We were young teens then."

"Well it's still got to be unused. Garret doesn't even graze his animals anywhere near there because of the marshes."

"Yes, but even so…"

"Look, it won't be for long," Joey said, firmly, "The little girl might already have been found. If she isn't then I need somewhere far enough away that won't be searched today. We only found the place by chance ourselves on a bike ride."

"And it was ramshackle then," Amrit replied, "God knows what it's like now."

"Well it's all I can think of."

Mike opened his eyes. The images in his mind had been so vivid. Even now he could smell the dampness of the barn that he'd taken his brother to and picture it as it was. It was a red brick building and had at one time been a place where animals had sheltered. There were a couple of disused stalls and iron hooks in the ground and on the wall that animals must have been tethered to. The remnants of old chains had been played with by Mike and Amrit when the place had been their den, attaching them to the hooks so they could swing on them.

He shivered now as he remembered using rope and chain to tie his brother up with. Jimmy had hated it and howled and wept but it was for his own good. He'd been able to walk a short way, far enough to get across to the grotty stable toilet in the corner, but he wasn't able to leave the confines of the barn. Mike loathed having to leave him there but there'd been no other choice. He hadn't known then that events in the village meant his brother was never going to return home again.

Chapter 22

Father

Daniel opened the suitcase he kept under his bed. His hands moved over the contents, touching them gently before timidly picking them up. It was a weakness the stuff he kept in there, that's what he'd always seen it as. How could these things have such a hold over him? He'd do his best to ignore them, sometimes successfully for months, but then a moment would suddenly come upon him like a craving, and he always gave in and had the lock undone and the case opened up again. It was open now because he was struggling to cope with his feelings for his daughters.

Although he now realised he didn't want Tania leaving the country Daniel had yet to speak to her about it, unable to find the right words to say. He was embarrassed about what he'd said and the way he'd treated her. How could he admit to his daughter that he'd got so much wrong?

She hadn't contacted him either. It was Sunday and Daniel wondered what she was doing now. Was she with Ráj? Had she told him about the argument? How did **he** feel about the new job in the States? Was he happy to see her leave?

Daniel sighed. There were so many questions and so much left unresolved but if Tania had gone ahead and made her decision, perhaps already booking her flights, what right did he have to tell her to stay. Tania had a life to live however she wanted to live it. Daniel was old, he realised that now. He ached in his limbs every day, he needed his stick to walk and even then he could only walk a short way before needing to rest. His life was almost over.

Perhaps in one way it will be better if she isn't here though, Daniel thought to himself, looking into the suitcase, this stuff can remain a secret even after I croak.

But it still had to be got rid of before then, of course it had. Daniel didn't want anyone to see, to know. He was too old to do it himself. The tatty, old case itself was heavy and he could just about manage to slide it out from under the bed but there was no way he could carry it away and dump it somewhere. Plus some nosey resident would be bound to see him and wonder what he was up to.

Perhaps Jessica would get rid of it for him. Could he trust her with something so private? Would she throw the case away without curiosity taking over, breaking it open to look inside?

Daniel sighed as his mind travelled back to Little Tenwick in nineteen eighty. He had stuff to get rid of that day too, the day his little girl was lost forever. That first night was the only chance he had, he knew that. Sylvia was out for the count with her sedative and Ray was in his room that overlooked the alleyway at the front of the house.

There was smoke, there had to be smoke. Daniel needed to burn the evidence of what he'd been doing that morning when Emma had burst in on him. She was the first person to see his secret and it had panicked him. He'd shouted at her and then… Daniel shook his head, not wanting to dwell on that particular part of the day.

People volunteered to help once they heard the news. Neighbours began knocking on other neighbours' doors to ask if they'd seen the little girl who was lost. Once it was realised she was nowhere in the village the police were called and the incident suddenly became serious. No longer was it a case of a child hiding, it was now a child missing.

With the police involved a proper search of the area was begun but it had to stop once it was dark. Daniel returned home that night, knowing what he had to do. It was dangerous with the entire village, the police and the press all looking at the Burrows family but the risk needed to be taken. If Emma wasn't found then the police would start asking other questions about the family, perhaps even get a search warrant for the house.

The back garden wasn't big and other houses surrounded it but they had tall shrubs all round the perimeter, making it secluded. No one would see the fire, only the smoke. Daniel had to hope no one would question it.

He'd felt a sense of relief when the fire took hold, closely followed by a sense of sadness that had then given way to revulsion. Why should he feel sad about losing the stuff? It was a powerful control it had over him, even then. It was pathetic.

No one had seen, at least no one had ever said anything. As time passed so Daniel knew he'd been right to do it. After the TV appeal for information about Emma, the newspaper articles began to change. Instead of focussing on the little girl they looked at the families, his and the McGills. They asked questions, left hints as to what they thought had gone on, just stopping short of being libellous. Daniel had seen other cases written about in the press. So often it seemed that the missing child had been killed by a member of the family, usually one of those that had tearfully asked for information in a TV appeal. Daniel knew he was sometimes looked at but at least the evidence of what he'd done that day was gone, burnt to a cinder and buried.

But those burned items had been replaced later on, when

Daniel struggled to let go of the past and had needed the help they'd always provided. Then those items had been destroyed too, only to be replaced over and over, repeating the same pattern whenever the urge was too great to ignore. Daniel hated feeling weak. It was why he didn't want to admit he was old. He wanted to be able to do all the things he'd done as a young man. Actually, if he was honest with himself, he'd be happy to be able to do all the things he'd still been able to do at sixty.

The stuff in the case tormented him like some force was playing with his emotions, laughing at the pathetic person he was for needing them like a fix. He never liked having those items in the house even when he craved them, but while they could bring him heartache, despair and embarrassment, they also brought him comfort and sometimes he desperately needed that, like tonight after realising he'd ruined his relationship with each of his children.

Of course there was still time to fix things with Tania before she left. He could even hold out an olive branch to Ray, not that either of them would necessarily want to forgive him, but Emma was gone forever. There was nothing he could do about that.

Daniel shook his head, sadly. Why did that journalist have to come along and rake up the past? She'd brought all his feelings of hurt and anguish back up to the surface. She'd made Emma real again when she should have remained a memory. Daniel couldn't face a real Emma. He couldn't admit his guilt to her. He was struggling enough with admitting he was in the wrong to Tania.

If only Karen Taylor hadn't phoned him on the day he was going to talk through his daughter's plans with her. The shock of what she'd said affected his mood. He could have had a great conversation with Tania about her future instead of getting upset and telling her to fuck off. He felt dreadful. It was the journalist that needed to fuck off. She'd even written him a letter telling him she was sorry to cause offence but would he still like to talk about the past. She wasn't sorry at all.

Tania, he really had messed up there. How could he have got things so wrong? As Daniel so often did, he wished Alice was still alive to help him through this, be someone to talk to. It was difficult to find someone to trust and confide in at the retirement village. Everyone had their own problems, usually illness or relatives not visiting. Daniel didn't really want to talk to any of them. He felt they would then discuss his problems with each other, something a bit juicier to chat about than rheumatism and which brand of blood thinner they were on.

There was Bob but they only met sporadically down the pub and Daniel didn't want to talk about his problems in there. No, he realised he was quite alone but that was his own fault. He didn't allow people to get too close.

Growing up with a father that believed real men didn't show emotions, that a stiff upper lip needed to be maintained no matter what one was going through, Daniel had revolted, ensuring he showed his own children all the love he had for them. Then Emma had been taken and Daniel hadn't known pain like it. While he'd managed to find love again with Alice he hadn't planned on having more children, especially a daughter. There was no way he was going to risk going through the pain he'd felt over Emma again. It had been an unconscious decision but Tania had suffered because of it, because Daniel had decided to take a leaf out of his father's book and keep that stiff upper lip at all times.

He pushed the items back into the case and closed the lid, locking it before sliding it back under the bed. He didn't want to feel the need for them tonight. Was that the reason he kept those items, as a way of avoiding experiencing emotion? No wonder he thought himself weak; a real man showed every emotion. Strength came from admitting you felt sad or lonely or were struggling to cope, it didn't come from ignoring feelings and keeping people that you were supposed to love at arm's length.

Daniel raised himself slowly up from the floor, leaning heavily on his stick and the bedside table. After he'd steadied himself he made his way through to the lounge and into the kitchen. He rifled through the top draw until he found a notepad and a pen. He needed to speak to Tania but he wanted to write down everything he desired to say first. It was time to tell his daughter how much he loved her.

Chapter 23

Mother

Sylvia made her way into the church. It was half an hour until the bus to Maldon was due. Even though she knew Marjorie wouldn't notice, Sylvia couldn't not go and see her friend today. She'd always gone every Monday and Friday to see her, ever since Marjorie's husband had died. She couldn't miss a Monday just because she feared bumping into Ken.

He'd continued to call and text her and Sylvia was just glad he didn't have her home number in case Ray picked up the phone. His last message on her mobile had scared her when he said, if she didn't respond he would camp outside her house until she spoke to him again. She didn't need that right now. It was bad enough thinking she was still seen as 'poor Sylvia' in the village. With the approaching anniversary she didn't want Ken giving the locals another reason to look at her, either as a foolish woman for thinking she could have a relationship at her age or, more worryingly, seeing her as some kind of rapacious cradle-snatcher.

She replied to him with a text. As she'd typed it she remembered wondering why an office would have a seventy year old security guard working for them and felt stupid now that the thought hadn't raised alarm bells at the time. In her message she told him that she wasn't ready to talk and used the excuse of Emma's anniversary as the reason, feeling guilty for doing so but she hadn't been able to think of another explanation that would have prevented him coming over.

Telling him the truth, that she was embarrassed and worried about what others would think, wouldn't have cut any mustard with him.

Sylvia walked up the aisle and sat down in a pew a few rows from the front. She was glad there was no one else there to see her praying. Well, it wasn't exactly praying as most people would do it in church. Sylvia saved that for nighttime and for the Sunday service. At times like this she just sat in the church and thought over things, knowing God was listening. Sometimes she would leave the church understanding her emotions. Other times she had to wait for an answer to come to her.

Her actual beliefs wouldn't sit well with the rest of the congregation, she knew that. Growing up she was taken to church every Sunday. It was something everyone did back then in a village. The church was a big part of the community, a place to meet. When Sylvia married and moved to Little Tenwick she continued to do the same thing. She wasn't sure what her actual belief in God was until after Emma was taken. In her anger she raged at Him, the old man with the white hair and long beard, for allowing her daughter to be taken from her after all her years of service. It was only later, when asking for strength to understand the situation that she realised her 'years of service' hadn't been about belief at all, it had just been a habit. Why, therefore, should the God of her childhood help her when she'd never been sure He was real?

As she began to find strength and understanding Sylvia started feeling God was a force rather than a man. She still referred to Him as 'He' but 'He' was a power now, an energy of good. She still believed in Jesus but felt he was a gifted healer rather than the son of God. She continued to read her bible but understood that a work that only contained certain versions of the same events, written by different people and which had been translated into many languages before English, had to be read with an open mind. It was like a piece of village gossip. Each person that tells it narrates it in their own way. Some will tell it verbatim, other's will add and embellish, and then there'll always be someone who doesn't know all the facts and will invent new ones to fill in the holes. At the heart of each person's story lies the truth but it can be shrouded in a hell of a lot of rubbish.

She'd once made the mistake of trying to explain this to a fellow member of the congregation who had been very short with her and called her a heathen. Since then Sylvia had kept her beliefs to herself. She still liked going to the local church and listening to the services. It did a lot for the local community and Sylvia enjoyed being a part of that. She hated seeing the arguments and fighting that occurred in the world in the name of religion. She wished that people, no matter where they lived or what their background was, were brought up from childhood with an open mind and given the chance to explore and respect all faiths before deciding what was best for them. At the end of the day, religion was meant to be about love for your fellow human no matter which faith you followed. If only there was a little more love and respect for each other, Sylvia felt, the world would be a much better place.

She'd come here today to deal with her anger. To Sylvia, being angry solved nothing. It was an emotion that could control you. Nothing was ever solved satisfactorily by being angry. God had shown that to her in the past and she needed Him to help her again now.

She started with the Ken relationship. With that she felt angry and embarrassed; angry that he'd lied to her but also angry at herself for not realising he was younger than he'd said he was. Hadn't she thought to herself that he would look a lot younger without that little moustache? She was embarrassed because Ken was nineteen years younger than she was, which was a huge age gap. What would people in the village think? They'd wonder what he saw in her, thinking she must have squirrelled away money over the years and that's what he was after.

Then they'd wonder where that money came from. Would they start suspecting her of having stolen from her cleaning clients? Would those people Sylvia used to clean for start wondering about items that had gone missing from their homes? She'd only stolen that one time, from Mr Prendergast at Honeysuckle Cottage, but she'd been desperate, at her wits end.

But Ken knew she didn't have money, Sylvia reasoned with herself. He owned his own house and was still working. So what did he see in her? That was the real problem. While she was worried about what others thought Sylvia was also wondering what a fifty-nine year old man could possible see in a seventy-eight year old woman. Ken had told her he thought her beautiful and enjoyed her company but perhaps that was just a lie, another one after lying about his age. Was he laughing at her or just some sort of pervert?

Sylvia shook her head.

No, she thought, that's not fair. Ken may have lied but he's not a pervert. I must rid myself of this anger, it makes my thoughts irrational.

It was the age difference, that was definitely the main problem with Ken. While Sylvia believed she looked okay for her age she knew damn well she didn't look anywhere near fifty-nine. She and Ken had made love. She'd enjoyed his touch, she'd enjoyed his body and the feelings being together in that way had brought to the surface. Now the thought of them together like that made her feel awkward, and yes, a little repulsed.

It wasn't right, that's what she felt. That was the overriding reason. This was wrong. Yes, Sylvia knew if it was the other way around and a seventy-eight year old man was dating a fifty-nine year old woman, people would be thinking, 'the old goat, good on him' but no one would be thinking of her that way. They'd think her some kind of dirty, old woman.

And that was where the anger was coming from, she realised. While it was an injustice, Sylvia felt an older woman and a younger man was still seen by too many people as wrong and the residents of Little Tenwick would definitely struggle to understand the relationship. The only solution to that, as far as she was concerned, was to end things permanently with Ken.

Sylvia sat up straighter in the pew. The decision was made but there was a genuine feeling of sadness and loss at that choice, even though she felt it right and proper. She moved on to the other reason for her anger. She hated being seen as 'poor Sylvia.' Why was it affecting her so much? Why did other people's opinions matter to her?

Because they do, she thought to herself. It was the curse of living in a small village. Everyone took an interest in your life and you couldn't escape that unless you moved elsewhere. Even then that didn't always work. On so many occasions Sylvia had heard mention of some villager who had moved away and learned about a situation they'd recently been caught up in.

She thought back over her time living in the village. She hadn't grown up far away but Little Tenwick was new to her when she and Daniel moved here after their marriage. They were seen as a nice young couple and everyone was pleased when Sylvia became pregnant and gave birth to Ray. His christening had been enjoyed by everyone.

Then had come the years of trying to have another baby. The trips to the hospital and the doctor's home visits didn't go unnoticed. Perhaps that was when she'd first become 'poor Sylvia.' But then Emma had been born and everyone was happy again for the young couple who had been through so much but had come out the other side. Of course they didn't know the marriage was already rocky.

When Emma had been taken there had been a united feeling of shock and anguish in the village. Nobody had seen a thing but that didn't stop everyone talking. You didn't have to witness something to gossip to someone else about it. There was blame laid at the McGills' door and plenty of chat about the incompetence of the young teacher. As gossip spread so the rumours grew, mostly about poor Jimmy McGill and the supposed times he'd shown anger to someone. It should have been comical but people started to believe it.

While no one spoke directly to Sylvia about that, Marjorie would keep her up-to-date on the latest gossip, hoping the absurdity of it all could bring a little bit of humour to her friend's life, even if just for a brief moment. The two had often laughed about the risibility of previous gossip, how a story could be blown out of all proportion but this time, Sylvia was a part of it and what was being said, especially about the McGills, was turning nasty.

Sylvia wished now that she'd had the courage to go and visit Sheila McGill to let her know she didn't believe that Jimmy had taken Emma but with the press and the villagers' eyes on her constantly, she'd have been spotted going into the McGill house and that might have made things worse.

She sighed as she sat in the pew. There it was again, worrying about what other people thought rather than putting herself first. Perhaps that was the problem, she always put others first. Kerry had asked her that day while cleaning in the vestry if she'd ever told the other members of the village what she felt about the way they looked at her and Sylvia admitted she hadn't. She was more concerned with the way **they** felt, worried they'd feel awkward if she talked about Emma. Shouldn't she have just gone ahead and talked? She was the one suffering, not them.

But there was more to it than just other people's opinions. Sylvia closed her eyes and looked inside herself. She was worried **she** saw herself as 'poor Sylvia' too. The loss of all those babies through miscarriage, the failure of her marriage, Emma being taken; they were all things she blamed herself for. Wasn't she just a big failure? That was the reason she didn't like seeing the pitying looks on other people's faces, she feared they were merely a reflection of her own feelings.

Once she'd conquered her anger after the abduction, when she'd reached the stage of being able to forgive whoever had taken her daughter, Sylvia had felt herself master of her emotions. God had shown her the way and rather than praying to Him to bring her daughter back, she prayed that Emma was okay and happy wherever she was. She thanked God for keeping her daughter alive and for giving her the faith to know she **was** still alive and living her life elsewhere.

But it was all lies, wasn't it. She'd never truly forgiven the person that had stolen her daughter from her and ripped out her heart. She'd never stopped being angry about what had happened. No mother should have her child torn from her in that way, it was cruel. She was a mother, aggrieved that her child had been taken and that the perpetrators had got away with it. Where was the justice? Where was the punishment for that disgusting evil, selfish person? Sylvia opened her eyes and felt the rage rush through her. She wanted revenge, she'd always wanted revenge.

Sylvia kicked the back of the pew in front of her, hard, the echo of the thud reflecting back to her in the open space. She instantly felt embarrassed at her outburst and was relived she was still alone. She looked up and apologised to her God for her anger but knew it had needed to be faced.

But why was she so angry now? She didn't want to undo all of the good she'd achieved over the years in dealing with her rage. What was it that was triggering it? Was it the interference of the journalist? Sylvia was still surprised she hadn't been contacted by Karen Taylor. Even Ray had stopped mentioning her.

No, it wasn't her, there was something else, something Sylvia hadn't faced up to. She took a breath and dug into her thoughts of the past, going deeper than she ever had before. She knew what it was. The memory had always been there but buried away in the furthest recesses of her mind. It was her fault wasn't it, Emma's disappearance. She'd convinced herself it was the thieving she was distressed about but it was more than that, much more.

Sylvia had seen her, she'd seen Emma as she emerged from Honeysuckle Cottage, her stash of items from Mr Prendergast in her shopping basket. Emma had been running towards her, crying; well, running towards home with one of her bunches loose, but Sylvia had stepped behind a tree to avoid her. She knew she couldn't be seen to be in the village when she was supposed to be on the bus on her way to Chelmsford. Her daughter had been upset and she'd longed to go to her but couldn't. Instead, as soon as she'd seen her daughter head up the alleyway for home, Sylvia had turned and fled past Honeysuckle Cottage on the edge of the village and crossed the stile into one of Garret's fields, walking and running the two miles to where she could board the other bus that would take her in the direction of Chelmsford.

Sylvia stood up from the pew and rushed for the door, head bowed to hide her tears. She hadn't known her daughter was going to be abducted, of course she hadn't, but if she'd only stepped out from behind the tree and held her arms out, Emma would have rushed into them and everything would have been okay. But she hadn't done that and her daughter was never seen again.

Sylvia crossed the green to go home. She couldn't go and see Marjorie now, not in this state. As she reached the alleyway to her house she couldn't help turning to look over at Honeysuckle Cottage. The tree she'd hidden behind was still there. While trimmed to stop it becoming too tall the thick trunk was just as it was. Someone could be hidden behind it now and no one would be able to see them.

Sylvia turned and walked up the alleyway, the same route her daughter had taken that day. What had happened to Emma after that? She stopped walking. That was the problem. That was what this was all about. Emma had been heading for home. She knew her mother wasn't there but her father was. It was Daniel she was going to see. Sylvia had never asked him what had happened because that would have meant revealing her own secret. There were only two houses down that alleyway, Sylvia's and Marjorie's. Surely no one would have been lying in wait there to abduct a child. Daniel must have seen his daughter that day. Why had he never admitted it? What had happened between them? Why was he so convinced Emma was dead?

Sylvia strode up to her front door. She needed to find out. It was time to face up to the past and the truth. All the worries, fears and stress about what had happened at the time had been the final nail in the coffin of their marriage. Sylvia didn't want all those emotions to eat away at her anymore. She'd allowed it to go on for too long. It was time to admit her truth and to ask some frank questions. Sylvia needed to visit her ex-husband.

Chapter 24

Brother

Little Tenwick to Windsor was quite a long journey to make to just say you were popping in as you were passing. Ray hadn't driven this far in years, not since he was married and his wife had wanted a holiday in Devon. They'd argued most of the way there, starting out with different opinions on routes to take as they left South Woodham Ferrers, and ending with why Ray was a selfish bastard not to want children as they approached Torquay.

At least today was different. Ray was in his Volkswagen Polo alone but he could have used an extra pair of eyes to read his written instructions of how to get to the sensory centre, having never bothered with a SatNav seeing as he rarely left Essex.

It wasn't often he took a day off. Ray had never been one of those people that looked forward to time off from work. To him it was a joy to get into the shop and get on with things. Days off, those were his problem. Head office forced him into taking time off when he'd rather be working. Being at home he got bored. He was sure his area manager, Elizabeth Chan had something to do with forcing him to use up his holiday rather than just losing it. She'd called him yesterday to say she was coming to visit on Friday.

Well if she thinks that's going to cause me an issue she's very much mistaken, Ray thought to himself as he drove through the M40 junction of the M25.

Ray prided himself on always being ready for an Elizabeth Chan inspection. She'd never just shown up without warning and he suspected she wasn't allowed to, but she'd always given him a very short notice period. Ray knew he always had one up on her because he never allowed anything to be out of place and his staff knew he could be out of his office doing one of his walks at any moment so they always toed the line. He was sure his efficiency was what put Elizabeth's back up. All she was interested in was sales and profits. He'd done some research on her and she'd been fast-tracked into her current position. To Ray that meant she hadn't had the proper amount of experience on the shop floor and he felt himself vastly superior to her.

Let her come, he thought, she'll be hard pushed to find any reason to chastise or fire me, the obnoxious bitch!

Ray smiled as he continued his journey. The motorway was busy but moving, with cars passing him on either side of the middle lane he was driving in. It made a change having something to do with a day off. He usually spent them with his mother and, although he often found it a trial, he felt Sylvia got a lot out of it. She enjoyed listening to him talk about his work while she cooked for the pair of them.

Once, in a moment of madness, he'd offered to take her away for a week's holiday to somewhere not too far away. She'd seemed quite keen until he began researching self-catering accommodation and then she'd become reluctant. Ray didn't know why. Perhaps travel scared her. He couldn't remember the last time Sylvia had been on a holiday. She barely left the village, apart from going to visit their batty, old neighbour at that rather basic nursing home. Ray had never been to visit but he had driven past it once or twice. He sighed as he thought about his mother. It seemed a bit pathetic to him, staying in one area for so long with not much going on in one's life.

"Thank God for my work," he said, aloud.

It was going to be a surprise for Caroline, him turning up. He really wanted to impress the chairman of the parish council and Ray was sure Geoffrey Delaney would definitely be affected by him knowing the head of the Small Hands charity. He'd spent a little time researching Caroline online and knew she'd made her charity a success. He didn't bother going into too much detail about what she actually did, something to do with helping challenging kids using lights and sounds, for him it was enough to know the charity was a success.

It had a board of trustees but by all accounts, Caroline was the one in charge so Ray assumed that meant she didn't have too much work to do in the day to day running. She had staff to man the ball pool. An impromptu visit from an old friend wouldn't eat into too much of her time. She'd be happy to see him. She might even invite him to lunch. Well, she wasn't short of a few quid.

Come to think of it, Ray thought to himself, meeting her wealthy husband wouldn't be a bad idea either. They must know lots of influential people. I could get to know people that could make Geoffrey Delaney and Mrs Barker-Smyth seem insignificant.

He grinned again. This was such a great idea. He only wished he'd thought about it sooner.

Ray hadn't originally planned this as a surprise visit. He'd tried phoning Caroline yesterday but had got through to a lovely-sounding woman named Fran instead who was the manager of the Windsor Centre. Ray alway liked talking to fellow managers, even if this one was only managing some type of children's playground. Whilst she'd listened politely to Ray explaining how he and Caroline went way back, she'd become friendlier when he'd asked her if a journalist named Karen Taylor had been in touch.

"Yes she did call," Fran had told him, "I only spoke with her for a few seconds but she seemed very nice and didn't deserve the ear bashing Caroline gave her."

"Ear bashing, really," Ray had been shocked, "I wonder why she was like that? I found her charming when she came to see me."

"She visited you?"

"Oh yes. Well I suppose I am one of the more important people in the story Karen is writing about. Caroline was on the periphery. I mean I know many people thought her responsible for the disappearance but really, it could have happened to any of the teachers."

"The disappearance," Fran had questioned, "Yes I'm sure that must sit heavy on her mind."

"I don't know why after all this time."

"Well I suppose she has a lot to lose really, if she was blamed for something today. She is a well-regarded person around here, as I'm sure you know, being an old friend. Why don't you pop in and see her as a surprise, she's here most days. She's out visiting the site of our new centre today but apart from that, she'll be in the office. She's always in the office. I'm sure she'll be pleased to see you."

As Ray took the slip road to the M4 he wondered if he'd been right to mention the disappearance to Fran.

But really, he thought, I barely said anything and the whole thing is going to be in a book anyway. If I were Caroline I'd be thinking about the attention I'd receive. Surely it can only help her charity.

He'd find out how she felt soon enough, he realised, as he took a surreptitious look at his hand-written directions. He wasn't far from the centre now. There were other things to talk about besides the past anyway. Ray had lots to tell her about himself and his rise to power at the supermarket. Weren't they in the same boat, both running successful businesses? Well, hers was a charity so not quite the same thing. It was her husband who had the business and had made a success of it. Yes, Ray really hoped he would get to meet him too at some point.

Turning onto the A355 Ray experienced a sudden feeling of uneasiness. Surely he wasn't nervous. He was a supermarket manager for goodness sake and used to dealing with people from all walks of life. As the road became the A332 Ray realised his uneasiness was with the past. He hadn't spoken to his mother about it in years, not wanting to listen to her going on about how much she missed her Emma. While he'd talked to Karen Taylor about the day of the abduction, she was merely a stranger. Today, for the first time in almost forty years, he was about to talk with someone who had been there at the time and who was involved in the story.

As Ray searched for a public car park his mind looked over the smaller details of the day of the abduction. Caroline had backed up his story that he had brought Emma to school as usual. He'd never discovered why she'd done that. After all, Ray knew that he hadn't taken his sister all the way to the front door that day. There'd been that incident on the way there, the tears, the frustration and then Jimmy McGill looming up from nowhere as he was wont to do, the oaf.

The last sighting of Emma in her brother's mind had been seeing his sister walking off hand in hand with Jimmy. He'd always assumed that was when the two had gone off together but then why had Caroline said Emma had been seen at school? Ray hadn't really cared before now, he was just glad that his sister was gone, but what had really happened? After all, if Emma had been to school then Jimmy must have taken her there and therefore he hadn't wandered off with her. So why did he disappear? What had he seen? Was Caroline's involvement in Emma's disappearance more than merely being a negligent teacher?

Ray got slowly out of his car. All of a sudden he wasn't sure if this was such a good idea. Caroline had been blamed for allowing Emma to leave the classroom but what if she was guilty of something much worse. Ray had said before that he wanted to shake Jimmy's hand for getting rid of his sister but now, faced with the prospect of actually meeting someone who may have been more involved than he'd realised, he felt scared. Then he thought about the casual vacancy on the parish council. It was something he'd craved for years.

I'm being silly, he thought, and letting my imagination run away with me. That's something mother does, believing her obnoxious daughter will return one day. I'm not going to turn into her. Pull yourself together Raymond.

He took a deep breath and headed for the main road. This was his chance to up his standing in the local community and he hadn't just driven ninety miles to turn round and go back again. Caroline Willis, or whatever her name was now, was the head of a children's charity. She was obviously a thoughtful person, not the sort to abduct and kill a child.

Ray felt his confidence return. This was the right thing to do. He was going to be warm, kind and charming and Caroline would be glad he'd popped in to see her. There was more to the past than just Emma after all and plenty of other things to talk about. Ray began to stride, feeling excited about how his future was going to change. This was going to be a success.

Chapter 25

Teacher

Caroline sighed contentedly as she hung up the phone to her solicitor. Contracts had all been signed on the new premises and everything was in place, ready for final exchange at the end of the week. Her solicitor had worked wonders getting everything sorted so quickly but it had taken Caroline a long time to find the right site in the first place. She hoped that would be enough for a while. She felt drained although whether that was due to overwork or to the emotional rollercoaster she'd been on recently with Hasanna and Oliver, Caroline didn't know.

She and Hasanna were back on track after an apology from Caroline. She'd told Hasanna she definitely wanted her to run the new sensory centre and to have an input into how she wanted it set up and developed. They'd travelled together to the site in Chadwell Heath, near Romford yesterday. It was a perfect place, on the train route that was going to be part of the new Elizabeth Line as well as being close to the main roads out to Essex, and near enough to the M25 for visitors from Kent.

Caroline had been given the keys so it was just the two of them looking round the shell of the building and the outside parking facilities.

"You know we don't need this amount of parking spaces," Hasanna had told her, as soon as they'd arrived, "We could easily create a garden here full of fragrance and colour and texture."

Inside she'd become even more excited.

"We could have a mezzanine," she said, her voice echoing off the walls, "Or maybe even a whole new floor. If we add a lift we can spread out the play areas, make them more accessible, or we could just put the offices and storage upstairs and give the whole of the ground level over to play and development; helping as many children as we can."

"Then you might want those parking spaces back," Caroline told her, smiling at her enthusiasm.

"Sod it, let's just build a multi-storey car park out there."

The two both laughed. Hasanna walked back to Caroline and kissed her.

"You really think I can run this?" she asked.

"Of course. I wouldn't have suggested it otherwise. You're more than capable."

"But won't Fran's nose be put out of joint, not being offered the new, larger centre to run? She is very good at her job."

"And she's settled where she is. Fran and her family live too far away for this to be a viable daily commute for her."

Hasanna looked around the vast open space again.

"To be honest I think I may need to move out this way too."

Caroline's heart beat faster.

"I realise that," she said, feeling wretched, "But you deserve this."

Hasanna smiled and gave her a hug.

"Hey it's not like I'm moving to another country. I won't be that far away. We'll still see each other."

Caroline smiled sadly back at her.

"But not every day. I don't want things to change between us," she admitted.

Hasanna sniffed.

"Everything changes," she said, "You can't stop it. I want

us to grow closer, don't you?"

She gently stroked Caroline's cheek.

"I'm in love with you," she whispered.

"Are you?"

"Of course. You think we had that big argument because we don't have strong feelings for one another?"

Caroline grinned.

"You're right," she said, "I want you to have this place, even though it means I will no longer see you each day. It's about you, not me. I guess that's love."

Hasanna smiled and they kissed again, longer and more passionately than before.

Back in her office, Caroline realised she was grinning at the memory. She looked across the room at Fran who was grinning back at her. Caroline felt herself turn red and she looked down at a piece of paper on the desk.

Fran had been grinning a lot this morning. It wasn't just a friendly smile, a smile you give in greeting someone or when you catch somebody's eye. It was a knowing smile, like she had a secret that she wanted you to know she had but she didn't want you knowing the details. Caroline found it annoying. Well, she often found Fran annoying but, as Hasanna had said the day before, she was very good at her job.

Things were less cheerful with Oliver. They'd had another huge row after he followed her home from the event that he'd invited that journalist to. While he was angry that she'd shown him up in front of clients and potential clients, she was angry at him for going behind her back and asking Karen Taylor along. In the end, Caroline had apologised for embarrassing him and he apologised for being deceitful but it was an uneasy truce. He'd surprised her by going to London on Sunday night and staying over on Monday as well, something he didn't usually do with one of his fancy things. They usually got a one nighter during the week. Either he'd found some young thing that wanted more of his time or he was still angry with his wife. Caroline suspected the latter.

She grabbed a sheet of paper and made a list of all the building contractors she'd used in the past, ready to contact them again and see if they would work over in East London and give her a quote for the work that needed doing. While happy for Hasanna to have input into the design, Caroline knew the basics of the building, such as plumbing and rewiring were needed first. There was a strict renovation budget that the charity needed to stick to.

"Everything okay?" Fran called over, still grinning.

"Everything is fine," Caroline replied, "Couldn't be better."

I'll wipe that smile off your face, she thought to herself, when I tell you your second in command is getting a better job than you.

"I'm glad," Fran said, "You've been looking a bit peaky lately. I was worried you were overdoing things."

"Not at all," Caroline told her.

Fran wasn't usually this chatty.

"I wasn't sure if that journalist had upset you; you know, the one that called last week. You seemed a little put out by the call."

"I was not put out," Caroline replied, firmly, "I just don't speak to journalists of her calibre. It's important the charity is represented by the quality press, not some gutter tabloid."

She was surprised that Fran didn't return to her work. Usually when Caroline became short with her she did just that. Today though she just nodded.

"Yes I agree," she said, "Some of these journalists just want a story and will come at any angle, dredging up the past or looking for secrets."

Caroline didn't like where this was heading but she couldn't just ignore it. She needed to nip it in the bud.

"Well Karen Taylor would have found it hard to find anything that way."

"Was that her name? What a good memory you have. It's strange that she just called up out of the blue though."

"She didn't," Caroline replied, before realising she should have just agreed as a way to end the conversation.

"Didn't she?"

"She'd been speaking to an old acquaintance of mine and my name came up, that's all. She wanted a story that I wasn't prepared to give to her publication. I doubt we'll hear from her again."

"Yes," Fran agreed, "We won't hear from her again. She's just disappeared."

Caroline heard the emphasis she put on the last word. What the hell did Fran know? Had Karen Taylor begun speaking to her staff, trying to find out about the past? If she had, Caroline would come down on her like a ton of bricks. In the mean time she had Fran to deal with. She stood up and walked across to stand in front of Fran's desk.

"Okay," she said, leaning over, pleased to see her manager recoil, "What is your problem? What is it you're getting at?"

"I don't know what you mean?"

"Yes you do. Don't play games with me, I'm really not in the mood for your childish taunts right now. Just tell me what you're implying. At least have the balls to tell me to my face."

"I really don't know what you mean," Fran pleaded, almost whimpering, "I'm sorry if I caused offence. I didn't mean to."

Caroline remained staring at her in silence until Fran turned to her computer screen to continue with her work. Caroline was gratified to see she looked a little teary. She turned and left the office, needing to put some distance between them.

She took a walk through the various play areas in the centre. Seeing the children smiling or laughing was such a joy. They were each going through so much in their young lives that to be able to give them and their families some pleasure, even just for a couple of hours, made Caroline's heart sing. It also made her realise that her problems were insignificant. She really shouldn't let Fran get under her skin. It was up to her to try harder with her employee.

In the quiet area Hasanna was watching one of the volunteers reading to several children. When she saw Caroline she walked over to her.

"I'm not slacking, honestly," she said, "I've been in with the counsellor and one of our families. I just stopped in here on the way back from showing them out."

"Okay, I'll believe you," Caroline told her, "This time."

She winked. Hasanna grinned and then indicated for the two of them to step outside of the room. Once out she said,

"I've had an idea that I want to run past you."

Caroline thought this was going to happen a lot now that Hasanna was going to be running the new centre. She liked it.

"When I take over the new centre," Hasanna continued, "I'll be moving nearer to it."

"I'm sure I can help with moving costs," Caroline said, "Probably not through the charity but..."

Hasanna shook her head.

"That's not what I mean," she interrupted, "Besides, the few possessions I own can fit in the back of my car. I rent a fully-furnished apartment. Anyway, I was thinking about us."

Caroline couldn't help looking about her, making sure they weren't overheard.

“Us?” she queried, in a hushed whisper.

“Yes. You said you would miss me when I go but it doesn’t have to be like that. You could come with me?”

Caroline couldn’t quite take in what Hasanna had said.

“Sorry, what?”

“You could come with me,” she repeated, beaming, “You could run the charity from your own office there and we could rent a place together to live in, you know, just to start with. If we like the area and being with each other we could buy something later. I’ll be earning more money, we could make it a joint thing.”

Caroline grabbed Hasanna’s arm to stop her talking.

“Hang on a minute,” she said.

“Sorry, I’m going on, I know I am, but I’m excited.”

“You want me to just come and live with you in East London and casually give up everything I have here?”

“Well I know it’s a lot to take in right now but, well, it’s an exciting idea isn’t it. Just think about it.”

Hasanna grinned before heading off. Another member of staff came up to Caroline, followed by a middle-aged man.

“Caroline,” she said, “You have a visitor."

Still Missing

by Karen Taylor

Chapter 3 (first draft - amendments)

The disappearance of Emma Burrows stood out for me when researching cases for this book. For a child to vanish from a tiny village which, ~~at the time,~~ was a place where everyone pretty much knew everybody else, seems remarkable. It ~~appears~~ would be extremely unlikely that a stranger from outside ~~would have just happened to pass through that day and~~ snatched a child, but Emma was known to favour adults over other children. But if a ~~he (or she) was~~ local resident took her, ~~then~~ how did no one ~~else not know~~ not see anything ~~about it~~?

~~I visited~~ Little Tenwick, ~~which~~ hasn't changed ~~much~~ in thirty-nine years. While the centre, where the school Emma attended is situated, is unusual in that there aren't many properties that face the village green surely, with a shop and pub and the time of day, there must have been someone that saw something.

~~Visiting the area raised more questions for me than provided answers.~~ I wanted to speak with those involved in the story at the time, all of those people, still living, that were part of both Emma Burrows and Jimmy McGill's lives. ~~I can't believe an entire village was part of a mass cover up~~. At the time everyone was in shock. ~~Today people all seem to know about the disappearance, even though they weren't all living in the village at the time.~~ The story is still part of ~~everyday~~ life here; a ~~huge~~ tragedy ~~where the after affects are still~~ felt and talked about daily.

Someone must know something. How in depth did the police investigation go at the time when the only suspect was

Jimmy McGill? Was there a lack of enquiry or just a lack of evidence; or was there a lack of truth being revealed?

Chapter 26

Accused

Mike was feeling a lot more confident behind the wheel after three days of practice. He only wished he could feel better about the destinations he was driving to but as each one was to do with the events of the past, they just filled him with dread as he journeyed towards them, particularly the one he was making today. His thoughts never drifted far from what happened thirty-nine years ago whether awake or asleep. On Saturday, the day he'd picked the car up, he'd returned from his trip to Little Tenwick feeling totally exhausted. Only a part of that could he apportion to jet lag, the rest being due to reliving the events of the day of the abduction whilst sitting quietly inside the church. After a restless and dream-filled sleep that night the following day had brought Eddie's arrival. It hadn't started out well.

*

Mike rose early on Sunday morning and went for a walk around the streets near the B&B to try and clear his head but it didn't work. His mind kept returning to Jimmy, remembering the moment when he'd left his brother tied up in a mouldy, old barn; howling because he didn't want to be there, the promise of a quick return with food and fizzy drinks unable to quell his agitation.

Mike returned to the B&B to have some breakfast so he could then take some paracetamol. He didn't get the chance. The owner, Mrs Jessop met him in the hallway.

"You have a visitor," she told him, "He seems a little agitated. He got a cab all the way here from Gatwick airport and was rather shocked by the cost. His mood didn't improve when I said you'd popped out so I've put him in my and my husband's private lounge."

Mike thanked her and felt the weight of what was to come as she showed him to the room. This was all he needed, Eddie being rude and the two of them getting thrown out of the B&B.

He opened the door. The room was small but cosy. There was a large fireplace and a picture rail running round the walls with decorative plates arranged along the top of it. The wallpaper on the chimney breast had a bold, dark grey stripe in it with the the rest of the room painted an off-white. A small TV stood on a stand in the corner and a three-piece leather suite was placed so that anyone sitting could watch it. On a coffee table in front of the fireplace was a hot beverage of some kind that was still steaming. In the armchair facing him was the sleeping form of Eddie. Mike stepped forward and gently shook his son.

"Eddie," he whispered.

Eddie opened his eyes. He started when he didn't realise his surroundings before his gaze caught his father.

"Dad," he said, sitting up, much more awake, "What the hell is going on?"

"What are you doing here?" Mike asked him, calmly.

"What am I doing here? My father suddenly decides to disappear off to England and then I discover that he's involved in the abduction of a young girl."

"How much do you know?"

Eddie rubbed his eyes.

"Only what I found online after I spoke with that journalist. Why didn't you ever tell us? Why didn't you talk to me about it, your own son?"

"Why, I'll tell you why."

Mike hated how quickly the anger welled up inside of him but somehow Eddie always managed to push his buttons. What the hell was he doing here? How long had he sat at the airport in Toronto before a seat became available? Had he travelled over three thousand miles just so he could berate his father?

"Because you have a great big chip on your shoulder and you overreact to everything."

"Oh really."

Eddie stood up, his voice becoming more audible as well.

"So how am I supposed to react to discovering my father's family were involved in a kidnapping?"

"And you get the facts wrong too when you're angry."

"I have a right to be angry with you for fuck's sake."

There was a gentle knock at the door. It opened and Mrs Jessop poked her head in.

"I'm sorry," she said, "But could you keep it down a bit. I have to think of my other guests."

"Having a good listen at the door are you," Eddie spat at her.

"Eddie!"

Mike turned to the lady and noticed she looked embarrassed. Perhaps she had been.

"I'm sorry," he told her, "We'll go out for a walk if that will help."

Mrs Jessop visibly relaxed. Mike indicated to his son with a nod of his head to leave the room and then he followed him.

The traffic was light on the main road which made the silence between the two men more palpable as they walked along. They came up to a park Mike had passed earlier and stepped through the gates. Birdsong replaced the sound of the sporadic cars passing on the road but neither man's mood was lifted by the beauty of the melodies. They found a bench in a remote part of the gardens, away from the children's play area and sat down.

"I'm still waiting for an explanation dad," Eddie told him, "What on earth has been going on with you?"

"That can wait," Mike replied, "I want to know why you flew three and a half thousand miles just to have a go at me. Couldn't you have waited until I came home? Do you hate me that much?"

Eddie snorted, dismissively.

"I've every fucking right to hate you."

"And you can stop with the language. It doesn't make you sound hard or intimidating."

"Jesus Christ dad, when are you going to realise I'm a grown up? I'm thirty-five years old with two kids of my own. Get off my back."

"I'll get off your back when you start behaving like an adult. Why do you still get into these strops? You huff and puff and complain that you're so hard done by. You sound like a stroppy teenager."

"Well perhaps that's because you've never given me any credit and still treat me like I'm one," Eddie told him, "You've been on my case ever since you found me drinking a beer when I was fourteen. It was one beer dad but you acted like I'd killed someone and then pissed on the body. You never let me forget it. You were never like that with Robbie."

"I didn't like either of you drinking," Mike told him.

Eddie snorted again.

"Come off it, you were much more lenient with him. If he told a story about getting drunk and falling over, you laughed. When I was drunk you treated me like a leper."

"Maybe that's because Robbie didn't change after a drink. He was the same person but you, you didn't drink because you enjoyed it, you seemed to want to become someone else, someone different to who you really are. And it never worked. You were nasty. Drink didn't agree with you. You became even more short-tempered. I feared you'd become violent. My dad was like that. I was terrified you were going to turn out the same way."

"Well I didn't know that did I," Eddie retorted, "You never said. You've kept this life of yours in England secret from me."

"I kept it secret from everyone, not just you. Why do you always single yourself out?"

"Because I'd like to know my father loved me," Eddie exploded, before standing up.

He took a few steps away from the bench. Mike was stunned into silence, the continued warbling of the birds and the distant laughter of children in the play area being the only sounds. Although still facing away, Eddie spoke again.

"Don't you get it dad," he said, quietly, "I want you to be proud of me. Mum was. She told me, but you…I never felt good enough. Robbie was the golden boy. Being fun to be around came naturally to him. The two of you always laughed together. Whenever you looked at me, the smile faded."

Mike felt tears sting his eyes.

"Of course I love you," he said, "I've always been proud of you, I thought you knew that. So you're not as lively as Robbie is, so what? My God, is that why you used to drink, to be more like him?"

Eddie still didn't turn round but Mike saw him nod.

"Oh Eddie. You don't have to try and be like your brother, and certainly not to try and impress me. You're you. You're a strong, independent man, a kind man with a smashing family that I couldn't love more. That's all down to you and Jill."

Mike saw Eddie's shoulders shake and realised he was crying. He stood up, walked over to him and cradled him in his arms. He didn't care if anyone else was about and what they thought of the scene. His boy needed him and he was here.

When Eddie eventually stopped crying the two returned to the bench and sat down, Eddie rubbing at his eyes with the base of his palms.

"I miss mum so much," he said.

"I know you do. I do too."

"I've felt so angry since she passed away. It wasn't fair. Can I be honest with you dad?"

"Of course."

"Sometimes I wished it had been you and not her."

Mike felt a stab to the heart but understood his son's anguish.

"I wish it had been me too," he whispered.

"I don't really mean it," Eddie added, "I just…the anger, I hate the anger."

Mike grabbed his son's face and turned his gaze towards him.

"I'm sorry," he said, "I'm so sorry. The anger is my fault. I've always feared it being in the family. My dad would get into a drunken rage and beat my mother. He never did it sober but that's no excuse. He didn't ever show any remorse. I'm like him, I know I am. That's why I beat the crap out of him when I was sixteen. It doesn't matter that he deserved it, I shouldn't have allowed the anger to control me too."

He sighed as he released his hold on his son and sat back further on the bench.

"I always wondered why my mum hated what I did to dad. After all the beatings she'd received I thought she'd be glad, be proud of me but she wasn't, and rightly so. I shouldn't have hit him. Oh, I should have threatened him, had him up against the wall to show him I was now stronger than he was but I lost control and became just like him. Mum must have seen that. She never treated me the same way again afterwards."

"You're not like him," Eddie said, "We all get angry but you would never have hit mom, just like I would never hit anyone, least of all Jill. Anger doesn't control either of us. All we're guilty of is not facing up to what made us feel angry sooner. We should have had this conversation years ago."

Eddie leaned against the back of the bench so that both men were staring at the scene opposite them. A robin was hopping around the grass on the edge of the path, only flying off when a squirrel came up, searching for food under the bin and between the legs of the bench. He made a dash for the nearest tree when a jogger ran by.

"Perhaps you should have had this conversation with your dad too," Eddie suggested.

Mike snorted.

"I don't think my father would have been up for an in depth conversation. All he knew how to do was drink and hit people he could control. No, he was a bully of the worst kind. Some people are just evil and beyond saving."

Eddie shrugged.

"Well you knew him and I didn't," he said.

Mike leaned forwards and placed his head in his hands.

"Are you okay, dad?"

After a few moments Mike sat up again and smiled.

"Yes, I'm okay," he said, "I just feel like a huge weight has been lifted from my shoulders. For years I've feared my father's genes, that I'd turn into him or my kids would. It turns out I just needed someone who loves me to tell me I was wrong.

Thank you."

The two men hugged.

"This doesn't get you out of telling me the truth about why you're here," Eddie said, after they parted.

"I know," Mike replied, "I want to tell you. I've come here to face my past. I didn't realise I needed someone with me to do it. I'm glad you're here, son, but let's go and eat first shall we, I'm starving. Then we can arrange your staying at the B&B. I have a twin room. I'll tell you everything then.

*

Eddie was sat in the passenger seat of the car now as they drove through Maldon. He knew this was the most difficult journey his father was making so far and he remained silent, leaving it to Mike to decide as and when he wanted to talk. He'd been the same on Sunday, waiting for his father to tell him all about the past after they'd eaten breakfast and he'd apologised to the owner of the B&B for his earlier outburst. Up in the room the two men had sat up on the twin beds, leaning back against the headboards. It was a few moments before Mike had found the right words to start.

*

"What you read in the newspaper articles, about Emma Burrows being abducted and everyone believing my mentally ill brother did it, was wrong. I mean I don't actually know what happened to the girl but it wasn't Jimmy that did it. I thought it was to start with. I found him with her purple hair ribbon."

Mike had been looking straight ahead of him but now he turned his head to face his son.

"I took Jimmy away. I was the reason he disappeared…and it was my fault that he died."

Eddie's eyes widened.

"Jesus dad, you didn't…kill him did you?"

Mike took a moment before replying.

"It was my fault," he said, "With the help of my friend, Amrit I hid Jimmy away in an old, disused barn. I thought I was doing the right thing but it was so wrong. When I got back to the village, after leaving Jimmy in the barn, I expected the little girl to have been found but she was still missing. The search was going to continue until nightfall and would carry on the following day if she wasn't found. I'd hidden Jimmy away to bring home later and then say he'd been home all day, but with the girl still missing and the place crawling with police and locals, I couldn't get him home again without being seen. It wasn't long before everyone knew that Jimmy was missing too and suddenly, what I'd tried to avoid happening, happened. Jimmy was blamed for taking Emma. Mum was distraught but I couldn't tell her what I'd done. I'd ruined everything."

Mike sighed loudly.

"I didn't know what to do next. Jimmy was a smashing guy. He'd been starved of oxygen at birth and had learning difficulties but he was the sweetest person. He loved everything and everyone. Even if someone did something bad, Jimmy would still see the good in that person. He shouldn't have been blamed but it was easy wasn't it, to blame the mentally disabled man."

Mike slammed his hand down on the bed.

"I hated that village and everyone in it. Mum had always proudly displayed her eldest son and didn't want him hidden away. Of course he did cause a few problems. Jimmy liked to be nosy but wasn't discreet about it, peering into windows, listening in to conversations, that type of thing, but at worst he was an occasional nuisance. When that girl went missing it was the excuse those bastards needed to blame him for something big, something evil. It felt like they'd waited years to 'get him' and now they could…and I was the one that had allowed it to happen."

Mike fell into silence. Eddie let him have a few moments before asking,

"So how did he die?"

Mike felt the lump in his throat.

"I left him too long in the barn," he said, "I hid him for three whole days. Only Amrit and I knew he was there. We'd visit him as often as we could, take him food, sit with him for a while. We had to take water as well, for Jimmy to wash with and to flush the non-functioning toilet. It was really grotty but he actually did remarkably well. Once he got used to something Jimmy was fine and he started seeing the barn as the norm. I knew I'd have to move him again soon as the search for the girl was getting nearer. I couldn't believe she hadn't been found."

"And you're sure that your brother had nothing to do with it?" Eddie asked, tentatively.

"Definitely," Mike replied, "If only I'd realised that straightaway rather than judging him…"

He stopped talking, lost in the memory of 'if onlys.' Eventually he shook his head and continued on with the story.

"Whenever Jimmy did something that he knew was wrong, he'd try and deny it to start with but then he would have to admit it. It was like he couldn't lie, that the feeling couldn't be contained in his body and he had to release it. If he'd done anything to Emma he would have told me eventually. All he said was that he'd taken her to school. I don't know why he would have done that. I assume he meant he walked along with the girl and her older brother, Ray. Ray took her to school that day as he always did on Wednesdays. He told the police that and the teacher confirmed it."

"What about the ribbon?"

"Oh, Jimmy stole that off of her. He loved coloured things and soft things. That was the only thing he'd done wrong that day."

Mike had begun smiling as he spoke about his brother's love for soft things but now that smile faded.

"He was innocent but I'd made him look guilty. I still didn't know what to do. The longer he was gone the harder it was to bring him home. The police would have been all over him and he would have struggled with that. I'd have been whisked off as some accessory to the crime and then mum would have been alone, struggling. I couldn't have that."

"What about your dad," Eddie asked, "Where was he?"

"Oh he was away with his fancy woman. He returned a week after the abduction, full of stories that he was about to die. He didn't give a lost girl any thought. He barely commented on his son's disappearance. Of course it turns out he was actually ill. He died a few months later in the home of his mistress. Can you believe she sent me a letter and asked for money for the funeral. I screwed it up and threw it away."

"So what happened to Jimmy?"

Mike felt the tears well up in his eyes.

"I went to the barn with Amrit on the Sunday morning. He'd gone the night before and we usually took it in turns but he came with me, knowing I wanted to move Jimmy again before the searchers arrived. When we reached the barn we walked in and found Jimmy lying dead on the floor."

Eddie gasped.

"He must have tripped on one of his ropes that we tied him up with," Mike said, his voice full of upset, "The poor guy had probably just been trying to stretch his legs. He'd hit his head on some kind of iron bar on the floor. I think it was probably a railing from a fence. There was so little blood, just a dent and bruise on the top right part of his forehead. God knows if he died straightaway or lingered. I hope it was straightaway."

"That's awful," Eddie said.

Mike nodded.

"Amrit got upset and started panicking and it was difficult to work out what to do next. I couldn't take Jimmy home like that. I couldn't explain what I'd done. I didn't even know how I'd be able to face my mother again. In the end we decided we needed to bury him. The girl was still missing and everyone believed he'd taken her anyway; if he didn't come back then it wasn't going to affect their opinion."

Silent tears were rolling down Mike's face.

"We hid him away in the back of Amrit's dad's van until later that night when we buried him a few miles away, at the site of some medieval ruin on the edge of the Essex marshes, near a place called Northey Island. There was barely anything left of the building, having been built too close to the marshes, just like the old barn I'd housed Jimmy in. We thought he'd be safe there. It was a strangely peaceful place that no one visited anymore."

Mike turned and placed his feet on the floor between the two beds.

"Recently I've been picturing that night, the darkness, the cold wind blowing into my face as I buried my brother in an unconsecrated grave before I returned home and stayed silent about the whole thing. I had to put up with the accusations about Jimmy, cope with a mother who was getting more and more upset, while trying to pretend that I knew nothing."

"That must have been hard."

Mike nodded.

"And then mum's back pain was finally diagnosed by a doctor. I'd struggled to get her to see one for months but the pain had suddenly got so bad that she relented. She hated hospitals and doctors, never went to one even after she'd been beaten by my father. I swear she might have had broken bones that she just let heal on their own. She was always so afraid that the medical profession would take Jimmy away from her. She didn't know I was the one who was going to do that."

Eddie turned and stood his feet on the floor so that he was facing his father.

"And what was the cause of your mother's pain?"

Mike looked into his son's eyes.

"She had spinal cancer."

Eddie's eyes became watery.

"Like mom," he whispered.

Mike nodded.

"That must have made you feel even worse," Eddie said, "When mom got her diagnosis."

"I felt I was being punished for what I'd allowed to happen to Jimmy. Your mum's death brought the past back. I'd never told her about what happened but while she was alive there was still the opportunity for me to do it. Then the chance was gone."

The two remained silent for a few moments.

"So what happens now," Eddie asked, "Are you done with the past? Can you return home?"

"Not quite," Mike told him, "I'm here for a week but that's plenty of time. I went to see my mum yesterday. I need to go and see Jimmy before I leave."

"Would you like me to come with you?"

Mike smiled.

"I'd like that a lot," he said.

*

For the rest of Sunday he'd let Eddie catch up on his sleep, often dozing himself, exhausted from the outpouring of emotional energy. On the Monday Mike had taken his son to Little Tenwick to visit his mother's grave again, putting off the trip he needed to make but was scared of doing. Now, finally, it was Tuesday and they were headed to Jimmy's resting place.

As soon as he turned onto the Mundon Road it felt familiar to Mike and his heart began to palpitate as the dark memories of that night thirty-nine years before tried to burst through to the forefront of his mind again. Although he'd been travelling in the other direction that night, Mike felt the same ominous feeling he'd had back then as he and Amrit risked being discovered burying a body. Eddie maintained his silence sat in the passenger seat, sensing his father's angst.

Mike turned down the tiny, barely-used lane he'd last driven down in the pitch black. He'd feared the area would be more built up now but the few houses in that place were still far enough away for the two of them not to be noticed. He needed to see Jimmy's resting place because he'd avoided doing it before emigrating to Canada. He should have come then, to say goodbye. Perhaps if he had then the past would have remained buried for the last thirty-nine years rather than always being on the edge of his thoughts, slowly eating away at him.

The lane travelled round several bends even though the area was open land and Eddie noticed his father seemed to anticipate each turn before it happened. Suddenly Mike stopped and turned off the engine. He got out of the car without saying anything. Eddie followed suit. The grassy space was muddy after the recent rain and the two walked gingerly across the ground until Mike stopped by what looked like a large rock that seemed out of place to Eddie.

"He's here," Mike said, not turning round.

"What, under that rock?"

"It's stone," Mike replied, mechanically, "From the building that was here hundreds of years ago. It used to be taller than this and more obviously part of a wall. I buried Jimmy beside it so that I'd have a marker. A lot of the old building was taken away but I guess the parts that were left must have slowly sunk further into the ground. Even this piece will be gone someday."

Eddie didn't say anything, detecting the note of sadness in his father's voice. In the graveyard yesterday his grandmother's gravestone stood out as a monument to her. Here, his uncle's plain marker was just part of an old ruin, ignored by everyone.

"I can't remember which side of it we dug," Mike said, looking at the ground, "Isn't that terrible?"

"Dad it was nearly forty years ago."

Mike didn't appear to hear.

"Maybe it was the opposite side," he said, stepping round to look at the other side of the rock.

He stopped dead and stared down at something on the ground.

"Dad?"

There was no response.

"Dad, what's wrong?"

Eddie walked round to where his father was staring at the ground, hoping he wasn't about to see remains of his long dead uncle risen to the surface. There was a large bouquet of flowers lying there. The flowers were still fresh.

"What's this doing here?" Mike whispered.

"It could be for anything…" Eddie began.

Mike looked up at him.

"Of course it's not just for anything," he snapped, "It's the sort of bunch you place on a grave. Jimmy's here. Who on earth has left this? Who else knows what happened?

Chapter 27

Brother/Teacher

"Remember me," Ray said, brightly.

Caroline's brow furrowed as she tried to recall who this man was who had just been brought over to see her.

"It's Ray," he said, "Ray Burrows."

She felt the blood drain from her face. What the hell was he doing here? As if he'd heard her thoughts he added,

"I was just passing and thought I'd drop in, take a look at the place you run. I saw it mentioned in one of the nationals, broadsheet obviously, I don't read the tabloids."

Ray looked around the area they were standing in, which was really just a corridor between rooms. Caroline realised the member of staff that had brought him to her was still there. She forced a smile onto her face.

"That's fine, Natalie I'll look after Mr Burrows now."

Natalie nodded and headed off. Caroline was trying to think quickly. She had no idea why this man was here visiting her. It was the last thing she needed. The past was already at the forefront of her mind but having someone from it, physically standing in front of her, was almost too much. She really wanted to think about what Hasanna had just told her about moving in together.

"Why don't we step into my office," she said.

She needed to get Ray away from her team before he began talking about the past in front of them. That could surely be the only reason he was here. Karen Taylor had mentioned it was

Ray who'd told her where she could be found. She didn't want this blabbermouth here at the centre.

As they walked to the office Ray started talking, telling her about the changes in Little and Great Tenwick and going on about his job at the supermarket like it was the most important branch in the chain.

"Is it still based in that small parade of shops?" she asked.

Ray beamed.

"Yes," he replied, "We're still there, serving the community as best we can, making a difference to people's everyday lives. Well, much like you're doing here."

Caroline didn't think there was any comparison but they'd arrived at her office door so she ignored what he'd just said. Fran looked up as the door opened. She still looked fearful until she saw Caroline had brought company.

"Could you leave us for a while please, Fran," Caroline said, "I need to use this office for a meeting."

"Oh, so you're Fran," she heard Ray say.

Caroline's eyes widened. So that explained her behaviour earlier.

"It was lovely speaking to you yesterday," he continued, "So nice to put a face to the voice."

He held out his hand and Fran reluctantly shook it. She looked sheepish and didn't meet Caroline's eye.

"I'll take my break now," she mumbled, before grabbing her coat and heading out the door.

Caroline indicated the chair in front of her desk for Ray to sit down in. He was still smiling and looking around the room, impressed with what he saw. Caroline found it annoying.

"So what is a manger of a village shop in Essex doing in Windsor?" she asked him.

Ray's smiled faltered at the slight but then he recovered.

“Off to a managers meeting,” he told her, “We’ll be discussing the future of the company; where it’s going, that type of thing.”

He’d been pleased when he came up with this excuse for coming. Caroline wasn’t taken in by it for a second. The only reason he could be here was because of what happened in the past.

“So, you’re doing very well for yourself,” Ray said.

“I’m sorry?”

“With your husband’s business and the charity, it was all mentioned in the article I read.”

Caroline didn’t like where this was heading. Why had he mentioned Oliver? What was this man after?

“We’ve had a couple of nice pieces written about the charity,” she told him, “But it’s not like we’re that well known. We rely totally on our donations to be able to keep the centres running. You can set up a direct debit to help if you like.”

She saw Ray’s grin falter for a split second.

“Or make a one-off payment.”

“Well that sounds great,” he replied, “I’ll look up the details when I return home after this…I mean after my company meeting. I’m very much involved in local, charitable projects myself. I’m about to join the parish council.”

“Are you.”

Ray tapped the side of his nose.

“It’s hush hush at the moment,” he told her, “But I’m being considered for the casual vacancy. I can’t see there are any other worthy candidates.”

“Well your secret is safe with me.”

The room fell silent. Ray looked about it again. Caroline sat and watched him. If he was here to dredge up the past then she would wait until he brought it up. In the mean time he could squirm for all she cared. After a few moments he said,

"So, erm, if I set up a direct debit to assist your charity, would you mind if I told our local parish chairman that I know you?"

"Sorry?"

Ray stopped searching the room.

"Well it might help my chances of getting on the parish council," he told her.

"I thought you said the seat was already yours."

"Well yes, but I don't want to be seen to take it for granted. If I'm associated with you, I thought it only fair I asked first, then it would reflect very well on me. It wouldn't be a lie would it, after all we go way back, don't we?"

Caroline's eyes narrowed.

"Are you trying to blackmail me?" she asked.

Ray's mouth dropped open.

"Of course not," he replied, shocked, "Why would you say something like that?"

"Come on Ray," she said, "We barely know each other. When I worked in Little Tenwick we didn't ever speak. You put that bloody journalist onto me and now you've turned up here out of the blue. You're hinting at the past while also going on about how well I'm doing and talking about my husband's business. What is it you want; is it money?"

"I don't want anything," he told her, almost whimpering, "I just want to get onto the parish council. It's been my lifelong dream to do that, to reach that pinnacle in the local community."

Caroline raised an eyebrow.

"Really, that's been your dream has it? That's the extent of your ambition?"

He nodded.

"My God," she said.

"What's that supposed to mean?"

"Nothing," she sighed, "If that's what you want then good for you but really, how could I help with that? I run a small charity on the other side of London from where you are. I have no influence in the Tenwick villages and wouldn't want to have. I also don't want to speak to your journalist friend either."

She started to stand up.

"So really, if that's all you came here for I'm afraid..."

"I don't understand," Ray said, shaking his head.

Caroline sat back down again.

"You don't understand what?"

He looked across the desk at her.

"This reluctance to speak to a woman writing a book? What is everyone's problem with it?"

Caroline shook her head in wonder.

"Ray, your sister disappeared," she told him, "She was never seen again. Don't you think that's something people would rather not talk about? The loss, the tragedy, the fear of what might have happened to her; it's unpleasant stuff, especially for those of you closest to her."

Ray waved his hand dismissively. It reminded Caroline of the gesture Oliver made and she instantly felt angry.

"It was thirty-nine years ago," he said, "Surely everyone is over that by now, I know I am."

"What? This was your little sister. She was part of your family, part of you. How do you get over something like that?"

Ray shrugged.

"Well you have to move on don't you."

"Yes move on, but not forget or 'get over it.'"

Caroline couldn't believe how unfeeling he was. She hadn't got over it and she was just the teacher.

"I'm sure your parents still struggle."

Ray tutted.

"Tell me about it," he said, rolling his eyes, "Mother still insists on her being alive. I can't believe she's that gullible. Of course Emma's dead, she has to be."

"Perhaps she finds it too hard to think like that," Caroline told him, forcefully, "Have you considered that? I mean, have you ever given a thought to someone else besides yourself?"

Ray's head whipped back to look directly at Caroline.

"And what do you mean by that? I've always been there for mother. I live with her at the moment because she enjoys having me there."

"I'm sure you're a bundle of laughs."

Ray's eyes narrowed.

"Let's not forget whose fault this all is," he said, "You were the one who was supposed to be in charge of my little sister when she was in school. It was a ridiculously small place in the back of beyond. You barely had a handful of kids to watch over and yet you still managed to lose one."

Caroline leaned forwards.

"And that's something I've had to live with for near on forty years," she replied, barely able to control her irritation, "It's the reason the past and your sister stay with me. Besides, I didn't even see her arrive that morning."

She regretted that last sentence but Ray was too angry to realise what she'd just admitted.

"Well you should have done," he told her, "My God she walked in with that oaf didn't she?"

Caroline frowned.

"What do you mean," she asked, "Are you talking about Jimmy McGill?"

Ray's face froze as he thought about what he'd just said. Caroline could almost hear his mind whirring as he tried to find a way to respond. In the end he decided on honesty.

"Oh alright," he began, "I didn't bring my sister all the way into school that day like I said I had, okay? When the headmaster brought me out of my class later on I thought it was because I'd been found out. Then he tells me my sister has gone missing and all the way back to Little Tenwick, in the secretary's car that smelled strongly of cigarette smoke, I was petrified that I'd be blamed for her wandering off somewhere. It was typical of that little bitch to get me into trouble."

Caroline was shocked by the transformation of the man in front of her. When he'd entered the office he'd just seemed an annoying prig. Now he was full of malice and his face was practically contorted with the anger he was obviously feeling.

"God I hated her so much," he spat, "She was a manipulative, self-centred, spoilt, little cunt."

Caroline gasped.

"She was five years old," she told him.

"And yet she still managed to turn my parents against me, so much so that I wasn't noticed. They barely acknowledged me, unless it was to do with her in some way, how I was her favourite person or how they thought it cute that she she wanted to hold my hand when I was forced to take her to school. Even her touch made me feel physically sick."

Caroline wasn't sure Ray still realised she was there until he looked right at her again but with such a look of loathing she recoiled in her chair.

"I hated Wednesdays when I had to take her to school. The little bitch had been particularly grizzly at home that morning because mother was in a rush and had accidentally pulled one of Emma's bunches while trying to tie her ghastly purple hair ribbons. That thing would cry at anything, it was so annoying."

Ray turned away, moving his head jerkily from side to side

as he spoke. Caroline thought he would spit at any moment, trying to get rid of the venom he'd amassed over the years.

"Actually mother had been short with her, which was very unusual. Usually nothing about 'perfect, little Emma' got on her nerves. That's why the little beast was sulking as we left for school. I practically had to drag her along the road. As we crossed the green Emma stopped dead and no amount of shouting from me could move her. I was ready to clout her one when I heard laughter and saw that bitch Michelle Monroe from my class and that annoying younger brother of hers who lived up behind the church. They were walking past the entrance to the primary school as they made their way to West Road where the school bus turned round after picking us up for the Comprehensive. That was all I needed."

Caroline wondered if Ray actually liked anyone.

"I can still hear her god-awful cackle now. 'Are you walking out with your girlfriend' she called over, with her brother adding, 'she's too mature for him.' I told Emma to come along but she refused. All I could hear was their laughter. 'Ray can't control his bowels let alone his sister.' This was the shit of a brother again. They disappeared from sight and I turned on Emma. I was so angry. She'd just embarrassed me in front of the mouthiest girl in my school."

Seeing Ray this angry while reliving the past made Caroline scared. What had he done to his sister? Was this the real reason why Emma had been upset in school and had run off? Had he hurt her so badly that she'd keeled over later and died, lost somewhere on her own? Could she, Caroline, have saved her if only she'd remained in the classroom that morning?

"I grabbed her," Ray said, his voice bitter with rage, "I squeezed her upper arms tightly. She looked petrified and I was glad. I told her she was going to stop being a little shit. She started crying again but that just made me angrier and I shook her. I shook her as hard as I could."

He stopped talking, lost in his thoughts. Caroline was horrified by the sadistic look on his face as he relived that moment. She was almost afraid to ask what happened next but she needed to know.

"And then what?"

Ray looked back at her again, the malice now gone and his expression back to normal.

"And then I found myself flat on my back," he told her.

She hadn't expected that.

"I didn't know what had happened at first. I'd felt something push me and I must have hit my head on the edge of the kerb because I could practically see stars. When I was able to glance up I saw him."

"Jimmy McGill?"

"Yes. He was looking at me curiously. Well he always looked at people curiously, the stupid, bloody idiot. And do you know what the little bitch was doing? She was leaning against him, sobbing. He looked down at her and touched one of her hair ribbons lightly before patting her back, I suppose trying to console her as he'd seen others do. Then he looked over at me. I guess to her, Jimmy looked like an adult, someone to trust, someone to turn against me."

"So he'd pushed you."

"Yes, and with some force. I could have been killed."

Caroline wanted to tell him that he could have killed his sister by violently shaking her but knew he wouldn't listen to that.

"He said to me, 'you hurt your sister.'"

Ray's put-on voice sounded offensive and made Caroline wince. It wasn't even how Jimmy had spoken.

"I shrugged my shoulders and told him, 'so' but the idiot couldn't understand that. I felt humiliated sat on the floor and was glad that Michelle and her brother weren't there to see me. I stood up and the little cow pushed herself further against Jimmy. Can you imagine that? She knew what she was doing, the manipulative fucker."

"She was probably scared of the man that had been shaking her."

"Well she deserved it! I was still her brother and the man she was holding onto was the local loony. I picked up my school bag and told him to take her to school because I no longer cared. I walked off to catch the bus. When I looked back the little gobshite was holding the idiot's hand and they were walking towards the school. I thought no more about it. I got to the bus stop and punched Michelle's brother. That felt good and she never made fun of me again, I can tell you."

Ray stopped talking and sighed.

"Is that all of it?" Caroline asked.

"Until I was brought back to the village and discovered that the police and some of the villagers were out looking for Emma **and** Jimmy. I didn't know what had happened but for now I was off the hook. And you told the police that I'd brought Emma to school. I never understood why you did that but I thank you for it."

Caroline felt her skin crawl. She didn't want to think about the lie she'd told and she certainly didn't want to think about it helping this disgusting man sitting opposite her.

"As the days passed and there was no sign of them I realised I didn't have to reveal what I'd done. My parents were both upset and thinking about Emma constantly, but at least they included me in their grief."

Ray smiled.

"Being held by my parents while they cried, I could have laughed. I was finally being noticed again."

He gave a laugh now and Caroline felt he expected her to join in. He was back to the prig that had walked into the centre a short while ago. She leaned across the table and spoke slowly but with menace.

"Not only would I not endorse you as a member of any parish council but I've half a mind to contact the one you want to join to tell them exactly what sort of repulsive, repugnant degenerate you are."

Ray looked shocked. Caroline continued.

"You will not tell them you know me or use me to endorse yourself in any way. If you do then I will take legal action, do you understand me?"

Ray's face twitched as he tried to find the right response. In the end he just stood up.

"I wouldn't let you endorse me even if you paid me," he said, nonchalantly before turning and walking to the door, "You were a lousy teacher and it can only be a matter of time before this so-called venture of yours fails. I don't need some child loser scuppering my chances of getting on the council. I bid you good day."

He left the office. Caroline took a deep breath and let it out slowly. She'd never felt affection for Emma Burrows before now, just guilt about what had happened. She'd been a whiny child but now Caroline knew why. How else had the poor thing suffered at the hands of her incredibly unpleasant brother during those first five years of her life? Even Caroline had felt afraid of him in the last ten minutes and she was sixty-two. How petrified had a five year old girl been? What on earth had Sylvia and Daniel been doing not to notice their son was demonic?

Caroline shook her head. She didn't know what had happened to Emma that day, whether she died or was taken by someone, but whichever of those scenarios was true, the result was that she'd been saved, saved from spending one more second with her psychotic brother.

Chapter 28

Mother/Father

Sylvia hadn't been to London in years, let alone travel across it and out the other side. She'd arranged the trip quickly before she could change her mind. She would have liked to have gone with someone but she didn't want Ray to know what she was doing yet, although he'd driven off somewhere on his own today anyway on his day off. She hoped he was meeting up with a friend and having a good time. If she and Ken had been speaking then perhaps she could have asked him to come along with her, maybe not all the way to the Cotswolds but at least as far as London. In the end she'd had to organise the trip on her own.

She left Little Tenwick early, the cab passing parents taking their children up the pathway to the primary school. There seemed to be so many of them now compared to when her own children went there. The school catered for ages four to eleven but classes back when Ray and Emma attended were tiny. Over the years there had been talk of it closing but new housing brought young families to the area and Little Tenwick Primary had survived while others fell.

Sylvia sighed. Now there would definitely be someone to notice an upset girl running out of school but in nineteen eighty it wasn't surprising no one had seen Emma…well, except for her own mother. Sylvia shivered. A busy village would also have seen her stealing as well but she shook that thought away too. She didn't want to think about that right now, not until she was face to face with Daniel.

The train into Liverpool Street was fine but the circle line to Paddington was daunting as it was on the same track as other lines and she had to keep checking the screen to make sure she was going to get onto the right train. It was rather packed when Sylvia got on and she couldn't always see past the passengers stood in front of her to know what station they were arriving at. She began to feel panicky, worried she'd miss her stop, but then the carriage cleared as everyone got off and Sylvia realised she was now at Paddington and she followed the rest of the crowd.

Paddington proved to be an even more frightening experience. Sylvia hadn't realised a train station could be so big and house so many people. They all seemed to know where they were going and rushed by her in different directions. At one point she had to head to the side of the main concourse so that she could control her breathing, fearing she was about to have a panic attack.

Fortunately another person stood nearby was able to point her in the right direction. Sylvia had already spent nearly two hours travelling and wasn't looking forward to another hour and a half to Kingham in Oxfordshire but this part of the trip proved to be very nice with beautiful scenery to look at out of the window, especially as she got nearer to her destination.

She hadn't told Daniel she was coming. That was probably stupid as he could be out or have gone away somewhere. Or he could be at home with his daughter visiting him whom he might not want to talk about the past in front of, but without a phone number the only way she could have contacted him was by letter and that would have taken too long and he might have refused to see her. She'd already booked her return journey and would only have about an hour at most with Daniel but Sylvia felt that was plenty of time to discuss what she needed to talk about.

At Kingham she took a cab to Stow on the Wold, taking her over the border into Gloucestershire. The retirement village that Daniel lived in looked plush and charming. While the new apartments were built like the traditional stone houses of the area there was no mistaking they were new, but it was still a beautiful development.

It took a little while for Daniel to get to the door, leaving Sylvia feeling worried that he was out and that her trip had been a waste of time and money after all. Then it opened. She'd have recognised her ex-husband anywhere. While he was grey-haired with thick, black glasses on, slightly stooped and leaning on a walking stick, he was still recognisably Daniel Burrows. Not expecting her, he stared for a few moments at first before recognition dawned.

"My God, Sylvia; what the hell are you doing here?"

"I've had warmer welcomes," she replied, and smiled.

Daniel returned it and chuckled.

"I'm sorry," he said, "But it's such a shock. I never expected to see you again."

The smile left his face.

"Oh my God, is something wrong? It has to be for you to come all this way. Is it Ray?"

"No it's nothing like that," she said, trying to placate him, "I just want to talk."

That sounded odd, even to Sylvia. Daniel's brow furrowed.

"To talk?"

"Yes, but I'd rather not do it on the doorstep."

"Of course."

Daniel stood back to let her in. It was very modern inside the ground floor property. Daniel led her through a door to the right into a large room that was lounge, dining and kitchen.

"It's a bit flash for an old codger like me," Daniel told her, seeing his ex-wife looking about the room, "But it's not a bad place to see out my final years. I've got everything I need. There's a restaurant on site if I choose to use it, and a communal lounge and a hairdressers. Not that I really need to visit there too often."

He pulled at his wispy hair and smiled. Sylvia felt stupid now for some of the awful things she'd imagined might have happened thirty-nine years ago. There was no way this man could have done anything to hurt his own daughter, but she still needed him to share the truth with her about what had actually gone on that day. There'd been too many lies and cover-ups.

"Let me get you a coffee," Daniel said, walking past her, "You must be exhausted after travelling all this way. Would you like something to eat?"

"No I brought a sandwich with me and ate it on the train. A coffee would be lovely though."

Daniel hung his walking stick on the towel rail at the end of the kitchen cabinets beside the sink and then limped about the kitchen as he filled the coffeemaker and got the milk out of the fridge. Sylvia sat down on the sofa, realising the comfy-looking armchair opposite that was sagging in the middle was where Daniel liked to sit.

She noticed the photos on the table beside his chair. There was the one of Emma taken not long before she disappeared. Sylvia had the same one in a frame at home. The photograph was crooked and Sylvia noticed that there was no glass on the front of the frame. An accident she supposed. There was also a picture of a lady taken when she was a young woman that had to be his second wife.

"Do you have a picture of your Tania?" she called out.

Daniel looked over at the little table and frowned, like he'd only just realised a photo was missing.

"Somewhere," he muttered, "I had an accident with the photo frames."

Sylvia didn't question him further, noticing her ex-husband's embarrassed expression.

"People don't print photos like they used to," she said, instead, "They're all taken on their phones these days and left on them."

She sat forward on the sofa as Daniel brought her coffee over before returning for his own mug and his stick. He had a packet of digestive biscuits under his arm and placed them and the mug carefully onto the coffee table before gently sinking down into his chair.

"What does she look like, your Tania," Sylvia asked.

Daniel gave her a smile.

"She doesn't look like Emma," he said, "That's what you were wondering wasn't it."

Sylvia smiled back, blushing.

"Well I noticed your wife in that picture with her blonde hair. I couldn't help thinking…"

She left the sentence hanging.

"Tania has ginger hair," Daniel told her, "A dark ginger, although it's more red these days. She's nothing like Emma. Tania has grown up into a strong, independent woman. I'm very proud of her…I just need to tell her that."

Sylvia decided not to follow that remark up with a question. It seemed like something personal. Daniel remained lost in his own world for a moment but then he regained his composure.

"This must be important," he said, to Sylvia, "Otherwise you wouldn't be here. While it's lovely to see you, couldn't you have just phoned?"

"I don't have a number," she replied, "Besides, I felt I

needed to see you in person."

Daniel looked concerned.

"Are you heading back home today?" he asked.

"Yes. I don't need to take up too much of your time. My taxi is returning at half past two."

She took a sip of her coffee and refused the proffered biscuit.

"You know the anniversary is coming up," she said.

"Of course," Daniel replied, "Thirty-nine years. It's not something I would forget, even with that sodding journalist contacting me."

"She contacted you?"

"Yes. I suppose she must have spoken to you first."

Sylvia shook her head.

"Actually no. She spoke with Ray but I told him I didn't want to speak to her. I assume he must have mentioned that to her. I'd have thought he'd have said not to contact you either."

"Why would he do that? We've not spoken in years."

"I'm sorry about that."

"It's not your fault," Daniel said.

"No," Sylvia told him, "But I'm still sorry about it."

Daniel replied with a nod.

"I do wonder why she didn't try and contact me though," Sylvia added, "After all, she's a journalist researching a story. I doubt she'd really take my feelings into consideration."

"Yes she phoned me and then sent a letter," Daniel told her, "Not that I've replied to it. I've thrown it in the bin."

Sylvia nodded. Daniel broke a digestive biscuit in half and dipped one of the pieces into his coffee.

"I did wonder whether to contact you," he admitted, "After she spoke with me. It brought the past back to life. I assume you're still on the old number. I didn't call in the end because, well I suppose I didn't really know what to say."

Sylvia smiled, sadly.

"Yes I suppose we're strangers to one another now," she said.

Daniel returned the same smile.

"Thirty-nine years," he said, "It goes by so fast."

"I know."

"I'm eighty now. How did that happen? These last weeks I've started to feel every year of it too. You look great, by the way."

Sylvia smiled, shyly.

"Oh I feel my years too," she said, "Especially first thing of a morning or when it's damp outside."

Daniel laughed.

"Listen to us," he said, "We're even talking like old people. I always promised myself I'd never get like that, telling everyone my age, discussing ailments and yet here I am; I've become my parents."

Sylvia laughed too.

"We don't change as much as we think we do," she said.

The smile left her face as she remembered saying the same sentence to Ken recently. She missed him.

"How's Ray doing," Daniel asked, "I know you kindly write to me about him but there's only so much you can put in a letter."

"He's fine," she said, picking up her mug, "Still living with me temporarily. He enjoys his work at the supermarket. He doesn't really talk much about friends, just his work colleagues, but I think he's happy."

"Has the village changed much? I'm surprised you stayed there, considering what happened."

Sylvia took a sip of her coffee before replying.

"Mmm, this is delicious. Well it seemed wrong to sell up after you continued to pay the mortgage. I've always been very grateful for that."

"I know. It was the least I could do. You did everything when I was unemployed. I hated it and didn't really help you out like I ought to have done, cooking dinner or cleaning the house. You still did all of that after you came home from cleaning other people's houses. I was lucky when I got my new job here in Gloucestershire and my career advanced quickly. When Alice and I married we moved into her house. It only seemed right to leave you the old one, make sure you and Ray were provided for."

"Well it was very generous of you. I still like living there, despite what happened. It's familiar. The village centre hasn't really changed that much, you'd still recognise it, although there is a lot of new housing on the outskirts."

"Where isn't there," Daniel said, dipping the other half of his biscuit into his mug, "It's the same round here, new properties going up, trying to blend in but obviously new, like this place really. Still, I'd rather see that than a load of soulless boxes."

Sylvia looked at her watch. Daniel noticed.

"I'm sorry," he said, "I'm rabbiting on and you're on a deadline. Would you like to tell me why you're here?"

All of a sudden Sylvia didn't want to. She was enjoying talking with her ex-husband and what she had to say would change the relaxed atmosphere between them. But she had no choice. She wasn't going to waste the trip.

"I need to know what happened on that day," she told him.

Daniel frowned.

"What do you mean," he replied, "You know what happened."

Sylvia shook her head.

"No," she said, "I want the truth. I know you saw Emma again after she left for school."

Daniel's face showed a brief expression of shock before he composed himself again.

"I don't know what you're talking about," he replied.

"Yes you do," Sylvia pushed, feeling incredibly calm, "Emma ran home from school, upset."

Daniel's fingers drummed the ends of his armrest.

"She was…," he began, before realising what his ex-wife had just told him, "How do you know that? You weren't there."

Sylvia took a deep breath.

"Yes I was," she told him, "I didn't go to Chelmsford until later that day."

"What? Why?"

"Because I was stealing from Mr Prendergast who'd passed away the day before."

Daniel's eyes widened.

"You were doing what?" he said, shocked.

Sylvia stood up. She always felt so restless when she was anxious. She began pacing the floor. For Daniel it was a reminder of his daughter; not Emma this time, Tania. She always paced the room whenever she was stressed or angry.

"We had no money," Sylvia said, "I had to do something, you wouldn't. Mr Prendergast was dead and had always promised me one of his antiques. His money-grabbing nephews and nieces who never came to visit were going to get the lot. I only had that one day to take what I wanted. I hated doing it but I was so scared of losing the house."

"We weren't going to lose the house."

Sylvia stopped pacing and looked down at her ex-husband.

"Yes we were," she told him, "We'd missed a number of

mortgage payments and the interest rates were so high. Your unemployment benefit and my scant cleaning wages barely kept us in food. You'd closed your mind to it, as you always did whenever there was a dilemma to face. You were the same when we were trying for a baby, not wanting to go for tests at the hospital, happy to blame all our problems on me."

"My God you haven't changed have you," Daniel told her, "You still think you're so high and mighty."

"I've never been like that."

"You were always like that," he snapped, "Always thinking you were better than everyone else, thinking you were the same as the people you skivvied for."

"Well my 'skivvying' was all that was putting food on the table. You can talk about being high and mighty, you'd have rather seen your family homeless than take a job you felt was beneath you. There was work out there, you were just too lazy to do it. No wonder I had to clean houses. No wonder I had to resort to stealing."

"I never made you steal."

"I had no choice," Sylvia shouted, at him, "Don't you see how desperate and wretched we were, even before Emma was taken."

Daniel turned his gaze away from her and Sylvia felt suddenly tired after the anger. She sat back down again.

"We blamed the divorce on the abduction but we weren't happy for a long time before that," she admitted, "Only the kids kept us together. Well, only Emma really. Ray was fifteen when she went and was already independent. When Emma was taken there was nothing left to keep us together."

"I miss her everyday," Daniel whispered.

"Then tell me what happened," Sylvia said, "I need to know. I've always needed to know."

"You don't need to know," Daniel told her, "Let the past die."

"I can't," she replied, "I can't let this go. I can't let Emma die. She's still alive, you know I've always believed that, but if I thought for one second that you'd…"

Daniel turned back to face her, anger on his face.

"Do you think I killed our daughter," he asked her, shocked, "Do you think me capable of doing that?"

"Sometimes," she admitted, "I can't help it. You lied to the police."

"So did you!"

"But you saw her after me. You were the last person to see her. Were you the last person to see her alive?"

"Get out."

Sylvia was momentarily stumped.

"What?"

"Get out of my house. I don't want to talk about this."

"And you think I do," she told him, incredulously, "You think I wanted to spend over three hours travelling here today just to rake up the past? I have to do this Daniel, for your sake as well as mine. I realise now that I haven't truly moved on in thirty-nine years and I'm sure deep down you feel the same. Tell me what happened."

"No."

"Then I assume you must have killed her."

"No."

"I'll go to the police."

"I was in a dress!" Daniel shouted.

The room fell silent. Sylvia heard the words but her brain couldn't arrange them into anything that made sense.

"What?" she said.

Daniel had turned away from her again. Sylvia saw him rub

at his eyes.

"I was wearing a dress," he said, so softly she had to lean forwards to hear him, "When she ran back home that day, I was wearing a dress."

"One of mine?"

"No of course not," he said, annoyed, "How on earth would I have fitted into one of yours. I had a couple of my own. I kept them in that heavy old suitcase of my grandparents."

Sylvia was still finding it difficult to believe she was having this conversation.

"You owned a dress," she said, aloud, more to understand it herself than to reply to Daniel.

"I needed to wear them, occasionally," he admitted, "It was something I'd always done."

"Why didn't you ever tell me?"

Daniel snorted.

"Yeah, right," he said, "That would have been an easy conversation to have, wouldn't it? Look at me Sylvia. I might be a wizened, old man now but back then I was six foot tall and pretty well-built. You think that sort of physique looked good in a dress? I looked hideous but I wasn't doing it for that. I just liked the feel of the material on me. I felt calm, relaxed. It helped me cope."

"You could have told me," Sylvia said, "We were husband and wife."

"Of course I couldn't have told you," Daniel replied, "My God, I know today anything goes but this was nineteen eighty. Well, it had been going on for years before that. I don't know why I do it. I've tried to analyse it but I've never come up with anything. It's not like I was spanked by nanny in a dress when I was a child or anything sordid like that. I just have a need sometimes to put on a dress. I'm ashamed of it but I've never been able to stop, no matter how hard I've tried."

"You shouldn't be ashamed," Sylvia told him.

"That's easier said than done. You remember what my father was like. I came from a home where men were men and women were there just to please the men. My dad already thought me odd because I didn't want to enter the armed forces like he and all his ancestors had done. He made his opinions known when I lost my job after the factory closed and you were out working. How on earth could I have told anyone that I liked to wear women's clothing? It was a shameful thing back then and I can't help still feeling ashamed today."

He grabbed his mug and took a gulp before continuing.

"Whenever I feel stressed or fretful, I put on a dress," he said, "At first I feel calmer, less worried, but then I catch a glimpse of my reflection in the mirror and I feel embarrassed, sordid, but even then I know I'll feel the need to put one on again another day. It's like a vicious circle."

Daniel fell silent as his memories passed through his mind. Sylvia would have let him have some time but she didn't have much to spare before the cab returned.

"So you'd put on a dress that day," she encouraged.

He nodded.

"I often did once I knew you were all out of the house. I hated not having a job, being unable to provide for my family. I tried to put on a relaxed front when you were at home because I didn't want you to worry but I was terrified. Putting on a dress helped me cope. Wednesdays was the best day because I knew you would all be out of the house for hours. I didn't expect to see her there."

Daniel's tears were rolling down his cheeks. Sylvia wanted to go to comfort him but there was nowhere for her to sit and she couldn't kneel down on the floor with her knee, not with the long journey home ahead of her.

“I’d just walked down the stairs to make a cup of tea. I didn’t aways wear the dress downstairs in case somebody knocked at the door but I thought I was safe that day for a while. I was still in the hallway when the door flew open and there was our little girl, upset and crying. She looked up at me with those large blue eyes of hers, her hair a mess, but all I saw was the confusion on her face. I was upset, embarrassed and angry at myself. I shouted at her. I shouted at her to get out. My voice was louder than I thought. I saw the fear in the poor, little mite’s face. I’d never yelled at her like that before. She turned and bolted. I rushed upstairs to change so that I could run after her.”

Daniel looked across at Sylvia.

“I thought she’d have just run out into the alleyway. I didn’t know why she was there in the first place. I suppose someone had upset her at school. She was a fragile, little creature wasn’t she. When I came back downstairs after changing and locking the dress away, I searched the alleyway first before heading off in the direction of the school. When I got there I found the teacher searching the grounds for her. I couldn’t say I’d seen her at home. I’d have had to explain why I’d scared her off. I didn’t know what else to do. That’s why I didn’t tell the police I’d seen her. I didn’t know anyone else had. That night I burned the dresses. I’m sorry Sylvia. It’s all my fault she’s gone. I feel so guilty.”

Sylvia stood up now and went over to him. She remained standing and cradled his head in her hands as he cried.

“I feel guilty too,” she said, soothingly, “I saw her and could have run to her but I didn’t. Now I know that only a few moments later she would have run back down the alleyway again, but I’d already crossed the stile into Garret’s field and was on my way to the bus stop."

"It's not your fault, Sylvia," Daniel said, sniffing, "You weren't to know I was going to scare her off."

Sylvia gently turned Daniel's face up to her's.

"It's not your fault either," she told him, "You weren't to know she was going to come home and you weren't to know she was going to disappear."

"I wish I knew the truth," he said, "Where did she go? Did Jimmy McGill take her? What happened to them? The not knowing has eaten away at me all this time."

"I understand. It's done the same to me too. But I believe she's still alive, I truly do."

Daniel sat back in his chair.

"I wish I had your faith," he told her.

He sighed.

"I still feel responsible," he said.

"So do I. It's easy to say, 'if only I did this or hadn't done that' but we do what we do at the time with what we know. We can't live our lives full of 'if onlys.'"

Daniel reached up and took Sylvia's hand in his.

"I've let it affect my whole life," he told her, "I don't speak to my son and I'm not as close to my other daughter as I should be."

He shook his head, sadly.

"I've been afraid to love her," he admitted, "My Tania. I loved Emma so much and the pain of her leaving was almost too much to bear. I couldn't go through that again. I felt Emma's disappearance was punishment for the dress thing."

"I felt I was being punished too, for stealing. Not that I kept the money that I received for pawning the items I took that day. I posted it back through Mr Prendergast's door for his family to find, with a note thanking him for the loan. Obviously I didn't sign it. We didn't need it in the end because the building society gave us some time off from paying the mortgage after Emma was taken."

Sylvia squeezed Daniel's hand.

"We're not either of us being punished though, not by God or whatever forces or power you believe in. We blame ourselves for allowing our daughter to go missing when we both had chances to save her but really, neither of us knew what was going to happen."

"That doesn't make it any easier for us to forgive ourselves though, does it," he said.

"No."

They both managed to smile again at one another. Sylvia let go of his hand and looked at her watch.

"Well," she said, "I suppose I ought to leave you be now that I've done what I came for. I don't want to intrude on your time."

"You're not," Daniel told her, "I'm mostly on my own here. My Tania comes in to see me when she can but I've not been good to her, especially recently. To be honest, I think I've lost her after all, just like I've lost Emma and Ray. My God, what a terrible father I must be."

"You're not a terrible father," Sylvia told him, "You never were. My God you loved Emma and Ray and I'm sure you love Tania too. You've always done your best for the children, Daniel, don't ever let anyone tell you you haven't."

"Tania told me."

Sylvia was momentarily lost for words.

"Well, it's not too late to iron out any problems. She lives nearby doesn't she?"

"Not for long. She's going to live in America."

"But she's not gone yet. Part of being a good parent is to

realise we're not perfect. We can make mistakes and we have to acknowledge them. Show her how much you love and care for her. You're still alive and she's still here. Talk to her."

"I'm struggling to work out what to say."

"Just start at the beginning. Write it down. You've got lots of time on your hands haven't you, you old codger."

Daniel managed a small chuckle.

"I'm learning to accept that's just what I am," he said, "An old man."

He looked back at Sylvia.

"What about you?" he asked.

"What about me?"

"You have Ray but is there anyone relationship-wise?"

Sylvia sighed.

"There was someone, is someone; was someone."

"Well that's not confusing."

She smiled.

"I mean there was someone who I met recently and who has made me happy but…I turned him away."

"Why?"

"Because he lied to me, about his age. Daniel, he's only fifty nine."

"Ooh a toy boy. Sylvia Burrows, I didn't know you had it in you."

"And that's what I'm worried about," she said, "People saying things like you just have."

"I was only joking."

"Yes, and that's what some of them will say too but it's not nice to hear."

Daniel tutted.

"Sylvia," he said, "You've just been berating me for not being open enough to tell you about my wearing a dress and yet now you're saying you've ended a relationship with someone who makes you happy, just because you're worried about what other people think."

"It's a small village, Daniel," Sylvia told him, "You know what it's like."

"Then move, if you want to. Or stay and tell the people that question your judgement to fuck off and mind their own business. It's your life not anyone else's. Your friends will be pleased to see you happy. If they're not, then they're not your friends. Come on Sylvia, we've both had enough heartache in our lives; too much. Surely if there's a chance of a bit of happiness then we should grasp it with both hands."

Sylvia patted his shoulder.

"What you say is right, of course. I don't know, I guess I feel a little embarrassed about it myself, the age difference."

"Alice was eleven years younger than me."

"Yes but it's different for a man isn't it. It shouldn't be, but it is. You marry a younger woman and people will say 'Good on him' whereas a woman marries a younger man and she's thought of as some ageing tart."

"Then tell this guy how you feel. You've told me to speak to my daughter, that works for you too. Talk to this man. Explain your feelings. Give it a chance. Jesus, we could both be dead tomorrow. Take a chance Sylvia. Live the life you want."

Sylvia had a lot to think about on the journey home. She was glad she'd visited Daniel, not just to hear his side of the story but because it was just nice to see him. It brought Emma closer to her than she'd been for a long time. She felt a kind of frustration at what had happened. Both she and Daniel had, just for once, not been able to help their daughter straightaway, leading to her disappearance. It all seemed so trivial, what they'd done, but the after effects were still being felt by both of them to this day.

Then there was Ken. Daniel was right, she was worried about what other people would think but she was also scared that she wouldn't be able to get over the age difference between them herself. Would she always be fearful of someone finding out Ken's age? Wouldn't that worry put a strain on whatever relationship they had? Perhaps she should do what Daniel suggested and tell Ken how she felt. That's if he still wanted to speak to her.

Still Missing

by Karen Taylor

Chapter 3 (first draft - amendments)

But what of those people who were, and still are, involved in the story of Emma Burrows. ~~How have the last thirty-nine years shaped them?~~ ~~Have they been able to move on or has the past remained with them always?~~ Do they pretend the past never happened to help them move on; staying away from the others involved in the story, not confiding in those people around them now? Is that even possible?

For the ~~family members~~ parents, Emma can't ever be far away in their thoughts. Sylvia and Daniel ~~are no longer together; their pain and suffering over the loss of their daughter too much to bear as a couple~~ divorced years ago. While Daniel married again and had another child, Sylvia has never escaped the past, choosing to remain in the same home that the family of four once shared with just her son, Ray for company. Back at home after a number of failed relationships he spends most of his time working in an insignificant supermarket in a quiet, neighbouring village.

But what of the other two remaining characters from this tragic story? ~~Are their lives still touched by the past?~~ ~~For~~ Caroline Willis, ~~she inevitably left~~ was forced to leave teaching behind her after being the person ~~many locals blamed~~ most people thought responsible for Emma's disappearance. She was, after all, the person in charge at the time and she'd abandoned her post. ~~It only took two minutes for the child to go missing but that was enough time.~~

Life ~~though, appears to have~~ has been ~~kind~~ exceptionally good to Caroline, who is married to a wealthy accountant in

Surrey. She now runs her own charity helping disadvantaged children, the guilt of the past ~~has stayed with~~ leaving her ~~spending her life~~ trying to help as many children as she can because ~~there was one she couldn't help~~ she failed to help one in the past with catastrophic results. ~~She may have money wealth and a great lifestyle, but has she found the peace she so obviously craves?~~

For Joey McGill, life surely ~~had~~ deserved to get brighter. Not only did he have to struggle with seeing the world blaming his brother for the abduction, within six months of the incident, both of his parents were dead, Sheila from spinal cancer and Tom from cirrhosis of the liver. His entire family were gone but there was no sympathy for him, not while Jimmy was thought of as guilty for one of the worst crimes most people can imagine; the abduction and murder of a child.

~~I wasn't surprised to discover that Joey had emigrated to Canada.~~ With nothing to keep him here except bitter memories, a fresh start in Canada was surely something he deserved but he's still ~~being~~ been touched by tragedy with the recent death of his wife from the same illness that took his mother.

For those involved there ~~must be~~ is a reluctance to talk about the situation but ~~surely~~ it should be faced ~~if there is more to tell~~. With so many unanswered questions about what went on ~~I can't see how any of the five people involved have been able to let the past truly rest~~ I believe there's more to this story than meets the eye.

Chapter 29

Accused

Naveena was happy to see Mike and to meet one of his sons. She talked about the old days when he used to visit the newsagents, laughing about how she'd fancied him as a young girl. There was no problem giving him Amrit's address in Basildon. She was sure he'd be happy to see his old friend again.

Mike was surprised to hear from Naveena that Amrit hadn't gone into property selling like he'd wanted to do all those years before (once his parents had finally accepted he wasn't going to be a doctor). He remembered his friend talking to him about it a lot, saying how more and more people were buying their own homes and that in the future, people would move from house to house as a way to make money, rather than just living in one place their whole lives. He'd been proved right but now it seemed he'd never taken advantage of the situation. Instead Amrit had become a court usher and had lived in the same home for years. It was quite the turnaround.

"Do you think Amrit could have left the flowers there," Eddie asked, as they drove along the A127 the day after the discovery, "It is almost the anniversary of Jimmy's death after all."

"No," Mike replied, "I spoke to him before I left Canada. He's terrified of anyone finding out the truth. He didn't even want me visiting him."

"Well this is going to be a fun reunion then."

Mike was silent a moment before confessing,

"I did tell someone about what happened."

"What? Well then why are we going to see an old friend who doesn't want to see you?" Eddie asked.

"Because it was my father I told…on his deathbed."

Eddie frowned.

"I thought you said your dad died with his mistress."

"He did. I went to visit him there. I was the only one who knew where she lived. I'd seen them together once while out driving."

"Why did you go and see him," Eddie asked, "I thought you hated him."

"My mum had just been told her cancer was terminal. I felt I ought to tell him. My God he'd probably caused it with all the stress and physical pain he'd given her over the years. I didn't want him back but, they were still husband and wife after all. I suppose I believed he had a right to know."

Mike sighed.

"When I got there Eileen told me he was really ill and that the doctor had just given him something to make him sleep. It was obvious she didn't want me seeing him but I insisted and eventually she showed me upstairs to the bedroom. I was surprised really. I know he'd told us he was dying but I thought that was just for attention. I assumed that was why he'd remained at Eileen's, because she gave him the attention he wasn't receiving at home."

He shrugged.

"I was just glad he'd stayed away. Mum and I had enough to deal with. Anyway, he was lying quite still in the bed. He could have been asleep or unconscious I couldn't tell. I sat there for a while, by his side but he didn't stir so I just started talking to him. I told him about mum and, before I knew it, I was telling him everything else that had occurred. I left nothing out."

"And what happened after?"

"Nothing. He never woke up so I just left. I didn't hear anything until I received the letter from Eileen just after mum had passed, telling me dad had died and asking for funeral money. The only person I told is dead and I don't even know if he heard me in the first place. Even if Eileen overheard she surely must be dead now too. She was as prolific a drinker as dad by all accounts. Amrit's the only other witness still alive. I guess he must have told someone. I need to find out who."

Mike was thankful for the SatNav in his hire car as soon as he pulled off of the A127. The Basildon he'd last visited didn't appear to exist anymore. He drove past retail estates full of large stores and restaurants, and then numerous new housing developments packed full of various-sized properties. Eventually the SatNav led him down a quieter road of what appeared to be ex-local authority homes. Amrit's maisonette looked the same as all the other brown-bricked terraces. The road itself was pleasant enough with trees growing along the pavements and each property having its own front garden, but Mike just felt that after almost forty years his old friend would have been somewhere…not exactly better, just different. Naveena said he'd been living here over thirty years but it seemed to be a place one ought to retire to, not move in when you were barely thirty.

Mike drove further along the street until he found a parking space that wasn't restricted for residents only. Walking back with Eddie he wondered if Amrit would be in. It was six o'clock in the evening. He may not be home from work yet. They walked up the path, past a neat lawn framed by a trimmed box hedge. He pressed the doorbell and waited. A few moments later the door opened.

The man was recognisable as Amrit but he'd changed a lot. Even at twenty he'd still retained his puppy fat but the man in front of Mike now, in his dark blue suit, was thin. His face was lined across his forehead and around his eyes. Coupled with his white hair he looked older than his sixty years. He didn't smile when he saw who was standing at his door, he just sighed.

"You couldn't help yourself could you."

While Mike hadn't been expecting fanfares and party poppers he was surprised by this resigned reaction.

"I suppose you'd better come in."

Amrit stood back and let Mike and Eddie walk past him into the cramped hallway. After closing the door he indicated with his eyes that the two of them should enter the front room. It was quite a large, square space but seemed smaller due to the clutter. A tattered-looking, brown cord sofa was pushed up against the longest wall facing the window where there was a dining table with one of its leaves folded down, a dining chair placed either side of it. Two armchairs, matching the sofa in both colour and age, appeared to have been squeezed in around various tables and display units. A TV too large for the room was stood on a mahogany stand beside a nineteen thirties, tiled fireplace. Mike sat down in one of the armchairs, Eddie took the sofa. Amrit greeted Mike's introduction of his son with a nod as he sat down in the other armchair facing his old friend.

"So, how long have you been here?" Amrit asked.

There was no offer of refreshments.

"Since Friday," Mike told him, "I came to visit mum's grave."

"What about the journalist?"

"I haven't heard back from her."

"Ah," Eddie said, "That might be my fault."

The other two men turned to him. Eddie looked sheepish.

"I told her we'd had a recent bereavement and to leave you alone. I'm afraid I was a bit abrupt with her and said **I'd** contact her when it was convenient again. Sorry dad, I meant to tell you that earlier."

Mike nodded to convey that it was alright. He returned his attention to Amrit.

"Who else knows what happened?" he asked.

"What do you mean? No one knows, apart from the two of us. Well, unless you've now blabbed to your family."

He indicated Eddie.

Using the word 'blabbed' made Mike feel angry. This was his story to tell to whomever he wanted. He wasn't spreading a bit of juicy, local gossip.

"Someone knows," he said, "And it hasn't come from me so it must be you. Come on, be honest."

Amrit looked puzzled.

"I don't know what you mean," he replied, "I haven't told anyone. Why would I? You know this scares me. I didn't even want you here. I work in the legal profession for goodness sake and I don't want this messing up my pension. I'm relying on that money for my old age."

"I'm so sorry I'm interfering with your 'career,'" Mike told him, sarcastically, "A court usher, doesn't that mean you just ensure the jury are sitting in their correct seats?"

Amrit snorted.

"Still the same old Joey," he said, "You still think you're a cut above the rest of us don't you. I didn't realise tightening nuts on car engines was the loftier career choice."

Mike stood up.

"And what do you mean by that," he demanded, "My God if it wasn't for me you'd have been beaten black and blue by every kid in school."

"And don't you always let me know about that. Jesus Christ Joey, we're both sixty years old but you're still in the playground."

"What's that supposed to mean?"

Amrit stood up as well.

"It means you still think of yourself as the boy you were in senior school, trying to control the other kids because you thought only you knew best and everyone had to be like you."

"So you'd rather I'd have let the other boys punch you?"

"Of course not but you seemed to think beating up the other kids and bossing them around still made you popular but really, who ever came to your house besides me?"

"Well," Mike began, suddenly flustered, "That's because of my dad's drinking and because people didn't understand Jimmy."

Amrit shook his head.

"Like hell it was. You didn't have any other friends besides me and even then I had to always be grateful to you. When were you ever grateful to me? I was the only person stopping you from being lonely but you never saw that. No one cared about your dad or your brother, they just didn't give a shit about you."

Mike stepped forwards but before he could do anything, Eddie was up and standing between the two men.

"Come on guys, listen to yourselves," he told them, "You're both sounding like a couple of kids. What are you doing, picking up where you left off? There's more important stuff to talk about."

Mike glared angrily at Amrit for a second more before sitting back down again. Amrit followed suit.

"That's better," Eddie said, returning to his seat, "Now come on dad, tell Amrit why you're here."

Mike took a deep breath.

"We went to visit Jimmy's grave yesterday," he told his old friend.

Amrit shivered.

"I can't go anywhere near the place," he said, "I don't ever travel along that road."

"I found it easily enough, even though there's just a small part of the old wall left. It looks like a rock, as Eddie said when we got there."

Mike took a beat before adding,

"There was a bouquet of flowers on the ground."

Amrit frowned.

"What do you mean?" he asked.

"I mean there was a bunch of flowers lying right where Jimmy is buried, like someone was remembering him. Now it wasn't us and it obviously wasn't you, so who left it there?"

Amrit looked thoughtful for a moment.

"I don't understand," he said, "I've never said anything to anyone."

"Well you must have said or done something to make someone realise," Mike told him, feeling frustrated, "It wasn't me. I was on the other side of the Atlantic not even telling my family. You were here. It has to be you."

"Well it wasn't!"

"Oh come on, who else could it be," Mike shouted, "For God's sake, try putting your brain in gear and start thinking."

"Dad!" Eddie said, but Mike ignored him.

Amrit was looking daggers.

"You'd better watch yourself Joey McGill," he whispered, coldly, "You think you know everything but you don't."

"Well what don't I know then? You've told me I was

unpopular, you've said I try and control you, you've explained I was the worst friend to you; what else is there for you to accuse me of?"

"Look, just because you're scared that doesn't give you the right to take your anger out on me," Amrit told him, "You think I don't know what being scared is?"

Mike snorted.

"Oh I know you know what scared is, hiding in the school toilets from the girl you were too afraid to ask out, not telling your parents that you struggled with the tutoring lessons they were paying out for because you feared your dad's wrath, almost wetting yourself when that dog jumped up at you outside the shop."

Amrit tutted.

"Every one of those examples is from when we were kids," he said, "Have you completely forgotten the four years after we left school? Have you forgotten me passing my driving test before you because you were too nervous to pass on your first attempt? Have you forgotten the time I fended off that crazed junkie in the shop when I was covering the late night shift? Have you forgotten that I put myself in a position where I could have been arrested because I helped you hide your brother after that girl went missing?"

"Of course I haven't forgotten," Mike spat.

Amrit shook his head and sighed as he pictured the past in his mind.

"You know, I sometimes wonder if you actually realise what I risked for you over those few days. I could have gone to prison for aiding and abetting a criminal."

"Jimmy wasn't a criminal."

"I was talking about you! You were the one hiding him whether he was guilty or not. Even innocent, the police would have needed to talk to Jimmy. You were obstructing police enquiries and I was helping you do it."

"And I thanked you for it."

"No you didn't."

It was Mike's turn to frown.

"What?"

"You never thanked me," Amrit told him, "You phoned me that day and I came running. I helped you hide your brother and then I helped you look after him until...Look, I knew you were grateful but you never actually thanked me. You just fucked off to Canada without a look back."

Mike stood up again.

"I did have other things on my mind," he shouted, "Like the deaths of my entire family. Sorry if that got in the way of me saying thank you to you. How about I do it now. Thank you."

Amrit tutted again.

"You're pathetic," he said.

"You can talk," Mike replied, looking around him, "Living in this dump with no partner or kids; who's pathetic now?"

Amrit stood up and was in Mike's face before Eddie could move.

"And who's fault is that," he snarled, "I helped you at your worst time and you repaid me by fucking off and leaving me. What was I meant to do? You talk about being left alone and not telling your Canadian family about the past, well boo hoo. At least you had a family. I was petrified of what I'd done and I had no one to confide in. I was so terrified it would all come out, that Jimmy's remains would be found, that I'd be blamed because you'd escaped the country. I hid myself away in a safe job in the legal profession, not going for promotion or anything like that so that I could remain hidden under the radar. I kept myself to myself. I couldn't let anyone get too close in case they got caught up in the fallout when it happened."

"Well that is pathetic," Mike said.

"Dad!"

"Well it is! It wasn't his fault, it was mine. If it had come out, I would have been to blame and probably brought back to this country to face charges. He had nothing to worry about."

"You don't know what it was like back then," Amrit told him, the anger now gone from his voice, "The rumours and the gossip continued long after you'd left the area. When you emigrated there were no McGill's left, just Joey's best friend. I moved out here but every time I returned to Great Tenwick to visit mum and dad and the rest of the family there was always someone in the shop who wanted to bring the past back to life, asking me all sorts of questions as if I knew all of the McGill family secrets. I was petrified I'd say the wrong thing. You went three thousand miles away. I couldn't do that. I had to escape the best way I could, by hiding here in this shit hole of a house."

Amrit turned away and looked out of the window. Mike sat down again, feeling sheepish. Nobody spoke.

"Look I'm sorry," Mike eventually said, "I didn't realise I'd left you in such a mess."

He saw his friend's shoulders sag. Amrit turned and waved his hand dismissively.

"It's fine," he said, "It's not really your fault. I've made my own decisions in life. Not all of them have been right."

He let out a long sigh.

"Perhaps I deserve everything I've received," he admitted to them, before turning to face the window again.

"Don't say that," Mike replied, feeling empathy towards his old friend, "All you've done is help. I'm the guilty one. I'm the only one that should have suffered."

"You're being too hard on yourself."

"No I'm not. You're right. I always thought I knew best and I've always tried to control everything but that's just because mum and Jimmy needed help. One of us in that family needed to be the strong one and I stepped up, but I ruined everything."

"Stop it Joey," Amrit said, his voice cracking.

Mike didn't seem to hear, too wrapped up in his own thoughts.

"I tried to help mum and I tried to save Jimmy but I messed it all up as usual. I made Jimmy look guilty and mum suffered so much that she went to an early grave."

"Please don't say anymore."

"I killed Jimmy."

"No you didn't."

"I did. I might just as well have struck him down myself."

Amrit span round.

"Oh for God's sake stop trying to control the blame as well," he shouted, startling both Mike and Eddie.

They stared up at him.

"You didn't kill Jimmy, she did!"

The whole atmosphere in the room changed; the temperature dropped, leaving an icy coldness that permeated throughout the space and wrapped itself around the three men. Mike and Eddie both shivered. Amrit had his hands across his mouth, like he was trying to stop another word from ever passing his lips again. His eyes filled with tears and when Mike stood up, his gaze followed him fearfully.

"What did you say," Mike asked, in a harsh whisper.

The room still felt so cold that he was surprised he couldn't see his own breath.

Amrit shook his head. He didn't move at all as Mike

grabbed him by the lapels of his suit jacket. Eddie got to his feet too.

"Tell me," Mike said.

Amrit's hands dropped from his mouth but he remained silent.

Mike shook him.

"Tell me!"

"Dad!"

Eddie grabbed hold of his father.

"You're not going to hear anything if you shake him like that."

Mike let go but didn't step away. Amrit's tears began to slowly course down his cheeks.

"Please don't make me say anymore," he whispered.

"Talk," Mike ordered, "Who is 'she?'"

Amrit bit his bottom lip before blurting out,

"Your mother. She knew what happened. She killed Jimmy."

A look of horror appeared on Mike's face as those words sunk in. His whole body filled with emotion, a rage for the events of thirty-nine years ago and for all the years of silence that followed. He couldn't really see clearly but he pulled back his fist and let fly with all the force he could muster. It was only Eddie's knocking him off balance that stopped him punching his old friend full in the face and probably breaking his nose as well as knocking him out. His fist still caught the edge of Amrit's left cheek which was hard enough to send the man spinning into the dining table behind him, the glass vase full of flowers on top of it crashing to the floor and shattering into pieces.

The fight left Mike instantly and he collapsed down onto the sofa. Eddie moved across to Amrit to see if he was alright and, checking that his father wasn't about to strike out again, left the room and returned with a cloth soaked in cold water, which he held gently to Amrit's face after helping him back into his armchair. After a moment Amrit took hold of the cloth himself and Eddie sat down on the sofa beside his father.

"I'm sorry," Amrit said, "I never wanted to have to tell you that. But you made me."

"What happened?" Mike asked.

He was staring at his hands, mainly at his right where his knuckles were red.

"Your mum was beside herself with worry," Amrit began, "Well, you knew that. I tried to pop in when I could during the day while you were at work. I thought I was doing the right thing. She was so upset. She showed it more to me than you. She didn't want you fretting about her."

He took a breath.

"I told her that Jimmy was safe, that you were looking after him. I thought her knowing you were handling the situation would calm her down, but it just made things worse. She was anything but calm, wanting to be taken to see Jimmy there and then. She wouldn't let me leave until I promised to take her. You were working late that night so we went then. As I drove there I started to believe that this was for the best, that it would be good for the two of them to see each other. It was the biggest mistake of my life."

He turned the damp cloth over and pressed the colder side against his face.

"She laid into Jimmy as soon as she saw him. I was shocked. I mean, your mum had been adamant about his innocence, declaring it to the police, the press and anyone else she saw whenever she was forced to venture out of the house, but she got hold of Jimmy that night and started asking where the little girl was and what he'd done to her."

"That doesn't sound like mum," Mike said.

"Tell me," Amrit replied, "I don't think she really believed it but there'd been so much talk in the village. I think she just wanted the whole situation settled so that she could bring him back home again. She was desperate for information, to know what had happened, but Jimmy couldn't tell her because he hadn't done anything."

Mike looked up. Amrit met his eye.

"We both knew by then, didn't we," he said, "That we'd got it wrong at the start."

"That I'd got it wrong," Mike admitted, "It wasn't you."

Amrit acknowledged the statement with a nod. He continued.

"Well, poor Jimmy couldn't understand why his mum was acting the way she was. You know what he was like with interpreting emotions. She was pulling at him and hit him around the head a couple of times. I was still in shock and rooted to the spot. I didn't know what to do. The next moment, to try and stop her I suppose, Jimmy pushed his mum away. He was strong and the push was hard. She fell backwards and hit the base of her spine against one of those large pieces of stone that had fallen out of the wall. I knew it had hurt her when she cried out."

A tear slipped down Mike's face. He wiped it and sniffed.

"So that was why she could no longer hide her back pain from me," he whispered, more to himself.

"Jimmy was even more distraught then," Amrit continued, "He could see his mother was hurt. He came towards her. He was still tied up but at that moment, Sheila was angry and scared. Without thinking she grabbed a piece of metal chain that was by her left hand and lashed out with it."

Amrit winced at the image in his mind.

"She was left-handed anyway, wasn't she," he said, "It was a heavy blow. Jimmy fell to his knees. I'll never forget that expression of puzzlement as he turned his head to face me. It was barely a moment but it seemed to happen in slow motion. His upper body fell forwards and crashed to the floor. He was dead."

Amrit pulled a handkerchief out of his pocket and blew his nose.

"It was awful. Your mum was grief stricken, throwing herself on top of her son and sobbing. She didn't want you to find out. She kept saying, 'Joey mustn't know. He'll blame himself.' I had to take charge of the situation. I moved the body and tried my best to make it look like an accident, like he'd tripped and hit his head on one of those iron railings that were strewn about the place. Then I had to drive your mum home and wait until the morning when I insisted on accompanying you on your visit to the barn. I couldn't let you find him on your own. I just hoped I'd done enough to make it look like an accident, that it was no one's fault."

Amrit got off the sofa and crouched down in front of Mike.

"But I failed," he whispered, "You still blamed yourself and I couldn't do anything to change that. I'm so sorry."

Mike looked back at his friend.

"Why didn't you tell me all this after mum died?"

"You wouldn't have wanted to hear that then. My God you've just hit me thirty-nine years later. Back then you'd have probably killed me. Besides, Sheila didn't want you to know. I wasn't able to prevent her or Jimmy from dying but I could honour that wish. You were heading off to Canada to start a new life. What was the point in telling you and risking you thinking differently about your mother? It was my secret to keep."

Suddenly Mike reached forward and took his friend into a hug.

"I'm sorry," he said, sounding muffled with his mouth against Amrit's suit-jacketed shoulder, "This has affected your life as much as mine. But it is all my fault. I shouldn't have involved you."

They parted. Amrit smiled, sadly.

"No," he replied, "It was my decision to help, my decision to tell your mum and take her to see Jimmy, my decision to try and hide what happened. You've nothing to blame yourself for. You're not a murderer Joey McGill. You did your best for your family and for your friend. You always did that and I'm sure you still do."

Amrit gave another long, drawn-out sigh.

"It was a tragic accident," he said, "It was all such a sad, tragic accident."

Chapter 30

Mother

Sylvia lay back against the pillow. She turned her head to the left and smiled at the man staring back at her. Ken leaned in and kissed her, tenderly. Their talk had gone well.

Things hadn't quite gone as she'd planned though. Upon phoning Ken after her return from Stow on the Wold, she'd discovered he was at the hospital where his mother, after a massive stroke, was not expected to last the night. She went up and sat with him until the old lady passed away in the early hours of Wednesday morning.

She'd held him afterwards as he cried but there was nothing more than that. She'd stayed with him the whole of Wednesday as well, for the first time not worrying about her son's work schedule. Besides, Ray had come home in a foul mood on Tuesday and it hadn't seemed to dissipate each time she phoned him to say she was still with her friend who needed her.

Thursday morning she and Ken had finally talked about their relationship.

"I understand why you might feel embarrassed," he'd replied, after she'd told him her concerns, "I would probably be ribbed at work about being with an older woman. But I wouldn't care because I know how special you are to me."

"I'm scared I'll still care too much about the age thing," Sylvia had admitted, "I don't want us splitting up further down the line when it will be harder to part."

"Sylvia," Ken had said, "We don't know what's in the

future. Perhaps I'll live as long as mum, perhaps I'll go before you, I don't know. We can't change my being younger or you being older, and we can't change falling in love with one another. What we can control is not living our lives full of 'if only's.'"

It was at that point, realising she'd said a similar thing to Daniel, that Sylvia had decided to give things a try with Ken. Right now, lying back in his bed, early Friday morning, she was glad she'd made that decision. She'd told Ray she was still staying with a friend after returning home briefly the day before to pick up some more clothes, but his concern had only been for his stomach and he'd complained about having to fend for himself. For the first time Sylvia had felt riled, telling him, quite forcefully, to either cook himself something from whatever was in the freezer or to bring something home from the supermarket. She realised she'd been doing too much for him this past year. Perhaps she always had.

Lying in bed with Ken, Sylvia was in no rush to get up.

"What are you thinking about?" he asked her.

"I was just thinking about Ray," she told him, "I've thought it before but now I definitely think it's time he stood on his own two feet again."

"Well of course he should. You shouldn't feel guilty about that. He's not a young child anymore."

"That's why I feel guilty. I'm worried I've treated him that way ever since Emma was taken. I wonder if I overcompensated because I was thinking a lot about Emma at that time. He was hurting too, I know that and perhaps I began treating him the way I'd treated Emma, as a five year old."

"You can't blame yourself for that," Ken told her, gently stroking her upper arm with the backs of his fingers, "He's had almost forty years to become the person he wants to be. He's been married hasn't he? He's an adult and, from what you've told me, seems happy with his life. That's got to be down to you."

Sylvia smiled.

"I want you to meet him," she said, "I want him to know about you."

"I want that too. It's a shame we didn't think to invite him to the lunch today."

"I'm looking forward to meeting your Uncle."

Ken looked sheepish.

"I was originally going to refer to him as my cousin before you found out my true age," he admitted, "Not that Uncle Gilt is that much older than me anyway. He was my father's youngest brother. He's only in his late sixties."

"So young," Sylvia teased.

They both grinned.

"I'm not sure I can refer to him as Uncle Gilt though," she said.

Ken laughed.

"You can call him by his real first name," he told her, "It's really only the family that call him Gilt because his initials are G.O.L.D."

Sylvia reached for her blouse from the chair beside the bed.

"Didn't his parents realise that when they named him?" she asked.

"I expect so," Ken replied, "But they wanted to name him after both his grandfathers. I suppose GOLD is better than GLOD."

*

Sitting at a table in a pleasant pub in Battlesbridge, Sylvia couldn't remember the last time she felt this happy. Ken's Uncle had been absolutely charming from the moment he picked both of them up in his rather nice Jaguar. He had no problem with her and his nephew dating and was just happy because they were.

It gave Sylvia hope for the future. While she knew there would be talk about her and Ken she remembered what Daniel had told her, those people that couldn't understand or accept the relationship didn't matter. It was her friends and family that mattered and she was sure they would love seeing her so happy.

Ken's Uncle had told her to call him Gilt and, sitting at the table enjoying dessert, Sylvia found now that it tripped off the tongue quite easily.

"So how many people come to your church on a Sunday," Gilt asked her.

Sylvia felt like all they'd done was talk about her today.

"It's usually pretty full," she told him, "At least two thirds. Never less than that."

"Well that's very good in this day and age."

"Well it is only a small church but we're getting people coming from further afield, like my friend Kerry. She says she doesn't like the vicar at her parish and it seems she's not alone. I'm not sure why. I've never met the man. I'm glad that they like to come to our church with our lady vicar though. I think it's important that religion and the church continue to evolve like everything else does."

"I totally agree with you Sylvia," Gilt said, patting her hand, "Opinions and values change. We can't live in the past."

Sylvia smiled. Uncle Gilt was such a nice man. He'd managed to put her at her ease as soon as they'd met and he listened intently to whatever she had to say before replying. Not everyone did that. Some people seemed only to be interested in their own opinions, rarely listening to anybody else and always interrupting during a conversation.

When coffee was brought up the talk turned to family as Ken told his Uncle about the arrangements he was planning for his mother's funeral.

"Do you have a big family, Sylvia," Gilt asked, after Ken had finished.

"Not really," she told him, "There are some cousins still alive around the country but we really only keep in touch at Christmas. No it's only my son, Ray and me really. Ken hasn't met him yet but I really must arrange something to rectify that. He works so many hours though at the supermarket."

"Which supermarket is that?" Gilt asked.

"The little one in Great Tenwick."

"Oh I know it well. We'll be passing right by there when I take you home. How about we drop in to say a quick hello."

"Oh," Sylvia said, "I hadn't really thought about that. I…"

She stopped as she realised she was automatically trying to find an excuse not to. That was wrong. That was her old way of thinking. She looked across at Ken who smiled back at her.

"Yes," she said, "Why not. I'm sure Ray won't mind. He can afford to take five minutes out of his day."

Sylvia felt good about the decision. She wanted her son to know about Ken and the sooner the better. Ray might take a little while to get used to the idea of her being in a relationship but she felt sure he would come around. It might help him see that he needed to move on with his own life as well. As she got back into Gilt's car after the meal Sylvia felt positive and contented. Life was moving forward for her and she was going to enjoy it.

Chapter 31

Brother

Ray was in a bad mood. He'd been in one since he'd left Caroline's office on Tuesday. How dare she speak to him the way she had. She certainly wasn't someone Ray wanted to be associated with.

No class, he'd told himself, nouveau riche on her husband's money.

Of course he blamed Emma. It was talking about her that had caused the tension between him and Caroline in her office in the first place. When was that little bitch going to stop ruining his life?

Sylvia was also to blame for his mood as well, as far as he was concerned. Why was she suddenly sounding so bright and bubbly after being tearful only a few days before? And what was all this staying out all night business with a friend, not giving him any consideration whatsoever? Was it really too much to ask for her to at least prepare some sort of dinner for him before she took herself off for the night? It's not like she had a job to go to so she wasn't busy, like him.

I might as well have stayed with Jackie, he thought to himself, sulkily.

He hated being in a mood like this, especially as Elizabeth Chan was due any minute. He liked to be calm and reasonable when she was here as he knew it really pissed her off. It was half past one and she'd told him she was coming at three but she always showed up early. He was ready for her, although the morning hadn't been without its drama with staffing issues. Two part-timers hadn't shown up for their shift. Carmel, his second in command had taken the phone calls when she arrived.

"Well what did they say?" Ray had asked, once he'd arrived.

Carmel had replied calmly, used to Ray's ways.

"Ted's ill with a bug and Janine isn't coming back."

"Well that's a bloody cheek," he'd said, "She ought to work her notice period."

"She hasn't finished probation yet. She can leave when she wants."

Ray had tutted, hating it when Carmel was right.

"I knew there was something wrong about her when I interviewed her for the role. I'm glad my instincts have been proved right. Well, we'd best get someone else in to cover. I want the area manager to see a well-oiled ship."

"I've already done that," Carmel had told him, "Bobbi is on her way."

"Bobbi? Oh Carmel, couldn't you have done better than that?"

"She was the only one available at short notice. She's a good worker and the customers like her."

"Yes but she sounds so common, hardly a good image for Elizabeth Chan to see."

Carmel had rolled her eyes and got on with getting the tills ready. Ray had retreated to his office where he'd sat for the rest of the morning, slowly seething as he thought about all of these damn annoying women in his life that caused him such grief.

He sat back in his chair now, his pencil plans for the expansion into the newsagents next door on the wall behind him. That was another reason to be angry. Ray hadn't been able to get the stupid computer to do what he wanted. He definitely needed to bring that up with Elizabeth. It was her responsibility as area manger to keep all of her stores up-to-date, technology-wise, and she was obviously slacking.

Karen Taylor was annoying him too. He'd heard nothing from her since their initial meeting, despite sending her several emails. Having explained his mother didn't want to speak to her, surely he was the one person she ought to be in regular contact with. After his visit to the sensory centre on Tuesday Ray was ready to tell the journalist a few home truths about Caroline Metcalf. Why hadn't Karen contacted him though? What sort of journalist was she? Didn't she want to get the whole story, well the whole story as he saw it? Was she disorganised or just crap at her job? Ray sighed. Another bloody woman messing with his life.

He got up and walked out onto the shop floor in readiness for Elizabeth. She stomped in fifteen minutes later on her stilettos, her long, black hair bouncing from side to side with each step, her brow furrowed.

"It's such a bugger to park an SUV out there," she said, as she walked straight past Ray into his office.

Well get a smaller company car then you stupid bitch, is what Ray didn't say out loud.

"We only have the few parking bays out the front," he told her, "But most people manage. Of course we could increase those if we expanded."

He stood beside his desk and tried to surreptitiously indicate his pencil plans with his head but Elizabeth was looking into her briefcase, ignoring him.

"There's been a lot of new properties built around here," he continued, "Which means more people and traffic. Still, that's good for us."

"Is it?"

Ray was surprised by the response.

"Well of course, it's obvious, isn't it?"

He realised that sentence sounded a little degrading. Elizabeth looked up at him and raised an eyebrow.

"I mean more residents means more customers," Ray added.

"Only if you actually bother to attract them in," she replied.

Ray smiled.

"Oh they come in," he said, loftily, "We're the only store around."

Elizabeth tutted.

"It doesn't look like it judging by your sales."

"Well obviously it takes a little time to develop a customer bond," he told her, moving behind his chair, "But it would help if we were a little larger. That's why I've been looking into expansion."

"That's funny, so have we," she replied.

Ray beamed.

"I'm so glad we're on the same page."

He stood aside and indicated his pencil drawings on the wall, proudly.

"What the hell is that," Elizabeth said, squinting at the pieces of paper from her side of the table, "Did some six year old kid do you a drawing?"

Ray's smile faltered.

"It's my plans for expansion," he told her, shocked she hadn't realised, "It's my ideas for knocking through into the newsagents next door."

Elizabeth blew a raspberry.

"You don't have to bother with any of that old shit," she told him, "We have bigger plans than that."

"Oh really," Ray said, sitting down in his chair, trying to look professionally interested in hearing what head office had to say.

"Yes," Elizabeth replied, returning to fiddling inside her briefcase, "The local council has finally given the go ahead for a large supermarket to be built up the road on a new retail park and we're opening a new branch there."

"Wonderful," Ray said, holding out his hands, "Have you got the plans in there?"

Elizabeth stopped rummaging and looked across at Ray, an amused expression on her face.

"Of course not," she said, "I was looking for a mint humbug. **I've** only seen the plans once. You think anyone would show you?"

"Well surely if it's going to be my new branch I ought to see it."

Elizabeth burst out laughing.

"Oh my God," she said, "You don't think for one minute I'd let you anywhere near our latest flagship branch do you?"

Ray frowned.

"So you mean you're going to keep this one open?"

"No of course not. What would be the point of that? No, we're already in talks with the people who are going to buy the newsagents next door. They want to expand into here and have a small grocery section and post office."

"What?"

Ray was confused.

"Naveena didn't tell me about that."

"I'm shocked," Elizabeth told him.

"But what about me," he asked, realising he sounded pathetic, "What am I going to be doing?"

His area manager shrugged.

"You can take a lesser role at the new place, or there might be the chance of early retirement or redundancy."

"But I don't want to retire, not yet. Why on earth aren't you giving me the new store? I've worked here all my life."

Elizabeth sighed as she sat up straight in the chair and gave him her full attention.

"That's the reason," she told him, "You've spent your entire working life in this one place."

She indicated around her with a repulsed look on her face.

"You have no experience of running a store the size of the new one. You're not used to change and you've only ever had to manage a handful of part-time staff at any one time. A vast store is a lot different to running one of these minimarts. Any of our managers could run one of these."

She stopped speaking as she noticed Ray just staring at her. He was obviously gritting his teeth and his head was shaking ever so slightly, like he had a tremor.

"What?" she asked him.

"How dare you," he hissed.

"I'm sorry?"

"How dare you speak to me like that," he said, his voice rising.

He stood up.

"Who the hell do you think you are?"

Elizabeth's brow furrowed again.

"I'm your boss," she told him.

Ray snorted.

"Boss," he said, almost spitting the word out, "Yes of course you are. You turn up once a quarter if you feel like it. That's not a boss, that's called a cushy, little number. I'm a boss. I run a tight ship, I take care of my staff, I take care of my customers. I look at the bigger picture. What do you do?"

"I suggest you shut up now," Elizabeth told him, "Don't give me a reason to have you fired before you could retire."

Ray laughed out loud.

"Don't threaten me, missy," he told her, "I know you don't like me. You'd have had me out years ago if you could but you know I'm too clever for you. You know that I'm the best at what I do."

It was Elizabeth's turn to laugh.

"What you do," she told him, "Is the same job you've done for thirty years since you were made manager here. You work in a teeny, weeny shop in the back of beyond. We've got managers out there earning a hell of a lot more than we pay you. They've got huge numbers of staff under them. Their stores make thousands and thousands of pounds each day. They rearrange stock, run promotions, take care of large budgets, analyse the local market to see what works best. What do you do? I'll tell you what you do, you open the door in the morning, sell a few groceries and then close it at the end of the day."

She shook her head.

"You really think you're some kind of big fish in a small pond don't you," she said, "Honestly Ray, take a look around you. Look at the peeling paint on the ceiling of this cupboard you call an office. Do you think that if you were so highly thought of we'd have let this store start to decay? We've been trying to get this new supermarket deal sorted for ages. It was only a matter of time until this place closed and the old nag that runs it put out to pasture."

Ray leaned forward across the desk.

"I don't have to stand here and take that from you. I'm about to become a member of the local parish council. I'll be able to get those plans changed, give the contract to a competitor. That won't look so good for you then will it. Now, you can get on with whatever it is you do here every quarter, none of us are quite sure what that is; I'm going out to ensure **my** store is still running perfectly as I do each day. Then I'm going to ring head office and go over your head about all this and tell them how you've just insulted me. Then we'll find out who's an old nag and who's the jumped up little tart."

Elizabeth sniffed, unconcerned.

"You do that," she told him, finally locating her sweet in her briefcase and unwrapping it.

Ray was livid as he stepped out onto the main floor. How dare she speak to him like that. Who did she think she was? She was barely even forty. What did she really know about running a successful store, or about life in general?

He hadn't planned on coming out to check the shop, he just needed to get out of the claustrophobic office and away from Elizabeth. As Ray walked down the central aisle towards the tills, Sylvia stepped out in front of him, beaming.

"Not now mother," Ray said.

She touched his arm.

"Hang on Ray, I only want a moment."

"What!"

Sylvia took a step back, confused by her son's anger. She indicated a tall, older man beside her who was also looking confused.

"Who's this?" Ray asked.

"This is Ken," his mother told him, "He's become a very good friend of mine and I wanted you to meet him."

Ray sighed.

"Really mother this isn't the time to introduce me to yet another of your little church friends. I've got a lot on."

"Ken isn't a church friend. Actually he's not really a friend. He's much more than that."

Ken held out his hand.

"I'm very pleased to finally meet you," he said.

Ray stared down at the outstretched hand, slowly taking in

what his mother had just told him.

"Oh my God," he said, looking up, still not shaking Ken's hand, "Are you telling me what I think you're telling me?"

"What do you mean?" Sylvia asked.

"You're telling me that you've got a boyfriend at your age?"

Ken put his hand down and Sylvia gently took hold of it.

"Yes," she said, "We met at the retirement home a few months back and we've become close."

Ray glanced at Ken before returning his gaze to his mother.

"Is he a resident?" he asked.

"No of course he isn't a resident," Sylvia snapped, angry now, "He's only…he's only fifty nine."

Ray's eyes widened.

"Oh my God," he said, dramatically throwing his head into his hands, "This is really all I need today. My job is in jeopardy, I'm surrounded by idiots and now my mother is making a fool of herself with some gigolo."

"Now just a minute son," Ken said.

Ray's head shot up.

"Don't you call me that," he hissed at him, "Don't you ever call me that."

"I didn't mean it like…"

"Not even my father gets to call me that anymore, only her, and even then that ought to be a privilege. She's not exactly been a great mother to me over the years."

"Ray, how can you say that?"

Tears had formed in Sylvia's eyes and were starting to slowly run down her face.

"What's wrong with you?" she whispered.

Ray was unmoved.

"Any decent mother would see when she'd hurt her son but not you, no never you. And the worst thing is you still don't have a clue do you?"

A small crowd of half a dozen people had gathered round them, all eyes on Ray. Sylvia buried her face in Ken's shoulder. He placed a protective arm around her.

"You stopped being a mother to me the day you brought that crying, little shit home from the hospital."

There were several gasps in the crowd. Sylvia lifted her head up and looked across at her son, tears rolling over her cheeks.

"I don't understand Ray. Are you talking about my Emma?"

Ray snorted.

"Exactly," he said, "**Your** Emma, your precious bundle of joy, your little miracle, your special child. What was I mother? What the fuck happened to me when she came along? I'll tell you. I ceased to exist. You stopped loving me."

"That's not true. I've always loved you. Emma needed more help. She was a baby, Ray. You were grown up."

"I was ten years old and I needed you, you stupid bitch!"

Ken stepped forwards.

"Hey now, watch your mouth."

Ray looked at him.

"And you can stay out of it," he shouted at him, "You know nothing, nothing about my life."

"Is everything okay in here?" a voice called.

Through the crowd walked Geoffrey Delaney.

"Oh Mr Delaney, it's you," Ray smiled, his anger subsiding.

Instantly he was in 'good impression' mode.

"This is nothing, just an issue with a couple of customers."

Geoffrey ignored him.

"Are you okay Ken? Sorry, it took me a few minutes to find a parking space. Sylvia what's wrong?"

Ray's mouth dropped open.

"You know my mother?" he asked.

For the first time, Geoffrey looked at him.

"We just had lunch together," he said, "My nephew here wanted us all to meet."

"Your nephew?"

Ray was confused and for the first time, noticed the crowd that had formed around them. Mrs Dunwoody was grinning from ear to ear, listening to every word. Elizabeth was stood beside her, obviously relishing the scene which just brought Ray's anger back. He'd show her though. Here in front of him was his saviour, the chairman of the parish council. He'd be able to show that woman exactly how much he was thought of around here.

"We just came in and this guy has been nothing but rude to his mother, Gilt," Ken announced.

"Oh well," Ray began, flustered, "Really, I've just had a couple of shocks and then…why did he call you Gilt?"

Geoffrey sighed.

"It's because of my initials," he said, "Geoffrey Owen Lionel Delaney."

"I'm sorry Gilt," Sylvia said, wiping her eyes, "Ray usually isn't like this."

"You call him Gilt too?"

Ray could feel the situation getting away from him. He gave Geoffrey one of his best smiles.

"Look Mr Delaney, this is all just a misunderstanding. I'm sure you won't allow this to colour your opinion of my joining the parish council."

Geoffrey let out a half snort, half laugh.

"Your what?"

"Well, I am being considered for the causal vacancy aren't I?"

Geoffrey frowned.

"Oh my," he said, "Of course you're not. What made you think you were?"

Ray was taken aback.

"Because I've been ingratiating myself with all of the members," he said, "I've been telling you how much I want to help the community and showing you everything that I've achieved here."

"Is that what you've been doing," Geoffrey said, "Look I'm sorry Roy but we need someone on the council who knows about the community, who has already done a lot to help it and who wants to continue to help it for the good of everyone, not themselves."

"And isn't that me?"

Geoffrey smirked.

"A village shop should be the heart of the community," he told him, "But this place is like a morgue whenever I come in. You could have made so much more of it, involving the shop in local projects and events. I've never even see an advert for it in the local newspaper."

"We don't need to advertise, we're the only store around here."

"And yet most local residents prefer to drive elsewhere for their groceries. Putting the shop aside, have you ever once volunteered your own time or services to help the needy in the community? Have you ever volunteered to help out at one of our charity events?"

"Well no but surely the parish council has other more important things to consider than charity, like running the town."

Geoffrey sighed.

"If you'd ever bothered to come to one of our meetings,

which are open to members of the public, you'd have a better idea of all the things we do. It's not about power or social standing."

He looked about the shop.

"Although why you think this place gives you social standing I don't know."

He looked back at Ray.

"You are not being considered to join the parish council and never will be. You are not the sort of person we need on there."

Ray couldn't believe what was happening. It all had to be a bad dream. He'd wake up in a minute, back in the real world where he was a well-respected member of the community, admired for his work ethic in his safe and secure job, and still with the chance of becoming a member of the parish council.

He closed his eyes and opened them again and realised he was still standing in the middle of his nightmare. All eyes were on him but for once, Ray didn't want to be noticed. He looked around the room at the expressions of shock or disgust. Elizabeth wore a self-satisfied smile. He'd just played into her hands and given her enough rope to hang him with. Geoffrey's countenance was that of a man looking at a nasty rash he'd just discovered. His mother was the only person not looking at him.

"This is all your fault," he spat at her, "You've ruined everything for me yet again."

"Hey," Geoffrey said, "No one has done this except you."

Ray ignored him and pointed at his mother before addressing the room.

"This woman," he said, "Abandoned me when I was ten years old. She lavished all her love and attention onto a screaming, spoilt, little gobshite. I was forgotten. It took the disappearance of Emma and my staying around doing everything for my mother to get her to notice me again."

"That is not true Ray and you know it," Sylvia shouted at him, wiping her nose with a tissue, "I've always loved you and been there for you. My goodness, you're back living in my house where I cook and look after you. I do it because I love you and because I don't want you to be lonely."

Ray laughed.

"Me lonely," he replied, "What makes you think I'm lonely?"

"Well, you never mention any friends or going out with anyone. All you ever mention is Bertie and he's your cat."

There were a few sniggers from the crowd which did nothing to help Ray's mood. Sylvia continued on.

"You're stressed out because of that journalist raking up the past. You're just upset because you still miss Emma. Admit it Ray, you've always loved your sister."

Ray snorted.

"Oh you poor delusional, old woman. You really don't get it do you?"

"Get what?"

Ray leaned forwards until his face was close to his mother's.

"I detest her," he spat, "I hate her. I've hated her since the moment she was born. I'm glad she was taken and I hope she's dead."

He didn't expect the blow or realise his mother could hit that hard. He looked back at her while rubbing his cheek. Her eyes were still watery with fresh tears but there was anger there too. He hadn't seen that expression since that first time she'd caught him hitting Emma.

Ray glanced around the room again. Everyone was staring daggers at him. As he looked back to his mother he saw Ken with both arms around her and Geoffrey Delaney patting her shoulder consolingly. Where was the sympathy for him? Ray tutted.

“Oh fuck the lot of you,” he said, “You can all go to hell.”

He pushed through the group of spectators and stormed out of the shop.

Chapter 32

Father

Daniel felt anxious. He hoped she'd come. He'd left Tania a message on her mobile phone, asking her to come over for a proper conversation without argument this time. He hadn't actually apologised for the previous row or said why he'd left it so long before contacting her, but he had admitted that the argument was his fault. Why did he find the words, 'I'm sorry' so difficult to say to his daughter? It was one of the first things a parent taught their child, to say sorry when they'd done something wrong. It should work the other way round too. It was like what Sylvia had told him, a good parent would acknowledge when they'd made a mistake.

Daniel had done a lot of thinking since Sylvia's visit on Tuesday. Finally admitting the truth to someone about what happened the day Emma vanished had helped him a lot. Sylvia was right, neither of them had been able to wholly move on with their lives while their secrets remained hidden. As her parents they'd naturally blamed themselves for Emma's disappearance. Every mother and father wants to keep their child safe and will always take the blame when something happens, even if it's just their child falling over and grazing their knee. But for Sylvia and Daniel there was the added guilt of turning away from their obviously distressed daughter in order to maintain their secrets. Daniel knew neither of them would ever be able to completely forgive themselves for that.

But it was wrong to live in the past and Daniel had another

daughter who had come to him for help and he'd turned her away as well. At least he could fix that, he hoped. He'd left the phone message for Tania on Wednesday morning. She hadn't replied until late evening and then that was just a brief text message, telling him she'd come on Friday after work.

Daniel had spent the last two days fretting, so much so that he'd half convinced himself she wouldn't turn up at all. He really wanted to make things right between them and hoped his purchase in Stow this morning of a new item for his apartment would help. Jessica had approved of it when she came in to clean earlier.

He knew he had an uphill struggle with Tania and that became apparent when she knocked on his door that evening rather than using her key and calling through.

"Thank you for coming," he said, as he let her in, feeling very formal.

Tania took up her usual place on the sofa.

"Would you like a coffee," Daniel asked her, remembering the last visit.

Tania sniffed.

"That depends upon how long I'm staying," she replied.

He felt the usual rush of emotion and the urge to react negatively but ignored it. Instead he smiled and said,

"Long enough for a coffee, I hope."

Tania nodded and Daniel headed for the kitchen.

"I know I didn't give you my full attention the last time you came," he called over to her, as he prepared the coffees, "But I promise tonight that…"

"The decision's already been made, dad," Tania interrupted.

Daniel felt his heart ache. So that was it then, she was leaving. He remembered Sylvia's words again about being a good father. He swallowed the lump that was rising into his throat and smiled over at her.

"Good," he said, "I'm glad. I'm sure you've made the right decision. I'm happy for you."

Tania didn't reply. Nothing else was said while Daniel busied himself with the coffee. He brought his daughter's over to her and then returned for his own. He didn't make eye contact as he sat down in his armchair. He took a long time taking a sip of his coffee before placing the mug down on the side table, preparing himself. Eventually he looked up again.

"Look Tania," he began, "I know I haven't always been there for you in the way you wanted me to be. I realise that now but I want you to know, I always did my best for you."

She still didn't respond. Daniel sighed.

"No that's bollocks isn't it," he said.

He picked up the wastepaper bin from under the table beside his chair.

"Look at this," he said, indicating the number of screwed up balls of paper, "This is the result of my trying to write down everything I wanted to say to you today. I couldn't get it right."

Tania frowned.

"I've not been a good father to you," he admitted, "And I'm sorry about that."

Finally, the words 'I'm sorry' had come out. Daniel felt he'd struggle to stop saying them now.

"I have no excuses," he continued, "And I've not got you here to beg for your forgiveness. I just want to explain to you what I've come to realise these last few days."

He stopped speaking, finding it difficult to know where to start next.

"I'm listening dad."

"Yes alright, give me a minute!"

Tania scowled.

"Sorry," he said, "Please let me get it right. You know I'm not one for explaining or showing my emotions and yet I actually cried yesterday in front of Sylvia."

"Who's Sylvia, one of the other residents?"

"No, my ex-wife."

Tania's eyes widened.

"Your ex-wife? What was she doing…"

Daniel held his hands up to stop her talking.

"Please," he said, "Let me explain."

Tania picked up her mug and settled herself further back on the sofa.

"I was scared to love you," Daniel blurted out, "I don't mean that I didn't love you, or don't love you, of course I do; but you have to understand, when Sylvia and I had Emma, we'd spent years trying for another child. I'd given up hope of it ever happening and then suddenly, there was this beautiful, little girl. She was our miracle baby and both Sylvia and I loved her so much."

Daniel saw Tania grip her mug tighter. He knew she was trying to control her own emotions and he couldn't blame her after the way he'd always spoken about her sister, but she needed to know how much Emma had been loved.

"She was very precious to us. We probably spoilt her a little too much but we couldn't help it. Emma was a delicate child and she always seemed in need of a hug which, as her father, I was happy to give."

Tania sighed.

"I know all this dad."

"Look, please let me get this out," Daniel told her, feeling a little miffed, "It's important, I promise you. You don't have children of your own yet. Believe me, there's an unconditional love that you just can't understand if you're not a parent."

"Really."

"Yes, really. You said the last time you were here that providing for a child's future was part of the parents' job description, well so is unconditional love. It's a love like no other. I need for you to know this so that you can try and understand what it feels like when the object of that love is taken away from you."

Tania looked down at her mug, feeling embarrassed for interrupting.

"Just like the love for a child is like nothing else, so the pain of losing one is like nothing else too," Daniel told her, "It hurts emotionally and physically. You never feel complete again. With Emma, one second she was there and then she was gone and none of us who were involved in her life know what happened. We can surmise, we can fear what happened but we'll never know. That's something else we have to live with. Imagine then what I felt when you were born. Here was a new daughter for me to love, but I didn't want my first daughter to feel she was being replaced, even though she wasn't around. I was also terrified of something happening to you like it had to Emma. I knew I couldn't go through that level of pain again."

Daniel tapped the coffee table with his stick so that Tania looked up at him.

"Of course I love you," he said, "But I always felt both guilty for loving you for Emma's sake, and scared of loving you for my own sake. That's not right and it's not fair on you but that's how I felt. You were so different from Emma right from the start. You always seemed strong and independent. I thought providing a future for you through working hard at the businesses we had was enough. I know I was using work to hide my feelings but I never realised how much it was hurting you. I'm so sorry."

"Oh dad," Tania sighed, "You haven't ruined my life or anything like that. I know I was loved. It's just that for me, I kept hearing about this wonderful other sister and you always seemed different when you spoke about her. I wondered what I had to do to get you to look at me the way you looked at her photo. There was another you and I wanted to know that dad. Once I was older I realised you seemed different because you were always sad when you spoke about her. That didn't stop me suffering with sibling rivalry. I was trying to compete with someone who wasn't actually playing the game and I was still losing. It was so frustrating."

Daniel stood up from his chair and opened his arms.

"Can I give you one of the hugs you've been missing out on?" he asked.

Tania's eyes filled with tears as she stood up. As he held his daughter in his arms, Daniel felt her body shudder as she cried and he held her that little bit tighter.

"I'm happy for your move to America," he whispered, "But I'll miss you so much."

Tania let go of her father and fished for a tissue from her jacket pocket.

"I'm not going to America," she told him, as she wiped away her tears.

"Sorry?"

"I'm not taking the job."

"But you told me the decision was made."

Tania nodded.

"And that was after I told you to go."

"I know," she said, "But after I left here the last time and calmed down a little, I realised that your anger showed you weren't coping with the past. I reckoned that wasn't just about Emma but about mum too. I couldn't leave you on your own. I knew you needed me, even if you weren't aware of that."

"But I treated you so badly."

Tania smiled.

"I'm a daughter," she told him, "It's in the job description to look after your parents."

Daniel grinned.

"I can't say I'm not happy that you're staying but I don't want to ruin your chances of a better life."

Tania shrugged.

"I like my life here," she said, "I hadn't thought about moving away before the job offer. I think I've made the right decision. Besides, Raj and I decided we didn't want our relationship to be across five thousand miles. We've realised we care about each other more than we thought. We're going to move in together."

Daniel didn't think his smile could get any wider.

"It's about time," he said, "I'm glad. Does this mean I'll soon hear the patter of tiny feet?"

"Only if we get a dog."

Daniel laughed.

"I'm just happy that you're happy," he told her.

"And I'm glad that you've been able to open up to me this evening. I know it wasn't easy for you."

The two of them hugged again.

"Dad," Tania asked, while they were still holding each other.

"Mmm."

"What the hell is that photo doing there?"

Daniel let his daughter go and turned to face the table beside his armchair.

"Oh, do you like it," he said, "I bought the frame today. A double frame to show off both of my beautiful girls. I only didn't have one of you before because…well, because you're still here. The one of your mother only went up after she passed away."

"Well that's a lovely thought dad but did you have to use that particular photo?"

"Well you and Emma are both five years old in them."

"Yes but Emma is a cute blonde. I've got the ginger hair and glasses and the crooked fringe."

"You're still beautiful," Daniel told her, "I took the photos into the restaurant at lunchtime today to show off both of my girls."

"Oh my God dad you didn't, did you?"

Daniel started laughing again.

"No of course I didn't," he told her, "I only put that photo in as a joke after I started going through the albums. I knew you hated it."

Tania grinned.

"I'll put a different one in later. I want to look at all of my girls each day in these photos."

"You can see me in real life dad," Tania told him, "Whenever you like."

Daniel beamed.

"Thank you," he said, "That means a lot. You know, I'm thinking that's it's time I tried to contact your brother, Ray. I don't know how he'd feel about that or if he'll be receptive, but I can only try."

"I'll help you, if you want me to."

"Thanks. Perhaps I'll speak to Sylvia about that."

"Oh yes, why was she here the other day?" Tania asked.

Daniel took his daughter's hands and they both sat down on the sofa.

"That's something else I want to tell you about," he said.

Chapter 33

Teacher

Caroline sat up at the island in her vast, bespoke kitchen. From where she sat she could choose to look out beyond the expensive dining table made from reclaimed teak, through the bi-folding doors and out onto the expansive garden. Instead she faced the other way and stared at the wall of four ovens, two built-in larder fridge freezers and an integrated coffee maker. Not that she was paying those much attention either.

She was thinking about Hasanna, what she'd suggested the day of Ray Burrows ghastly visit and the conversation they'd had earlier this morning. Caroline had been so affected by it that she hadn't gone into work today. The charity would have to manage on its own. But of course it could do that because of all the well-trained staff at the centres, both paid and unpaid. Caroline didn't really have to go in each day like she did. It was only at certain times, like recently while looking for new premises, that her workload increased. So why did she still pay daily visits to the centre? Perhaps it was just guilt like Hasanna had told her this morning, guilt at her lifestyle, guilt at the state of her marriage, guilt at the past.

Oliver had spent last night in London. After being away Sunday and Monday Caroline was a little worried when he disappeared again on Thursday but she put it out of her mind to deal with later and had headed off to Hasanna's apartment. It hadn't been quite the fun evening they'd both wanted. Hasanna was still on a high, thinking about her new job and the proposition she'd made to Caroline about living together. Caroline found her enthusiasm annoying but tried to hide it by staying quiet. It didn't work, as she recalled again now.

"I don't understand," Hasanna said, after asking Caroline why she seemed unhappy.

"You want me to give up everything I've worked for over the years to come and try living with you."

"Well, yes," Hasanna replied, "I mean I know it won't be as easy as all that and you'll need time to sort things out but…yes, I want you to leave everything behind and come and live with me. I love you Caroline. I want us to be together. I think it's a great idea."

"But we've only been together a couple of months."

"And I already love you. I want us to be together, don't you?"

Caroline took too long in replying and saw the tears spring to Hasanna's eyes.

"It's not that I don't," she quickly said, "I'm just in shock. I wasn't expecting this."

"You love me, don't you," Hasanna asked.

Caroline wished she would stop talking about their love. She was starting to sound needy and desperate and Caroline didn't like that. It was strength she admired, not neediness. She'd seen that in Hasanna just as she'd seen it in Brenda Goodwin and Oliver.

"There's more to this than just love," she said, "Do you even realise what you're asking me to give up? I'm married, I have children, I have a house and an interest in my husband's business. I have a life away from the charity."

"You have a husband you don't love, children you rarely see and a materialistic lifestyle," Hasanna threw back at her, clearly annoyed, "Am I not worth more to you than that?"

"That's not what I'm saying and you know it. This is a major step and it's happening really fast."

"Well you're the one who keeps telling me how much you'll miss me when I move east. Is that because you love me or do you just enjoy the sex I give you that your husband doesn't want to anymore?"

"How dare you!"

"I can't believe you're not even one bit excited by the idea," Hasanna moaned, shaking her head.

Caroline sighed.

"Look, you've shocked me, that's all."

Hasanna didn't seem to hear.

"I thought I knew you. I thought the charity was more important to you than the lifestyle you and Oliver have."

"Well why can't I enjoy both," Caroline asked her, almost pleadingly, "I worked bloody hard to achieve the lifestyle. It's not wrong to enjoy the fruits of one's labour is it?"

"Is that what I am, a fruit of your labour? If I wasn't here would you be flirting with some other cute employee?"

"Now you're being ridiculous."

They were stood in Hasanna's tiny square kitchen area off of her lounge. The cupboard doors were dark wood, definitely from the nineteen eighties. The worktops had been replaced at some time with a basic, white laminate. Hasanna turned away from Caroline now and walked into the lounge. The furniture was as dated as the kitchen, a sagging, brown sofa, a small pine dining table with mis-matched chairs and a nineteen seventies, wooden display unit that had a pull down door hiding a drinks cabinet. Caroline couldn't help turning her nose up at it.

"I'm being ridiculous, am I," Hasanna said, turning back to face her, "What do I really mean to you Caroline? Am I someone to love or just a passing whim? You need to choose what you want."

Caroline stepped into the lounge and sat down on the sofa.

"You're not a passing whim, it's just that…"

"It's just what? You know, you haven't actually told me you love me."

"Of course I have," Caroline replied, indignantly, "When we were at the new site we told each other."

Hasanna shook her head.

"No, I told you that I loved you. You told me you wanted me to have the new job and would miss me and assumed that was love. It's not the same thing as saying it. Why are you afraid of saying it?"

"I'm not."

Hasanna sat down beside her.

"When was the last time you said it to someone? When was the last time someone said it to you besides me? You and Oliver muddle along in your privileged lifestyle, your kids don't live nearby or keep in touch that often; do you feel unloved? Do you cling to the wealthy lifestyle because that's all that's left of your marriage? Do you not think you deserve to be loved? Did something happen in the past to make you feel that way?"

Caroline opened her mouth to reply but no words came out. In her mind it was thirty-nine years ago and she was in the grounds of the primary school, frantically searching for Emma Burrows alongside Brenda and Daniel; the little girl missing because Caroline hadn't been doing her job properly and had abandoned her post for an illicit liaison.

In the space of a few seconds her mind travelled across that whole school year when she'd been stuck in Little Tenwick but desperate to flee. There'd been the looks from the locals, the comments and her job disappearing as colleagues took over her duties. Then there was Brenda Goodwin, the woman that had supposedly loved her, who'd been only too keen to entice the pretty, young teacher into a physical relationship and who, as soon as Emma Burrows had gone missing, placed all of the blame on Caroline, taking none for herself; too worried that the affair would be discovered and she'd lose her husband, her job and her standing in the village, all the things she'd worked for…

Caroline gasped.

"What's wrong?" Hasanna asked.

She couldn't reply. She looked at the woman sat beside her and felt the hot tears begin to roll down her face. How had this happened? How had she allowed it to happen? Nearly forty years later and history was repeating itself, except this time Caroline had taken the role of Brenda Goodwin, the woman too scared of change, too scared of losing a reputation and perhaps, too scared of love.

Hasanna looked concerned. She reached out and touched Caroline's arm.

"What's wrong?" she asked again.

Caroline shook her head.

"I'm so sorry," she said, "I'm treating you appallingly."

She struggled to say anything else and just hugged her girlfriend to her, enjoying the feel of Hasanna in her arms.

They'd gone to bed and made love before falling asleep, both waking early the following morning. It was in bed, as the day dawned outside, that Caroline told Hasanna all about the disappearance of Emma Burrows and her role in it. She left nothing out, the relationship with Brenda, her lie to the police about how long she'd been away from the classroom for, and her recent conversation with Ray.

Hasanna had been agog, looking at her like she was watching some thriller at the cinema. At one point Caroline asked if she wanted popcorn. When she finally finished talking the sunlight was penetrating in through the curtains. Caroline laid her head on Hasanna's shoulder, enjoying the feeling of her girlfriend's hand gently stroking her thigh. She felt lighter and more relaxed after making her confession and waited patiently for a response to what she'd just said.

"I don't really see why you've allowed this to affect your whole life," Hasanna finally admitted.

Caroline sat up straight.

"What do you mean?"

Hasanna looked at her.

"You still feel guilty, don't you?"

"Of course I do. Because of my incompetence a little girl went missing and was likely killed. God knows if anything was done to her before she died. I don't like to think about that but it's a possibility. I left a family devastated and I lied to the police. You bet I still feel guilty."

Hasanna shook her head.

"No, that's not what I mean," she told her, calmly, "I mean that you feel so guilty that you believe you don't deserve to be truly happy. The lavish lifestyle you profess to love, it's just a pretence. You told me it was Oliver that always wanted it and you helped to achieve it, but I don't think you truly enjoy it."

"Didn't we have this conversation before," Caroline replied, testily, "Isn't it you that has a problem with my money?"

Hasanna sighed.

"I don't have a problem with your money, as I told you," she said, unperturbed, "But you do have a problem. How do you spend it, your money?"

"Sorry?"

"What do you do with it?"

"Well, we enjoy it," Caroline admitted, "We have nice meals

out and we have holidays, a winter sun one, a summer trip and an autumn city break."

"Exactly," Hasanna told her, "You go away in the winter, but is that ever to Australia to visit your son? The city break, is that ever to Manchester to visit your daughter?"

Caroline didn't respond.

"No it isn't," Hasanna continued, "You spend time off from work with a man you've told me you no longer love. You miss your children but you don't make the effort to be with them. Why? Because it would make you happy and that's not allowed."

"That's not it," Caroline said, "It's complicated. We're…"

She couldn't think how to continue. Hasanna spoke again.

"You just accept that your children aren't part of your life, even though you have enough money to visit them or to pay for them to visit you. While Oliver works to make money your guilt makes you work all the hours God sends for a charity, trying to atone for what was actually just an error of judgement thirty-nine years ago. Yes, it was a terrible thing to happen but you weren't to blame. Whoever took the little girl is to blame. Why keep punishing yourself? It's ruining your life."

Caroline bit her lip to stop herself crying again.

"And then there's me," Hasanna added, "This guilt of yours is stopping you loving me."

"Don't say that," Caroline said, "I love you. I told you that last night while we were making love."

Hasanna shook her head again.

"You won't allow yourself to love because you don't think you deserve it. That's the whole problem here. You feel you deserve to be alone, to be in a loveless marriage, to not have family around you because that family in that village are still missing their daughter. If she'd been found then that would have been okay, but she wasn't and so you've continued to blame yourself for nearly forty years. You cling to the lavish lifestyle because that's all that's there. It's not what you want in life but you've made do."

Hasanna sighed again.

"You know, I think we could be truly happy together but I don't think you'll ever allow that to happen because you can't handle that amount of happiness. That level of euphoria has never been the norm for you and it scares you. Deep down you think it's wrong to feel that way but you do deserve it Caroline, you so deserve it."

Caroline wiped her eyes with the back of her hand.

"I am scared," she whispered.

"But what of? Leaving Oliver, being with me, or feeling happy?"

Caroline remained silent, not knowing what to say.

"The choice has to be yours to make," Hasanna told her, "For us to be together you have to face up to the past thirty-nine years, think about who you are and what you've become and who you want to be. I know it won't be easy, to change patterns that have been part of you for so long, but you don't have to be unhappy. If you want to come and start a new life with me in East London then great, but if you feel you can't change and can't truly release yourself from the guilt, then stay with Oliver and carry on as you are. But I won't hang around then to be some bit on the side."

Caroline cradled Hasanna's face.

"I don't want you to be my bit on the side either."

Hasanna smiled.

"The ball's in your court then."

Caroline sighed as she sat on the stool in her kitchen. Hasanna had headed to work and she'd driven home, stopping for a large cappuccino and a berry muffin at Pret on the way. She was still lost in thought when she heard the front door open. Oliver walked into the kitchen with his overnight bag, whistling. He jumped when he saw Caroline sitting there.

"Hello darling," he said, brightly, "You gave me quite a start. Not going to the centre today?"

"No, I don't really feel like it."

"Good, let someone else do the work. If you can't take a day off when you're the boss then what's the point, eh."

He placed his bag onto the floor by the door and walked over to the coffee machine.

"How about I make you a cappuccino," he said.

"Thank you."

Caroline was surprised by his cheerful demeanour. They hadn't exactly been on good terms lately.

"I was thinking about our autumn city break next month," Oliver called out, his back to her as he got milk out of the fridge, "How about Prague this year? I know you've always wanted to go."

"Erm, yes, yes I have always wanted to go there."

Caroline didn't know what else to say.

"Good," he said, "I was looking at hotels on my iPad on the train home this morning. There are some lovely five star ones. I think we deserve a treat. Things have been tough lately haven't they."

"Yes they have," Caroline admitted.

Oliver turned to face her. His expression showed concern.

"I've not handled this old abduction story very well have I. I've not considered you in all of this."

Caroline was shocked by this admission. Why was Oliver being so understanding, and now of all times?

"Well it's not an everyday occurrence is it," she told him.

He smiled.

"No, well hopefully we're through it. And if that journalist tries to publish anything we don't want her to, we'll sort it out together."

Caroline smiled.

"I'm not going into work today either," Oliver continued, "How about you come to Wentworth with me. We could have lunch there."

"That would be nice."

"And perhaps you could take a look at their gym while you're there, see what you think. Prague will only be a matter of weeks away you know. We ought to get in shape for it."

Still Missing

by Karen Taylor

Chapter 3 (first draft)

~~*Trying to get those involved in the Emma Burrows story to open up to me has proved quite challenging in most cases. I realise my questioning will open up old wounds but surely a fresh look at the past would help those wounds heal for good. Time moves on, technology moves on and police procedures move on. To those not involved, thirty-nine years may seem too far after the event to bother with, but to those that were affected by the abduction, surely a chance to perhaps answer some questions, to re-examine the past, should be an opportunity to grab with both hands.*~~

~~*To me, looking in from the outside, those involved seem scared to even look back at what happened. For Emma's parents that is understandable but for the others that were on the periphery of involvement, their hesitation to speak to me makes my journalistic brain become thoughtful. I've been fascinated by this case because of the lack of evidence and suspects at the time but the wall of silence that I'm up against now actually speaks to me.*~~

~~*Most people believe Emma is dead. Perhaps that is true after the number of so-called sightings diminished as the months passed by after the disappearance, but where there is no proof surely there should be hope. While Sylvia is certain her daughter is alive, why are others so certain she is dead? I can't help wondering if there is other information that never came to light that, if it had, might have had some bearing on the case.*~~

~~*If that's true then there is almost forty years of guilt of not speaking up at the time to be carried around. That would weigh*~~

~~*a person down and could make them reluctant to talk now. If the past hasn't been settled then no one can properly move on. Thirty-nine years may have gone by but time alone doesn't provide absolution.*~~

WHY WILL NO ONE TELL ME THE TRUTH!!!

Chapter 34

Mother

It was a silent journey back to Ken's house. Geoffrey drove while Ken sat beside Sylvia in the back seat, holding her hand and letting her deal with what had just happened in her mind. When she was ready to talk he'd be there for her.

Sylvia had been shocked by Ray's outburst in the supermarket. How could he say all of those horrible things? He loved his sister, he had to love her, everybody had. She hadn't meant to hit him but she couldn't help it. He was being so cruel and with the recent stress and worry about the past and the anniversary coming up the following week, all of the emotion had overwhelmed her. That wasn't like her and that wasn't like her Ray either, she knew him. What sort of mother would she be if she didn't know her own son? He was all Sylvia had since Emma's disappearance.

She hadn't neglected him, had she? While Ray had been angry today it didn't mean he was lying during his outburst. Emma had been so long in coming that of course Sylvia had lavished attention on her but Ray had been ten years old, old enough not to feel insecure about his sibling, surely. He'd never said anything, not once. Wouldn't he have turned to his mother if he'd been unhappy in any way?

Once in Ken's lounge Sylvia began voicing her opinions to him.

"Do you think I neglected him? Should I have got him some help after Emma was taken? I just thought he was quiet because he was a teenager, not because he was distraught. Maybe I shouldn't have taken that job as a dinner lady, helping all those other kiddies when my own son needed me."

"I can't really answer those questions for you, Sylvia," Ken told her, gently, "I can only imagine the horrible situation you were in. It was a difficult time for all of you back then. All I can tell you is that I think you're a wonderful woman, kind, caring, loving and I'm sure you always did your best for your kids."

Hearing those words, Sylvia burst into tears. Ken cradled her on the sofa until she was finally able to talk again. She told him then what she'd told Daniel, all about what she'd actually been doing that day her daughter disappeared.

"I've always felt so guilty about it," she said, "But talking with Daniel I could at least start to see that what happened was an accident Now though, after what Ray said, I can't help feeling I'm to blame for everything. I didn't go to my little girl when I should have and I didn't notice my own son was hurting. I'm a terrible mother."

"Oh Sylvia," Ken sighed, still holding her, "I can't believe you're a terrible mother. So Ray didn't like his sister, so what. That's what siblings are like when they are young and it's about time he grew up. Perhaps if Emma hadn't vanished they would have grown up together and had the chance to become closer, but that opportunity was taken away from him. He never had the chance to learn to love his sister and so whenever he thinks about her she is still five and he is still fifteen. That isn't your fault."

"I just feel like a failure right now."

"I understand that but you're not. My God look at you. You went through one of the worst things any parent could go through and you've come out the other side. You've spent your life being a strength to so many other people, always helping where you can, making their lives richer. You've done everything for Ray and it's his problem if he can't see that. Don't think of yourself as a failure Sylvia, you're amazing."

He kissed her on the forehead and she managed to smile up at him.

"Thank you," she whispered, "I'm so glad you're here."

He smiled back.

"Perhaps I'm meant to be," he told her, "Perhaps I'm meant to be a shoulder for you to cry on at this time."

"I need it with Ray leaving," she admitted, "I know he'll be at home right now, packing his bags and moaning about everyone. He was the same when he left Jackie. I'm scared about where he's going to go. Perhaps I should phone him."

"You said yourself that it was time for him to leave, for his own sake. Maybe this is the push he needed. Let him go Sylvia. I'm sure he'll be in touch as soon as he's calmed down, and you'll be there waiting for him."

He held her tighter.

"Terrible things can happen in this world Sylvia but it's how we cope with them that's key. You know that yourself. You told me you prayed to God for strength to understand and deal with the situation and you got that. I know you miss your daughter every day but you've got on with your life. You don't just function on a daily basis, you live. That's all part of the strength in you."

Sylvia sighed.

"I've always believed Emma would come back one day," she said, "I've always thought that was why me and Daniel have gone on living, getting to this age."

She looked up at Ken.

"But she's not going to come back is she?"

Ken shook his head.

"I would doubt it," he told her.

Sylvia nuzzled into his neck. She thought about that journalist poking her nose into people's business. She hoped the woman would leave them all alone now. The truth about the past had been faced by those that needed to face it. It was done with. There was nothing left to say.

"I can't change the past," she said, to Ken, "But I can affect the future. Will you come to church with me on Sunday? I want you to meet my friends."

Ken smiled.

"I'd like that," he replied.

Chapter 35

Brother

Ray threw everything into the two suitcases he'd arrived back at Sylvia's with after leaving Jackie. Everything still fitted in. He'd neither bought nor got rid of anything in the past year.

He was still furious at everyone. His mother had once again taken Emma's side by striking out at him, Elizabeth Chan was going to sack him and that pompous prig of a parish council chairman had embarrassed him in public.

My God I'm glad I don't have to suck up to that odious creature like the rest of the council have to, he thought to himself, I always knew there was something about Geoffrey Delaney I didn't like. I pity the rest of them.

He kept most of his hate for Emma. This was all her fault. She'd managed to turn everyone against him even though she wasn't here. How was she able to do that? Why had that journalist decided to look into the story just at the moment he was about to join the parish council? He wouldn't be speaking to her again. He hoped her book bombed. Her interference had brought Emma back and everything had gone wrong. Why wasn't he taking over the new shop? He was the obvious choice. He didn't believe all that shit his area manager had spouted about budgets and staff numbers. His might be a small shop but it had stayed open all of these years where many had failed. Surely that counted for something?

He slammed the lids of the two cases shut and carried them awkwardly downstairs to the hallway, ready to put into the boot of his car. He stomped into the kitchen and took a carrier bag out of the cupboard under the sink. He opened it up and selected a number of items from the fridge, knowing he would be too upset to think about cooking over the next few days.

He put the bag beside his suitcases in the hallway and walked into the lounge to make sure he hadn't left anything in there. He looked around the room and sighed, flopping down into the armchair. How long had it been since the room had last been decorated? A man his mother knew at the church had done it. Ray never did anything like that. That sort of manual work was meant to be paid for not learned, as far as he was concerned.

Sylvia hadn't wanted it changed at all, feeling the need to keep things as they had been when Emma was here but the years had passed and Ray thought it ought to be done. He smiled now as he remembered that he'd secretly wet the top corner of a strip of the old paper so that it began to peel off, forcing his mother to redecorate.

The smile disappeared as he thought about today. What on earth was Sylvia doing making a fool of herself with some man? She was old, she didn't need a boyfriend. What had put that notion into her head? She couldn't be lonely, not with her son around. Ray didn't understand it at all but still, if his mother was about to make a fool of herself he was glad he wasn't going to be here to see it.

He stood up and walked back out to the hallway. He picked up his suitcases and the carrier bag full of food, ready to move onwards. He didn't move very far. He slowly lowered the luggage to the floor again and sat down on the bottom of the stairs.

Where was he going to go? What was he going to do? The supermarket had been his life. Running his shop had been his empire, his way of being in control, being respected. Except that he wasn't, was he. His area manager despised him, the chairman of the parish council thought him a joke and his staff would all transfer to the new store and forget him. Sylvia had someone else to share her evenings with and Ray was alone.

That was the problem. Despite all his moaning about people, Ray didn't like being alone. That was why he'd always gone on to another relationship after the previous one had ended. He'd come back to Sylvia's after Jackie because he was fifty-four and thought there weren't going to be other women out there wanting to get together with him now.

He looked at his suitcases. That was it, that was his whole life there, packed away into two small items of luggage. It wasn't much of a legacy. Ray didn't know what to do next. Fifty-four was too old to start afresh. He wanted his old life not a new one, even though he believed everyone in it had betrayed him.

The cat brushed past him as it walked down the stairs. Ray smiled and grabbed it, holding it close to him as it struggled.

"At least I still have you, Bertie," he said.

The cat bit him.

Chapter 36

Father

Daniel felt his heart thumping as he slipped on the navy blue, long-sleeved dress. While the usual feeling of calm enveloped him as the material brushed gently against his legs and stroked his back as the zip was done up, he also felt a nervous panic rising within him. Tania was sat in the lounge waiting for her father to emerge.

Telling his daughter about the dresses had been the hardest part of explaining why Sylvia had visited but soon she knew the whole story, about Sylvia's desperate attempt to obtain money, his need to put on a dress and how both of those things had helped lead to Emma's disappearance.

Tania remained silent throughout, listening intently to everything her father said, knowing he needed to say it all just this one time. At the end she'd hugged him and thanked him for taking her into his confidence. Daniel, too full of emotion, had cried.

With everything in the open the two of them had found it easier afterwards to talk about things.

"I really don't know why I do it," Daniel had said, "It's only the dress I like to wear. I've never bought shoes or stockings or underwear and I've never wanted to wear make-up."

"Perhaps those items are more sexual and that's not the reason you do it," Tania had responded, "You say you feel the urge to wear one when you're anxious or stressed out. To me that sounds like the dress is a sort of comfort blanket."

"I suppose it is. I still don't really know why I have this need. I guess I've never wanted to analyse it too much because I've always felt embarrassed. I can still remember when I was a child and playing dressing-up with a friend at home. I had on an old skirt of my mothers and we were both laughing when dad walked past the door. He took one look in the room and shouted, 'Get that thing off, you little nonce.' Well that was the end of dressing up. My God he was a pig of a man. I don't know how my mother put up with him but she did. She was the only one who could stand up to him."

"Well maybe that's it," Tania had said.

"What?"

"I saw a programme once that said cross-dressing men often admire and imitate women. Perhaps a dress represents your mother and her strength at being able to stand up to your father."

"My God, we're getting a bit deep here aren't we," Daniel had replied, "You could be right but to be honest with you, I feel too old to start analysing it all now. I may not need to wear one again now that I've finally faced up to all the secrets of the past."

"Maybe not but you shouldn't feel ashamed if the desire stays with you."

"We'll see," Daniel had replied.

They'd remained silent until Tania announced,

"Do it one more time."

"Sorry?"

"Put on a dress, in front of me."

Daniel's eyes had widened.

"What on earth would either of us get out of that, apart from my embarrassment and you feeling physically sick?"

"I'm being serious dad," Tania had told him, "You've faced

up to everything and I'm proud of you, but you obviously still feel ashamed when you shouldn't. I think that's because you started associating the dressing up with Emma leaving. Your daughter was the only person to ever see you like that and then she was gone. Well, you have another daughter. You can wear a dress in front of her and I promise she won't be disappearing afterwards."

Daniel had taken some persuading and he certainly wasn't going to do it that night. Now it was Saturday afternoon and here he was, looking at his image in the mirror with his daughter sat in the other room, waiting for him.

Daniel had picked the most conservative of the dresses he owned. Arms were covered and most of his legs too. He forced himself to keep looking at his reflection. Every other time he'd seen himself he'd felt revulsion, today he wanted to see himself as just a normal man with a need.

The three dresses Daniel currently owned had been bought after Alice died. There was no denying that they'd helped him cope with his grief. Sometimes he'd needed to put one on just to make it easier to cry. He felt guilty for Alice being the one to go rather than him. She'd helped nurse him through his pneumonia but he hadn't been able to reciprocate that, her heart attack taking her away from him so swiftly.

Would he get rid of these dresses after today? Daniel didn't know for sure. He didn't want to repeat the pattern again of destroying the dresses only to find he still retained the need to wear one at a later date. Maybe he should keep them a little longer, just in case. He knew Tania would dispose of them in secret for him when he was no longer here.

It felt different today, not wearing a dress out of a need for some comfort. Perhaps that was why it was easier to look at himself in the mirror. He still felt he looked ridiculous and he was terrified that Tania would laugh at him when he entered the lounge. She wouldn't mean to but she might not be able to help herself. That couldn't be helped now though.

Daniel sighed as he took once final look in the mirror only this time it was because of the reflection of the old man staring back at him. He'd resigned himself to being old. That morning he'd been appalled to discover that he rather enjoyed the game of bingo he'd been conscripted into as he entered the communal lounge.

But he felt he didn't have much to complain about. While he would always blame himself for Emma's disappearance and would always feel frustrated that he didn't know the truth about what happened to her, he also had another daughter who loved him and whom he loved too. She was a clever, resourceful, kind woman; the most precious person in his life and she was here for him no matter what. She was already checking into what that journalist could and couldn't write about in her book. It was all going to be okay. Daniel took a deep breath and walked out of the bedroom.

Chapter 37

Teacher

Caroline stayed behind at the Windsor Sensory Centre to fire off a few final emails. Being the last one there she turned off the lights as she walked through the corridors towards the backdoor and the staff car park. After setting the burglar alarm she stepped through the door and locked it behind her. Now was the moment to take that step forward. She felt scared.

Hasanna had already given notice on her rented apartment in Hounslow and was almost finished packing up her stuff, ready to head east. It was barely a week since they'd discussed the future after Caroline had told her all about Emma Burrows, but when Hasanna made a decision, she didn't hang around. Caroline smiled as she got behind the wheel of her Mercedes roadster and switched the engine on, pressing down on the accelerator pedal to make it roar. She thought what she was doing was right for her. How many years had she put off making the change?

It was a chilly, overcast evening and Caroline could see a light mist around the street lamps as she drove. She thought about the small bag in the boot. It contained only the bare essentials. She didn't want to start the new adventure with an array of designer outfits. Hasanna had been right, it wasn't her.

The roads were still busy and, as she sat in a queue at a set of temporary traffic lights for roadworks, Caroline reflected on the last few months since Hasanna had become an important figure in her life. They'd been happy ones despite the recent upheaval due to that bloody journalist, not that she was so worried about the book now anyway. As Hasanna had told her, a book about missing persons cases was hardly likely to have a wide circulation and Emma Burrows was only going to appear in one chapter, if at all. Caroline had agreed and doubted she'd even get a mention, having threatened to sue if she was spoken about.

She followed the other cars through the roadworks, even though the temporary set of traffic lights had just changed back to red again. She was tooted by the first car waiting to come through in the opposite direction as she passed but she didn't care. She had an appointment to keep.

As Caroline reached the gates she slowed down and took a deep breath. It was strange. It felt like this was the moment where, if she went forward, there would be no going back on her decision; the path for her future would be set and couldn't be altered again.

She smiled and shook her head, feeling she was being too melodramatic. She put her foot on the accelerator pedal and drove forwards.

Caroline thought about Hasanna as she changed her outfit. She knew she'd be happy, working for that children's charity in India. She could get hands on with many different roles. It was so the right move and Caroline was pleased she'd been able to help her find it and so quickly, the charity being desperate for someone with Hasanna's skills and experience. She'd been surprised when Fran told her she wanted to move her family across London to run the new branch of the sensory centre when it opened. Apparently her husband had family out that way and they wanted to be closer to them. It looked like everything was going to work out. Caroline would run the Windsor office for the foreseeable future.

She left the exclusive changing rooms at the Wentworth Health Club and went to find her personal trainer. It was time to finally make that change to her life and start getting fitter. The long weekend city break to Prague with Oliver was all booked now and Caroline knew both he and she would feel better if she was a few pounds lighter.

Chapter 38

Accused

Lake Huron wasn't as calm as a few weeks before but neither Mike nor Ben minded. There was a chill in the air and Mike knew it wouldn't be too long until he took the boat out of the water and stored it away before the biting Canadian winter took hold.

He'd come up to the cottage on his own this weekend, well, he'd insisted on it and his family understood why. He'd told them all about the past. He and Eddie had flown home on the same flight last Friday and they'd sat down together to share the news that same evening. There'd been shocked expressions and a few gasps but Mike had found it easier to tell them the truth having Eddie by his side.

As he sat in his boat now, Mike thought again about Amrit's bombshell. It had taken him a while to accept what his mum had done. He wished she'd told him the truth. It was hypocritical, he knew that; after all he hadn't told her the truth as he'd known it. But as it turned out, Sheila had actually known everything that had happened and she'd never said a thing.

How had she managed to cope with that? Mike knew what it was like to keep a secret. He'd felt so frustrated and guilty because he was unable to prove Jimmy's innocence. Now he knew his mother must have felt exactly the same way. It had to have contributed to the rapidity of her death. Perhaps in a way though, she'd welcomed it, knowing she would soon be with her Jimmy again and he wouldn't be alone.

On their last few days in England, Mike and Eddie had travelled out to where the old barn had been located. It had been demolished at some point and the whole area given back to nature. The space was open, peaceful and beautiful. They'd also returned to Little Tenwick and crossed the old stile into the field where the copse was. Eddie had asked if his father wanted to go inside it to find Jimmy's hiding place but Mike had shaken his head. He wasn't sure whether, after thirty-nine years, he feared discovering some dusty, old treasures inside the dead tree trunk or feared finding it empty.

They'd also gone out for a meal with Amrit the night before their flight home. It was a little difficult at first but after some wine they'd all relaxed. They'd said their goodbyes and there was talk about keeping in touch and visiting each other but they all knew it wouldn't happen.

Karen Taylor sent Mike an email on his last day, telling him she was sorry about the loss of his wife but asked again if he wanted to talk to her while he was in the country. He'd politely declined, explaining he was done with the past and didn't wish to revisit it again. She hadn't replied to that.

After they'd boarded their flight and as the plane had taxied to the runway, Eddie asked his father,

"Do you think you'll ever come back again?"

Mike had shaken his head.

"I don't think so," he'd replied, "I thought I'd left Joey McGill behind all those years ago but he stowed away in my luggage. I brought him back and now he's staying here where he belongs, with the rest of his family. I'm Mike again and my life is in Canada."

Eddie had smiled.

It was Saturday now, the 28th. Four days before had been

the anniversary of the disappearance of Emma Burrows. Today marked thirty-nine years since Mike had found his brother dead in the barn. He wanted to be alone to have time to grieve for his whole family, his mum, his brother and his wife. Who knew, perhaps he'd even give his dad a thought.

As he sat in the boat, his mind full of memories and his heart full of emotion, he pictured the bouquet of flowers left at Jimmy's burial site. Mike still didn't know who'd left it there and he supposed he never would. There was no point wasting time worrying about it anymore. It was something destined to remain a mystery along with what had happened to Emma Burrows. He was out here now to grieve. Tomorrow he would drive home and have dinner at Jill and Eddie's. He was already looking forward to it.

Chapter 39

Abducted

She found it easier to find the right spot than she thought she would. Her father's letter had been so accurate, so detailed. She got out of the car and began walking, bouquet of flowers in hand.

Her father's letter was in her pocket now. She had it with her at all times, she wasn't sure why. Maybe it kept him close. Perhaps she just didn't want anyone else finding it. It told her everything.

Andrew Jones, that was the name of her father. He hadn't been born with that name and neither had she been born with hers. They'd both become Jones thirty-nine years before.

The rock in front of her looked completely out of place in the flat, open, marshy landscape. It was only as she got closer she realised it was made out of stone and had at one time been part of a wall. This was definitely the place then.

She hadn't known of the letter's existence until her father's solicitor placed it into her hands. Her dad's first stroke had led to vascular dementia and she'd been slowly losing him ever since. He'd been everything to her, father, protector, best friend. Even though he was still alive, just, in many ways he was already gone.

It was some of the things he'd said after his first stroke that concerned her . While he reminisced about their life together he also began mentioning other memories that she wasn't a part of, names and places that meant nothing to her. Obviously she knew her father had had a life before she was born but they'd never discussed it. Now his travels to the past were spoken about with such passion that he sometimes cried. The people in it were obviously important to him.

It was after a second stroke had put him back in the hospital that she'd confided in her dad's solicitor, telling him of her concerns about who these people he spoke about were and what had happened in her father's past. Perhaps they were people she needed to contact. That was when he'd handed her the sealed letter which her father had written a number of years before with instructions it should only be passed to her if she started asking about the past. The solicitor knew nothing of what was in it, having only known them since their arrival in Sussex twenty-nine years before.

I'm so sorry that you've discovered something that means you now have to read this letter. Please believe me when I say you are definitely my daughter, even though biologically you're not. When I took you that day in the village it was an act of rescue, not abduction.

She'd been angry after her first read-through of that letter, shocked and angry. Her whole life had been a sham. She wasn't who she thought she was. Her father had robbed her of her true life and given her some other one. How could she ever forgive him for that?

She hadn't gone to visit him in the hospital for over a week after reading that letter, only returning after he contracted a chest infection and his condition had worsened. Seeing the reedy, emaciated, old man lying in the bed, almost disappearing into the pillow, her anger at him dissipated and she wept guilty tears. He had no recollection that she hadn't been to see him.

She leaned against the rock as she thought back over her life. It had only ever been the two of them. She had a faint memory of a woman being there with them when she was very young but her father had always told her that her mother died in childbirth. So who was this other woman? She thought she knew now because of the letter. He'd left nothing out. The whole story was there, how she was taken that day, who else was involved and who he'd been at the time.

She understood her father's restlessness now, why they never stayed in one place too long when she was a child. He mentioned in the letter that they'd spent time on the continent but she couldn't really remember specific places or people. She'd never had close friendships because as soon as she got to know someone they were off to live somewhere else.

Only when she was fifteen did she finally persuade her father to settle so that she could attend the same school for two years to study for her GCSEs. They were in Sussex at the time, a big enough county to hide in being split into East and West. She was pretty sure that was the only reason her father agreed to her request. Although there were friends then, after being used to travelling around, she never let them get too close. She wished now she had. She felt so alone.

That was probably the reason she'd considered contacting her real family. Her father was disappearing before her eyes and she needed someone to be there for her. In her mind it was all lovely, the family that had never stopped loving her holding out their arms to welcome her back into the fold, but she soon realised it wouldn't be like that. Too many years had passed by. If they were still alive her birth parents would be old now, like her father. Their lives had all been disrupted nearly forty years before when she went missing. To reappear now would just disrupt them again and she put thoughts of contact out of her mind. Besides, no one could replace her dad.

There was a puddle on the ground beside the rock and she

saw her reflection in it. She shivered as she remembered looking at the photograph of five year old Emma Burrows for the first time. She'd had several memories in her mind that she could never quite connect with her own life, being brutally shaken, a doll with purple hair, and an image of a little, blonde girl with bunches tied up with purple ribbon. She'd thought the child was perhaps a long lost temporary friend from one of her many schools but there she was in the newspaper article online, staring back at her. It was her and yet she couldn't identify as her.

She'd never felt she looked like that. She only remembered the fat child with dry, brown hair and glasses. She'd never even known her father dyed her hair. She'd just assumed he was shampooing it for her and believed him, when she started doing it for herself and turned blonde, that hair could just change colour like that. She'd trusted everything her father had told her. That was why the letter had felt like such a betrayal at first.

Her father had never been much of a cook and they'd survived mostly on takeaways and readymade meals. Plus there had always been treats. In her teens, living in Sussex, she took over cooking duties and the pair of them ate more healthily, the childhood weight dropping off her. Stopping the treats had proved harder. She enjoyed those. Her father had always rewarded her with some kind of confection whenever she did something well, like passing a spelling test at school or tidying her room. Part of the treat was seeing her father smile, knowing she'd made him happy.

When I got you to her house I started giving you information for your new identity. I'd thought it all through on the way there. I made it into a game, giving you treats whenever you got something right; your new name, my new name, the fact I was now your dad.

She stood up and walked around the rock, wondering if there was some way she could work out the exact spot of the grave. She really wanted to lay the flowers in the right place. It was important to give Jimmy McGill some respect. By God, he'd received very little of it during his life. He was the innocent one in the story of Emma Burrows. He'd had nothing to do with her abduction but had been blamed by so many. That was wrong and it was something she struggled to forgive her father for. He'd allowed that to happen.

So who was the father of the woman currently looking for an unmarked grave? Who was Emma Burrows now? Emma Burrows was called Sarah Jones, a former air hostess who now trained cabin crew at Gatwick Airport. Her father, Andrew Jones was a retired builder who'd always been happy to take on any work he could get. Sarah Jones loved her father with all her heart but she didn't love the man he'd been and couldn't associate the two of them as being the same person. How had Andrew Jones once been Tom McGill?

Chapter 40

Abductor

My Darling Sarah

I'm so sorry that you've discovered something that means you now have to read this letter. Please believe me when I say you are definitely my daughter, even though biologically you're not. When I took you that day in the village it was an act of rescue, not abduction.

Yes, you read that right. I took you away from your real parents when you were five years old. You can read the newspapers from that time if you like but I'm going to give you the real story of what happened. Too many of the people involved lied about what happened that day, scared that their secrets would be discovered. The truth has never been revealed, even to this day. It makes me believe I was right to take you.

Firstly, know that I used to be a terrible man. I was a drunk, I beat my wife and I rarely had time for my two sons. I was planning to disappear around the time I took you. I had plans in place that I'd been slowly making over the previous four years, ever since my youngest son, Joey had beaten me up for hitting his mother. It had been a wake-up call but not in the way it should have been. I wish it had cured me but I continued to drink and to beat my wife, just a little more secretly than before. I don't think she ever told Joey that. Being beaten by my son didn't make me sorry for what I'd done, I just felt humiliated and knew I wanted to get away from them all. I was still drinking and believed faking my death would make them realise what they were missing. I'm cringing while writing this my darling, hating that you have to know about the awful, drunken, violent man I'd been.

I knew someone who knew someone else who could get me new ID. They'd already made me up a passport in the name of Andrew Jones. Back then a child appeared on a parent's passport as a name only so it was easy to then give Andrew Jones a daughter named Sarah.

So how come I rescued you. You were called Emma Burrows. The newspaper articles will tell you about who you and your family were. I'm not going to do that here. Just know that you were five years old and things weren't quite as everybody thought.

Everyone believed you were abducted by my eldest son, Jimmy. He was twenty-five at the time but he had mental health issues that occurred during his birth when he was starved of oxygen and he remained a child in many ways. When he wasn't born the perfect son I'd expected, I blamed my wife. I felt unhappy each time I looked at my disabled boy. Drink made me feel happy for a while. Back then it was under control but when Sheila became pregnant again I was afraid the same thing would happen. Having one disabled son could be seen as tragic but two would look careless. I didn't want to be laughed at by my friends who were all able to talk proudly about their children and what they were doing or had achieved. Jimmy, as far as I could see, was achieving nothing.

Sheila was so proud of Jimmy and would parade him around the village. That just embarrassed me even more. I hadn't become the wife beater then although I still didn't treat her well. My drinking only really increased during the second pregnancy when I began adding spirits to my beer consumption. Sometimes I was happy, sometimes I just grew angry. When I was angry I drank more to try and get me back to happy. I didn't realise I had a problem.

When Joey was born completely normal I was too far down the alcoholic path to turn round and come back. All I could see was that Sheila's love for me had been transferred into her two boys and as they grew up, so they returned that love to her. I was left out in the cold. I'm not trying to excuse myself, I'm just trying to tell you what I was feeling back then. I blamed the drink. As far as I was concerned I was the victim. Before the drink I'd never hit my wife so it had to be the drink that was doing it, never mind that the anger had been there beforehand. The fact I knew I was hitting my wife when drunk didn't stop me drinking. It was entirely my fault but I didn't see it like that.

I can still remember the first time I hit her. Joey hadn't long been born. Sheila and I were watching a five year old Jimmy trying to kick a football, me in a drunken stupor. He was still learning co-ordination and missed the ball each time, falling over but getting back up to try again. Sheila found it delightful, I was embarrassed. Eventually I stood up and tried to kick the ball away from him to stop him doing it. In my drunken state I too missed it. Sheila laughed and then Jimmy copied her. She didn't laugh for long. After that it became a regular occurrence. Hitting my wife made her notice me. The fear of what mood I would come home in meant I was always in her thoughts. It wasn't all about the boys anymore. I could control her. It made me the man of the house again.

Yes it's pathetic and I hate having to write this down but you need to know the whole story. I stayed submerged in alcohol for the next twenty years, not realising it had taken control of me rather than me controlling it. Sometimes now I can't help fearing what would have happened if I'd stayed any longer with the family. Would Tom McGill have killed his wife quicker than her cancer did?

Returning to the day I took you, as Tom McGill I was on my way home after another argument with my girlfriend, Eileen who lived in a different village in Essex to the one you and I lived in. Little Tenwick was a quiet place. I didn't really like it. It was a typical village with everyone putting their noses into other people's business, thinking they knew what went on but actually understanding nothing.

I'd walked home overnight after Eileen threw me out of her house. Arriving in Little Tenwick early I took the shortcut through the gap in the fence by the primary school. I saw your teacher, Caroline Willis in the headmistress's office. The two of them were kissing with the headmistress's hand up Caroline's jumper.

I don't mean to shock you, talking matter-of-factly like this, but you need to know the facts. I already knew they were having an affair. I knew a lot of the secrets going on in that village because I had a spy. Jimmy was a nosy bugger, always listening in to people's conversations or watching them, even in their homes. He didn't always understand what was going on but he enjoyed telling me all about what he'd seen. It was the only time I indulged him.

I passed the school and entered the centre of the village. It was pretty deserted as always. I saw you being taken to school by your brother, Ray. I was by the entrance to the church hidden by one of the yew trees. Your parents thought the sun shone out of that boy's arse when he was actually a nasty bastard. He was jealous of you, a typical fifteen year old who thought he was a grown up but just acted like a spoilt child. Jimmy had seen him trip you up before now. That day he was more upset than usual after an altercation with some school friends and I saw him shaking you. I still hate him for that, knowing the dreams you used to have afterwards. Anyway, I was about to go to you myself when I saw Jimmy rush over and come to your rescue, pushing your brother away.

Ray was a bloody coward and rushed off, leaving you with Jimmy. I watched him gently walk you across the road and up the path to the school. I actually felt proud of him that day. I turned and set off for the pub. Although it was early, if the landlord was in a good mood, he'd usually let me in. I knocked and waited around for a while but there was no answer. I was going to go home instead but then I saw movement in the large house beside the pub.

It was your mother, Sylvia in Honeysuckle Cottage, except she wasn't cleaning it as usual, she was stealing from the old guy that lived there. I watched her from behind the wall between the pub and his front garden, causally helping herself to his curios. Just as she emerged from the house with her basket I heard a noise behind me and you were running towards us, crying. I did't know what had upset you until I noticed one of your bunches had fallen down and your purple hair ribbon was missing. It had to have been Jimmy. He liked taking brightly coloured things. Obviously Caroline Willis was still in the arms of the headmistress rather than being in the classroom where she should have been. That was why a five year old child had been able to leave school with no one noticing.

I was expecting Sylvia to run to you. She was a bit 'over the top' with you usually, too emotional, too clingy; but she didn't. I was shocked to see her hide behind a tree, your own mother. You turned up the alleyway to where your house was and she turned and legged it across the field with her contraband. So much for saintly Sylvia!

I crossed the road to start walking to my home. As I passed your alleyway I heard a shout and looked up it. It was your father, Daniel who'd shouted. I could see him through the narrow window in the hallway of the house you all lived in. I caught sight of the dress he was wearing. That was another secret Jimmy had seen but didn't understand. Daniel had always been a placid man and I'd never seen him that angry before. He shouted at you to get out. You were upset and yet your father told you to go.

You fled from the house and back down the alleyway. You looked so distraught and then you saw me. I suppose I was recognisable as a local but I hadn't expected you to fly at me, throwing your arms around my legs. I instinctively picked you up and you clung to my neck and sobbed, finally getting what you'd wanted all along, some comfort.

Right there and then I knew what I had to do. I wasn't the only one that needed a fresh start, you did too. The decision seemed so natural. I know I'd been no great shakes as a dad to my sons but it felt right that I could be there for you now. I didn't think about how to do it or what the outcome of my decision would mean for anyone else, I just knew I could be your dad and raise you. You'd needed someone that day and I'd been the only one there to comfort you.

My heart melted. I'd never felt like that before. It was as if all the hate I'd carried for the last twenty-five years, ever since my wife had presented me with a sub-standard child, had gone, vanished into thin air by your hugging me. You were the perfect child I should have always had. I know how awful that sounds my darling but that's the sort of selfish, self-centred man Tom McGill was.

Instead of returning home I left the village with you the same way I'd arrived. We took two days to get to Eileen's, what with me having to carry you most of the way across fields. I daren't risk cadging a lift. There were enough barns around there to sleep in overnight and I managed to steal some food for us. You were quite happy being with me. We were on an adventure.

When I got you to her house I started giving you information for your new identity. I'd thought it all through on the way there. I made it into a game, giving you treats whenever you got something right; your new name, my new name, the fact I was now your dad.

Eileen was shocked when I turned up with you and even more shocked that I never touched alcohol again. I had to be strong for you and I realised getting drunk had always been a weakness for me, a way to hide away from my life and responsibilities. You saved me as much as I saved you my darling.

Of course it wasn't all perfect. I'd become anxious about what I'd done. It would wash over me like a wave. I'd stolen you away from your family. I'd taken a child. I was an alcoholic man who hadn't bothered with his own family and had causally left them behind without a backwards glance to try and raise another child on my own.

I'd stopped drinking abruptly and suffered because of it. I couldn't sleep, I would sweat profusely and shake. I tried to hide all of this from you. Sometimes I wondered if you were real or whether I was just hallucinating that I'd stolen a child.

Eileen wasn't keen on having you there. She was petrified we'd be discovered and that she would get into trouble for something I had done. We had a strange sort of relationship. Eileen was already an alcoholic when we met but I'd definitely made things worse. She enjoyed the company of men and was quite happy to sleep with them if they paid for her drinks all evening in the pub. When I was there we'd go on a bender for days and then we would argue. There was never physical violence between the two of us. Eileen wouldn't have stood for it anyway. If a man attacked her she would fight back. She'd been arrested a number of times because of it, once going to prison after leaving a man with glass in his face and a knife in his shoulder. Tom McGill might have hit his wife but he was a bully rather than a thug and too cowardly to try it with anyone who was his equal or stronger than him.

I knew I had to return to Little Tenwick one last time to show my face. It would have looked suspicious if I'd disappeared permanently at that time. I didn't like having to leave you alone with Eileen but I had no choice. I told her I didn't want her drinking or bringing a man back to the house while I was away. I think she was still so disturbed by the change in me, seeing me sober and wanting to raise a little girl that I'd stolen, that she agreed.

Back in Little Tenwick it was less of a problem acting the part of drunk Tom McGill while secretly sober than I thought it would be. I was still suffering effects from going cold turkey. I was irritable, I was having mood swings and also emotional outbursts, which wasn't so different to the normal Tom. I put it around that I was dying from cirrhosis of the liver but no one seemed to believe me or cared. Of course I was the only one who knew where you were, that you were safe and Jimmy hadn't taken you so I wasn't concerned like the rest of them were. I had been shocked on arrival to discover Jimmy had disappeared and was being blamed for taking you. I didn't know how that had happened but I also couldn't do anything about it. A couple of days later I left my past behind me for good and returned to be with you.

Does that sound callous? Believe me, I'd caused the McGill family more hurt and pain while living there. Leaving them was the best thing I could have done for all of us. I assumed Jimmy would be found soon and everything would be okay.

Eileen had coped looking after you and even kept up your lessons. You were already calling yourself Sarah. When I arrived back you were so happy to see me again and rushed to hug me. My heart melted again just like on the day you flew at me for comfort. I knew what I was doing was right, especially when you called me dad for the first time. I didn't give your real family any more thought after that

While at Eileen's I discovered what happened to Jimmy. My other son, Joey had hidden him away, believing he'd hurt you because he had one of your purple hair ribbons. Joey always thought he knew best. He'd never liked me. I know Tom McGill wasn't easy to like but Joey had always been his mother's son, trying to do his best. He really messed up with Jimmy though. The poor lad was left in a barn where he fell over, hit his head and died. Joey told me all this on a surprise visit when we had to quickly hide you in the cellar and I had to pretend to be dying upstairs. It was all I could do not to react when he told me what he'd done, taking on the blame as usual. He buried his brother in secret beside the ruin of an old medieval building, off the Mundon Road near Maldon in Essex

By the time we left Eileen's a month or so later she was glad to see the back of us. She no longer wanted to be with me, finding a sober Andrew Jones who only had eyes for his daughter, boring compared to a drunk Tom McGill whom she never knew what he was going to be like after a drink, fun or argumentative. But Tom McGill was now dead, officially too thanks to the guy that had arranged our new documents. Eileen wrote a letter to Little Tenwick to let them know about my death just before we left. I was glad to be leaving too. Seeing her drunk when I was sober gave me an insight into the person I had been. It was the wake-up call I wished had occurred after

Joey beat me, but then if it had I wouldn't have had you in my life, my dear Sarah.

You didn't resemble Emma Burrows anymore. The treats I'd given you when playing games had added weight and Eileen had shown me how to dye your hair. I'd also given you some weak prescription glasses. We went across to France for a while until I felt it safe to return to England. I had trouble settling though. While you didn't really resemble Emma Burrows anymore I was always scared of someone finding out the truth and so I moved us around a lot. We spent time in Scotland and the north of England before heading to the west side and Wales. My work was sporadic. Before the drink I'd been a decent builder but now I was taking labouring jobs wherever I could. We never had much in the way of money but we had each other.

I was still afraid when we finally settled in Sussex years later. You were now blonde again and slim. I was petrified you'd be recognised as an older Emma Burrows. I was also terrified about you leaving me. It only seemed like the day before you'd been five and now you were a teenager and fast becoming an adult. You were my whole world and I didn't want to lose you.

I suppose the selfish side of Tom McGill had stayed with me. It was hard to see you leave school and become a stewardess and spend time away from me. I felt sick every time you flew, having nightmares about plane crashes that would take you away from me forever. We'd been through so much together, not that you knew quite how much, until now.

But you did stay near me. When you bought the little, two-bedroomed house in Haywards Heath years later I was so proud, especially when you moved me in too. You finally had roots. During our lean times together I did sometimes fear I'd done you wrong by taking you away from a family and a community, and that perhaps I'd held you back. Travelling around so much had left us both with few friends and only each other for family, but when we moved into the house I felt I'd done the right thing.

We have been happy together over the years haven't we my darling. I'm just so sorry if you are reading this. Please remember that I love you more than anything. You don't have to be blood to be family. I've always tried my hardest to be the best dad to you that I could. I think I've done a good job. You are a fantastic person Sarah and I couldn't be prouder of you.

I love you, my darling girl.

Dad x

Chapter 41

Abducted

Sarah leaned against the rock again and surreptitiously touched her jacket pocket where the folded letter lay. Had it really been a rescue? She didn't know. She couldn't remember that other life and so couldn't decide whether she would have lived better as Emma Burrows rather than as Sarah Jones. As Sarah Jones she'd had a good life with a father that loved her. Many people weren't that lucky.

When she'd thought about contacting her real family Sarah had wondered if they were really like her father had portrayed. He hadn't painted them in a good light but neither had he done the same about himself. It was very easy to pass judgement on others without knowing all of the facts. Perhaps Sylvia had been driven to stealing, maybe Daniel had psychological needs that only wearing a dress could assuage.

She'd read the newspaper articles from the time of the abduction, noting the differences between the reports and what her father had told her. So many secrets. Sarah wondered whether, if each person had been honest about themselves, she would have been found. If that had happened then her father would have been arrested as Tom McGill and gone to prison, probably returning to drink. Her abduction really had been a rescue for him and that was something to be glad about.

Of course as Tom, what her father had done caused her real parents untold pain. Sarah could only imagine the heartbreak they must have felt. It was another reason not to make actual contact. To reveal who she was would bring nasty and selfish Tom McGill back to life and kill off kind and loving Andrew Jones. Sarah was physically losing her father fast enough already, she didn't want his name to vanish and to have her memories of him tarnished as well. He might have stolen her but he'd still given her life and it had been a happy one.

The breeze coming in off the North Sea was decidedly nippy but Sarah wasn't ready to move off yet. She pulled her jacket a little tighter around her, being careful not to squash any flowers in the bouquet. They reminded her of her hospital visits. While sat by her father's bedside after the second stroke, Sarah had tried to imagine what he must have gone through over the years. Had the fear of the truth being revealed ever truly left him? Had he constantly worried about either of them being recognised? With that level of worry she was surprised he hadn't had a stroke sooner.

She sometimes wondered if he'd looked any different as Tom McGill. Jimmy had been the only member of the family to have his photo printed in the newspaper articles at the time. Tom had changed her appearance so surely he must have changed his own as well to become Andrew. She only had a handful of photos of him and there were none from before she was born. Most of the time though she tried not to think about the man her father had been. She'd seen a loving, gentle side whereas his wife and sons had lived with a monster. Could a man really be so different when alcohol took over? There had been occasions over the years when she saw him become angry at a particularly difficult situation but he'd never been aggressive towards her. It made her feel a little guilty now.

While her father had never been one for computers she remembered his abject fear of the rise in social media websites where long lost friends and family could get back in touch with one another. Now she could understand why he'd been afraid, not that he'd had to be. As he'd mentioned in his letter, with all of the moving around they'd never been in one place long enough to make friends. For Sarah her job as cabin crew regularly took her away from home too and, even now, her role as a trainer meant she worked with different people all of the time. There weren't any long lost friends she wanted to contact and so she'd never been tempted to create an online presence.

But it had been through the internet that she'd found Karen Taylor. As Sarah looked across to Northey Island in the distance she thought back to that day she'd typed 'Emma Burrows' into a search engine and Karen's blog had appeared, mentioning all the cases she was researching for a book.

Initially it had scared her. She'd already decided she didn't want to reveal herself and suddenly there was this journalist who could potentially open up a can of worms. Sarah wanted to let Emma rest. To all intents and purposes Emma Burrows had died in 1980 aged five. It was at that moment that Sarah realised she needed to say goodbye to the little girl she'd discovered she'd once been. Only then could she move on. To do that she had to visit each person involved in the life of Emma that her father had mentioned in his letter, but she would only do it in a way that didn't disrupt any of their lives.

It proved quite easy to locate the Burrows family who were all still alive. Sylvia and Ray were living in the old family home and Daniel she found in the Cotswolds, his name often mentioned on the internet in relation to the restaurant he'd once owned. She worried about seeing them, fearing an emotional attachment that she wouldn't be able to switch off again.

Her first visit though was to Caroline Willis. Karen Taylor had mentioned her charity in one of her blog posts before deleting it. Caroline regularly held open days at the sensory centre she ran in Windsor. Sarah went and listened to one of her speeches. She seemed a very efficient and kind lady but there was obviously unhappiness in her life. Several times in her talk she mentioned her husband but not with any affection. Sarah only saw her smile when she spoke to the rather striking lady with the copper-coloured hair that also worked at the centre.

Sarah posed as the daughter of a potential new resident to the retirement village in Stow on the Wold to see her birth father, Daniel. She hoped he would somehow be pointed out to her while being given the grand tour. She was glad she was able to get a feel of the place where her birth father was living out his final years. Entering the communal lounge she thanked an old man who stood back to let her pass through. It was only when a member of the cleaning staff who'd following them in called out a greeting that Sarah realised the man was Daniel Burrows.

She took a surreptitious look at him while he spoke to the member of staff before quickly turning away when he glanced back in her direction. She didn't feel he looked happy that day and she couldn't help feeling sorry for him. After he'd left the room she casually asked the woman giving her the tour about him, saying he looked familiar. She was pleased to hear he had another daughter. It didn't cross Sarah's mind that she was related to her, she was just glad he had someone in his life.

Sitting on the rock was becoming uncomfortable and Sarah stood up. It was difficult to believe her trip to see her birth father had only been yesterday. She hadn't planned on driving to Essex straight after her visit but she'd read Karen Taylor's latest online blog on her phone while sat in the visitor car park at the retirement village. Karen mentioned a contact for Jimmy McGill was going to be flying in and staying in Chelmsford. Sarah knew it could only be Joey. Everything seemed to be slotting into place for her. Visiting him there meant she could also go to Little Tenwick at the same time to see her mother and brother.

Joey McGill felt special to Sarah. Even though her father didn't speak about anyone in a particularly good light she had instinctively warmed to the younger son mentioned in the newspaper articles and on the pages of her father's letter. It was odd really, seeing as he'd beaten up his father and had abducted his own brother, but he'd done those things for the right reasons. He'd tried to help and protect others. She felt he was more her brother than Ray Burrows was.

She phoned round a number of Chelmsford hotels she found online, wanting to confirm the details of the McGill booking. She finally struck lucky when she spoke to a Mrs Jessop who owned a small B&B. Discovering Joey was arriving that day she phoned the number again a short while later as she drove through Burford and managed to book a room for herself too. Sarah was there yesterday evening, sitting in the dining room when Joey, now calling himself Mike, walked in.

She'd tried her best to hide her nerves but her heart had still thumped loudly in her chest. There was no reason why Joey should recognise her, after all Daniel hadn't, but she was in closer proximity to him, sitting in the same room.

Sarah had wanted to speak with Joey. She wasn't sure why really. He wasn't an actual relative, unlike her birth parents and brother, but she just knew she had this need. Perhaps it was because he was a link to her father. While she didn't like to think about it, Andrew Jones and Tom McGill were the same man and this one person that had flown in from Canada was his blood relative, someone that knew him in the past. He was family as far as she was concerned. Although he didn't resemble his father he was a part of Tom McGill and so was a part of Andrew and Sarah Jones as well.

She didn't have to make up much of a back story to tell him. She really was on an extended leave from her job training cabin crew while her father was ill, she just wasn't on a training seminar. He'd talked warmly to her about his late brother and it made Sarah want to hug him. For a moment she'd wanted to shout out who she really was and to tell him his father was still alive and a changed man but she couldn't. Instead she'd excused herself and returned to her room.

Sarah's hand holding the bouquet was cold so she swapped it over and placed the cold one in her jacket pocket. She'd decided not to see Joey again this morning at breakfast. She imagined that if they'd sat together in the dining room, in the light of day, he might have picked up on some facial feature or a mannerism that would have revealed who she was. While she wore coloured contact lenses her eyes were still blue and her hair remained blonde. Also she was wearing a purple blouse and everyone knew that was Emma's favourite colour.

Sarah didn't like rushing off but feared saying a proper goodbye to him. For what he represented to her she might have burst into tears and that would have looked odd. As she'd told him last night, she could cry at anything. It was best she remained the kindly stranger and let him head off back to Canada and his own family.

The morning had been busy. After locating a florist to buy the bouquet Sarah had headed off to Little Tenwick. Her final look at her mother was almost across the bonnet of her car. From the newspaper articles and online maps Sarah knew exactly where the house was that she was brought up in. She was planning on driving past the alleyway first but then a distraught-looking woman had suddenly rushed out of it straight into the road and Sarah had had to slam on the brakes.

She knew instinctively it was Sylvia. There was a recognition, like remembering an old face from years ago. She looked so downcast as she stared into the car that Sarah thought about getting out to see if she was okay, even touching the handle of the driver's door. But then Sylvia called out an apology and stumbled off. Sarah watched her go, a tear falling from her eye. Thinking about that moment again now, by the rock, she wasn't sure if it was a genuine feeling of attachment to this woman or that she represented the one thing Sarah had missed out on during her life with Andrew, a mother. She hoped Sylvia had happiness in her life.

She'd discovered Ray was manager of the supermarket in the neighbouring village and stopped off their to see him and buy herself something to eat. It was a very brief visit. In the few minutes she was there Sarah realised her father's description of him wasn't wrong. He seemed an odious man with a high opinion of his own self worth.

He actually bumped into her while she was reaching for a packet of biscuits on the top shelf. There was no apology, so intent was he to talk to a woman buying scotch at the tills. When she overheard him mentioning Karen Taylor's book and his feigned affection for his sister she couldn't help hoping that his true feelings for Emma would soon become public knowledge.

After that gratefully short experience Sarah had made her way here to visit the one person she wanted to see more than any other. She placed the bouquet of flowers gently on the ground. Poor Jimmy. She wished she could remember him, to recall him gently holding her hand as he walked her to school that morning but she couldn't. His photo in the newspaper articles hadn't made her recall any memories, just like the picture of herself hadn't. Perhaps it was for the best.

Sarah took one final look across the open land to Northey Island. She wondered if Karen Taylor would actually put the Emma Burrows story in her book. She was struggling with the information according to the blog and Sarah felt that wasn't going to change even with Joey being here, but actually she was glad about that. It was the right time to let the past rest. Sarah Jones had been born as a five year old girl in nineteen eighty as she left Little Tenwick. She'd gone on to live a happy life with her beloved father, Andrew. The past was the past. She hoped everyone involved in the abduction story could accept that and move on.

She took one last look at the flowers on the ground.

"Goodbye Jimmy McGill," she said, "Rest easy."

As she turned she caught sight of her reflection again in the puddle.

"Goodbye Emma Burrows," she said, "Rest easy."

She walked back to her car ready to return to her ailing father in Sussex. Sarah realised that visiting these people from her past hadn't just been about saying goodbye to Emma Burrows, they'd been about saying goodbye to Tom McGill as well. In the car she took out the letter and tore it up into pieces. Her father was Andrew Jones. They'd spent the last thirty-nine years together, often travelling around the country. After all he'd done for her she needed to be by his side now, as he made his final journey.

Still Missing

by Karen Taylor

Chapter 3 (first draft)

As we have seen from the earlier chapters, people go missing all of the time. Even with today's technology it's still possible to disappear. But what of a child's disappearance? That's a completely different story. In the case of a missing child there's a sense of urgency to find them, a fear of what's happening to them the longer they are gone. There's a euphoria of elation when the child is found unharmed and a sense of utter desolation as worst fears are confirmed when a body is discovered.

But what happens when the child or their remains aren't found? How long should a search continue? To the family it should never end but to those on the outside, perhaps with a feeling of guilt, they must wonder if manpower and money should be thrown at something that now seems like a fruitless search. And what happens after many years have passed? Are those that were involved still affected by the past or are they able to move on with their lives?

Wayne Nicholls was eight years old when he went missing on 18 July 1987. He was a member of a large family living just outside of Stoke-on-Trent. On the day of the abduction he and his three siblings had all been at school...

Author's Note

While the story takes place in real counties in England, the villages of Little Tenwick and Great Tenwick are fictitious, as are the ruin on the Essex marshes looking out towards Northey Island and the retirement village in Stow on the Wold.

The Small Hands charity is also fictitious and any resemblance to a real charity is purely coincidental.

Author's website: www.stuartboneauthor.com

Printed in Poland
by Amazon Fulfillment
Poland Sp. z o.o., Wrocław

63929025R00213